Praise for the novels of
SUSAN KRINARD

TOUCH OF THE WOLF

"A vivid, talented writer with a sparkling imagination . . .
Touch of the Wolf is full of wonderful surprises."
—Anne Stuart

BODY AND SOUL

"A master of atmosphere and description . . . Krinard uses
her lyrical prose to weave a fascinating tale of
reincarnation and redemption."
—*Library Journal*

TWICE A HERO

"The reading world would be a happier place if more
paranormal romance writers wrote as well as Krinard."
—*Contra Costa Sunday Times*

PRINCE OF WOLVES

"Written with tremendous energy, it exhilarates the senses
and intoxicates the soul."
—*Affaire de Coeur*

PRINCE OF SHADOWS

"Rising superstar Susan Krinard dishes up yet another
mind-blowing reading experience in this explosive spin-off
of her already classic *Prince of Wolves*. . . .
[This] daring innovator and extraordinary storyteller . . .
creates another towering landmark in imaginative fiction."
—*Romantic Times*

Also by Susan Krinard

TOUCH OF THE WOLF
BODY & SOUL
TWICE A HERO
PRINCE OF SHADOWS
STAR-CROSSED
PRINCE OF DREAMS
PRINCE OF WOLVES

once a
WOLF

Susan Krinard

BANTAM BOOKS
New York Toronto London Sydney Auckland

ONCE A WOLF
A Bantam Book / July 2000

All rights reserved.
Copyright © 2000 by Susan Krinard
Cover art copyright © 2000 by Franco Accornero

No part of this book may be reproduced or transmitted in any form
or by any means, electronic or mechanical, including photocopying,
recording, or by any information storage and retrieval system,
without permission in writing from the publisher.
For information address: Bantam Books.

ISBN 0-553-58021-3

Published simultaneously in the United States and Canada

Bantam Books are published by Bantam Books, a division of Random House, Inc.
Its trademark, consisting of the words "Bantam Books" and the portrayal of a
rooster, is Registered in U.S. Patent and Trademark Office and in other countries.
Marca Registrada. Bantam Books, 1540 Broadway, New York, New York 10036.

PRINTED IN THE UNITED STATES OF AMERICA

OPM   10   9   8   7   6   5   4   3

*This book is dedicated to the wonderful people,
cultures, and beauty of New Mexico,
the Land of Enchantment.*

*Special thanks to Zahara Medina
for her help with the Spanish language.*

once a
WOLF

one

I t really is the most wonderful news, Lady Rowena," the middle-aged matron said, smiling with benevolent indulgence upon her hostess. "All society is looking forward to the wedding. And as for short engagements"—she made a dismissive gesture—"everyone knows they are the ideal."

Lady Rowena Forster returned Mrs. Arthur Van Rijn's smile and offered her and her two daughters another serving of tea. The young ladies accepted with just the right degree of formal grace.

"My girls have benefited so much from your tutoring," Mrs. Van Rijn said, observing her daughters with pride. "I quite despaired of them ever becoming proper ladies before you took them under your wing."

"It was my pleasure, I assure you," Rowena said. And, indeed, the girls were attractive. But they would have been accepted in society, polished or not, because of their family's standing among the aristocracy of New York—the aristocracy which, three years ago, had welcomed Lady Rowena Forster into its midst.

When Rowena fled her arranged marriage in England, she had gone to the one place where her brother Braden, the Earl of Greyburn, would never have thought to look for her: America. She had lived quietly for a time, relying on the generous inheritance she'd received from a distant relative. But then word had come from England that Braden no longer demanded her marriage to the American of werewolf blood chosen for her. Though the Cause of preserving the werewolf race was still his life's work, he no longer forced others to be an unwilling part of it.

All at once Rowena found herself free. She could go back to England, but there were painful memories there she was not prepared to resurrect. And soon after she came out of hiding, she found that New York society was only too glad to embrace an earl's sister from England. She had slipped easily into the routine of a winter Season and summers at Newport or Southampton. After nearly three years, she was an established member of the elite.

But the social round, and a strong commitment to several charitable associations, was not enough to fill the vacancy in her life. The husband, children, and normal, *human* life of which she'd always dreamed were still denied her.

Until the man she had least expected to meet had come into her circle and offered companionship, unique understanding, and the answer to her dilemma.

"It's so gratifying that you have decided to settle here in New York," Mrs. Van Rijn went on. "We should all miss you terribly were you to return to England."

"As I should miss you," Rowena said with a tiny nod. "We shall visit England several times a year. Mr. MacLean no longer has any need to personally manage his family's holdings in Texas."

"But of course. He would be quite beyond the pale to expect you to live among savages." She set down her cup and folded gloved hands in her narrow lap. "Mr. MacLean is a true gentleman."

Yes, Rowena thought. *A true gentleman.* No one in New York could dispute that, least of all herself. He was the fantasy of every unmarried woman in New York: immensely wealthy, handsome, charming, impeccably attired and mannered, a generous patron of favored charities, possessing the friendship of husbands on the Stock Exchange and blessed with his family's substantial land ownership since long before the War of Secession.

The fact that Cole MacLean had lost his arm in the War, fighting for the South, was not held against him. It made him seem the more dashing to admiring young ladies.

How ironic that those ladies had lost him to the one woman who hadn't wanted anything to do with him at first. Cole was, after all, the very man her brother had intended her to marry; that knowledge had made her avoid him assiduously for nearly a year. Then she'd begun to learn that he was the single perfect mate for her.

Yes, quite perfect.

"I'm sure you have many preparations to make," Mrs. Van Rijn said, rising. "We have imposed too much on your time."

Rowena snapped out of her musings and stood with a muted rustle of skirts. "Not at all, Mrs. Van Rijn. Your company, and that of your daughters, is always most welcome." She offered her hand. "I trust that I shall see you again soon?"

"We will be attending Mrs. Peacock's Farewell Ball," Mrs. Van Rijn said. "We shall see you there. And then, of course, we will be leaving for Newport." She pressed Rowena's hand. "Your wedding will be the highlight of the summer Season."

Rowena murmured words of gratitude and exchanged good-byes with the two Van Rijn daughters. Her parlormaid, Kate, showed them to the door.

Rowena watched from the window until the Van Rijn

carriage was lost among the many others negotiating the busy street, and only then allowed herself a moment to sigh and lean against the nearest chair. The stream of callers had been endless since the formal announcement of her engagement to Mr. Cole MacLean. She had been brought up to receive multiple guests with perfect aplomb, and yet it was almost as if she were eager to be rid of the prescribed rituals that amounted to little more than pretty words and self-satisfied pretensions.

She shook her head. She must be weary indeed to have such contrary thoughts. Cole would not appreciate them. He expected her to be the exemplary hostess, a credit to his standing and situation. When she and Cole were married, life would be much the same, if not more challenging. She couldn't let herself falter, not even when the children arrived. Children who would never know of their beastly heritage. Wasn't that worth every sacrifice?

Suddenly aware that Kate was still in the room, Rowena dismissed the girl and climbed the stairs to her bedchamber. She went at once to the wardrobe and drew out the heavy wedding gown that had been finished just days ago.

The gown was of white mousseline and silk brocade stitched with pearls, its virginal purity appropriate in spite of Rowena's years. Few in New York would guess that she had reached the age of thirty, and no one challenged her complete respectability.

The dress was beautiful, extravagant, and extremely expensive. Cole had commissioned it from Worth himself on a trip to Paris. He'd told her that it was essential to display wealth as well as possess it; to do less would damage his reputation among their peers. Rowena had questioned him about the necessity for such exorbitance wasted on a gown she'd wear but once. A few coolly reproving words from him had silenced her on that subject.

She shuddered to remember how she'd behaved with Cole at the beginning. The bad habits she'd accumulated in a lifetime of defying her brother soon became disagreeably apparent. She reacted to any challenging masculine authority with discreditable spite and sarcasm.

Cole had been the one to point out to her that her manner was overly bold, her speech much too pointed and hardly fitting for a lady of delicacy and rank. In fact, it smacked of the vulgar beast she wished to overcome.

He was right. He was always right. It was not his business to change; she must do the adapting. She had not been forced to marry him; she had chosen, after two years of his acquaintance. He had given her one final reason above all others to accept his proposal of marriage.

He alone *knew* what she was. She need never fear that some slip would reveal her shame, or that her keener senses, however she struggled to keep them in check, might betray her. She would not be burdened with knowing she deceived some ordinary man who believed that she, too, was normal.

Human.

Cole was not human. But Braden had been mistaken in assuming him to be a willing participant in his Cause. Cole had grown to feel the same distaste for his werewolf blood as Rowena. He wouldn't let his wife stray one step from humanity. He alone could keep the wolf at bay—and protect her from herself.

A gentle voice sounded deep in Rowena's mind: *"But do you love him? Love is the most important thing in the world."*

Of course Cassidy, Braden's young wife, had never spoken those exact words to her, not at Greyburn in England nor in the girl's letters to New York. But had she been here now, she would have said something very similar.

Cassidy hadn't lost her innocence in marriage to the earl, or in embracing her werewolf nature. She still believed that love could solve every problem.

It had no place in Rowena's plans. Once she had hoped to

love, but no longer. Love and passion were too closely entangled. Passion lay close to the animal nature, the uncontrolled wildness that was the beast. Rowena had long ago decided that she would die rather than foster that monster within herself.

Romantic love, anger, yearning, desire: Ardor of any kind was behind her. Her sole desire was for stability, and ordinary children who would look to her for guidance.

Surely that was enough.

Carefully Rowena restored the gown to its place, as if she could put troubling thoughts away just as easily. Her uncooperative mind moved to the latest rumor—subtle, generally ignored—that Cole had engaged in some less-than-honorable business practices.

Of course all men in his position had enemies, those who would look for blots in an otherwise spotless reputation. Such envious busybodies would speak of dark secrets and hidden motives. But Cole's only dark secret was his *loupgarou* blood, and he had renounced that forever.

Rowena sorted through her gowns to choose the one most appropriate for tonight's dinner party at the Greenwells'. Cole would be there, of course—his last engagement before leaving on business for Chicago. She would stand at his side as living proof that he had nothing of which to be ashamed.

She smiled at her own conceit that Cole needed her protection. He was a man who stood unshakably firm and dignified in the face of his anonymous detractors, and would scorn the support of a woman. Just as he'd scorn her if she ever suggested such support.

Ringing for Kate, she removed the pins from her hair and studied her face in the dressing table mirror. In a month, she would no longer be Lady Rowena Forster, but Mrs. Cole MacLean. Her old identity would cease to exist. Cole made it possible. He made it inevitable.

She shivered and looked away.

· · ·

The girl entered the alley without hesitation, a plain shawl drawn over her hair and her slender form wrapped in a nondescript cloak. She paused beside a haphazard stack of crates, searching the darkness.

Tomás Alejandro Randall moved into her view, and she took an involuntary step backward.

"Faith, you gave me a fright!" she said with a quick laugh.

"You, Kate? I doubt it." He took her hand in his and kissed her work-roughened fingertips.

She snatched her hand away and pulled the scarf from her bright streak of hair. "You'll not be liking what I have to tell you this time."

"Ah, but Kate—any news you bring is good if it means that the waiting is over."

"Then you'll be pleased," she said. "MacLean is to leave on business to Chicago immediately after the Greenwells' dinner party, and Lady Rowena's to join him in Newport in a week. The marriage will take place as planned, in less than a month."

Tomás leaned against the damp brick of the alley wall, intent on the study of his buffed fingernails, slipping easily into the character he must play one more time. The casual pose was a mask. Inwardly his heart raced with excitement, and only the practice of years kept the grin from his face.

The waiting *was* over. The time to act had come at last.

"You've done well, *querida*," he said. "You've more than earned your reward."

Kate snorted. "Is that all, then? It doesn't trouble you that none of your carefully planted rumors about MacLean succeeded?"

"I would have been surprised if they had." He pushed away from the wall and brushed off the tail of his coat. "Lady Rowena is a stubborn woman. Once she's set her mind on something . . ."

"She's set her mind on MacLean, sure enough, and won't listen to any ill said of him. He could charm the birds out of the trees, that one—like a snake. But you won't let this bird fly, will you?"

He lunged toward her without warning and seized her hands. She gave a muffled shriek as he spun her around and caught her close against him, his lips almost touching the curve of her neck.

"Would you fly away from me," he whispered, "if you were the bird?"

"You're mad," she said, her breath coming a little too fast. "You truly intend to go through with this? You'll risk your life, just for revenge—"

"Ah, you do care." He kissed the corner of her mouth and released her. "Never fear, *mi pelirroja*. I live for such adventures."

"No." She tugged the scarf up over her head and clutched it about her neck. "You live for a past that's gone, Tomás Alejandro, and for the chance to die." She backed away. "I've played the role you asked of me. I've been the lady's maid this six months, and spied for you. At heart she's a good woman. All I want now is what you promised. I won't be any further part of this—"

"But you'll do one last thing for me. Will you not, *mi vida*?"

Her shoulders sagged. "What more do you ask?"

"Not much. Simply make sure that I am admitted to the lady's house after the party tonight."

"It's a good thing I'm leaving myself, or I'd be out on the street for letting a strange 'gentleman' in without an introduction."

"But you are leaving. This is your final task for me. And when it is done, the lady will fly freely enough into my golden cage."

"God help her, then."

"She's lived a life of privilege, and you've had to fight for everything you ever possessed. Do you still find so much pity for her?"

"Yes. She's just a pawn in your private war, rich or not."

"A very valuable pawn, to be treated with the greatest consideration." He reached within his vest and drew out a small, heavy leather bag. "Here's a token of my esteem. When I come calling at the lady's house, you'll have the rest."

She snatched the bag from his hand. "If it weren't for my brother and sister—"

"At least you have family left alive, Kate O'Neill." He looked at her and saw not a young colleen of pale skin and red hair, but the dark-tressed, dark-eyed woman who had raised him, and loved him, even when she had nothing left to live for but vengeance against the murderers of her mate— his father.

How different things might have been if his parents had lived. But the MacLeans had swept into their peaceful lives and left chaos and death in their wake. Only one Randall remained.

The old sorrow returned, sharp and unwelcome. Tomás endured it until it passed. He smiled at Kate, showing his teeth.

"Whatever the MacLeans want," he said, "I will make them pay double to get it. Whatever they gain, I will take away from them. They won't forget the Randalls while I live."

"And when you're dead?"

He shrugged. "We all die, señorita. It's a matter of when and how well."

"Then I hope you do it far from my sight." She turned to go and stopped, shoulders rigid. "Damn you, Tomás."

"And *buena suerte* to you as well, *mi amor.*"

She gave a harsh laugh that made a parody of his. "You've seduced a hundred willing women, Tomás, and not one of them has ever touched your soul. I think this time you've met your match. You'll not capture this lady's heart."

"It is not her heart I mean to capture. *Venga, vete!*"

She jerked a nod and hurried from the alley.

Tomás followed her to the street and turned in the opposite direction, drawing in the stifling scents of a New York
evening. At the moment he was but one of many average
men who walked the street on unknown business in this respectable but unremarkable part of the city. Tonight he'd be
someone else entirely. And a week from now . . .

A week from now he'd become once again what the
MacLeans had made him: a scoundrel, an outlaw, an enemy.
He was prey to no doubts, no regrets. Only inaction and
helplessness had the power to trouble him, and he was subject to neither.

Within a few hours he'd arranged two first-class fares in a
westbound Pullman Palace coach and was completely familiar with every segment of the journey to Kansas City. From
there, the Atchison, Topeka and Santa Fe would take him
and the lady to the very border of New Mexico Territory.
Where his men would be waiting.

That was, of course, if all went according to plan. And it
would. There was just the small matter of winning Rowena's
initial cooperation.

He returned to his modest hotel room and took inventory
of his wardrobe. Every piece of it was appropriate to a well-
bred but unostentatious English gentleman. The tailors who'd
served him in the past two weeks were convinced their customer was, in fact, of the British peerage, just returned from
a sojourn in the Wild West.

He dressed meticulously in pristine white shirt, silk waistcoat, cravat, cream trousers, double-breasted frock coat, and
top hat; checked his watch; and examined his reflection in
the mirror.

He knew what Rowena would see, and that she would believe the story he intended to tell her. Had she been more

open to her werewolf nature, perhaps she'd have recognized him by scent alone. But he trusted that her willing blindness would make it possible for him to deceive her . . . just as long as necessary.

And then she would be his.

two

The gaze of every distinguished male at the Greenwells' select dinner party had been fixed on Lady Rowena Forster
from the moment she'd walked into the marbled entrance
hall on Cole MacLean's arm four hours ago. The same eyes
were upon her now, as she and Cole made their good-byes
and waited for his carriage to take them home.

Cole was content that they should watch her, even if it
meant the fools didn't pay him the respectful attention to
which he was accustomed. Let them look their fill and sali-
vate in feeble envy. She was as much his property as the diamond studs on his shirt, his Savile Row suit, and the mansion
on Fifth Avenue. He'd snatched up New York's greatest marital prize with little more effort than it took him to pry the
most secret financial information from the mouths of the
richest investors in the city.

And all because Lady Rowena Forster trusted him. Trusted
him, above all others, because he knew what she was and
didn't reject her for it. Because they shared the same repudi-
ated heritage. And because she didn't know that he had no
intention of disowning the one part of that heritage that made
him her superior. And, in a few weeks' time, her master.

She'd been meant to be his years ago, when the marriage was first arranged by her brother in England. He didn't let what was his slip from his grasp.

He paused at a gold-framed mirror in the entrance hall to adjust his tie and caught Rowena's pale reflection beside and slightly behind him. She presented a pleasing contrast: light to his dark, slender against his broad strength, retiring where he was assured. One would never know, to look at her now, how much she'd altered in the two years since he'd taken her in hand.

She had been a slight challenge at first. The very pride and aristocratic hauteur that made her such an elegant ornament on his arm had also fitted her with a sharp tongue and defiant nature. Not that most of Society realized it; she was too skilled at negotiating the social milieu, a valuable asset in a wife. But he had recognized it at once, and relished the game of bringing her to heel.

He met her gaze in the glass, and she was the first to look away. That was one outward sign of how well he'd succeeded. At their first introduction she'd seen him as yet another plebeian, social-climbing American from the savage West, doubly damned because of who and what he was. She tried sharpening her tongue on him once or twice, and then he'd begun blunting her edge.

He'd started by implying that only he would ever understand her, or the animal impulses that lived under her skin no matter how much she repressed them. He told her that no ordinary man would want her if he guessed her true nature. He showed her that he alone could help her to live entirely free of the werewolf taint—if she trusted him to guide her in all things. She was not strong enough. He was.

He didn't even have to use his will to make her believe.

He taught her to defer to his taste, recognize her natural inferiority, and admit how desperately she needed him. The very gown she wore tonight was his selection, its muted color and lines deliberately selected to soften her appearance—and submerge her personality—still further. Day by day, month by month, he wore down her increasingly subtle insubordination, disguising his intentions in the pleasures of courtship. He knew what she feared most: losing her one chance to have a normal, "human" life. That was his power over her, now and always.

It was almost too easy.

She was very quiet as they moved among the other guests, letting him do the talking. He smiled and exchanged a tame witticism with the Dowager Greenwell. He wondered dispassionately if she had any notion that her husband's fortunes were on the wane, and that fabulous diamond necklace she wore about her wattled neck might be in jeopardy. Greenwell had been remarkably indiscreet with certain sensitive information, monetary and otherwise, and at this very moment, all unwitting, he was paying for it. Paying Cole MacLean.

Every man here had contributed to Cole's growing fortune and breathtaking rise to influence and authority. Most of them had no idea how much he'd taken from them, simply by using the mental abilities he had been born with. A few suggestions planted in a wealthy man's mind, and he considered Cole his best friend and financial advisor. A slight focusing of Cole's will, and a banker or investor or speculator let slip the latest confidential stock tip, or passed on the rumor of a company in pecuniary difficulty, or babbled about a personal affair that left him open to blackmail from an insidious unknown source. None of them ever connected his mysterious difficulties to the gentleman from Texas.

Lady Rowena had done her part, however unwittingly. The moment she'd begun to respond to his carefully orchestrated courtship, society's women had fully opened their doors to him, the former Climber whose education, charm, and carefully acquired refinement had never been quite enough to breach that last barrier.

But the barriers had been breached, and that led to still

more opportunities. Opportunities for unlimited power, the power that was his by right because he could take it.

He smiled to think of his father fumbling about in this rarified atmosphere like a furious longhorn bull in a china shop, and of his brother Weylin disgusting the high-toned ladies with his working cowman's clothes and unpolished speech.

But of course Father was long out of the way, and Weylin was occupied running after El Lobo in the Territory. The entire MacLean fortune, and future, was in the hands of the one MacLean capable of making a mark on not only New York, but the world.

The name Cole MacLean would be remembered. And feared.

"Your carriage has arrived, sir."

Cole tipped the attentive footman with a negligent gesture and led Rowena out to the carriage. She climbed in with practiced grace, a creature of exquisite proportions and impeccable lineage, born to the privileges he'd won with patience, talent, and grit.

Her fortune was as good as his. She already relied on his advice, and placed in his hands the funds she bestowed on her numerous charities. Most of which never reached their intended recipients, but that was something else of which she remained ignorant. He didn't plan to waste their money—*his* money—on the weak. Let her go on believing he shared her devotion to homeless children and reformed women of the street.

He settled into the seat beside her and took her gloved hand. "Did you enjoy the party, my dear?"

"Indeed. All the more because you were able to attend." She smiled at him with well-trained attentiveness. "I know you must leave tonight—"

"But we shall be together again," he said. He kissed her hand. "Then we'll never be apart. The next few weeks will move more slowly than molasses in January."

"One of your quaint Texas phrases?"

He was alert to the brief return, however mild, of her old sarcastic wit. "Very quaint," he said coldly. "I'm delighted to have entertained you."

Her smile faded. "I didn't mean to suggest that anything you say is less than—that is, I—"

It amused him that she never stuttered or lost her sureness of speech except in his presence. He squeezed her fingers a little harder than necessary. "I know you'd never mock me."

"Of course not." She fell silent. He kept his grip on her hand. She knew better than to try to pull it free.

"I trust you to keep quietly to the house while I'm gone," he said. "I want you at your best for our wedding. You needn't lift a finger; I've made all the arrangements."

"Yes, Cole."

"I'd prefer that you have as few visitors as possible. You're hardly young enough to have a chaperon, and I confess to being a bit jealous."

She said nothing. He trapped her hand between both of his.

"You will do as I ask?"

"Yes." Her face was carved of white marble, nearly expressionless. He relaxed. It wasn't that he didn't trust her out of his sight, but he enjoyed the testing. Especially when he sensed that her English lady's mask hid something he thought all but stamped out.

"Well," he said. "Here is your house."

He waited for the coachman to open his door and then helped Rowena out himself. She stumbled over her skirts, an uncharacteristic awkwardness.

"I've heard that you've given unofficial lessons in deportment to a number of young ladies," he remarked, leading her to the door. "Perhaps you should take a few yourself."

She flushed. "I am sorry. I was not careful enough."

He shook his head. "I expect better of you, Rowena.

You'll be setting the example for all New York. Never let down your guard."

Her Irish maid let them in the door. He gave the girl a calculating glance behind Rowena's back.

"It's a pity I can't stay," he said, drawing Rowena into his arms. She remained slightly rigid and prim, as he'd anticipated. Sometimes he was tempted to keep her off balance by trying a bit of "inappropriate" behavior. Not that he'd be satisfied with whatever pale shadow of sexual gratification she could provide; she was a virgin, naturally, and raised to think of sex as a duty that must be borne in order to produce children.

And though he might take pleasure in teaching her to perform as he wished, he didn't want her broken enough for the world to suspect less than marital bliss between them. So she'd have her children, and he'd find plenty of women, willing or otherwise, to appease him. Rowena was the sort to turn a blind eye to infidelity, as most women of rank did in her country. She wouldn't even raise the subject.

As long as she stayed just as she was now, he wouldn't have to waste any more effort on her once they were married.

On impulse he changed his planned chaste kiss on the cheek to one full on her mouth. She held completely still and let him do as he would. Not the slightest spark of passion marred her control. He let her go and pushed her away.

"I see I need never doubt your absolute propriety," he said sardonically. "Be on time in Newport. You know how I hate to wait."

She nodded, fixing her gaze on the floor. The maid rushed ahead of him to open the door as he strode toward it. He brushed the girl's breasts with his arm and smiled.

"Good-bye, my dear," he said, as much to the maid as Rowena. "I'll see you again before you have a chance to miss me."

He forgot his fiancée the moment he was out the door.

·   ·   ·

"There's a gentleman to see you, milady."

Rowena glanced up, distracted, from her letter-writing. Kate stood near the door, the silver card tray in her hand, looking ill-at-ease.

The clock in Rowena's boudoir showed nearly two A.M. It was well beyond a decent time for gentlemen to call on ladies—for anyone to call on anyone else, for that matter—and she was frankly amazed that Kate had answered the door. The girl should be in bed. Just because Rowena had not been able to sleep since Cole's departure did not mean that she expected her servants to share her insomnia.

And Kate had behaved most oddly, unless . . . She beckoned the girl forward. "Is it an emergency?" she asked.

"I believe so, milady. It seemed so to me. I'm sorry if I—" She blushed. "I'll tell him you are not receiving—"

Rowena shook her head and plucked the card from the tray. It bore a name she didn't recognize: Mr. Thomas A. Randolph. The right end bent down indicated that he had come in person. Most extraordinary; they had certainly not been introduced.

"Did he say why he had come, Kate?"

"He is a gentleman—from England, I think. He seemed most upset."

A gentleman from England. Instinctively Rowena went on her guard, though her relations with Braden had been pleasant enough for the past two years. Nevertheless . . .

"Please tell him that I shall join him as soon as possible," Rowena said.

"Yes, milady." Kate bobbed a shallow curtsey and left the boudoir. Troubled, Rowena made a hasty toilette and went downstairs to join her unanticipated guest in the parlor.

She saw at once that Kate was right: He was, indeed, a gentleman, from his flawless bearing to the shine on his shoes. His handsome face, tanned by the sun, was drawn in grave lines.

"Lady Rowena," he said, bowing slightly, "please do forgive me for seeking your acquaintance in so abrupt a fashion, and at such an untimely hour. But I have just arrived in New York, and you see . . ."

He hesitated, and Rowena studied him further. He wore a neatly trimmed mustache. He was tall and lithe under the well-tailored suit, with a breadth of shoulder that nearly matched Cole's. His face was decidedly attractive in a way utterly unlike her fiancé's—tanned, angular, less heavy in its lines. His hair was dark brown, his eyes the same, his voice pitched in a pleasant baritone. His accent was that of the English upper class; everything in him bespoke character and breeding.

A series of odd thoughts tumbled through her mind: a sense of recognition, a glimmer of curiosity, a tingle of personal interest, as if she ought to know him far better than a stranger. She had been well acquainted with handsome, cultivated men of his kind in the past, and never thought twice about it. He was different, somehow.

She wasn't even annoyed at his outrageous intrusion. What had Cole made so very clear in the carriage? He didn't want her to have visitors while he was gone. What would he say to this man's untoward arrival on her doorstep so late at night?

Her lips thinned. She knew what he would say. Such an offense against propriety would truly shock him—in spite of the fact that he had kissed her with a peculiar, almost hostile intensity just before he left.

That must be her imagination. He'd done nothing wrong, nothing that any fiancé might not attempt a few weeks before a wedding. She was not so naive. But she had been restless and vaguely . . . yes, angry . . . since she and Cole had returned from the party. Especially when he constantly reminded her how far she fell below his expectations. She sometimes felt that he regarded her as no more than a pretty bauble to display for his business and social acquaintances.

How ridiculous. Such thoughts were proof that she needed his guidance. Still, she felt an odd relief that he was not here at the moment. And this was, for a few more weeks, *her* house.

She wasn't yet Mrs. Cole MacLean.

She quickly recalled her guest, and smiled. "Please think nothing of it, Mr. Randolph. I understand you have come on a matter of some urgency."

"Indeed. Thank you, my lady." He waited for her to sit and then took his own seat opposite, holding hat and gloves in his hands. "Lady Rowena, I must be frank. I am here on behalf of your brother, the Honorable Quentin Forster."

"Quentin?" Rowena kept herself firmly in place, though her heart gave a leap. "Is he well?"

Randolph gazed down at his hat. "This is indeed awkward, Lady Rowena. You and I are not acquainted, but I have known your twin brother well since he came to the States. We became friends while traveling in the West." He looked up, and his eyes captured hers. "You have not heard from him in some time?"

"No. No, I have not." She stared at him as if she could force him to speak the news she dreaded. "Is he . . . please, tell me—"

"I beg your pardon, Lady Rowena," he said, rising. "He is safe, for the moment. But I have come to you because I did not know where else to turn. Quentin is in great difficulty. He . . . has fallen in with unfortunate acquaintances, and I fear for his life and his health."

I knew. Rowena sat rigid in her chair, subduing any semblance of alarm. *I knew something wasn't right, but I didn't want to admit it.* It was that old bond they'd always shared as twins—coming and going, erratic but always there. Sometimes it spilled from the quiet corners of her mind into powerful images, emotions too intense to bear . . . as had happened when Quentin was in the Indian Army.

But over the past year she'd sensed, without any definite proof, that he was in trouble. His most recent letters had held a tone of veiled desperation that none but she might have recognized. He hadn't responded to her last few missives. And she'd been neglectful and selfishly preoccupied enough not to pursue her shadowy apprehension.

She sent Kate for refreshments and struggled to maintain her poise.

"I am grateful that you have informed me of this," she said. "Can you tell me more?"

He shook his head. "The situation is complicated, and a lady such as yourself—" He cleared his throat. "Life is very different in the West. It is difficult to explain—"

"Kindly attempt it, Mr. Randolph."

He paused at her brusque interruption. "Very well. I shall speak bluntly. Your brother has become very fond of, even dependent upon spirits. He is reckless in pursuit of games of chance, and has made many enemies. I am afraid that he has lost interest in his own welfare, and is . . . forgive me . . . seeking his own death by any means possible."

Rowena closed her eyes. *Ah, Quentin, are you still so trapped in a past you would never share even with me?* Everything Mr. Randolph said reinforced her unacknowledged fears, and she had absolutely no doubt of his sincerity.

She faced him again. "You've come to me for help."

"Yes, Lady Rowena. Having heard of you from Quentin, I believe you alone may influence him to give up his current path and return to civilization."

Rowena stood, unable to contain her agitation. Anger welled up in her—at this stranger and his sudden appearance, at Quentin, at herself for not realizing sooner that he needed her.

And at Cole, for gradually supplanting everything else of meaning in her life.

"Then you are suggesting that I go to my brother," she said.

"Yes. I would not have come so far on such a mission had I not believed it to be the only way to rescue him." He withdrew a folded paper from his pocket. "Quentin did not know of my reason for coming to New York, but he did write this."

The paper was a letter, written in Quentin's hand, addressed to Rowena. It assured her, briefly, that the bearer, one Mr. Thomas Randolph, was a trustworthy friend and that his introduction to Lady Rowena Forster was fully endorsed by her brother. Quentin went on to ask that all hospitality be shown to Mr. Randolph in New York.

Rowena gave the letter back to Mr. Randolph. "I do not doubt your credentials, Mr. Randolph. You are perhaps unaware that I am to be married next month."

"I did not know, Lady Rowena. I just arrived in New York this evening, and came to you straightaway. I am sorry that my inopportune arrival may disrupt your plans."

She looked at him sharply, studying his face for mockery. She found none; instead, her heart warmed unexpectedly at his personal concern. He must be a good friend indeed, and deserving of all her courtesy.

If Cole were here . . . That thought kept invading her mind. If Cole were here, he'd tell her that she must not, under any circumstances, behave impetuously, not even on behalf of her brother. He would tell her that her worry was unfounded, typical female overreaction. He would pat her hand and tell her that he'd look into it—in his own time, of course, considering his own very full schedule. Nothing was to delay or interfere with the marriage.

She set her jaw. Cole would ask her to choose between her twin brother and his own convenience; it was as simple as that. She fully recognized the wrongness of her tendency toward rebellion, and thought it overcome. Now she saw that it was not. She was ashamed, but not quite enough. Not tonight.

"If my brother needs me," she said, "of course I will go to him. Where is he?"

"In southern Colorado, Lady Rowena."

"That is some distance from New York, is it not? It will take a few days to arrange my departure. I must—"

"I beg your pardon, my lady, but I am very much afraid that any delay may prove disastrous for your brother."

Kate arrived with the tray of refreshments, and Rowena offered them to her guest. He declined, but she hardly heard him.

"I took the liberty of obtaining two first-class accommodations on a westbound train leaving early this morning," Mr. Randolph said. He stepped toward her, one hand raised in supplication. "Lady Rowena, I beg you to trust me. Quentin's life may depend upon it."

Trust him. Rowena was well aware that to leave New York on the spur of the moment with a total stranger, being herself unmarried and engaged to another man, would provoke gossip and speculation of a most unflattering kind. Only her immaculate reputation would protect her—that, and Cole MacLean. He must be told, but she could not reach him now. She would telegraph Newport at once and write a long letter that would be waiting for him there when he arrived.

He would be very angry. She would have to appease him a great deal when she returned, humble herself completely. With any luck, the wedding itself would not have to be postponed. With any luck, she'd have Quentin in hand and returning with her on an express train back to New York within the next few weeks.

And she was perfectly safe from any imposition by Mr. Randolph. He was an English gentleman, and she was a lady.

"Thank you, Mr. Randolph," she said. "You have considered every necessity. It seems all that remains is for me to pack."

"If you will accept my advice, Lady Rowena, bring only your plainest garments and a minimum of trunks. You may be required to ride both on horseback and in very primitive vehicles. There will be few luxuries where we are going."

She lifted her chin. "I would scarcely expect catering from Delmonico's, or pretty phaetons in the desert."

His face broke into a broad smile that transformed him into yet another stranger—a man utterly different from the polished British gentleman, feral of spirit and reckless of gaze—one who sent a shiver coursing down Rowena's spine. But the flash of teeth and challenge was gone in an instant, hidden by a shallow bow.

"I salute your courage and fortitude, my lady. Quentin is most fortunate in his sister."

"As he is fortunate in his friend," she said. "And now, if you will give Kate your direction, I will finish my own preparations."

"I can send a carriage for you in a few hours—"

"Perhaps it would be best if we meet at the station, Mr. Randolph."

"Indeed." His eyes revealed a spark of humor. "I'll give your maid all the particulars."

"Then I wish you a good night, Mr. Randolph." She offered her hand. "Until morning."

"Until morning—or, as we say in the West, *hasta mañana*." He lifted her hand to his mouth, but instead of merely kissing the air above it, he pressed a kiss on her knuckles. The effect of the gallant, old-fashioned gesture was like his grin: startling, mischievous, and too intimate for comfort.

"In spite of the unfortunate circumstances," he said, releasing her hand far too slowly, "I believe this will be a most pleasurable journey." He retrieved his hat and gloves and followed Kate into the hall.

His parting words left Rowena nonplussed. She sat down in the nearest chair, reviewing all that had passed since his arrival. It was quite fantastic enough that she should find herself leaving for the wilderness but a month before her wedding, but there was something about Mr. Randolph that didn't quite fit.

She couldn't define her sense of apprehension. It wasn't until the very end of his visit that the vague presentiments of danger began. She might almost have ascribed it to . . . instinct.

No. That was a word she rejected as thoroughly as her werewolf blood. Nor was she one to let her imagination run away with her. It was hardly possible that he was *loup-garou.* There was none of his name in England. Perhaps it was simply that Mr. Randolph had been influenced by the uncivilized climes in which he'd traveled, like Quentin. As Quentin's friend, he might well have a touch of the rogue about him. But he hadn't done anything to make her doubt his honor.

Why, then, did his grin and his kiss remain so vivid in her mind?

Surely it was because they'd met in England, perhaps long ago, and neither of them remembered. That would account for it.

But it didn't explain why her heart pounded as if she'd just had a brush with some dark menace—or come too close to the beast within herself.

Oh, Quentin, she thought. *What have you done?*

Once before she had turned away from a duty imposed upon her because it conflicted with her own deeply held principles. Now she was driven by those same principles—the need to help bring order, upright behavior, and human moral dignity to the world she inhabited. There was no room in her vision of life for unbridled passion and careless abandon, for the coarse or blatantly sensual, for anything that might promote chaos and inevitable suffering.

One day she would raise her own children to be productive members of human society, and teach them to lead admirable lives of taste and restraint. Until then, she must respond to those unfortunates who needed her help—most of all her own brother.

And no foolish misgivings about Mr. Thomas A. Randolph could possibly interfere.

She shook off her doubts and summoned Kate to help her pack.

three

Weylin MacLean caught the westbound train in Dodge City, all too aware that once again he'd failed to track down the outlaw called El Lobo.

Rumors had sent him on a wild-goose chase from New Mexico Territory, farther east than he'd ever ventured. Having come to yet another standstill, he wasn't inclined to return to such "civilized" country short of Apocalypse.

He found a seat, a safe distance away from ladies who might be offended by his rough dress and lack of a recent bath, and gazed out the window. It was foolish to think that El Lobo would have reason to travel east. He was as much a man of the frontier as Weylin himself. He might have some skill at disguise, but he wouldn't last long in . . . New York, for instance, where Cole had turned himself into a rich dandy and had all but rejected his Texas roots.

Strange to think that Weylin had more in common with El Lobo than with his own brother. Strange, and uncomfortable. Cole would expect another report on his progress in catching the desperado, and he wasn't going to be happy. That was the single responsibility Cole left to his brother;

"one of the only things you're any good at," he'd said last time he came back to the Territory.

Weylin had failed. Again. He had no right to criticize Cole, who'd made the family name something to be reckoned with all over the States, and had increased the MacLean wealth a hundredfold. All Weylin managed was taking some small part in running the ranches in New Mexico and Texas, and he wasn't even in charge. He'd never wanted to be.

He permitted himself a rare sigh. Cole was the one who wanted power. He'd always been that way; that was what caused the fights between him and Father. And it was after Kenneth died that Father started to groom his youngest son to succeed him—not Cole, who was most suited for it.

No wonder Cole resented him. At least the will hadn't been changed before Father was murdered; Cole got what he wanted. He ran the MacLean empire, even if from a distance. And that left Weylin to take revenge for Father and the loss of MacLean property.

"The problem with you," Cole had said more than once, "is that you're a coward at bottom. Father coddled you too much. He kept you out of the War; he let you turn tail when we went after Fergus Randall for killing Kenneth. I had to do the dirty work. But that's past, Weylin. I won't soil my hands anymore. You bring Randall in, dead or alive, and I'll know you're still a MacLean."

A MacLean. That was worth being, no matter what people said about Father's methods. He'd been a hard man. You had to be, out here.

Ruthless, Weylin thought. *You have to be ruthless, as much as El Lobo. Think like him. Forget about honor and justice.*

But he couldn't forget. That was what Cole didn't understand. Just like Father wouldn't have understood.

Weylin rested his head back against the seat and closed his eyes. *I can damn well be a MacLean and still care about the law, Cole, even if you don't.*

It was Cole's mistake, thinking he was any less committed, any less resolute in his mission because he did things his own way.

He pulled his hat low over his forehead, settled his gun more comfortably at his hip, and let himself drift. He dreamed of an endless chase, always a step behind a dark brown wolf who laughed at him with jaws agape. He dreamed of tossing his lariat again and again, only to have it fall short while the wolf laughed again.

And then the dream shifted. Suddenly he, not the wolf, was one step ahead. He could smell El Lobo's scent on the wind. The hairs on the back of his own neck twitched in response. He heard his father's voice: *We don't have to turn into varmints to rule this country.* And Cole's: *Becoming a beast is a waste of the power we were born with. We're superior, not animals.*

Which meant they were superior to the Randalls, who'd always run as wolves. Weylin suppressed the desire to hunt El Lobo in the wolf shape he'd nearly forgotten. He let his keen sense of smell guide him. El Lobo was close, very close. . . .

He jerked up in his seat, the scent still in his nostrils. His spine thrummed with awareness.

El Lobo. He got up and moved into the aisle, hardly aware of the eastern ladies who whispered about him as if they'd never seen a westerner before.

He knew with absolute certainty that El Lobo was on this very train.

Tomás had forgotten, over the years, just how beautiful she was.

Beautiful. He had seen heads turn and eyes follow him enviously when he escorted Lady Rowena through Grand Central Station and onto the train. Men had bowed and stammered in her presence, as if she were royalty and they'd forgotten all their democratic American principles.

But they didn't know Lady Rowena Forster. She was indeed beautiful—and about as warm and womanly as a marble statue. Her hair was richly blond but tightly coiffed in a conservative style, and her face never revealed a single untoward emotion. Her traveling suit was simple but à la mode, hugging her slender figure but revealing not a single inch of skin from neck to toe tip.

She belonged in one of those vast overdecorated drawing rooms so beloved of the wealthiest New Yorkers who sought to copy the European aristocracy.

At least that was what she believed.

Now, as the train approached the Kansas-Colorado border, she occupied herself in gazing out the window at the passing scenery as if it fascinated her. Tomás knew from experience that her goal was more to avoid him than observe the landscape.

He settled back in his upholstered seat and studied her out of the corner of his eye. Even near the end of a long train journey she managed to keep herself stiffly upright, her back seldom touching the seat. For the past several days she'd remained detached, regal, unfailingly polite and distant as the moon.

The fact that they shared a berth in the sleeping car had done little to encourage her to speak to him, except to inquire further about her brother. Fortunately, he knew just enough to hold her at bay. And her long silences gave him every opportunity to recall in detail what she'd been like in England.

Of course he'd known her then under different circumstances, when she'd been forced to extremes by her elder brother's expectations. And "know her" was too presumptuous a phrase. He'd left England before her escape to America.

Here, at last, she considered herself safe. Safe to be the proper human lady. Safe from the werewolf heritage she re-

fused to accept, because Cole MacLean had convinced her
that he shared her revulsion for the shapeshifter's way.

Tomás laughed silently. How well MacLean had deceived
her. He'd revealed only that side of himself he wanted her
to see.

And what had she revealed to MacLean? That took a bit of
imagination. The lady was scarcely an exhibitionist, either of
form or feeling. If she ever let that gorgeous hair fall about
her shoulders, Tomás was not privileged to see it. Each night
she retreated behind the curtains of her lower bunk and, for
all he knew, slept fully clothed, corset and all.

But in the long, idle hours traversing the civilized East,
changing trains in Chicago, and setting out at last across the
open plains, he amused himself with quite a contrasting vision.

Lady Rowena Forster. How shocked she'd be if she knew
what he was thinking.

In his imagination, she was no statue but a soft and passionate woman. She was neither prim nor proper. Instead
of the close-fitting basque and corseted skirts, she wore a
white embroidered blouse, short-sleeved and loose about the
shoulders. The faint outline of her nipples lay like a shadow
beneath the cloth. Her skirt was full and richly colored, falling just to her ankles. Her feet—currently shod in dainty
boots—were bare.

She looked at him, her eyes laughing. There was fire in her
cheeks, the fire of a woman on the brink of arousal.

Ah, yes. Now her eyes were becoming heavy with sensual
invitation. Slender fingers brushed at hair that was unbound
and disheveled as a gypsy's. She bent toward him, and her
breasts pushed against their loose confinement.

"Tomás," she whispered.

Her lips were lush and moist, half parted. He moved to
seize her in his arms, but she backed away with a teasing
smile. With a twist of her hips she unbuttoned her skirt and

tugged it down until it fell in a puddle at her ankles. Her legs were long and shapely. Only the long *camisa* covered her, ending at her upper thigh.

Her motions then were deliberately seductive. She ran her hands over the pliant cotton of the *camisa,* molding it to her body. Slowly she began inching the blouse up over her thighs, her hips, her waist. The curls that guarded her womanhood were as golden as her hair. She lifted the bunched fabric above her breasts, revealing taut nipples of dark rose.

With a final dramatic gesture, she pulled the blouse over her head and flung it away. Moonlight caressed her curves like a hungry lover.

Tomás knew she was about to Change, and when she did, she would deny him what she'd so clearly promised. He lunged toward her. She skipped back, showing her teeth in challenge.

"Catch me," she said. "If you catch me, I am yours."

"Mi flama," he said, matching her smile. "You'll surrender to me—"

"Are you unwell, Mr. Randolph?"

Tomás started out of his pleasurable dream to the sight of Lady Rowena's deep blush. He became aware of two things at once: that he was profoundly aroused and uncomfortable, and that he'd been staring at her hard enough to draw her away from her implacable examination of the countryside.

But no. It couldn't be his stare that produced that color in her cheeks and brought such alarm to those cool eyes. He shifted in his seat and recalled his fantasy. If she had been privy to his musings, she might have reacted so. The way any ordinary woman not made of ice would do.

Was it possible that she had guessed his thoughts?

"Mr. Randolph?" she said, a little catch in her voice.

He considered possible answers. *Alas, I am quite unwell, my lady, but you have the cure to my illness. Shall we repair to the baggage car?*

"I was merely admiring the scenery and became . . . distracted," he said. "You seem disturbed, Lady Rowena. May I fetch you some water?"

She looked away sharply, her hand at her collar. "I am just eager to reach my brother."

"Of course," he said. To see her truly eager about anything would be most gratifying. But her brief moment of vulnerability had passed. Once again he was left to watch her pretending she didn't notice him. He sighed and attempted once more to summon up the wanton lady of his imagination.

But she had fled, bound up in her corsets and confining skirts. *What will it take to transform you, my Lady Ice? If a kiss were enough, MacLean would have tried it. He'd never buy the wares without testing them first.*

The image of MacLean kissing Rowena shattered Tomás's lazy amusement. For an instant he saw, too explicitly, his enemy invading his waking dream, standing between him and the Lady of Fire. It was MacLean who seized her in his arms, MacLean who covered her body with his own.

Demonio. Cole would never have her, Fire or Ice. If anyone were to quench that fire or melt the ice, it would be El Lobo.

The small hairs tightened on the back of Tomás's neck, and he found himself on his feet, standing over the lady in question. His fingers were curled to grab her in full view of every other passenger in the car.

And she was staring up as if at a monster.

Something within him snapped. The grim, jealous creature that had possessed him let go, and he fell into his seat again. In the same moment Rowena virtually leaped from her place and slid past him.

"If you will excuse me," she said, "I must . . ." Her sentence went unfinished. She hurried away down the aisle, past the curious and pointed gazes of her fellow travelers.

Tomás met the stares one by one until every voyeur found

something better to do, and then had a good laugh at his own expense.

Ay, Dios! He could hear Sim Kavanagh's voice now: "Caballero, if you're going to lose your head, never do it over a woman."

His head was still in place, but his mind was another matter. Or perhaps a more southerly part of his anatomy was to blame.

He relaxed and closed his eyes. Why fight it? Rowena was hardly his kind of woman, nor had he ever been required to beg for a lady's favors. In this case it might actually help to imagine her as his Lady of Flame, lest reality douse the very first ember. She'd take her own life rather than admit to a werewolf's passion.

If MacLean managed to steal her back before Tomás was finished with her, he was likely to discover his privates frozen between the sheets.

His mouth twitched between a smile and a frown. Let *that* horse be saddled when he caught it. And catch it he would. There was nowhere for Rowena to go until they reached La Junta, which should be in a handful of hours. The end of the journey, and the beginning of a new one. Lady Ice was in for quite a surprise.

For the first time he noticed that she'd left something of herself behind in her haste to escape. The white satin fan lay half open and forgotten on her seat, absurdly delicate. A careless move could crush it.

It's an unusual marble statue that needs cooling, he thought. *Or were you just beginning to thaw?* On impulse he snatched up the fan. The pristine folds carried Rowena's unique fragrance.

There was no denying that she owned an intoxicating natural perfume under all her feminine armor. Lady Ice would never let him near the source of that bouquet, but the Lady of Fire . . .

He moved to her seat to stretch out his legs and was idly

fanning himself when he registered the first hint of an entirely different scent.

Danger. It rose above the odors of someone's recent meal, bodies closely mingled, and ever-present smoke. His body snapped to attention before his mind could focus. The porter who obstructed his view of the aisle came level with his berth, and he recognized the man who stood at the opposite end of the car.

They called him lucky, the men who followed him. But no luck of his brought Weylin MacLean to this train on the very day that would see the start of the MacLeans' ultimate humiliation.

It was beyond belief that Weylin had tracked him to and from New York. He was sure that the younger MacLean had never set foot in the city; he'd have acted immediately if he knew Tomás was on board. He couldn't have recognized Lady Rowena.

That was as far as Tomás's luck held. At any moment Weylin would catch his scent and look across the car, and then there'd be hell to pay.

The Randalls had already paid their debt to hell.

Lady Rowena would know nothing of his sudden alteration in plans, but that would be remedied soon enough. He tucked the folded fan in his coat. *Enjoy your freedom while you can, my Lady Ice. This is not good-bye, but simply* adiós.

He rose casually, taking the porter's arm and using him as a shield to block Weylin's view.

"There's a man at the other end of the car," he said. "Tall and light-haired. It's very important that you don't let him come any further into the car. If you do, there will be trouble. Do you understand?"

The porter blinked and nodded. "Don't let him come in."

"*Excelente.* And now I will be going." He patted the man's arm and started for the rear of the car.

He didn't know what drew him to glance back as he reached the door. Weylin looked directly at him and stilled in midstep. His gray eyes narrowed. The porter hurried to confront him, but Tomás didn't wait to witness the outcome of such an unequal contest.

He had long since determined the most convenient exits for a possible hasty departure. No one saw him jump from the train, more cleanly than any human could manage, and roll among the prairie grasses unhurt. He stripped out of his fine suit of clothes, and Changed.

The world changed with him, becoming a place of myriad smells, sounds, and sensations that only *un hombre-lobo* could appreciate. Warm wind ruffled his brown coat. He nosed the pile of discarded fabric as if it were the bleached skeleton of another life, left for some wayfarer to discover.

On four feet he began to run—not the steady ground-eating lope of ordinary travel, but a dead gallop that would see him to La Junta before the train arrived.

Rowena stood on the railroad platform in La Junta, Colorado, her trunks at her feet, and uttered a very ladylike curse.

The dusty town bustled, oblivious, all around her. This was the railhead, the end of the line while tracks were being laid across the empty prairie to the somewhat more established town of Trinidad, near the New Mexico border. So she had been told.

She'd also been told that the next single-car passenger train to the end of the line, a few miles northeast of Trinidad, would not depart until dawn tomorrow morning. And there was no telling if Trinidad was to be her final destination.

She remained in ignorance of such details—including where in this Godforsaken place she might find a dish of fresh tea, not to mention her brother—because Mr. Randolph had disappeared. Once the train had reached the station she'd fully expected him to turn up, apologizing for his dreadful manners.

He had not, and she couldn't account for her inexplicable reaction toward him a few hours ago, or his peculiar behavior afterward. Certainly she'd caught him staring at her—it wasn't the first time—but until that moment when he'd looked ready to pounce, he hadn't given her legitimate cause for concern. She'd been the one to ignominiously flee from him, as flustered as a schoolgirl.

The indecent mental images had appeared without warning and insisted on following her all the way to the ladies' dressing room. No amount of tepid water applied liberally to her cheeks had chased them away. It was almost as if someone else had planted the bizarre thoughts in her mind.

She would never dress the way she'd seen herself in the first unwonted vision. It was like looking at some warped distortion of her own reflection. Barefoot, loose-haired, wanton.

And that was not the worst. There were the feelings that came with the picture. Heat, yearning, recklessness, and . . . yes, desire. She guessed that must be what she'd felt, for it was unlike any emotion she had ever experienced.

Desire. She wished desperately for the fan she'd somehow managed to misplace. The closest she'd ever come to that sensation was when she was forced to Change in fleeing from her imprisonment at Greyburn three years ago.

She'd vowed never to be driven to such extremes again, and had kept that vow. There was no reason in the world why the mere presence of a stranger should provoke any disturbance in her usual composure.

It was all quite ridiculous. She was not prone to wild flights of imagination, especially not of that sort. What would Cole think of her now?

She knew the answer to that question and did her best to put it from her mind. She tilted her parasol against the afternoon sun and smoothed her face of expression. She would not be so affected again—not by all the Thomas A. Randolphs of the world.

Randolph, however, had not returned to witness her renewed self-possession.

Instead, she found herself quite alone in a place that said very little for her brother's taste in habitat. The town had all the unruliness of a barbarian outpost. Rough men in dirty, ill-fitting garments rushed up and down the unpaved street on some mysterious business or other. The buildings on every side had a haphazard look about them, as if the inhabitants were eager to claim themselves civilized without going to the bother of planning.

It was not a place in which Rowena wished to make a long stay. If Randolph remained absent, she must find someone else to locate Quentin. She hadn't come so far to run back to New York with her mission unaccomplished.

Unless Cole came after her. And she would not think about that.

She began to study the passersby with greater attention. There was a man who might possibly approximate a gentleman; his clothes were clean, at least. *That* man had a respectable-looking woman on his arm, if any such creatures existed here. And as for that fellow there—

"Excuse me, ma'am," a low voice said. "May I be of assistance?"

She looked up into the shaded face of a true Western specimen, complete with broad-brimmed hat and deeply suntanned features. He lifted his hat just enough for courtesy and regarded her, unsmiling.

Instantly she found herself comparing him to Mr. Randolph. His trousers, shirt, and waistcoat were simple and worn, far from those of a dandy. He was rangy and loose-limbed, with sandy hair that gave him a youthful look. But he had a certain quality about him that she had recognized in Randolph only toward the end: a tough independence that didn't reveal itself so much in externals as in attitude.

She found, however, that she could face this stranger with none of the unease she'd felt with Randolph. There was no point in standing on ceremony. "Thank you," she said. "I would appreciate being directed to the nearest respectable establishment that serves refreshments."

He touched the brim of his hat again. "That would be the Kit Carson Hotel, ma'am." His gaze dropped to her trunks. "Were you waiting for someone?"

Though her incautious decisions had not been particularly successful of late, she decided to risk another. "The gentleman I was supposed to meet has been . . . somewhat delayed. You do not, by chance, know a Mr. Thomas A. Randolph?"

The transformation in his expression was brief and startling, reserved courtesy replaced by keen attention. "Randolph?" he repeated sharply. His right arm moved, pushing his loose coat open, and she caught a glimpse of leather, mother-of-pearl, and silver. She'd heard that firearms were a required item of apparel on the frontier.

"Mr. Randolph was to help me locate my brother, Quentin Forster," she said, observing him carefully.

"Forster?" he said. "Might I know your name, ma'am?"

"Lady Rowena Forster. Have we met before, sir?"

"No, ma'am . . . but I didn't expect to meet my brother's fiancée in Colorado. I'm Weylin MacLean."

Rowena absorbed the information with surprise that she was just able to contain. Weylin MacLean, Cole's younger brother. She'd heard about him, of course, but had always been told that he was running the family business in the West.

Well, this was certainly the West, and Weylin MacLean was in his element. The only resemblance he bore to his cultured brother was a slight likeness in the eyes and a sense of determination. He didn't have Cole's aura of driving power; even his accent was different, a drawl that she supposed must come from his Texas birth.

She offered her hand. "It is a pleasure to make your acquaintance, Mr. MacLean," she said, "however unexpectedly."

He barely touched her hand and released it. "I just came in on the train myself," he said. "Cole didn't tell me you were traveling West."

"I'm sorry that we didn't meet. Were you in New York?"

"No, ma'am. I was on other business." His gaze measured her dispassionately. "Cole doesn't know you came out here alone."

He certainly must by now, Rowena thought, hiding a shiver. She didn't intend to explain herself to Cole's brother. "I was not alone, Mr. MacLean. Mr. Randolph was escorting me. He was perfectly honorable—until he disappeared."

Weylin grunted. "I'd never doubt a lady's word." He bent to pick up her lighter trunk, tucked it under his arm, and then grabbed the second. "You're here, and you're to be my brother's wife. I'll see you safe until you go back to New York."

"I should hate to put you to any trouble."

He didn't answer but started away from the station across La Junta's main street. Evidently he was no conversationalist, and that suited Rowena just fine.

Nevertheless, her mind was crowded with questions by the time Weylin had checked her trunks with a clerk at the hotel and found her a secluded table in the dining room. The place was hardly elegant, but she knew from the train's short meal stops that it was far from the most primitive. The clientele was mixed, ranging from well-dressed men who might have been at home in New York to the most disreputable of ruffians and females of dubious virtue. All seemed to accept each other as social equals.

Weylin secured a waiter, who was able to provide Rowena

with tea. She sipped it with genuine appreciation as he sat down in the opposite chair.

"How did you meet Randolph?" he asked abruptly.

His request was less a command than an exhibition of his utter lack of gentility. She met his gaze coolly.

"He came to see me in New York," she said. "My brother Quentin has been traveling in the West. Mr. Randolph told me that he knew Quentin in New Mexico, and that he was in trouble. He was certain that only I could influence Quentin to leave his hazardous pursuits."

"And you believed him."

His comment stung. She was beginning to realize that she might have made a serious misjudgment, for which she could do nothing but blame herself. "I had every reason to do so," she said. "He spoke of my brother as only a friend could." She chafed at his silence. "Why should a stranger wish to lure me west, Mr. MacLean? Do you know something about this Randolph that I do not?"

Weylin studied her as if she were an annoying inconvenience that he might dispose of with minimal attention. "I know he's no gentleman."

"Then perhaps you might tell me what he is."

"It's enough to say that you were duped, ma'am, by a scoundrel."

If he hadn't been Cole's brother, she would have issued a chilling set-down. Once upon a time, that is—under Cole's tutelage, she had lost the knack. And Weylin might report on her behavior. She smiled with her best feigned courtesy.

"I see. What of my brother?"

"I've never heard of your brother."

Rowena gazed at her gloved hands and saw how tightly they were clasped. She eased them apart and sipped at her cooling tea. "Since I have come all this way, Mr. MacLean, perhaps I might impose upon you to help me locate him—or at least be sure he is not in the vicinity."

"I'm afraid that I have other business, Miss Forster, and you can't stay in La Junta." He summoned the nearest waiter and asked for the check. "There's a decent family with a ranch halfway to Trinidad. I'll take you there, and send a telegram to Cole. If he's not on his way here by now."

Rowena felt less than cheered by the prospect of facing an angry Cole alongside his overly plainspoken brother. "Then it makes more sense for me to remain in town," she said. "You did offer your protection."

"I can't have a woman involved in my business," he said. "If Cole were here, he'd say the same. You'll have womenfolk with you at the Bailey ranch."

She supposed he thought she should be grateful for his 'concern.' "I was under the impression," she said, "that one of your ranches is in the north of New Mexico Territory. Is that not directly south of here?"

"South and several days' ride. Did you come equipped for that, Miss Forster, when you lit off from New York?"

"I have been riding since I was a child."

"You're a gently bred lady, Miss Forster. Cole has told me that many times. You wouldn't last more than a day out here."

She flushed, remembering how willingly she'd accepted Cole's insistence that she have no part in his family's business in the West. She should be in complete agreement with her future brother-in-law.

It was mortifying that the first argument that came into her mind was the least acceptable, the one she refused to consider: that she was far more than any merely *human* woman. She would sooner be lost in the desert than admit that aloud.

"Nonetheless, Mr. MacLean—"

"It's not open to discussion." He rose and adjusted the collar of his coat. "Would you care for a meal while you wait, Miss Forster?"

"No, thank you."

"Then please remain here until I come back." He touched the brim of his hat and strode out of the dining room.

It appeared that she'd misjudged Weylin MacLean in one respect; he was good at giving commands, like Cole, and he was just as determined to protect her from her own folly.

She wondered why she had begun to resent it.

Nearly two hours passed before Weylin MacLean returned with a hired carriage. It was not an attractive vehicle, consisting primarily of a flat bed resting on four wheels fitted out with a benchlike seat in the front. Weylin called it a "buckboard."

"It'll get us where we're going," he said, lifting her trunks into the boot of the conveyance. "If we start now, we'll make the Bailey ranch by nightfall."

Delightful, Rowena thought. She'd stooped once to arguing with him; she would not do so again. There must be some other way to learn if there was any truth to Randolph's news of Quentin.

Weylin tied his speckled mount to the buckboard and helped her onto the hard wooden seat. He shook the reins over the scruffy horses and set off down the street toward the edge of town. Rowena tilted her parasol against the bright afternoon sun, studying every face they passed. Not one was familiar.

Turning southwest, Weylin directed the buckboard along the barely visible dirt track that passed for a road across the plain. The land here was broken with low hills and dry washes, desolate in the extreme. Prairie grass, spattered with wildflowers, stretched for miles to the east, north and south, while mountains edged the western horizon with a faint blue rim.

Of all the places Rowena had passed on the journey West, none was so daunting as this. She had seen prairie rolling past the train window, but hadn't ventured beyond the limits of each depot where they'd made brief stops. The very openness made her shiver as if with some strange foreboding. At first nothing seemed alive save for the grass, clumps of unfriendly cactus and a distant line of stunted trees. Gradually she became aware of small brownish rodents popping up from holes in the ground, the flash of a rabbit's tail, birds she thought must be larks, and a sort of hawk skimming across the sky.

She wished she hadn't looked up to watch the hawk in its flight. The sky was enormous. It arched overhead like an ocean tipped upside-down. She thought that it might fall and drown her at any moment.

How could any man tame this country? How could anyone hope to remain civilized so far from human mastery?

That was the danger. She knew there were Indians here, and natural forces formidable to any traveler. But those were merely physical perils. The greatest risk was that one might lose one's self . . . one's boundaries and inhibitions, the very qualities that raised people above the beasts.

The powerful, almost erotic image of herself remembered from the train filled her mind. *That* stranger might belong here. She never would.

She realized that she had been staring blankly across the prairie for several miles when her eyes caught movement to the south. Figures—mounted men. They were only dark spots now, but she knew they were drawing nearer.

"Mr. MacLean," she said.

He followed her gaze and his hands twitched on the reins. His nostrils flared.

"Who are they?" she asked.

"Hold on," he said. As soon as she had grasped the side of the seat, he urged the horses into a faster pace. The buckboard rattled and threatened to shake Rowena's teeth from their roots.

He was trying to escape the riders, and even she could see how futile the effort was. "Who are they?" she repeated. "Why are you running?"

But he was lifting a rifle from the bench beside him while controlling the horses one-handed. Rowena twisted to look behind at their pursuers.

Four men, she counted, and one riderless horse. As they came nearer, she could have no doubt that the buckboard was their intended goal.

"Can you handle horses?" Weylin asked. Before she had a chance to answer, he thrust the reins into her hands. All her attention turned to guiding the horses, but out of the corner of her eye she could see Weylin brace himself on the seat and raise his rifle to his shoulder.

Violence. How she hated it. The last time she had been involved in violence, the very world had been crashing down about her ears. She hated it, and all the raw emotion it exposed.

"No," she whispered. She heard Weylin hold his breath as he prepared to fire. The report of the rifle left her nearly deaf. When she could hear again, the thunder of many sets of hooves told her that the mounted men were directly behind them. She thought Weylin had fired several more times, but she didn't know if he'd hit his mark. She found herself wondering why their pursuers were not firing in return.

She was likely to have the answer soon enough. One moment Weylin was taking aim again, and the next the rifle was torn from his hands.

"Stop the buckboard!" someone shouted.

She glanced at Weylin, whose face was almost pale under his hat. He nodded to her, and she pulled back on the reins. The lathered horses obeyed readily. She guided them into a trot and then a walk. By the time the buckboard stopped, the pursuers had surrounded them.

Three riders aimed pistols and a rifle at Weylin MacLean. Two of them she guessed to be of Spanish descent from their clothing and dark hair and eyes. The third was not unlike Weylin in appearance, but he stared at her with something very like hatred.

The fourth man held in his hand a long rope, and at the opposite end of that rope, caught in a noose and lying in the grass, was Weylin's rifle. He grinned brazenly down at her from a fine gray horse, his face tanned and handsome. His clothing was virtually all black, from scuffed boots to flat-crowned hat. She knew at once that he was the leader.

"Randall," Weylin said.

The rider let go of the rope and made her a bow from the saddle. "Señorita," he said. "Forgive this untimely intrusion, but I must ask you and Mr. MacLean to get out of the buckboard."

His voice had a musical lilt to it, and a certain uncanny familiarity. Under his gaze, Rowena's heart beat faster than it had during the chase itself.

"Who are you, sir?" she demanded. "What do you want?"

"Don't you know, Miss Forster?" Weylin said. He jumped down from the seat and helped Rowena onto the grass beside the track. He took her elbow in a possessive grip and stared up at their captor.

"It *was* you on the train," he said. "I don't know what you're planning, Randall, but you won't succeed."

His words took several seconds to register in Rowena's mind. "*It* was *you on the train*." Her memory pieced together fragments of conversation and observation: Weylin's reaction to her mention of Thomas A. Randolph—his grim and obscure pronouncements: *"I know he's no gentleman . . . you were duped, ma'am, by a scoundrel."*

A scoundrel. A counterfeit gentleman with a smooth voice and handsome features and rich brown hair.

They could not be the same person, this bandit and the obviously cultured Mr. Randolph. She gazed at him and he looked back with frank calculation, dark gaze measuring her form from hat to hem. It was the same stare as the one that had left her so flustered on the train.

Could a man transform so completely? The mustache was gone, and he looked the very epitome of a dashing dime-novel desperado, ready to sweep swooning maidens off their feet. He wore a dark coat over a waistcoat of black leather; his collarless shirt of wool topped by a neckerchief. His trousers were secured at the waist by a black sash and tucked into knee-high boots, well worn but shining with recent polish. The only expected attribute he lacked was a gun.

Trembling, she closed her eyes and breathed in deeply. The scents of horse and dust and grass and Weylin MacLean were strong, but she still remembered how to isolate one smell from all the others.

And the bandit's was the same. The same as Randolph's, overlaid with the leather and rougher fabrics he wore.

"Randolph," she whispered. "Randall . . ."

"A thousand apologies for the deception, my lady," the bandit said, "but it was necessary at the time." He drew something from his waistcoat: her lost fan, slightly crumpled and incongruous in his bare brown hand.

"*You.*"

"El Lobo, at your service," he said. He swept his hat from his head in an elegant salute. His hair was rough and curling, no longer smoothed in place by expensive pomade. "You need have no fear of me, my lady. But I must ask you to come with us."

She laughed. The sound unsettled her, so raw and vulgar in the silence. With an effort she regained her dignity. "You asked me in New York, Mr. Randolph—Randall—but I do not think that I shall accept your second invitation."

Randall tapped her fan against his chin and glanced at his companions. One of the Hispanos lifted his rifle and casually pointed it at Weylin.

"Mateo is an exceptionally good shot," he said. "I would hate to have to do an injury to Mr. MacLean."

"You bastard," Weylin said without inflection, but his eyes were deadly.

She looked at Weylin with surprise, recognizing his reaction. She had seen that look before, and she knew what it meant. This man Randall was Weylin's enemy. A personal enemy.

"What is happening, Mr. MacLean?" she asked Weylin. "Why did this man lure me away from New York?"

"All your questions will be answered in time, Lady Rowena," Randall said. He dismounted smoothly and picked up Weylin's rifle, loosened the rope, and tossed the firearm to one of his men, who caught it in midair. He coiled the rope, hooked it over his saddlehorn and brought forward the riderless horse. The mare was outfitted with a sidesaddle; he had been prepared for a lady rider. "It is time we were going."

"You are . . . kidnapping me," Rowena said. "You cannot be serious."

"But I am. It is one thing at which we outlaws are expert. Didn't MacLean warn you?" He smiled, showing clean white teeth. She remembered that look, though he'd let it slip only once or twice in his former guise. "We have room for a few of your necessities, if you would select what you require from your luggage." He gestured toward the rider who stared at her with such hatred. "Unless, of course, you would prefer Sim do it for you."

He was not joking. The man called Sim rode to the buckboard and threw her smaller traveling satchel onto the grass. Randall gave her a pair of rough leather saddlebags, large enough for a few toiletries, undergarments, and perhaps a tightly rolled chemise or nightgown—certainly not for even a simple dress or riding habit.

"So now you make war with women," Weylin said. "I knew you were a killer and a thief, but not a coward. Your fight is with me—"

"And with your brother," Randall said, "But I have no wish to kill you. The time when you and I meet man to man is not yet. If you please, señorita."

Rowena felt her skin go hot with chagrin as she repacked what she could under so many hostile male eyes. Randall took the bulging saddlebags and passed them to Sim. He held out his hand. "Come."

As if in a dream, Rowena looked at Randall's outstretched hand. It was long-fingered, brown, and callused—not the hand of a gentleman, as she would have seen on the train had he not been wearing gloves. She had the sensation of having opened the lid of Pandora's box.

And she was afraid. Not of the guns, or of a fate generally ascribed to women who fell into the clutches of outlaws. She was afraid of this man. This "El Lobo." The Wolf.

The fear was not one she could explain. The last time she had been with him, she had felt the beginnings of it and fled. It might have been a premonition of coming disaster; now it was redoubled. It was the same feeling she had on this endless prairie, as if the very openness of it might swallow her identity and replace her with the wanton of her vision.

The wanton who hadn't existed before they met.

Behind those laughing eyes was real purpose. She knew the look of a man bent on revenge. Revenge against . . .

Cole. His face loomed in her mind. What lay between this stranger and her fiancé? She had never heard of El Lobo, nor of a man named Randall. She was caught in the middle of something of which she had no part or knowledge.

What would Cole wish of her now? Would he urge her to resist, leaving all her female delicacy behind? She couldn't imagine it. Surely he'd expect her to swoon, or pretend to do so. A continual faint might be the best protection she could hope for.

No. Such an act was repellant to her. Cole was not here; how she behaved was in her hands alone. At least she could maintain her dignity, and Weylin would report to Cole that she had not given him cause for shame.

Slowly she set her hand in Randall's.

Even through her glove she felt the heat of his touch, a vivid tingle of awareness as clear and sharp as the atmosphere. He leaned very close; she held her breath. Good God—he was not about to . . .

Her hat flew from her head and came to rest in the grass several feet away. Randall's hands settled intimately on her head, feeling for the pins that held her coiffure in place. His fingers were expert. In one fluid motion her hair tumbled free and flowed down, stray wisps catching on her lashes and lips.

"Ah," Randall said, capturing a strand between his fingers. "*Espléndido.* Like golden flame."

It was as if he held her tethered with that light touch. She tried to speak, but her throat had gone dry as the desert. Some almost inaudible sound alerted her in time to see Weylin surge forward.

"No, Weylin!" she cried.

He stopped. Triggers eased back into place. Randall released Rowena's hair, grasped her about the waist, and swung her up into the saddle, holding firm until she was properly positioned. Only then did he turn back to his enemy.

"Peace, MacLean," he said. "I simply wished to see what Cole finds so alluring. I think I am beginning to understand."

"Please don't trouble yourself, Mr. MacLean," Rowena said, trying to ignore the sensual feel of hair loose about her face and shoulders. "There is nothing this man can do that will affect me in the slightest."

Randall remounted with a flourish and saluted Weylin. "Tell Cole that I'll be sending him a message very soon." He rode up alongside the buckboard team, examining them critically. "These aren't worth taking, I think." He drew a long, wicked-looking knife from a sheath at his belt. With a few expert cuts he separated the horses from their harness. Weylin's horse was similarly released from the back of the buckboard. A single bloodcurdling yell was enough to send the animals dashing east across the prairie.

Sim dismounted and stalked toward Weylin, a length of rawhide cord in his hands. Weylin stiffened but did not resist as the other man pulled his hands behind him and bound them tightly. With a sudden twist of his foot, Sim hooked Weylin's leg and sent him tumbling to the ground. He bound Weylin's ankles just as thoroughly as his arms, and stood back to examine his handiwork. Weylin lay still on his side, his face devoid of expression and his gaze fixed on Randall.

El Lobo tossed Rowena's fan to the earth at Weylin's head. "If you begin now," he said, "you may get back to La Junta by midnight."

"I'll track you down, Randall," Weylin said. "Come hell or high water, I'll find you in whatever hole you hide in, and bring you to justice."

"You can try, amigo." He wheeled his horse about and the others followed, drawing Rowena's mount along with them. *"Adiós!"*

"You'll leave him out here alone, bound and with no mount?" Rowena protested, raising her voice to be heard over the hoofbeats.

Randall flashed her a grin. "He'll free himself eventually. And he can run faster than any horse, if he chooses," he said. "He is as much a werewolf as you . . . or I."

four

The lady did not seem overly surprised. She glared at Tomás, tight-lipped, and he wondered if she'd suspected all along.

Most werewolves of sufficiently strong blood and experience were able to recognize another of their kind. But Rowena had forsworn those inhuman powers. She had let them fade away of her own free will.

"You and the MacLeans are enemies," she said. "Like my elder brother and the Boros—" She cut herself off and stared straight ahead, bright hair whipping about her face.

The Boroskovs, she meant—her family's Russian *loup-garou* rivals, who three years ago at the werewolf Convocation in England had challenged the Earl of Greyburn's rule.

Yes, the lady would understand the nature of vendettas that could exist among those of the *hombres-lobo*. They burned hotter, more mercilessly, than any merely human conflict. They could last for generations, until the last combatant was dead.

The Randall-MacLean feud wouldn't end until Tomás himself lay under the earth.

He slowed his horse to a walk, and the others followed

suit. "Didn't you know that your fine Cole MacLean has many enemies?"

"I have no idea what you're talking about."

"Of course he would not tell you. The stories are hardly to his credit."

"What sto—" She caught herself. "I know nothing of your . . . conflict with Mr. MacLean. Weylin called you a thief and a scoundrel. If *you* are an example of Cole's enemies—"

"Only one of many. Most were not so fortunate as I; they are human. I do my very best to even the odds."

"By kidnapping women?"

"By kidnapping a very special woman," he said, admiring her fine seat in the sidesaddle. She didn't let so much as a hint of panic show in her bearing or voice. "We'll see very soon how well Cole values you, Lady Rowena. It should be an interesting experiment."

She breathed out harshly, as if she had a flash of doubt as to her own worth in her fiancé's eyes. "You intend to hold me for ransom?"

"Cole MacLean owes my family more than his entire fortune can redeem." He heard the fierceness in his voice and deliberately relaxed. "No doubt you're burning to hear the full account of my infamous past, and why I call the MacLeans my enemies. It is a long and complicated tale, best told in front of a warm fire with a full belly." He waved at one of his men, riding several yards away. "Perhaps Carlos will regale you with a song of El Lobo, horse thief and desperado, terror and scourge of the MacLeans and their fellow *ricos* of northern Nuevo Méjico."

"El Lobo," she said, mocking the words. "How very appropriate."

"I do not deny what I am—unlike you, my lady."

Abruptly, and without any warning at all, she sawed her reins to the side and wheeled her mare so tightly that the animal half reared in its effort to obey. Mateo cut her off before she'd gone more than a few lengths eastward and grabbed the reins from her hands.

She returned like a defiant prisoner, flushed and angry enough to set the prairie aflame. Tomás sat back in his saddle and studied her with satisfaction. She had no idea how undone she looked at the moment, how near she came to his imaginary Lady of Fire. How much of her precious self-control was illusion?

He would take pity on her and not tell her. Yet.

"I'd thought to trust you with your own mount," he said. "But since you are so impetuous, my lady, Mateo will lead you." He nodded to Mateo, who took her reins. They rode to catch up with the others.

"You never knew my brother at all, did you?" she asked.

"Not well, my lady," he said, "but we have met. And I knew your devotion to him would draw you with me as nothing else could."

"You played your role most excellently," she said, bitterness in the words. "But why did you leave me on the train?"

"When Weylin MacLean appeared, I thought discretion the better part of valor. I knew I would find you again."

"So that you could use me against the MacLeans." She laughed. Possibly she meant the sound to be feminine and careless, but it came out clipped and strained. "You are mad. Cole will not be intimidated by your threats."

"*Quizás.* But beyond Raton Pass and to the west of New Mexico—" he made a wide sweep of his hand southward, encompassing the mountains rising to the southwest. "That is my realm."

"You speak as if you were a king. Of what, pray tell?"

"Of my own fate, my lady. Of this moment." He grinned just to goad her. "That's enough for me. But of course it's most inadequate for a spoiled English noblewoman. I regret that you may find the living a little rough until your fiancé reclaims you. If he loves you, he won't make you suffer long. He does love you, does he not?"

"He is to be my husband."

"And you love him."

"I am your prisoner, not your guest. I have no interest in continuing this conversation."

"Then you won't object if we move faster." He signaled to his men and urged his horse into a canter. Rowena adjusted with natural grace, her body flowing with the horse's motion while her face remained unyielding and closed. They rode across the prairie, alternating between a walk and easy lope, until the sun brushed the mountains.

Tomás was well aware that Weylin made no idle threat when he promised to hunt them down. He'd been pursuing Tomás for years without success. At the end of this day's work, Cole would have no choice but to become personally involved. His pride was at stake, and his manhood. No longer could he afford to rule the MacLean interests from the safe distance of New York.

The battle was about to be joined in earnest.

In the meantime, Weylin had scant hope of finding them soon. Tomás knew of many small, hidden places—villages and arroyos and *cuevas*—that the MacLeans had never discovered. There was an abandoned village at the mouth of a narrow canyon off the Purgatoire River ten miles northeast of Trinidad, a place to provide shelter and rest the horses until just before dawn. Tomorrow night would see them in New Mexico.

They reached the empty village just after sunset. Tomás called his men together among the crumbling adobe walls and gave them their instructions, handing over the ransom demand he'd written for Cole MacLean. They'd see that it reached the main MacLean ranch in Colfax County.

Mateo passed Rowena's reins into Tomás's hands and turned west with Carlos. Sim hung back.

"You shouldn't be alone," he said. "If MacLean finds you here—"

"You know that I can look after myself, *mi amigo.* I need you to handle the Rialto gang when they come for our horses."

Sim turned his head and spat with great eloquence. "Then I hope you get some pleasure out of her." He looked at Rowena, who returned his stare as if she felt the full weight of his hostility. He wheeled his mount and rode so close to her mare that the animal shied and would have unseated a less skilled rider. Rowena snatched the reins and brought the mare to a trembling stop.

Tomás dismounted quickly and caught the mare's bridle. "Easy, *querida,*" he whispered in her twitching ear. "Are you all right?"

Rowena pushed a heavy mass of pale hair from her face. "Are you addressing me?" She glared at his extended hands and grimly suffered him to help her down. "Your friend is ill-mannered. But that is exactly what I ought to expect."

"Sim? It is true that he's no gentleman." He neglected to release Rowena, testing the feel of her body in his arms. Her hair was indeed glorious, even tangled by the wind. It lent a softness to her features that belied her haughty airs. Her willowy curves were well fettered in corsets and unyielding fabric, but he sensed the pliancy and warmth beneath.

This was no ice figurine he held. All at once it was much easier to imagine that his fantasies of the lusty Lady of Fire could become real. Remove those layers of binding cloth, add a few caresses, and it was just possible that the lady would ignite.

Eminently possible.

His mouth felt very dry. She ought to be fighting him tooth and nail. She was certainly not afraid of him. But she remained absolutely still in his arms. "Sim . . . has a rather pointed dislike of women," he said.

"As you do."

"I, dislike women?" He bent closer, studying the plump slopes of her slightly parted lips. "Ah, no, *dulzura*. Far from it."

Belatedly she stiffened and pushed him away. "I pity the poor creatures who suffer your appreciation. But I don't imagine the sort of company you frequent is very discriminating."

He laughed and rubbed his jaw. "*Ay!* I didn't know that they taught such repartee to English ladies. But of course you're no ordinary English lady."

Her face was ghostly in the dimming light. "Since you can have no experience of respectable ladies, sir, your suppositions are absurd."

"Then I must rely on you to correct my misapprehensions," he said. "I promise to be an eager student."

In answer she marched to the nearest adobe wall and pressed against it, folding her arms across her chest. "What is this place?"

"Once it was a village. Now—" He shrugged. "Now it is simply shelter for the night."

"We are staying here?"

Tomás gathered the horses and tied them to a weathered post. "The houses may be crumbling, but I thought you might prefer this to the open prairie."

"How very considerate of you. Don't you fear pursuit? I do not believe that Mr. MacLean was speaking idly when he promised to hunt you down."

"Your concern touches me greatly, señorita, but I could not expect either you or the horses to travel all night."

She shifted against the wall. "You sent the others away."

How careful she was to keep her tone indifferent. He hid a smile. "My men have work to do. We'll meet them in New Mexico." He untied rolled blankets from behind the cantle of his saddle, unsaddled his gelding and the mare, and set out their grain. He drew provisions from the saddlebags, carrying them into a hut missing its northern wall and most of the roof. Rowena made no move to follow.

"I regret that I have so little to offer you, my lady," he said. "I won't risk a fire tonight, and I cannot leave to hunt. But I've bread and cheese and strawberries—"

"I am not hungry."

"But you may wish to rest—unless, of course, you prefer to escape. In that case, you should prepare to Change. It is many miles back to La Junta."

Her silence was answer enough. No, she would not Change—not even to escape, not even if he invited her to do so.

He left the food laid out on a blanket and went to join her outside. "At least come out of the wind, my lady."

"I am not cold."

"And I think I might be warmer away from your natural chill, but I prefer to have you in my sight." He took her arm. "Luckily, you're not unpleasant to the eyes."

"Kindly spare me your dubious compliments," she said. She shook off his arm and walked ahead of him into the ruined house, snatching up one of the blankets as she passed. She laid it in the corner farthest from his. Her clothing was no better fitted for crouching than riding, but she managed to make a pillow of sorts and sat down as rigidly as if she'd been in a hard-backed chair.

Tomás made himself comfortable and used his knife to cut off a wedge of cheese. "And to think I went to the trouble of getting all this for you," he said, gesturing to the bread and strawberries.

"I'm very sorry. What do you usually dine on—raw meat?" His night vision could just make out the flush that rose to her cheeks the moment she finished speaking.

He examined a juicy strawberry. "I am a wolf. Perhaps you identify with another kind of animal. Shakespeare wrote about such a creature in one of his plays. In Spanish, we call it *La Fierecilla Domada*. You would call it *The Taming of the Shrew*."

Her blush deepened. "An outlaw who knows Shakespeare," she said. "I am duly impressed."

"I know many things," he said. *And I believe I may come to know you well, my Lady of Ice, before our acquaintance is finished.* "In answer to your question, my men and I are usually content with tortillas, frijoles—beans, to you—and chiles." He popped the strawberry into his mouth. "Are you quite sure you are not hungry?"

She turned her face away and began to shove her hair about, attempting to untangle the knotted strands with her fingers. Tomás sighed and went in search of her saddlebags. She looked at him warily when he dropped the bags beside her.

"I have never known a woman to be without a hairbrush," he said, untying the flaps. Rowena made a halfhearted bid to snatch the bags away, but not before he found what he was seeking amid the folds of cloth and female gewgaws. "Ah." He examined the handsome brush with a practiced eye. "Expensive."

"Do you care to calculate the worth of the few belongings you've left me?" she said. "Perhaps you intend to sell them as you plan to sell me?"

He raised his hands, palm out. "*Paz*, Lady Rowena. It is true that such a thing might feed a village family for a week, but I will not take it from you. And if selling you were my intention, I'd find you a far better master than MacLean." He presented the brush with a little bow and backed away.

Her thanks was hardly effusive; he might have mistaken it for a curse. Golden hair made a screen about her face as she went to work. Tomás chewed a piece of bread and observed her struggle, almost moved to pity. After a handful of minutes she partially reemerged, eyes glittering with something very like savagery.

"You wished to learn of ladies?" she said between her

teeth. "Here is your first lesson. There is a reason we keep our hair up when we ride."

"So I see. *Lo siento;* I am sorry. It was just too great a temptation to resist."

"And of course you never resist temptation."

"As seldom as possible." Once again he wondered if she realized how provocative her banter sounded. It frankly surprised him, for it was not what he remembered of her in England. She had not behaved so when she'd thought him a gentleman of her own class and country.

A man like Cole MacLean would not tolerate such boldness in his woman. He'd regard her as an inferior, like every other creature on the earth—his property, made to defer to him in all things. No, she could not have spoken so to Cole. Nor would he have suspected she wished to.

Either she simply considered Tomás too far beneath her to watch her tongue, or it was all the defense of a woman who was too proud to acknowledge fear or disadvantage, even to herself.

She spoke of temptation. Was she tempting, caught up in a battle with her own fair tresses, all but spitting with frustration? *Por Dios,* she was.

He got up again and walked toward her. She drew back.

"It might be easier if you had help," he said, crouching beside her.

"From you?" she asked with a lilt of incredulity.

"I often brushed my mother's hair when I was a boy. Hers was very thick and black, and it was beautiful, like yours."

An odd, almost wistful expression crossed her face, as if she had never considered that he might have a mother. "She must grieve over the life you lead."

"My mother is dead," he said, and shrugged. "Long ago. But some things one doesn't forget." He pulled the brush from her hand and caught up a lock of her hair. Tension sang through the strands. She jerked back.

"If you move, you may cause yourself discomfort," he said. "This will go much faster if you cooperate." He began to stroke, barely touching, the way he would groom a half-wild horse.

Strange to think that such a one as this needed gentling. She regarded herself as a fine and proper lady—yet wouldn't a lady flutter and faint in the hands of an outlaw? She would not be a wolf, but her spirit was too strong to remain in the cage she had designed to hold it.

Or had Cole fashioned that cage himself?

He finished with one small section of her hair and gathered up another. Each strand was delicate, touched with lighter and darker hues. It seemed to slide through his hands as if it had a life of its own.

And Rowena didn't stir. He could not have said why she chose to surrender. It was, at best, a reluctant capitulation. Perhaps this restrained sensuality was one of the few such indulgences she permitted herself.

But her gaze never left his face, and with each stroke of the brush he felt a corresponding tug in his own body, an increasing desire to bury his hands in the quiescent flame of her hair.

It was seldom that he pondered deeply on his own thoughts. He was a man of action, not reflection. He'd assumed on the train that his plans for his captive would be more work than pleasure—except the pleasure of trampling the MacLeans' nonexistent honor. His Lady of Fire was just idle fantasy.

He was beginning to change his mind.

Lady Rowena did not behave like a shrinking virgin. For an instant he entertained the thought of her lying naked in MacLean's arms; he remembered the moment on the train when he'd envisioned MacLean kissing her, and his bizarre reaction of possessive rage.

He could feel it starting again. *Ridículo;* she could not

have lain with a man before marriage. Not as she was in New York, or in England. Not his Lady of Ice.

"You."

Her voice brought him sharply back to himself. He let her hair fall. She swept it behind her shoulders and gave him a frown that would have made any lesser man tremble.

"I *know* you," she said. "I am sure of it now. We met before you ever came to New York." She stood up. "Who are you?"

He'd known the time must come when she would recognize him, if ever she acknowledged even a fraction of her werewolf senses. He rose to face her.

"I have been many men, señorita."

"In England," she said. "You were there. At Greyburn." Her face transformed with memory. "The Spaniard—"

"Don Alarico Julian Del Fiero, also at your service."

"What a fool I've been," she whispered. "Braden wrote to tell me that the man who claimed to be Del Fiero—you—" She shook her head. "The real Del Fiero wrote to Braden months after the Convocation. He never made it to England. Something prevented him—some*one*." Her eyes sharpened with accusation. "You took his place!"

"You have unmasked me, my lady."

"You helped Braden fight the Boroskovs, and disappeared. Now I see why you know so much about me. But . . . Braden knew nothing of your family. He was searching for *loups-garous* all over the world. You could have come openly, but instead you chose to hide—"

"You wonder why, Rowena? It was because of you."

She felt for the wall behind her. "I don't believe you. We never met—"

"But I knew of you, my lady. I knew you were destined to be Cole MacLean's bride, as arranged by your brother the earl. How ironic that you fled that marriage only to accept it three years later."

The color drained from her face. "Cole. Of course." She paced away from the wall and turned back, fists balled at her sides. "You hate the MacLeans enough to travel all the way to England . . . to interfere with Cole's marriage?"

"Bravo, my lady. Your mind is as quick as your tongue. I've watched the MacLeans for years—and I knew how ambitious he was to increase his position and fortune with a bride of such great family. Since it's my pleasure to frustrate Cole MacLean's ambitions, it was essential that I learn all that I could about Lady Rowena Forster."

Her chin jerked up. "And what did you learn?"

"That you were a proud and stubborn lady. That you despised the thought of marrying another of your kind. That you wished to be merely human, and that you would do almost anything to attain that wish."

Rowena's discomfort was manifest. Her normally frank gaze avoided him entirely. "You did not even speak to me."

"There was no need. I observed. I saw that there was little chance you'd willingly be MacLean's bride. I found it necessary to leave England following the battle with the Russians, but I learned soon after that you had disappeared, before your would-be mate ever arrived to claim you."

"Did you also prevent Cole from coming to England?" Her words held the bite of sarcasm, but his silence wiped the mockery from her face. "Braden told me later that he telegraphed to apologize . . . a sudden family crisis—"

"For which you should thank me, my lady. His 'crisis' gave you the time you needed to escape your fate. Unfortunate that you didn't follow your original plan to avoid him; it would have saved us both much trouble. But you were in a foreign country, and alone, when he found you. He made you believe that he could give you the kind of life you want. Is that not so?"

"He was not what I feared when my brother arranged our marriage. It was *my* choice to accept his proposal."

"And that is why you are here tonight, Rowena. I could not permit MacLean's scheme to succeed."

"Then this feud between you is worse than I imagined. It is an obsession, madness—"

"There is a certain satisfaction in madness. But you've never allowed yourself to discover that, have you?"

"I saw what it did to my elder brother, with his great 'Cause' of saving the werewolf race. At least he had a noble motive. But you—"

"You know nothing of me, señorita." He moved closer. "That could be remedied."

"You wish to explain to me why your cowardly act against my fiancé is justified. You wish to win my sympathy and cooperation. I have no interest in the lies of a thief and kidnapper."

"And killer. Don't forget that."

She flinched almost imperceptibly. "I do not see your gun. Don't all outlaws carry guns?"

"I've never much liked them. I prefer the use of other methods—"

"To murder? How many men have you killed, Mr. Randall?"

"I thought you were uninterested in my story." He shrugged. "If MacLean redeems you, you can ask him. *Sin duda,* he'll tell you the unvarnished truth."

"You truly have no shame at all."

"Why should I? I am not like you, Rowena, afraid of half of myself."

He knew it was the one subject she could not face calmly, no matter how much she tried to dismiss it. He saw the repressed panic in her eyes, panic she fought with the very spirit she wished to forswear.

As if she could.

"I am not afraid of myself—and certainly not of you," she snapped.

"*Muy bien.* Then I suggest you eat and then rest. We

have a long ride tomorrow." He went back for the food and wrapped it in a napkin. "Permit me to attend you, my lady. I did steal you away from your servants. Can a lady feed herself?"

In answer she picked up the bread, took it in both hands, and awkwardly tore off a piece. Delicately she nibbled on one end, though it was clear to him that she was hungrier than she'd ever admit. She examined a strawberry and ate it in several bites. She reached for the knife he'd left beside the cheese.

Her hand shook as she pointed the blade in his direction. "Stay away," she said. She scrambled to her feet, the weapon clumsy in her fist. "I'm going out to get a horse. Don't follow me—"

Tomás closed the distance between them in two steps and covered her hands with his. The knife's point made a crease in his shirt.

"I believe I would follow you anywhere," he said. He worked her rigid fingers open and eased the knife from her grip. "And I would be devastated if you hurt yourself, *mi rubia.*"

For a moment he saw the fierce battle within her, swirling like tiny golden sparks in her eyes. Her attempt at violence shocked her, and yet she despised her failure to fight him.

She wanted to fight, but in that very wish the wolf lay waiting.

Her hands went limp in his, and she closed her eyes. "Let me go."

"I cannot." Impulsively he bent forward to breathe in the scent of her hair. "Rowena, Rowena. It is a beautiful name." He brushed hair from her face and let his hand linger there. "Sir Walter Scott, is it not? She was the lover of a great knight."

"She was faithful to her betrothed."

"Even when she doubted him."

"You have no power to alter my beliefs," she said. She stepped back, freeing her hands. "You have no power at all. Good night." She turned her back on him and retreated to her blanket, her cold dismissal hanging between them like river mist.

But it was not the coldness that stayed with him as he gathered up the remaining food and wrapped it up for the next morning. It was the fire in her eyes when she'd threatened him with the knife, and the bold wordplay she employed to defy him. It was the many contradictions in what she was and what she believed herself to be.

Above all, it was the promise of what she could become.

How much would it take to push her to the very brink of her control, to that border where she would have no choice but to accept the wolf within herself? How would she react when she was forced to choose between passion and principle?

MacLean wanted Rowena, but it was not for that tantalizing hidden ardor. He must control her as he controlled every other person in his life. He would want her to be the perfect hostess, an ornament, a trophy to add to his prestige. He would pretend to be what she wished only until she was bound to him for all time. He would never let her become all she could be, and in his keeping she would never be tempted. He would make her believe he could provide exactly what she needed to be safe.

Unless another man made her want something more than safety.

A man like Tomás Alejandro Randall.

He sat down against the wall opposite Rowena's and gazed at her elegant marble profile. Suddenly the work he had set for himself did not seem quite so arduous. To seduce the lady, to see her come willingly to his bed to spite Cole MacLean . . . that had been an end in itself. But his interest was becoming much more personal. He had never been able to resist a challenge. Rowena would be one of his greatest. She would surrender, not only to him, but to her own Lady of Fire—embrace the wolf within him . . . and within herself.

Until he had truly been alone with Rowena, he had not been able to see the obvious. He wanted her. His loins ached with the images that rose in his mind, the same that had obsessed him on the train. Her passion, when he awakened it, would be incandescent. They would burn together. No matter if the flame consumed itself quickly. It would be glorious while it lasted.

He laughed silently. *Ah, my Lady Ice, you'll sigh my name with desire soon enough. I won't win you with stories to rouse your sympathy and righteous sense of justice. That would be too easy. You'll accept me as I am, as you believe me to be—outlaw and thief and scoundrel.*

And Cole MacLean would lose again.

Tomás shook out his own blanket and prepared himself for very pleasant dreams.

five

Rowena was already awake by the time Randall came to rouse her. She imagined that she'd slept a few hours, at least; her body was stiff and creased from the confinement of her clothing, but she was perfectly alert.

She had to be.

They rode south out of the abandoned village before dawn. Randall sat his mount easily, occasionally glancing her way but offering no further conversation. He allowed Rowena to guide her own mare—and left her to her unwelcome thoughts.

Again and again, scenes from last night came back to haunt her. His peculiar gentleness. His mention of his mother. The way he'd brushed her hair so intimately, when she'd done nothing to resist. His utter lack of anger when she'd threatened him with the knife. The way he'd called her a shrew. The way he'd called her beautiful.

In England, he had been a gentleman as Don Alarico. He'd defended her brother, fought for him. And it had all been part of his revenge.

She did not know his reasons for hating Cole MacLean. She had told herself she didn't wish or need to know. Why, then, did she feel almost ready to beg him for an explanation?

Why did she shiver with the memory of his touch?

God help her if she were so weak, so depraved as to fall prey to the crude charms of a man like Randall. He was merely playing games with her, goading her because she was here and Cole was not. He had no interest in her as a person, only as an object to be used. She must treat him likewise, as an unpredictable enemy.

Yes, enemy. If he was Cole's, he must be hers.

But there was no point in thinking of Cole. He was too far away to help her. She forced herself to consider the landscape as they ventured closer and closer to the mountain pass. For some time now, twin mountain peaks had been visible on the western horizon. Soon more mountains came into view to the south, presided over by a flat-topped peak which Randall identified as the marker for the pass that would lead them into New Mexico. Rowena was relieved to see an end to the prairie.

Randall circled the bustling town at the foot of the mountains and cut back in at the southern outskirts, joining a well-worn trail that crossed a bridge over the Purgatoire River. This was clearly a main route over the mountains; Rowena saw both single riders and merchant caravans with laden wagons and trailing livestock. Randall rode as if he had nothing to fear, as if daring Rowena to call for help.

And if she did? How many other innocents might be dragged into this conflict? It was not a risk she was prepared to take. There must be another way, a better time.

So she held her peace as they began to ascend, leaving the slower wagons and conveyances behind. At one point the trail turned to pass a ranch in a small valley, where several wagons had stopped at a chained gate to pay a toll. Randall pushed the horses across country until they were well beyond the toll gate.

For many miles they wound upward on the road, through canyons and dells and gorges and over hill upon hill. On

every side, scattered like the spots on a leopard, were dwarf
cedars that gave off a pungent scent, mingled with equally
short pines. Plants with leathery, spearlike leaves grew
among the grasses, unlike any that thrived on the moist
slopes of England. Stunted oaks, taller pines, and groves of
trees not yet in leaf appeared as the road climbed higher.

At last they reached the summit. New Mexico Territory
lay spread before them, flat-topped mesas and buff-colored
plains blotched with darker patches of foliage and the mean-
dering silver stripe of a river. It appeared to be every bit as
much a desert as the one they had left behind in Colorado.

New Mexico was where Braden's wife, the former Cassidy
Holt, had lived during the latter part of her childhood.
Rowena almost wished she had Cassidy by her side now,
to advise her with that clear-eyed innocence unsullied by
her own pain and struggle.

But wasn't it Cole she needed, Cole who would tell her
what she should do?

A lovely and simple melody insinuated itself into her
thoughts, carried by a rich baritone voice in a language still
new to her, mysterious and enchanting.

> *"Les encargo a mis amigos,*
> *antes de acabar de hablar;*
> *Unos son los que las sacan,*
> *y otros las van a gozar."*

Rowena found herself so lost in the flow of music that she
was startled by the sudden silence when it came to an end.
Randall was gazing at her, lips pursed in a soundless whistle.

"You choose a peculiar time for singing," she said.

"Don't you ever sing for the sheer joy of it, Rowena?"

"I sing when it is appropriate to do so."

"Of course. Appropriate. In church, or at those gatherings
of the fine and proper ladies in the drawing room." He guided

his horse so close to hers that their legs nearly touched. "Don't you want to know the meaning of my song?"

"I am entirely indifferent."

"I'll tell you anyway. It's called 'La Calandria'—'The Lark.' It is the tale of a lark who promises to marry the sparrow if he will help free her from her cage. But when he does, she flies off and leaves him." He sighed. "Such is the way of women. At the end, the sparrow sings:

> "I should like to warn my friends
> before I end this discourse;
> Some come to rescue them,
> but others will enjoy them."

Rowena felt her face grow hot. He was baiting her again, quite deliberately. Was he suggesting that Cole, when he recovered her, would not "enjoy" her?

Was he suggesting that someone else would do so?

"Do you see Mr. MacLean as a sparrow, Señor Randall?"

"*El buitre* befits him better—the vulture. I might call you La Calandria, if you sang a little more sweetly."

"I should call you a bantam cock for your arrogant crowing."

"But you could not play *gallina* to my *gallo*."

"I do not speak your language."

"*Gallina* means coward as well as hen."

It was a most dubious compliment. "How strange that you find it necessary to compare me to some animal or other. You would take great satisfaction in making me every bit as disreputable as you are."

"Under the right circumstances," he said. His voice dropped to a husky whisper. "In a candlelit room with a comfortable bed and the stars shining outside the window—*sí, luz de mis ojos,* I would like that very much."

His meaning was insultingly blatant. In all her time with

Cole, she hadn't thought beyond their marriage and the children she would have one day. The necessary method of producing those children had simply not been of importance, or a subject befitting speculation.

Randall's words did what Cole's presence could not. She tried to quell the images that assailed her mind: a room, just as he described, smelling of flowers, and dark save for a handful of candles, with a large bed in the center. The bed was occupied. El Lobo lay on it, bare to the waist, and in his arms was a woman with golden hair, as naked as he. . . .

"Stop it!" she cried.

"Rowena?"

He *knew*. He was doing this to her. *He* was planting these images in her thoughts—using the werewolf power of influence their kind possessed. She'd lived as human too long to fight him off.

She swayed in the saddle; he caught her arm. An incredible sensation swept through her in that moment, an ecstatic pulsation that began and ended in the most intimate parts of her body. It left her breathless and weak and terrified.

"Let . . . go," she gasped.

His unexpectedly swift obedience made her focus on his face. The pupils of his eyes were huge, and he looked as if someone had given him a hearty knock alongside the head. She only wished she had been the one to deliver the blow.

Oddly enough, he had no glib words ready for her, even when his gaze cleared and he seemed to see her again. Instead, he muttered something about hurrying the pace and set his horse at a trot down the sloping trail, scarcely glancing behind to make sure she followed. Her arms and legs shook so badly that she never considered the possibility of riding in the opposite direction.

At noon, without having shared a single word in many hours, they reached the foot of the pass. Rowena saw the crude buildings of another ranch, well attended by travelers, but Randall brought them to rest in a narrow canyon just off the road. He watered the horses and offered her the remaining bread, cheese, and fruit. She found herself too hungry to resist, even on principle, but she made very sure not to touch him in the exchange.

The one thing she wanted more than anything was a bath. Her skin was sticky, and dust filled all the wrinkles in her clothing and her hair and her mouth.

A rivulet of brownish water flowed down the center of the canyon, but she knew perfectly well that she had no choice but to persevere without such civilized luxuries as cleanliness. Bathing anywhere within several miles of El Lobo was out of the question.

Fortunately, he was preoccupied with his own concerns. Instead of riding on, he kept them concealed in the canyon and watched the road expectantly. Just as afternoon began to wane, a party of riders approached from the south.

Rowena immediately recognized the two Spanish men who had first accompanied Randall. They led a pair of fresh horses. Tomás went out to meet them and returned with the animals. He stripped the tack from their original mounts and transferred Rowena's sidesaddle to one of the replacement horses, all without a word to her. After so many hours, she found his silence almost more vexing than his indecent insinuations.

"What now?" she asked.

"We go to meet my men and complete a transaction."

"An illicit one, no doubt."

"*Sin duda.*" He smiled at her, and her heart quite foolishly stopped just for an instant. Whatever his odd response to her when they'd last touched, he was over it now. The return to their sparring was a relief.

"Does that mean you agree?"

"Would I dare to contradict a lady?"

"I wonder if there is anything you would not dare."

"I often wonder the same of you, señorita."

"I intend to keep you guessing, señor."

"Then I look forward to the game."

She knew perfectly well that giving him tit for tat was un-ladylike and exactly what Cole deplored, but she couldn't seem to help herself. And it was safer than the alternative. "You aren't accustomed to losing, are you?"

He gestured to the newly saddled gelding with a shallow bow. "I warn you, Rowena. Men like me never play fair."

For that she had no answer. She allowed him to help her mount, steeling herself against his touch. This time there was no peculiar reverberation in her body, only that keen awareness that never went away.

They rode to join Randall's men, who tipped their hats to Rowena and closed in around her. The four of them and the two spare horses followed the dusty road southwest for most of the afternoon, over arid, broken plains flanked by hills and mountains to the west, their serrated edges touched with snow. They paused for rest and water, and then continued on until nightfall, skirting villages and any other place where travelers gathered. They made camp beside a stream, where Rowena was provided with blankets and a saddle for a pillow. She washed her face and arms in the stream, wrapped herself in a blanket, and spent the night sitting up against the trunk of a tree. No one disturbed her, not even Randall.

At noon the next day they turned west away from the road, following a track that wound its way through a maze of arroyos, the word New Mexicans used for small canyons. It was late afternoon before Randall called a final halt in yet another of the nameless gulches.

A band of perhaps twenty men was waiting there, a collection of disreputable ruffians all heavily armed with every variety of knife and gun. Randall appeared a polished gentleman compared to the least unsavory among them. That, she considered sourly, must be the man called Sim. He rode to meet Randall.

"Rialto's men are tired of waiting," Sim said.

"Go get the horses," Randall said. Sim nodded and rode further into the canyon with several of the men. When they emerged again, they were herding a score of handsome horses.

"Mateo," Randall said, "please watch over the lady while I conduct our business."

"Who are those men?" Rowena asked. "Yours?"

"Rialto's gang? I wouldn't have them if they begged. But they do pay well for good horses to sell in Arizona."

The roughest looking man in the bunch, complete with piratical eye patch, broke away from the others and strode toward Randall. "You kept us here long enough, Lobo."

Randall dismounted. "*Bienvenido,* Bill Hager," he said with an ironic salute. "I think you'll find these horses worth the wait."

"They better be." Hager paced a wide circle around the herd, hand conspicuously near the butt of his pistol, muttering and spitting as he examined the animals. He was scowling when he returned. "Half of them are MacLean stock."

"The finest in New Mexico," Tomás said. "I told you they were worth your time."

Rowena reined her horse forward. "You stole these horses."

"I'm surprised you ever thought otherwise," Randall said. His expression hardened. "This is no place for a woman. Mateo, take her—"

"Well, well. What's this pretty little bird?" Hager caught hold of her mount's bridle and leered up at her. "Not hardly your type, Lobo, from all I've heard. Ain't she a bit ree-fined?"

"None of your business, Hager. You're here for the horses—"

"Might be interested in some honey to sweeten the pot."

"This honey comes with a sting."

"I beg your pardon," Rowena said. She stared into Hager's dissipated eyes. "I am Lady Rowena Forster, and if you touch me, you will find yourself in considerable trouble."

Hager grinned around blackened teeth. "Damnation! Miss High-and-Mighty Furriner. Ro-wee-na. Haven't broke her yet, Lobo? I'm just the man for the job." His smile vanished. "How much?"

"More than you can afford."

"With you there's always a price."

"Not always, amigo. Not always."

"She must be somethin' pert' special, then. I wonder why?"

"Ask the MacLeans," Randall said.

"Yer stealin' their women now, Lobo?"

"I plan to steal everything they claim."

Hager's face underwent a series of transformations. "Well, then. I don't figure she's worth that kind of quarrel with the MacLeans."

"Or with me," Randall said lazily. "She's my woman."

Rowena sucked in her breath. The brief sentence sharply recalled the vision of the bed in the candlelit room. "I am nobody's—"

"As you said, Hager," Randall interrupted, "she needs a little breaking. But I prefer a gentler method."

"Your 'method' seems to work on them horses," Hager said. "All right. Rialto told me to strike a deal."

They fell into negotiations, tossing out offers and counter-offers. In the end, they appeared to reach a mutually satisfactory agreement. Hager's men closed in around the herd, and Hager himself passed Randall a heavy leather purse.

"It's all there," Hager said as Randall weighed it in his hand. *"Naturalmente."*

"Honor among thieves," Rowena said.

"Not honor, but self-interest," he said. "Hager knows he can't cheat me."

"Does he know *what* you are?"

"There are rumors," he said with an air of exaggerated mystery.

"Which I am certain you encourage, regardless of the consequences."

"Consequences? What are those?"

She bit her lip on a retort, aware of Hager's gaze on her. After a moment Hager walked away, and his gang drove the herd out of the canyon toward the outbound trail, while the remaining three men, including Carlos and Mateo, came to join their leader. Sim sent her a poisonous glance and then ignored her.

They set off again, returning at last to the main road reaching ever southward. Rowena was becoming familiar with the tree-dotted and desiccated terrain, though she felt no love for it. The sun began to sink behind the mountains that could be seen along the horizon to the north and west, the vast range Randall called the Sangre de Cristos.

"So," Rowena said to him when they were riding side by side, "you make your living by stealing horses."

"You knew I was a thief, and worse."

"It is my understanding that horse theft is a capital offense in the West."

His grin was blinding. "You are worried about me."

She ignored the comment. "I am not a horse, Mr. Randall—"

"Will you not call me Tomás, Rowena?"

"I never gave you permission to use my name."

"Formality doesn't agree with me."

"As little as good manners, it seems. You actually have a name other than 'El Lobo' or 'Randall'?"

"Did I fail to properly introduce myself?" He executed a half bow in the saddle. "Your servant, Tomás Alejandro Randall." He pronounced the first name with an accent that made it sound quite different from an everyday Thomas. The middle name was obviously Spanish.

"Tomás," she said. It did not sound like the name of an outlaw. She shook herself. "As I was saying, I am not a horse."

"Though you are a fine, high-bred creature."

"You said something to your larcenous cohort that I most firmly dispute. I am not 'your woman,' nor will you break me."

"I am grateful to see that Cole MacLean has not succeeded in doing so. I doubt it is from lack of trying." He sighed. "He and Hager cannot appreciate a woman like you, Rowena."

"And you do? Was that why you chose to humiliate me?"

He stopped his horse and turned to face her. "No." His voice grew very soft, very dangerous. "You do not understand our country and our ways. Until you do, I must protect you."

"Protect?" She laughed.

He reached across the space between them to touch her cheek. "I did not lie when I said you were beyond price, Rowena."

She blocked the overpowering sensation of his caress with a staccato rush of words. "Except the price that Cole MacLean will pay to get me back. What is that, Tomás? A thousand horses? Twenty bags of gold and silver?"

"Justice," he said, dropping his hand.

"And if he will not pay? Will you sell me to a man like Hager?"

"I thought you were sure of your lover, Rowena."

"I was simply curious as to what depths of depravity you might sink."

"I, too, intend to keep you guessing." But the disturbing tenderness in his dark eyes gave the lie to the mere suggestion that he would do anything to hurt her. "I know it's been a long day. We have only an hour to ride, and we'll reach the village where we spend the night."

"Another abandoned ruin?"

"No ruin, my lady. It may not be what you're accustomed to, but it is full of life . . . and *hospitalidad*." He touched the brim of his black hat and rode ahead, leaving Mateo to guard her.

He was true to his word. They turned into the hills off the road, and traveled for slightly more than an hour along a rutted trail just wide enough for a narrow wagon. As twilight fell, they passed the first humble hut on the outskirts of a modest town nestled in a narrow valley.

The village itself was a collection of adobe houses strung along the road, which ran parallel to a stream. The houses were built like the ones in the ruins, but their walls and roofs were neat and intact. Small fields of what Rowena presumed to be American maize and scraggly wheat stretched out behind the houses toward the stream. There were no fences, and no two-story buildings. Rowena guessed that the inhabitants lived off this rugged land from day to day as best they could, with little surplus for luxuries.

A spotted dog ran from the low doorway of one of the larger houses to bark at the strangers, trailed by a middle-aged woman in a simple skirt and blouse. She shielded her plump face with her hand, as if sunlight glared in her eyes, and broke out in a wide grin.

"*El Lobo!*" She clapped her hands together. "*Silencio, Ruidoso.*" The dog sat down, panting. "*Juan, sal! El Lobo está aquí!*"

Tomás signaled a halt. He waved to the woman just as a boy in loose trousers and shirt darted out of the house. The child made as if to run to Tomás, but the woman grabbed him by the arm.

"*Visitando tarde! Vé a decirselo a los otros!*"

With a visible pout the boy ran off, spotted dog at his heels.

"Ah," Tomás said, breathing deeply. "I can smell the frijoles.

We'll eat well tonight." He dismounted, handed the reins to one of his men, and came to stand beside Rowena's horse. "Permit me to help you down."

She was just stiff enough to need his assistance. She stepped away and caught her balance as before the woman came to greet them.

Her welcome was effusive, and Tomás returned it with a kiss on one of her plump cheeks. They spoke to each other in Spanish far too rapid for Rowena to pick out more than one or two half-familiar words.

Feeling very much the outsider, she occupied herself by studying the village. There certainly wasn't much to see. An old man leaning on a cane was hobbling down the street as fast as his twisted legs would allow; a pair of young women in similar dress but much slimmer than the first hurried to the corner of a distant house, peeped around the edge, and giggled like schoolgirls. Their eyes were all for Tomás.

"Rowena."

She turned belatedly back to him.

"Lady Rowena, this is Señora Asunción Valdez." He spoke again to the woman, who beamed at Rowena and answered warmly. "She welcomes you to Rito Pequeño, and to her house."

It would have been impossible to misinterpret the woman's friendliness. That she and her village were willing to shelter an outlaw like Tomás was equally clear—unless these people were somehow unaware of his activities. In either case, Rowena would not forgo common courtesy.

"Please thank her for me," she said.

"You can thank her yourself. The word is *gracias.*"

"*Gracias,* Señora Valdez," Rowena pronounced carefully.

The woman burst into a renewed flood of Spanish. Tomás listened and nodded with half-closed eyelids.

"She's very curious about you," he remarked when the woman hurried back to her house.

"And what did you tell her?"

"That all will be revealed tonight. Soon the men will come in from the fields. The village will hold a *baile* for us— a dance, you would call it." He grinned. "The people will use any excuse for a dance."

"You are very popular here."

"I'm fortunate to have many friends throughout the Rio Arriba. If you choose, you can make them your friends as well."

"How can they be mine when they are yours?"

"You'll find," he said, easing closer, "that you and I are not such enemies, Rowena." He'd no sooner come with a hair-breadth of brushing her lips with his than he was turning smoothly to greet the old man with the cane, who seemed as delighted to see him as Señora Valdez had been. Rowena was left speechless.

There followed a steady stream of visitors, barefoot boys at first, and then men of various ages, and shy girls and women who hung back while Tomás and his men found stabling for the horses. Rowena was the subject of many curious glances and whispered speculation. Tomás's men were known to the villagers, and some wandered off with acquaintances. Sim Kavanagh stood along at the edge of the milling crowd, smoking a cigarette. His baleful stare caught Rowena more than once.

If she were less a lady, she would confront that man and demand to know the reason for his dislike. But to acknowledge his stares was beneath her—as much beneath her as fluttering about Tomás with coy glances and hooded eyes like several of the pretty señoritas. Tomás had a jaunty word and a wink for every one of them.

None too soon, the well-wishers went about their business, leaving a trio of staid older men who spoke to Tomás with dignified formality. Tomás introduced the elder of them as Don Pablo. He tipped his hat to Rowena. She nodded.

"Don Pablo insists that you and I stay in his casa," Tomás said. "We will dine with him." He turned back to the men and withdrew something from his waistcoat. Rowena recognized the leather bag of coins he'd received for the stolen horses.

At first Don Pablo refused the bag, looking both hopeful and embarrassed. But Tomás pressed it into his hands with a coaxing grin. *"Para los niños,"* he said.

Don Pablo bowed his head, the telltale moisture of tears in his eyes. *"Dios le bendiga, Don Tomás. Dios le bendiga."*

"De nada." Tomás pretended not to notice the old man's emotion. He excused himself with a slight bow and took Rowena's arm to draw her away.

"Was that for my benefit?" she asked.

"Perdón?"

"You wanted me to witness the disposal of your ill-gotten gains, did you not? I see that I misjudged you." In spite of herself, the words rang with mockery. "El Lobo is simply an American Robin Hood—stealing from the rich to give to the poor."

"Do you find that so ridiculous, my Lady Ice?"

"Don't call me that."

"But it suits you so well." Under his light tone and idle half-smile lay a core of steel. "Your English Robin Hood stole from nobility just like you, my *lady*." He gestured at Señora Valdez's house. "Don Pablo and Asunción, who have invited us to eat at their table, were not always poor. Once they were among the *ricos* of the Territory. They owned much fine land, and many sheep. When the Americans came, some like them began to lose what they'd had since the old days under Spain and Mexico. They didn't understand the new ways and new laws, and the lawyers found it easy to trick them. Don Pablo and his people were driven from his family's land, and started again in this village, where life is much harder. He cares for the people who once worked for him as best he can. I am merely trying to give back a little of what was taken from him."

An unexpected suspicion crowded into Rowena's mind. "You aren't suggesting that *Cole* had something to do with this man's situation?"

"Not Cole, but another much like him."

She released her breath. "I am sorry that fortune treated Don Pablo so poorly," she said. "There is still much about this country I don't know. But you are clearly an educated man, Tomás. I doubt that *you* were ever among the poor."

"Have you finally developed an interest in my past?"

"If I did, would I find justification for criminal behavior?"

He laughed. "I have a premonition that before you and I part company, you'll find yourself on the wrong side of the law at least once, *mi rubia*."

"I should hate to disappoint you. Why not let me go, before you learn how mistaken you are?"

"When your company is so very . . . stimulating?" His grip on her arm became a slow caress from wrist to elbow, a stroke she felt keenly through her snug sleeve. "I don't know how I managed without you to keep me in my place."

"Your place is in a jail."

"I'd far rather be in your bed."

six

His shocking bluntness sent a stab of alarm and heat racing along Rowena's spine. *Games,* she reminded herself. *He's good at playing games, to see what sort of reaction he can get. Just like Quentin.*

The thought of Quentin cleared her mind at once. A rogue her brother might be, and recklessly whimsical, but he was no criminal. She apologized silently to Quentin for the comparison.

"I presume you'd like to bathe before dinner," Tomás said, as if he'd commented upon the weather. "Asunción will be happy to help. Come."

Whatever else he might do or say to discompose her, he hadn't lied about Don Pablo's hospitality. Asunción set about fussing over Rowena like a mother hen. Her attitude was respectful but without formality; she carried herself like one still surrounded by the wealth Tomás implied she had lost. She hung a blanket over the open doorway of a small, square room adjoining the *sala* or main chamber of the house, providing Rowena with complete privacy to wash with the use of clean rags, rough soap and a tin tub filled with warm water. She hadn't felt so wonderful in ages.

She did what she could to freshen her clothing as well, rinsing out her spare drawers and chemise, and then had time to rest. The room was unfurnished save for a little table, a cupboard, a crude bench, and rolled blankets or mats set along two of the walls. One deep window, its sill awash with bright potted flowers, let the last daylight into the room. In its very simplicity was an unforeseen beauty. Outside she could hear the children of the village laughing and preparing for the *baile* after dinner.

Children. She closed her eyes and let herself sag against the wall. The high, happy voices reminded her of the babies she longed to have—children who would certainly never know poverty. Not like these. Was Tomás so terribly wrong to want to help people who did not enjoy the privileges of the rich?

Yes. There were ways other than stealing and killing; she and Cole had funded several charitable organizations in New York. Any good Tomás did was undone by the methods he employed to achieve it.

What had driven him to this life, and to such hatred of Cole MacLean?

You don't care, she told herself desperately. *You don't care at all.*

During a long hour of uncomfortable reflection, the scents of exotic cooking penetrated every room in the casa. Rowena's mouth was watering when Asunción came to fetch her.

The dining area was dominated by one big, battered table obviously built by someone with a rudimentary knowledge of carpentry. The chairs did not match. The plates were chipped and the cutlery plain, but Rowena knew that the Valdez family had set out its very best for her and Tomás.

Three children, two young women, and a middle-aged man joined Don Pablo and Asunción at the table. Tomás declined the head seat and guided Rowena to the center of the table, where they would be surrounded by their hosts.

Aware of her deficiencies in language and her unfamiliarity with the ways of Tomás's people, Rowena tried not to let her nervousness show.

She was the one at a disadvantage here. Surely these folk didn't know she was an unwilling captive, and she had no way of telling them. Tomás could say anything he liked without fear of contradiction.

It seemed that he wished to test her. He would learn that she could pass any devious trial he set her.

Tomás named each of the elements of the meal: tortillas, frijoles, mutton in a stew with red chile sauce, and coffee. Everyone was courteous but informal; Rowena couldn't remember the last time she'd dined so casually, or on such unusual fare. There was much genuine warmth and chatter among the family members, and she felt an ache of unexpected longing. Meals at Greyburn—or with Cole—had never been like this.

She was just about to take a spoonful of the mutton stew when she realized that Tomás was watching her with keen anticipation. She took a careful bite and stopped. Slowly she swallowed and turned to him with a pleasant smile.

"Delicious," she said.

"You don't find the food too . . . spicy? I know that the English prefer a bland cuisine."

"Please tell our hosts that the food is excellent." She took another bite. The strong flavors danced on her tongue like a piquant melody. So much for Tomás's assumptions.

"Very good," Tomás said under his breath. He spoke in Spanish to Asunción and Don Pablo. They smiled and nodded. Rowena felt absurdly pleased that she'd pleased them.

After the main courses had been served, Asunción and her daughter brought out sweet dumplings called *buñuelos*. The young ladies, perhaps sixteen and eighteen years of age, were far more interested in Tomás.

The elder of the two began to chatter in rapid Spanish,

asking Tomás any number of questions and using the pauses to flirt with impudent boldness. Tomás made no attempt to discourage her interest and gave the girls full attention, passing compliments to the younger girl that made her blush.

After a time Rowena realized that the elder girl was staring at her. She lifted her chin.

"Please ask the young lady if there is something she wishes to ask me," she said to Tomás as she finished her *buñuelo*.

The girl promptly answered Tomás's question. He covered his mouth on a cough.

"Carmen wants to know if you are able to see the sun."

"What?"

"There's a folk legend in this country that says those who are very fair cannot see the sun."

It was an absurd myth—but no more absurd than that of human beings who could change into wolves. "Please assure Miss Carmen that I can see the sun quite well. I simply prefer the shade."

"Perhaps that is your problem, Rowena," he said softly. "This is a land that rewards those who love the sun. You may find it easier to accept its heat than hide from it."

"I thought that the people here came in from the sun at noon."

"They respect its power, but they are not afraid."

"You cannot seem to decide whether or not I am a coward. Fortunately, I have yet to develop any interest in your opinion of me."

Don Pablo chose that opportune moment to speak. The women cleared the table, and it was soon apparent that the whole family was preparing for after-dinner festivities. Tomás offered his arm and led Rowena outside, followed by the children and adults of the Valdez family.

The evening was fair and warm, and so the *baile* was to be held in the open area behind Don Pablo's house. Already many of the villagers had gathered there, including a man with a fiddle and another with a guitar. They tuned their instruments to much laughter and happy conversation. Children ran about freely. Women in brilliant red or yellow skirts sat on benches that formed a loose boundary of the earthen dancing floor. Tomás's men were there—all but Sim Kavanagh.

Don Pablo opened the celebration with a welcoming announcement. He gestured Rowena and Tomás, the guests of honor, toward the two heavy carved chairs reserved for them. The musicians began without fanfare. Their melody was uncomplicated and rhythmic, similar to the one Tomás had sung yesterday. Rowena recognized a waltz, vastly different from anything she'd ever heard in England. Couples formed quickly. There was no more formality here than there'd been at dinner: no dance cards, no scrutinizing of rank or social suitability, and no chaperons other than the older women who watched from the sidelines. Even the children danced.

Before she had a chance to sit down in the fragile hope that she'd be ignored, a young village man in well-worn shirt and trousers approached with an invitation. It was impossible to refuse without blatant discourtesy. She flung a helpless glance at Tomás. He was already dancing—with the elder Valdez daughter, who fluttered her lovely eyes at him.

Blast him. He could certainly dance; she remembered that last evening before the battle at Greyburn, when she had played waltzes on the piano in the drawing room and "Don Alarico" had asked Cassidy to join him.

Far better that *she* should dance with a stranger. She allowed the young villager to lead her to a clear space on the floor. The man was eminently respectful of her; his manners were impeccable, despite his humble appearance. Soon they were only one more part of the mass of color spinning to the quaint and pretty music. The stiffness in her spine began to relax.

When one melody ended another began almost without

pause, but this time Don Pablo himself claimed her. He was more vigorous than the young man and less strictly proper. He swung her about with a gleam in his eye, as if he knew a secret she did not. That was nothing new.

He guided her past another laughing couple. Rowena recognized Tomás with a new village girl in his arms. She gazed up at him with a sort of odious infatuation.

"Seguramento no está celosa de su marido, señora?" Don Pablo asked.

"I beg your pardon," she said. "I don't understand."

He shook his head and chuckled. *"No se preocupe. Todo occure como Dios quiere."* The song ended, and she found herself passed like a sack of grain to the next man.

That man was Tomás. He pulled her close with the manifest intent of provoking her. Her heart fell into the trap and tripled its speed.

"I am proud of you, my lady."

"Then I can die in peace, knowing that my life had purpose."

He clucked. *"Vamos, vamos.* Don Pablo thinks very well of you, and so do the others. They say you're worthy of El Lobo, for all your foreign ways."

"I don't dare guess what inordinately high opinion they have of you. They must not know what you are."

"A thief?"

"A . . . werewolf."

"It surprises me that you dare speak the word. What if it should corrupt the purity of your resolve?"

"Will you answer my question?"

"Don Pablo knows. A few others suspect. I see no reason to frighten those who do not."

"Then you admit it is a shameful thing to be."

"Al contrario. It is very useful to a man in my profession."

"You have made my case perfectly." She smiled up at him

and stepped away as the third song came to a close. The musicians stopped to rest and take refreshment. Older villagers gathered about the guests while younger men and women drifted off to snatch a moment or two of furtive courtship.

If not for the way she continued to notice every pretty young partner Tomás chose, Rowena might have enjoyed the rest of the *baile*. Rank and position had always been important to her, yet for a time she was able to forget the vast gulf that lay between her and these good people.

The dancing and celebration went on until well past midnight. People drifted back to their homes reluctantly, exchanging exhausted but happy farewells. Rowena and Tomás were shown back into Don Pablo's house, where Tomás was offered a nightcap while Asunción made up a bed in another room.

Rowena took advantage of the privacy to wash and pull her crumpled nightgown from her saddlebags. It was much the worse for the journey, but she couldn't bear another night in her corset and traveling clothes. She undressed as best she could. The cambric was cool against her skin. At least tonight she would sleep in a bed, however lumpy it might prove.

A small mirror hung from one of the thick walls. She'd put up her hair last night, by feel alone, with the extra pins she'd had the foresight to pack in the saddlebags. It was a perfect fright. She let out the pins. Most of the tangles were gone—thanks to Tomás.

Even handling her own hair brought back the feel of his touch, his surprising gentleness. She tried to banish the memory with hard, painful jerks on the last remaining knots. The method proved ineffective. Grimly she persevered until her hair fell thick and shining at her back.

Already her skin had begun to take on the subtle glow of a tan. Tomás had told her that she ought to enjoy the sun, which was ample reason not to. If he thought he could mold and shape her to his specifications for his own amusement . . .

The vivid Indian blanket hung over the doorway shifted aside at the touch of a hand. Tomás walked in without warning and paused to gaze at her, hands on hips.

Rowena snatched the blanket from the bed and wrapped it around herself. "What are you doing here?"

He yawned behind his hand and tossed his hat on the bed. "Looking forward to a good night's sleep."

"Leave at once!"

Off came his coat, leaving him in shirtsleeves and waistcoat. "But this is our room, *dulzura*."

"*Our* room?"

He unbuttoned his waistcoat. "This is not a hotel in New York." He folded the waistcoat and placed it over the back of one of the room's two chairs, the other of which was already occupied by Rowena's things. "Don Pablo insisted on giving us his room."

"This is *his*—"

"The only one with a real bed. I had no intention of straining his hospitality, so I simply told him"—he unwound the sash at his waist and released the upper two buttons of his shirt—"that we are newly wed."

He'd caught her unaware too many times with such outrageous pronouncements. "You have lost your mind," she said calmly.

"In what way? I've eaten well and danced and now I'll share the night with a beautiful woman." Another button came undone. Dark, curling hair showed in the vee of his open shirt. If he continued, he'd very shortly be naked.

She'd seen unclothed men in the past—her brothers, when they Changed, though she'd avoided them at such times when she grew older. Braden had always claimed that there was no disgrace in nudity among their kind.

This was not the same. She and Tomás were both *loups-garous,* but he was not preparing to Change.

Cole had never appeared before her with more than his

coat removed. She hadn't considered what he might look like beneath the expensive and respectable attire. Now her unruly imagination was well on its way to completing the job of undressing Tomás.

His chest and shoulders were broad, but not heavy. He would be sleekly muscled under the shirt, long and lean. His hips were narrow, buttocks firm. His legs would be made for riding and running. And as for his—

"I'm glad you like what you see," Tomás said. He pulled the hem of his shirt from the waistband of his trousers. "Don't you think it's your turn?"

Horrified at her own thoughts, Rowena stepped back and bumped into the bed.

Tomás left his shirt hanging loose and sat down in the chair. "You don't mind if I remove my boots?"

She struggled to keep her gaze from straying to his chest. "Very well. If you insist on remaining here, I will find somewhere else to sleep—"

"And insult our hosts? I think not." He stood his boots in the corner of the room and laid his stockings over them. His bare feet were soundless as he crossed the room. "What would become of my reputation if it were known that my new bride abandoned my bed?"

Rowena edged around to the back of the bed. "You should have thought of that before telling such a ludicrous falsehood."

"But they were all so pleased for me, that I'd won such a lovely bride."

"I doubt that the señoritas were pleased," she said. "You have falsely claimed a victory you could not possibly achieve, not in a hundred lifetimes."

He leaned on one of the plain wooden bedposts. "Be warned, my Lady Ice. I can't resist a challenge."

"Don't come any closer."

"And if I do? Will you fight me?"

"That's exactly what you want, isn't it? That's what you find . . . exciting."

"I'm far more interested in what you find exciting, Rowena. What brings the fire to your eyes and the color to your cheeks, besides aristocratic indignation." He leaned far over the bed. "Shall we try an experiment?"

She was not hard-pressed to guess what sort of "experiment" he had in mind. "You lied about me to these good people. How many times have you lied to *me* since you revealed yourself as a thief and outlaw?"

"Odd as you may find it, I have not lied to you."

"I find that not merely odd, but inconceivable."

The teasing, half-dangerous gleam in his eyes went out like a snuffed candle. He straightened and pulled off his shirt with unnecessary force. The muscles in his back and arms flexed and rippled as he flung the shirt over the chair.

Rowena refused to retreat even an inch when he came for her. He scooped her up effortlessly; she compelled her body to go limp and boneless. The blanket slid to the floor. She thought her body would shake apart with the violence of her heartbeats.

But his gaze didn't stray to her breasts and hips and legs so clearly delineated under the fine cambric. He all but dropped her into the bed. His arms formed a cage to either side of her; his breath scorched her with its heat.

"As inconceivable as you may find it," he said roughly, "I have never taken an unwilling woman." He threw the blanket over her and drew it up to her chin. "This room is too chill for me. I think I'll seek warmer company."

"Those many doting señoritas?" she snapped. "I doubt that Don Pablo will thank you for despoiling his daughters."

"Do not worry. I prefer a woman of experience—and full-blooded passion. *Hasta mañana.*"

Long after he'd left the room, Rowena lay rigid and bitterly cold in spite of the mild evening air.

"Don Tomás!"

He woke with a pounding head to the urgent voice and blinked against the bars of light filtering into the stable. The horse with whom he'd shared the night stomped and snorted as if to agree with his opinion of the morning.

More than just his head ached. He'd attempted to sleep—hours after leaving Rowena—in the crowded village barn while fighting an arousal that had become his constant companion. It was his worse luck that he woke with the same arousal.

And what had he expected last night? An easy conquest? Where was the challenge in that?

He groaned and spit straw from his mouth. No; he hadn't really believed Rowena would share her bed. Not without considerably more encouragement. But it had been worth a try.

He found himself remembering the curiously potent touch they had shared in the pass, jolting him like lightning out of a clear sky. It had been like the culmination of the act of love, though they'd done no more than brush each other. He hadn't known what to make of it.

Maldición! Such thoughts were not helping. *Now,* mi amigo, he addressed his uncooperative member, *if you'll just go away until I need you . . .*

"Don Tomás! Are you here?"

He sat up, scrubbing at his hair. They should have left the village before dawn, in case Weylin had managed to find their trail. If the caller were one of his men, he might have reason to worry. But this one was female, and elderly. Don Pablo wouldn't send an old woman to warn him of danger.

"I'm coming," he called out, reaching for a shirt that wasn't there. Well, *la mujer vieja* had undoubtedly seen as much as Rowena had, and appreciated it more.

He found the woman waiting just outside, wringing her hands. The instant she saw him she launched into a monologue that took all Tomás's concentration to follow. He nodded, smiled, and assured her of his help. When she had left, he visited the stream and washed himself quickly. Then he went in search of his men.

Rowena was awake, groomed, and dressed when he found her. Someone had already provided her with coffee, which she was drinking as if she sat at ease in her morning room at Greyburn. It was as if nothing had happened between them.

"Are you ready to leave?" he asked tersely.

"Good morning," she said with exaggerated courtesy. "I've been up for some time."

"So have I." He noticed that someone—Asunción, undoubtedly—had replaced his soiled shirt with a clean one. He put it on and tied his sash. There'd be gossip soon enough about his failure to share his "wife's" bed, even if Asunción herself kept quiet. He wouldn't be here to listen.

"We ride west," he said, "to the village of Los Milagros."

"For another bestowal of your largesse?"

He was not in the mood to trade barbs with her today. The old woman had given him an excuse for action, and it was exactly what he needed. He finished dressing and escorted Rowena from the room. Without explaining his purpose, he warmly thanked Don Pablo and Asunción for their hospitality, left the children each with a coin, and kissed the eager daughters on their smooth cheeks. His men, accustomed to sudden departures, had the horses saddled and ready.

To her credit, Rowena hung back to thank the Valdez family and the villagers who'd stopped by on their way to work in the fields and pastures.

Asunción presented her with a straw hat to shade her fair skin, and after a moment Rowena opened her saddlebags and drew out her ivory-handled hairbrush. Asunción's daughters were delighted with the gift. Rowena had done surprisingly well here. Nevertheless, it was fortunate that she spoke no Spanish.

He shrugged away his idle thoughts and leaped into the saddle. Mateo helped Rowena to mount. Sim appeared from whatever lonely den he'd spent the night in, and they rode west to the shouted farewells of the people.

It was not long before they reached Los Milagros. How the old woman had come to know of the trouble here, Tomás could only guess. The reason for concern was obvious as soon as his band rounded the mesa that bounded the village to the east.

The girl was surely no more than seventeen years of age. She was small and delicate, with dark hair unruly about her face and feet bare on the rocky path. The men who drove her could have been folk from any local village. Their faces were twisted with hatred. They'd already hurt the girl, and they were not finished with her yet.

But they hadn't reckoned on Tomás.

He gestured his men to retreat. They dismounted out of sight of the village and the men on the path.

"What is going on?" Rowena demanded after Mateo had helped her down. "Who are those people?"

Tomás took her arm and led her to a place where they could observe the path. "An old woman in Rito Pequeño told me there was trouble in this town. Do you see that girl?"

"Of course." She shaded her eyes. Her voice tightened. "What are they doing to her?"

"They say she is a *bruja,* a witch. Such women are feared. This one is being driven from her village."

"A witch? She's just a child!" Rowena started out from cover, oblivious to danger. Tomás pulled her back.

"Yes. But the terror of *brujería,* witchcraft, is strong among many people. *Brujas* are said to cause the evil eye and take the forms of animals. It is not unknown for witches to be put to death."

Rowena turned such a fierce look on him that he was caught between surprise and admiration. "And do you intend to do anything to stop this?"

In answer he began to shed his clothes, watching her expression run the gamut of outrage, alarm, and gradual realization. She turned her back on him quickly, but he could hear her breath grow faster and deeper. Once, he was certain, she glanced his way just before he stripped the last bit of clothing from his body.

He would have liked to savor the small victory, especially after last night. But that would have to wait. Closing his eyes, he let the Change come. His body grew light as air, formless, at one with the earth and sky . . . and *shifted*. The potency of a wild hunter's heart pumped through his veins. The transformation was an instant of sheer ecstasy, and he let the wolf take him.

This was freedom. This was the ability to live life in the moment as no man ever could. But his human mind remained to guide him, and he knew his purpose.

He burst from cover and charged directly for the men and their captive.

Numb with pain and despair, Felícita did not know at first why her tormenters were shouting.

She lifted her gaze from her bruised and dusty feet. A sleek shape, dark brown and black, was running toward her. It might have been a dog, except that it was much too big and too fast and its teeth were bared in a grin no dog had ever worn.

Once, long ago, she had seen a wolf. They were not common now, even in the mountains. She thought that this must be *un lobo*, even so. She should have been afraid.

The men were afraid. One of them yelled a warning. Another tried to point his old pistol and then dropped it in panic. The other three, armed only with the switches they'd used to beat her from the village, had sense enough to run.

Felícita stood very still. The wolf ran past her, chasing the men as they scattered. The warm morning breeze touched her neck where the switches had cut her bare skin above the neckline of her *camisa*. If the wolf killed her, at least it would be quick.

But when he came back for her, he was no longer running. He approached at a trot, long-limbed and relaxed, with his tongue lolling just like a dog's.

His eyes were different from any animal's she'd ever seen. He sat down directly in front of her, speaking with those strange eyes as men spoke with their mouths—or their souls. She tried to answer, but no sound would come out.

The wolf whined in his throat. He touched her fingertips with his warm, moist nose and started down the path the way he had come.

He wanted her to follow: She could feel that in him the way she felt things in people. She was too weary for surprise. If she could but think. Her mind was cloudy after days of fear and isolation. For as long as she could remember, her uncle had always told her what to do. The men in the village must have been waiting for Tío's death, so that they could make her go away. Only she had nowhere to go.

The wolf paused and looked back, head cocked. From behind him came a figure—a woman, pale, and dressed like a fine lady from the city, walking very straight in her tight clothes.

She wasn't afraid of the wolf. She passed him by without a glance and came straight to Felícita.

"Poor child," she said. "Come with me."

The language was not Felícita's, but she knew it. Tío had taught her the Anglo tongue, so that one day she could go among the people in the cities and earn money as she did in the village. There were many more people in the city, Tío said, who would pay much when they learned of her powers.

Powers. That was what he called her ability to see into the hearts of others. People came to Los Milagros—people who had heard of the girl who could tell fortunes just by looking at a man or woman. Most were villagers, sometimes outsiders like this lady, though never so grand. She would look into their souls and tell Tío of their desires and fears, and he put these things into words and gave them stories to make them happy.

She hadn't thought there was anything wrong in making people happy. She hadn't understood that people were also afraid of the things she knew. Afraid enough to want to hurt what they feared.

Tío hadn't explained that part of it. He had kept her sheltered, protected, like the carving of a saint in an alcove.

The foreign woman knelt awkwardly and touched her arm. "Do you understand me? Come. You'll be safe."

El lobo stood at her side like a tame demon, adding his silent plea to hers. Perhaps the pale lady was a real *bruja,* just as in the stories. If she was, it didn't really matter. Felícita was already damned.

She let the pale lady take her hand and lead her down the path and around the bend where it passed Mesa Baja. The wolf disappeared as if by magic. Men were waiting with horses in the shade of an *alamo.* They stared at her, but they weren't afraid. The lady made her sit down under the tree and offered water from a metal bottle.

After a while, when her mouth was less dry and the lady had bathed her face with a clean cloth soaked in the water, a man came to join them. He was tall, and very handsome. Felícita flinched, but he shook his head and dropped down onto his haunches a safe distance away.

"How is she?" he asked in *inglés.*

"She is in shock, I think. They hit her." The lady's voice was angry, but the anger was not for Felícita. "She must be properly cared for."

"*Naturalmente.* She seems to trust you."

"She needs a woman to care for her. Ask her if she speaks English."

"*Hablas inglés?*" he asked Felícita.

She stared at him, unable to answer. She couldn't seem to make words come anymore, in any language. Her throat closed up even when she thought about it.

"I am Tomás," he said gently in Spanish. "Can you speak?"

Somehow he had guessed. She shook her head and tried to ignore him. If she could just pretend she was alone in her own little casa, where no one could ever find her . . .

It was too late. No matter how much grief it brought, she couldn't stop the knowing. Already she began to see into his heart.

But there was a change this time from all the times before. Tío had kept a wall around her, to guard her soul as much as her body—an invisible wall as strong as the thickest adobe. None of the other seekers who had come to the casa could touch her through that wall. Their feelings and the images they made in her mind were remote, impersonal, a play she watched from a distance. Until the men of the village had come for her, the ones who called her *bruja,* and drowned her in their hatred.

This Tomás did not make her afraid. He was completely unlike the villagers she'd known all her life. He was like . . .

Like the pale lady. They were the same, yet not.

She let the images form. This Tomás . . . was a blaze of summer sunlight bright enough to hide the storm clouds waiting over the horizon. Most people would never think to look beyond the brightness and warmth. But no . . . the sun came up exactly the same every day. Tomás was a flickering candle that might shift direction or go out in an instant. He might pretend, but he was afraid to be the sun.

The lady pulled at Felícita just as strongly. She was a cactus growing on the hill, prickly on the outside and standing alone. If one was patient, one could find the fruit she hid with her spines, and the beautiful flowers that came each spring. But she would not see herself that way, because she thought she belonged in a fine garden where all the flowers grew in rows and never strayed from their places. She was a caged wild bird that was afraid to fly.

Not a bird. A wolf, like the wolf that had saved Felícita. A wolf that would not accept its own shadow.

Felícita covered her face with her hands. Tío's walls had crumbled to dust. The pictures and emotions in Felícita's mind were too strong, too clear, too personal: sun, candle, cactus, bird, wolf; need, fear, sorrow, secrets . . .

"I believe she cannot speak," Tomás said. "She understands Spanish at least, but—"

"She must understand kindness," the lady said, *en inglés*. She set her hand on Felícita's shoulder. "My name is Rowena. I'd like to be your friend, and help you."

Tomás scooted closer. "Were you alone in the village, *muchacha?*" he said in Spanish.

Felícita nodded, still too numb for grief.

"There was no one to help you?"

She shook her head.

Tomás sighed and glanced at Rowena. "The old woman who told me of the girl is a distant relative. She said that there was an uncle in the village. He must be gone, or this would not have happened."

"I should hope not." She stroked Felícita's hair. "What of this woman in Rito Pequeño? Could she take the child in?"

Felícita tried to cry out. Tomás looked at her searchingly.

"It would not be wise," he said. "Rumors of this will spread quickly. Others might come after her."

"Because of some ridiculous belief that she is a witch?"

"Is it so ridiculous in a world that holds our kind?"

The lady frowned. "She is not—"

"Not one of us, no. But she is—" he cocked his head, "unusual."

"All the more reason to pity her."

"As you pity yourself?"

The color rose in her cheeks. "You certainly didn't help by appearing as a wolf in front of those men. They will think she summoned some sort of familiar. I suppose you could not resist a dramatic gesture, whatever the cost."

"It doesn't matter what they think. They will not trouble her again."

"Then you agree that we should take her with us?"

"You've appointed yourself her guardian. Can you trust her in the company of villainous outlaws?"

"The alternative is leaving her here, and that I will not do."

The feelings coming from Tomás and Rowena swirled around Felícita's head like a relentless wind. She felt very small in the midst of it. When these two looked at each other, when they spoke . . . it felt like a fight that was not a fight, a drawing together and a pulling apart. In the center of each was a hidden need for which the other had the only answer.

And she knew she had to go with them. She could not see into the future; she had not foreseen Uncle's death or the way the villagers turned on her. It seemed that she could look into every heart while her own remained a mystery.

Tío had raised her, cared for her, told her what she should do each day from waking to sleeping. Her life had been free of choices—until the wolf and the woman came to save her.

But there was still no choice. This man and this woman were somehow bound by the same *destino*. She, too, was bound. She could no more walk away from them than she could bring Tío back to life. They had not come to her as the others had, to ask for the secrets of their fates. But if she could help them—she, worthless empty vessel that she was—maybe she could learn to help herself.

"Will you come with us?" Rowena asked.

She nodded and took the lady's hand.

The old man shook his head emphatically. *"No, no he visto a nadie."*

It was the fourth denial in the past half hour. Weylin sent the *viejo* on his way like the others and started east toward home. He'd come to the end of this trail.

No matter how careful and casual he'd been with his questions, the villagers were suspicious from the start. Randall might have warned them against him, knowing full well he wouldn't be slow in following once he worked out of his bonds, but Weylin thought it more likely that they were defending the outlaw of their own free will.

Randall had stopped here, of that Weylin had no doubt. He hadn't bothered to disguise his trail as far as this village. He challenged his pursuer with his very carelessness.

That was nothing new. Time and again, Randall had kept one step ahead of Weylin. The people who sheltered and aided him—men, women, and children—seemed to regard him as a kind of everyman's hero.

An outlaw, a killer like Randall, could never be anything but vermin. He bought the loyalty of these people with trickery and theft. Weylin had already ridden a careful circuit around the town; Randall's outbound track had been wiped clean with brush, the scent confused by livestock recently driven from one end of the village to the other.

So Randall had escaped . . . again.

Weylin removed his hat to mop the sweat from his forehead. He didn't bother with cursing. He'd lost too much face as it was, when Rowena was taken.

But he was stubborn. And patient. Very, very patient.

Under the circumstances, he knew it was time to go home. Cole would be at the ranch any time now, if he'd received the lady's message. He wouldn't let her run off without coming after her. He'd want to take command of the hunt.

That wouldn't be as easy as Cole surely believed. He might know the business end of the Randall fortune and New York society, but he'd been too long away from the frontier, running things from some fancy office back east. He was likely to go charging off half-cocked, thinking he could buy or compel what he wanted. Like Father.

Cole just might have made a mistake in his choice of mate. Weylin didn't know much about women, but he knew when they were trouble. Damn the lady for her arrogance and gullible lack of common sense. He hoped she'd keep her head with Randall.

Her head, and everything else.

With a click of his tongue, Weylin turned his gelding toward the edge of the village. The people watched him pass, their scents giving them away even when they hid from his view behind thick adobe walls.

Just as he passed the last house, a small boy darted out from a doorway and shouted a taunt that rang in the hush like a tolling bell. Weylin reined in the gelding and dismounted and grabbed the boy before he'd run two steps toward safety.

The boy hung in his grasp, defiant and terrified. Weylin set him down. "That isn't polite," he said softly in the boy's language. "Why are you angry? Have I ever done anything to you?"

Lower lip quivering, the boy shook his head. "But Papá said you are hunting—"

"Alonso!" A man who must have been the boy's father came running out of the house. He caught Alonso's arm and gave him a shake. "*Lo siento, señor.* Please forgive the child for his rudeness." He turned Alonso and marched him back to the house under the lash of a round scolding.

Weylin observed until they had gone and mounted again. It was too bad . . . too bad a promising lad like that had to fall under the spell of a killer. If Weylin ever had a son of his own . . .

He cast that thought from his mind. He had a job to do. When he'd brought Randall in—then he could think about a wife and children. When he'd earned the right.

I will bring you back, he promised Randall. *Justice always prevails in the end.*

seven

On the third afternoon following the witch-girl's rescue, Tomás informed Rowena that they were almost "home."

They had traveled, ever westward, among countless arid mountains and valleys, stopping each night wherever a camp could be made away from human habitation. They'd circled well south of Santa Fe, one of the larger towns in the Territory, and turned north and west until they reached the wide, cultivated valley of the Rio Grande. The river was a vast ribbon of muddy water, tinted by the earth through which it flowed. They crossed where it ran shallow and the current was not too swift, climbing the sandy slope on the opposite bank. Here, in the county known as Bernalillo, there was hardly a village worth the name.

Rowena had become inured to the primitive conditions of western travel—drawing water for drinking and bathing from nearby streams, washing by hand those portions of her clothing she could, sleeping with a minimum of privacy and only a bedroll for comfort, simple food cooked over an open fire.

She had avoided Tomás assiduously, but she couldn't escape her awareness of him. If he could push unwanted images into her mind, as he had done several times before, it was no wonder that he could manage so small a thing as to make himself a continual presence in her thoughts. If she should choose to call on her werewolf powers, she could shut him out.

But she would *not*. Nor would she concede that she felt anything for him but the strongest disapproval for his behavior.

Except where the girl was concerned. Rowena had derisively compared Tomás to Robin Hood, but she hadn't expected him to begin rescuing the persecuted. He certainly hadn't gained much for himself in the transaction . . . unless it was his intention to win *her* approval. *That* he would not find quite so easy.

Whatever his motives, she was reluctantly grateful. Having the girl to care for made it possible to concentrate on something other than her own indefinite future. She saw to it that she and the child had an area of each night's camp separate from that of the men. She made the girl eat, and encouraged her to overcome the shock of her ordeal by speaking to her constantly of the everyday things all women understood, regardless of position or language: the importance of keeping hair neat, maintaining dignity in the face of adversity, and ignoring the failings of the male gender.

The girl didn't participate in the discussions. She remained mute, though her face and eyes and hands were eloquent of sorrow and loneliness. That was something Rowena understood. Because the girl needed a name, she began to call her Hope—the gift she most wanted to bestow.

During the long nights, lying sleepless under the stars, she wondered why she felt so protective of a girl she didn't know. It wasn't merely the sense of responsibility born of a lifetime of *noblesse oblige,* the duty of the privileged to aid those of less fortunate estate. Nor was it the maternal desire that made her want children of her own; Hope was nearly a woman, scarcely more than ten years younger than Rowena herself.

No. There was something about the wilderness, this vast untamed country, that bared the soul. She had sensed it the first time she'd crossed the prairie in Weylin's buckboard. She hadn't grasped then how intimately acquainted she was to become with this cruel and terrible landscape, and the men it had shaped.

When she found her own reflection in the unsparing mirror of the New Mexico sky, she knew why she would defend Hope with her life. It was because they were alike. They were both outcasts: the girl because of foolish superstition, and herself because of what she'd been born. Neither of them had asked for their fates.

The difference between them was that Rowena had not given up. She continued to fight the stigma of her birth. No one would ever have cause to drive her out because she was a monster.

And as long as she had anything to say about it, no one would ever again do the same to Hope. She would find a place where even one accused of witchcraft could be safe and happy.

It only remained to win through the current predicament. The place where they had come to rest this warm afternoon was a tablelike ridge called a mesa, so common in this country. They'd been gaining altitude steadily all during the day's ride, and from the abrupt edge of the mesa, clothed in tall pines and thick grass, one could look down into a steep canyon cut into reddish rock, splashed with a strip of bright green to mark the course of a stream. Hardier plants clung tenaciously to the cliffs and crumbling slopes.

"Just a few more hours," Tomás said, riding up to join her. He nodded toward Hope, who sat alone at the edge of the mesa lost in her own hidden thoughts. "How is she?"

"Well enough. She is eating now, and showing interest in her surroundings."

"Thanks to your care of her."

So he had noticed. Rowena avoided his gaze. "Someone must. I . . . did not thank you for saving her life."

"I didn't expect your thanks."

"I see. Then you didn't do it to gain my appreciation for your . . . chivalry?"

He laughed. "I should not be surprised that you came to that conclusion, but you overestimate your influence on my behavior. Not everything I do is for your sake. The whole world does not revolve around Lady Rowena Forster."

Stung, she quelled her immediate response. "You will forgive me if I have some cause to doubt your motives."

"Ah, yes. I'm *un malo hombre,* a bad man. Such men do not save damsels in distress."

Something in his tone, an almost bitter self-mockery, surprised her. It was very much out of character. Had she judged him too harshly?

She prided herself on being just and fair, in expecting no more of others than she demanded of herself. There had been times, before she left England, when she had failed in that standard because of her own self-absorption and pain. She had misjudged good people and regretted it ever after.

She was falling prey to the same pitfalls now. Good Tomás might not be, but he was not entirely villainous. She had already seen ample evidence of that and chosen to ignore it.

"It was decent of you," she admitted.

"I believe that is the finest compliment I've ever received."

"Don't let it go to your head."

"What of my heart?" He leaned close. "I do have a heart, Rowena. I doubted yours until I saw you dancing in Rito Pequeño, and with the girl."

The man could do more to raise a blush on her cheeks with such a lukewarm statement than any other could with words of high praise and gallantry. "Why should you care if I possess a heart or not?"

His eyes grew hooded as he started to answer, but he was

interrupted when Sim Kavanagh joined them. After his earlier hostility, Kavanagh seemed bent on ignoring Rowena.

"Ramón says there's still no pursuit," he said. He drew a pair of red neckerchiefs from his coat pocket and passed one of them to Tomás. "I'll handle the girl."

His pointed stare toward Hope left no doubt as to his meaning. Rowena had noticed him watching the girl several times during the past few days. On each occasion she'd deliberately put herself between him and any view of Hope.

"What is he talking about?" she asked.

"It's necessary for you and *la muchacha* to be blindfolded from now on," Tomás said, "as are all those who first come to El Cañon del Rito de las Lágrimas."

"You've brought other captives here?"

He smiled. "Wait and see."

"I can hardly do so if you blindfold us."

Kavanagh dismounted, tossed his reins to one of the other men and stalked toward the oblivious girl. Rowena forgot her own concerns. If any of Tomás's men seemed most like the savage killer wolf of myth, it was Sim Kavanagh.

"Leave her alone!" she ordered.

Hope turned at the sound of her voice. She shrank from Kavanagh, who was preparing to grab her.

Rowena all but jumped from her saddle, stumbled on her skirts, and started for Kavanagh. "Hope—"

For an instant she and Kavanagh stood face to face. Rowena's heart pounded with dim understanding of her own recklessness and untoward aggression. She could not think clearly any longer. The civilized worlds of New York and England might have been in another universe.

"Don't touch her," she said, forcing her voice to a near-whisper.

She fully expected Kavanagh to ignore her. She didn't know what she might do if he did. Attack him? The mere notion was ludicrous.

But he did not ignore her. His hand went to the gun at his waist; his icy, pale eyes bored a burning path into hers.

And then he backed away. His mouth turned up in a contemptuous snarl, but he was the one to retreat. Rowena was stunned at her primitive exaltation in the victory. Just as if she, like her elder brother in England, had fought a deadly battle with tooth and claw. . . .

Her voice shook when she spoke. "Come with me, Hope."

"If you wish, you can blindfold her."

Tomás stood at her shoulder. She hadn't even been aware of his approach. Her momentary triumph burst like an overfull balloon; surely Tomás had driven Kavanagh away, not she. He would not need to use words.

She turned on him. "How can you abide a man like that in your company?"

"Don't outlaws belong in the company of outlaws?"

"But he is . . . you are not—"

"Not like him? It's true, I never hired out as a *pistolero* to fight other men's battles." His face grew serious. "Do I seem different to you, Rowena?"

She swallowed and tried to regain her sense of moral superiority. "No. Not at all."

"You are right." His smile was almost harsh. "It is simply that our methods differ." He brandished his neckerchief. "The girl?"

"Her name is Hope." She snatched the cloth from his hand. "Hope, child—" The girl stood as frozen as she'd been when Kavanagh went after her. "It's all right. Oh . . ." Pride was useless now. "Tomás, would you explain to her—kindly, if you please . . ."

"Of course." He spoke to the girl in musical Spanish, drawing from her the rare hint of a smile. He ended with a question. Hope nodded solemnly.

"She agrees that you can blindfold her," he said. "She isn't afraid." There was real gentleness in his voice. "Hope, you say? It is a good name. *Esperanza.*" He passed his neckerchief to her.

Esperanza was a much prettier name than Hope, Rowena decided; she wouldn't quarrel with Tomás's choice. Trustingly, Hope—Esperanza—turned about and let Rowena tie the blindfold over her eyes. Then strong, graceful hands were on her own hair, sliding cloth over her head and into place, adjusting with light touches until the blindfold rested as comfortably as possible.

Rowena knew a moment's panic. This was what her blind brother, Braden, lived with every day. But two sets of warm fingers grasped hers like lifelines—Esperanza on one side, Tomás on the other. An unexpected sense of serenity stole through her, as if she had become whole for the first time in her life.

"I'll help you mount," Tomás said. "Esperanza first." She heard him move away. Her body hummed in anticipation of his return; without sight, her other senses doubled in acuity. She could feel him draw near before she heard his footsteps.

"Trust me," he whispered in her ear. He lifted her easily and set her in place, adjusting her legs and skirts. Her mouth was too dry to allow protest. "Hold onto his mane," he said. "Gobernador knows the way to our canyon."

She had little choice but to trust the horse—and Tomás. She clung to Gobernador's mane like a child on her first riding lesson. "Esperanza?"

"She does very well," Tomás said ahead of her. "I will look after her."

She found that she believed him. The horses began to move. For a time they traveled on flat ground, and then the trail begin to descend sharply. The distinctive smells of the pines and cedars of this country, and the ever-present reddish dirt, filled her nose. She heard the constant song of birds, and the increase in their numbers told her that they must be approaching the watercourse.

If she gave way to her wolf side, she would be able to discern the path almost as if she could see it. It would be so easy to do, so natural. Small animals scurried out of their way. A hawk cried out overhead. Saddle leather creaked, and the men talked in low voices. Tomás whistled a song; the sound bounced from rocky walls that closed in about them.

Smells, sounds, sensations. They became her world—a world that bore no resemblance to the sweet wet green of England. But she was not afraid. She was not even angry.

Anger had been so much a part of her life. She'd been angry since Tomás, in his guise of Mr. Randolph, had abandoned her on the train. And if she looked farther back in time, she had been angry all during her last years in England.

Only in New York, with Cole, had she found a kind of peace. She must remember that. This contentment was illusion.

The path continued to descend, and then reached a level space. Rowena sensed that they were in a narrow canyon, with great cliffs to either side; they had descended from those very cliffs. She could smell water and growing things more lush than any on the plateaus and mesas.

"I will ride ahead now, to prepare for your arrival," Tomás said beside her. "Esperanza will come with me."

"No!" Her horse sidestepped in response to her sudden agitation.

"You'll see her again." His fingertips brushed her cheek. "Soon." He spoke in Spanish to his men. Some of them rode off with him; two others remained.

One of them was Sim Kavanagh.

"I know what you are," he said in a sibilant whisper.

She held herself very tall in the saddle. "Do you, Mr. Kavanagh?"

"You're trouble, *Lady* Rowena Forster. You're Tomás's big mistake."

"As incredible as it may seem, we are in agreement," she

said. "However, it does you no good to speak to me. Tell your friend—"

"He is my friend." His horse pushed into hers, causing both animals to snort and jostle. "You're a woman. No woman ever brought anything but grief. And one like you—" She heard him spit. "You're the worst kind."

His hatred was palpable. Tomás had told her that he had no use for women, but this went beyond so simple an explanation.

"You have considerable gall to criticize the worth of another," she said, "given your profession."

"My profession," he said. His voice was as flat as the top of a mesa. "Do you know what that is, sweetheart? I'm a killer."

"Like . . . like Tomás."

"Nothing like Tomás. He doesn't know what the word means."

"That's not what I've heard."

"From the MacLeans?" He grunted. "I don't give a damn what you believe. You and MacLean deserve each other."

"Thank you."

His hand shot out to grip her wrist. "Tomás has some crazy ideas about you, woman. It's like he's walked right into a trap with his eyes wide open. I'm not going to let you destroy him." He jerked her, hard. "Do you hear me?"

"I could scarcely avoid it."

"You're one uppity bitch. If I had my way, you'd never have come this far. But you won't be here long enough to make any difference."

"I am delighted to hear it."

He released her. "You wouldn't be the first female I've killed."

He meant it. Rowena suppressed a shiver. "Your *friend* might object."

"He'd never know." He pulled his horse aside. "Stay away

from him, woman. Keep up your high-and-mighty airs. Just stay away from Tomás."

Before she could answer he was riding off down the trail, leaving her wreathed in a cloud of dust. She coughed behind her hand to hide a curse.

"*No se preocupe, señorita,*" said a soft, accented voice. "He . . . will not hurt you."

"Mateo?"

"*Sí.* I . . . speak *un poco de inglés.*"

"A little English." That meant he'd understood Sim's threats, and had chosen not to interfere though she'd been left in his care. Was he afraid?

It was hardly fruitful to ask. "How long are we to wait here, Mateo?"

"No more waiting. If you will come . . ." She thought he must have attached a lead rein to Gobernador's bridle; in moments they were on their way again. She found that her heart was still racing from the confrontation with Kavanagh.

Coward, she accused herself. *He is only human.*

And then she shuddered that the thought had come so easily. For it meant that she was *more* than human. It meant that she had gone one step closer to forgetting what she had sworn years ago.

She tried to put the whole thing from her mind. The path was level now, traveling the length of the canyon she could not see. The scent of water grew stronger, and there was moisture in the air. The trail passed under areas of cool shade as well as open sky. Several times she heard distant voices. But just when she thought Mateo was leading her toward them, he veered aside and began to climb again.

They stopped at another flat area. Rowena sensed a wall or cliff very close, as if she could reach out and touch it.

"*Aquí, señorita,*" Mateo said. He helped her dismount.

"Where are we?"

"The place where you will sleep tonight," he said. *"Por favor."* He took her hand and placed it on a smooth wooden pole. "We must climb."

She felt the length of the pole and found the horizontal rungs that joined it to a parallel shaft. A ladder. A primitive ladder leading up the face of the cliff.

"Climb this?" she said.

"If you please, señorita."

She did not please, but neither would she be compelled. Gingerly she put her foot on the lowest rung. Mateo set his hands at her waist and gave her a boost. Too late she remembered that she would be at a disadvantage with Mateo below her. There was no help for it but to climb as quickly as possible.

Her skirts were a substantial hindrance and she had to feel her way, but climb she did. The ladder reached above ten feet. At the top she found the well-worn edge of a natural rock platform. On hands and knees she crawled onto it. The sense of being surrounded by rock was overwhelming. She stood carefully, wary of banging her head on a low ceiling.

Mateo came up behind her. She heard the scuff of his boots, his breathing, and then the creak of what might have been hinges. Just as she was about to ask him the first of several urgent questions, she heard the unmistakable closing of a door.

"Mateo?"

She tore the blindfold from her face. The room in the cliff was a cave, shaped by nature and enhanced by human hands. The floor was rock, as was the blackened ceiling and two of the "walls." The only light came from small windows left in the outward-facing wall, built of fitted bricks that nearly blended in with the rock itself. The threshold, where she'd first entered, was fitted with a plain wooden door. A door that was closed, and undoubtedly locked.

She was quite alone.

Her first instinct was to find any way of escape. She could see well enough in the semidarkness, but the confinement reminded her far too much of her last months in England as her brother's prisoner at Greyburn.

She tried the door first. It was, indeed, locked. If she called on her werewolf strength, she could break the lock—or the door itself. She backed away before the temptation became real.

The tiny, square windows were too small to permit egress. From each of them she could see, at last, where the long road from La Junta had taken her.

The canyon was, as she'd observed from above, fairly narrow and with high walls on either side. The opposite wall was a more gradual slope, west-facing and rocky. The band of green down the center of the canyon was as verdant as any in England, brilliant with new growth. The rest of the canyon floor was more open, scattered with pines and clusters of rock. To the left, almost out of sight, she could see what looked like adobe houses and cultivated fields running out from the stream.

People lived here. This was not merely an outlaw's hideout. Why, then, had she been left in this prison?

She turned away from the windows and examined the cell. The saddlebags with her belongings lay by the door, where Mateo had dropped them. For the first time she noticed the rugs and furs heaped on the floor, the candles, and the basin, towels, and jug of what must be water. There was even a plate of strawberries. Someone had prepared this cell for an inmate.

Along the far wall and halfway up the ceiling she found markings unlike any she'd seen before. Rustic drawings. Hieroglyphs rendered in red and black and white, of circle and line. The shapes were primitive and yet oddly fascinating: animals, birds, people, and other figures she couldn't name. They seemed to dance across the wall as if they were alive.

Others had sheltered in this very cave long ago, people who knew no writing or true culture. They'd left their indelible mark; their presence infused the rock itself, just as the smoke of their fires had blackened the ceiling.

They had been like the animals they painted. She could feel it. They had lived as part of nature, thousands of miles and years away from what she knew as civilization. If she stared at the drawings long enough, their spirits would seep into her soul, and she'd have no way to stop them. . . .

Rowena backed away from the painted wall and stood, shivering, against the man-made bricks opposite. An hour passed, and then another. The canyon sank into shadow. She began to wish desperately for the company of another human being. Anyone who could remind her that this cave was simply that—a natural feature adapted by savages, and not a preternatural realm haunted by ghosts who would strip away her humanity.

How she hated what Tomás had done—was doing—to her.

She wished that he were with her now.

The light dimmed and left the cave in darkness.

"And you let him get away."

Cole crumpled the telegram in his fist and threw it across the parlor at the expensive antique mirror that hung above the fireplace. The ball of paper bounced from the glass. "Just the same as always."

Weylin showed no reaction—certainly no chagrin at his miserable failure or Cole's scathing words. He gazed at Cole with that steady, placid stare, like a cow chewing its cud.

Damn him.

Cole strode to the sideboard and poured himself a whiskey, straight, and then went to the window overlooking the carefully tended garden and outbuildings beyond.

Double-Bar-M, the first big MacLean ranch in New Mexico

and the largest in Colfax County. He hadn't been back here in years, but seeing it still gave him satisfaction. All of this was his, for miles in every direction: rich, rolling grassland as far as the eye could see, high-quality range to foster strong, healthy beeves; good water; the promise of a new railroad to make the outfit profitable beyond his wildest dreams—and, above all, power. No one crossed a MacLean in this county. Or in the entire Territory.

Except for Tomás Alejandro Randall.

He drained the glass. "After all these years, you still can't bring him in," he said, not bothering to face his brother. "He's just too smart for you—is that it? A Randall, smarter than a MacLean." He resisted the urge to spit. After the years in New York, where he'd learned to be a gentleman as eastern society defined the word, he wasn't about to resume old habits.

That was the difference between him and Weylin. He had fulfilled his ambitions. Weylin was still the stupid cowboy he'd always been, with his muddy boots and sweat-stained hat. He wasn't even able to accomplish the one task set for him.

"I just received a letter from Randall, outlining his ransom demands," Cole continued, slowly, as if he were speaking to an idiot. "All he wants is a million dollars. And a public admission that we stole the Randall land—among other things."

Weylin scuffed his boot on the floor. "What would you pay to get the lady back?"

"He won't get a plugged nickel from me." He spun on the heels of his highly polished shoes and regarded Weylin with contempt. "Who made our fortune? Who won the MacLeans as much wealth and prominence as the Astors? *I* did. I took us from being ranchers like a thousand other Texans and made the MacLean name big all over the nation."

Weylin shifted his weight from one leg to the other,

unhurriedly, and met Cole's stare. "How did you make that fortune, Cole?"

It was happening again, though they'd seen each other seldom enough since Frank's death. Weylin didn't say much, but his few words had a way of cutting Cole to the quick.

"What the hell are you talking about?"

"You know." Weylin's eyes looked almost grim. "Once we worked the cattle together. We built the ranch from nothing. It was hard labor, but it was honorable. We earned what we had with our own hands."

"And I earned mine with my wits." Cole slammed his glass to the floor. The heavy crystal shattered. "That's what you're shy on, Weylin. You've never gone further east than Missouri. Your education ended in grade school. You can't tell stock shares from livestock." He laughed. "So much for being Father's favorite."

Weylin shook his head. "Kenneth was Pa's favorite."

"Kenneth and Father are dead. I'm still here. And I'm the head of this family." He returned to the sideboard for a fresh drink. "At least Father wasn't soft. You're soft, Weylin. They'd eat you alive in New York. You think because you can ride for a week straight through the desert on a handful of water that you're a man?"

"I'm a MacLean."

"You squander the name. I've used my advantages to the fullest. It's my right. It's every man's right to take whatever he can—"

"Not every man is a werewolf."

So Weylin wasn't as ignorant as he seemed. Little as they'd discussed Cole's business in New York, Weylin knew Cole wasn't a man to let puerile scruples about his inhuman nature prevent him from taking full advantage of that nature. It was so easy to manipulate ordinary humans, especially when the subject was money—or greed.

But Cole hadn't Changed since the loss of his arm. He

preferred to remain in human shape, and save his superior skills for the human world.

Their father had seldom Changed. He'd found it difficult, and so discouraged his sons from the act because he couldn't bear to be outdone. But he'd used his other abilities to find, hold, and keep men and cattle at a time when Texas had been struggling for survival after the War. He just hadn't gone far enough.

Weylin had followed Father's wishes and given up Changing years ago, but *he* wouldn't take advantage of his other werewolf powers. All because of that pathetic personal code of fair play, picked up the devil knew where. Certainly not from Father.

For a moment Cole wondered if Weylin knew how he'd promised Rowena never to use his werewolf abilities, or Change, or be anything but strictly human. No. Rowena wouldn't have discussed such a personal matter in the short time she was with Weylin. Before Randall took her right out from under Weylin's gun.

"You're right," he said at last, riding high on the wave of his scorn. "Not every man is a werewolf. But there are plenty of men like you—the ones who'd hold the strong back from shaping their own destinies. You're a relic, Weylin. You and your kind don't belong in the world that's coming."

"Maybe I don't want to belong in your world."

Cole snorted in disgust. "We're wasting time. Randall is the subject of this conversation . . . and how you failed to keep him from stealing my wife."

"She's not your wife yet."

"What is it? You don't think I can get her back when you failed?"

Weylin gazed calmly out the window from his place by the fine French settee.

"You listen to me," Cole said. He threw the second glass into the fireplace and stood nose to nose with his brother. "I was willing to let you prove that you had some worth to this family besides doing what any second-rate hired hand could do. I thought that once you were deputized by the sheriff, you'd have the guts to go after Randall and mean it. You washed out. Now I'm going to get him my way. Whatever it takes."

"What does it take, Cole? This isn't New York."

"Humans are the same everywhere. I'll find the scum who've helped him and make them cooperate—"

"Even when it makes you the same as Randall?"

Cole hit him. It wasn't his hardest punch; Weylin only swayed and held his ground. He didn't try to fight back.

"He murdered our father," Cole said. "Fergus Randall killed Ken. He took my arm. I want the Randalls wiped off the face of the earth."

Weylin touched his jaw indifferently, as if someone else had felt the blow. "Do you love her that much?"

"What?" Cole floundered, twisting his thoughts to follow Weylin's question. *Rowena.* He meant Rowena.

Love. How amusing. Weylin, never one for the ladies, still harbored a boy's old-fashioned notions of romance.

"She's mine," he said distinctly. "I don't give up what's mine. And I'm not returning to New York until I have it back. All of it."

He thought the conversation was over. Weylin's gaze was blank; he'd gone inside himself the way he often did since Father died. But just as Cole started for the parlor door, Weylin stopped him.

"You think I don't care what he's done?"

Cole turned. Weylin was anything but bovine now; all at once the wolf was raging in his eyes. "I want him as much as you do," he said. "But I'm a man of the law, Cole. You saw to that, so that whatever I did would be nice and legal." His smile held neither menace nor cynicism, but it was chilling just the same. "I'm duty-bound to warn you . . . if you commit a crime to kill Randall, I won't look the other way."

Caught between amazement and rage, Cole burst into a laugh. "Is that a threat, brother mine? Do you think I should be afraid of you when Randall pisses on your boots?" He stopped laughing when he saw the look on Weylin's face.

He considered, briefly, if he'd underestimated his brother. They were of the same blood, the same Scottish Highlander heritage infused with Texan grit and werewolf power.

If Weylin ever came close to guessing the truth about Frank MacLean's death . . .

But he wouldn't. No matter what he said, Weylin would never turn against family. He salved his conscience and made himself feel more like a man by standing up to Cole. It was all bluster.

If it ever became anything more, he knew what would happen.

Cole relaxed. "Go on, Weylin. Work some beeves or run in the desert. I have a man's job to do."

This time Weylin had nothing to say.

eight

The ancient cave dwelling was in total darkness when Tomás unlocked the door and stepped inside. The candles had not been lit; there was no movement.

Only the sound of breathing, and the scent of fear.

Rowena was afraid. Tomás felt immediately that her dread wasn't the kind that could be conquered with the sharp-tongued wordplay she so frequently practiced on him; he'd never sensed that she was really afraid in the way many women would be. He had admired her stubborn pride.

He hadn't expected her to be afraid now. When his keen night-vision found Rowena curled up in the corner, her knees drawn to her chest as far as the gown would allow, he felt ashamed.

Again she made him feel shame, when his mind had been readying for far more pleasant emotions.

"Rowena," he called softly.

The faint glitter of her eyes focused on him. "So," she said, her voice trembling, "you've come back."

"Far later than I planned. I apologize."

"I assumed that you . . . meant to leave me here."

Alone was the word she left unspoken. "No longer than

necessary, *mi rubia*. Though I am fond of this place, it's no fit dwelling for a lady."

"Ah. Something upon which we can agree."

Bueno. Her spirit was returning. She sat up a bit straighter against the rough brick wall.

"It is, however," he said, retrieving the candles at the far end of the cave, "the kind of place that you might come to like in spite of yourself."

"I think it most doubtful."

"It requires that you open your heart to the ancient music in these rocks. They are the bones of the earth. We, more than anyone except the original inhabitants, can hear their song."

"We?"

"You know what I mean." He lit a candle and set it down a few feet away from Rowena. The light splashed across her face, and he could see the marks of strain etched in sharp relief.

He considered the blankets and furs that she'd left where they lay. The blankets seemed the safest choice, under the circumstances. He chose a colorful Navajo weaving and knelt to offer it.

"Wrap yourself in this," he said.

For once she didn't argue. She settled the heavy cloth about her shoulders, stroking the pattern with one fine-fingered hand.

"It's beautiful," she murmured.

He grinned, pleased beyond all reason. "The Navajo are the people who live east of these mountains. They are known for their expert weaving. For a time, a young Navajo woman lived with us in the canyon. She taught this weaving to others, and then went on her way." He traced a bright geometrical design with his finger, moving up the length of Rowena's arm. "It was difficult for her at first. The Navajo believe that all shapeshifters are evil witches. It took much courage for her to accept me without fear or hatred."

Rowena met his gaze. "Perhaps her people have reason to hate and fear such creatures."

"As much reason as the villagers who attacked Esperanza?"

"Where is she?"

He'd given her too easy an escape from their conversation. "She is well, and you'll see her tomorrow. But tell me—do you think that all such judgments of evil are just?"

She looked away. "You know I do not. There is no evil in Esperanza."

"Then it's possible that people make mistakes in their judgments, no matter how strongly they believe."

"Are you suggesting that you've been the victim of such mistakes?" she said with a little of her old asperity.

"Perhaps your greatest fear is that *you* might become such a victim, Rowena."

She glanced at him sharply. "I shall never be."

Because you're afraid to live fully as what you are. He laughed inwardly at his own philosophizing. Rowena had many unwonted effects on him, not least of which was this tendency to reflect too deeply and seriously on affairs of the mind and heart.

Far better to savor the pleasures of the body.

She suddenly seemed to notice his hand on her arm, and flinched without drawing away. He chose to accept that as progress. He kept his touch feather-light.

"What is it," he asked softly, "that you fear in this place?"

It was yet another sign of change that she didn't flatly deny possessing any fear at all. But neither did she answer.

"Is it the darkness? I can make more light—"

"It's not the darkness," she said in a very low voice. "I can see as well as you."

An admission. An admission, however small, of her true blood.

As if she realized she'd given him another victory, she donned her haughty mask. "No one enjoys imprisonment."

"Especially not our kind," he said. "But your brother imprisoned you, didn't he? He, who should have known best how it would be."

"He . . . thought he was justified in doing so."

"And you hated him for it."

"No. Yes." She dropped her face in her hands. "Please—"

"He did it so you would marry a man you didn't love. The same man who sought and claimed you when you thought you had escaped."

"I did not know Cole in England."

"You don't know him now, either."

"I will not listen to your slander."

He sighed. "So it's imprisonment you fear. As I do."

"You?

"My freedom is dear to me. I run as I please, and no man is my master. That is why I won't let the MacLeans steal it from me."

"Even if death is the alternative?"

"Death," he whispered. He smiled at Rowena. "My mother's people do not speak of the dead."

His distraction succeeded. "Your mother's people?"

"My mother's father was Chihenne Apache. He captured my grandmother in a raid and married her, according to the ways of his people. When she returned to my great-grandfather, Don Arturo, with her child, he accepted her. Others would have turned her away. She was much loved, and so was her daughter."

"Your mother."

"Doña Adelina. A fierce woman, and proud. Much like you."

She did not know how to react. The original Lady Rowena Forster would have seen it as an insult. But now . . .

"Who was your father?" she asked.

"His name was Fergus Randall. He was a Scot, from a long line of Scots who came to America over a hundred years ago. The Randalls settled first in the Carolinas, and then in Kentucky. Fergus's father established a mercantile house in St. Louis. As a young man, my father was one of many who came over the Santa Fe Trail to trade with Nuevo Méjico, when it was still under Mexican rule."

"Is that how he came to meet your mother?"

"Yes. He went into a business partnership with my great-grandfather, Arturo de Ribera Navarro. And he fell in love with Adelina. Arturo told me that their marriage was one of the life-bonds that sometimes form between *hombres-lobo*. They could not be separated, except by death."

Rowena stared down at her clasped hands. She didn't want to be reminded of what she was. What *he* was as well.

"Surely . . . you knew your father."

"When I was a boy. My mother outlived him."

He wondered if he'd tell her the truth if she should ask how his father had died. Would she believe him? Or would she consider it one more trick to win her good will, to turn her against Cole MacLean?

"The MacLeans are also Scots," she said. "Cole once told me that they settled in the Carolinas."

Was she beginning to understand? "The Scots have long memories, and they are masters of the ancient feud. The same is true of the people of this land. They do not forget an enemy, just as they will never betray a friend."

Rowena would not meet his eyes. It was always the truth that most frightened her, the truth she did not want to see. She did not pursue the subject. "Your mother's father was an Apache. I have heard that they are among the most ruthless of the Indians in this country—"

"And some say that they only defend the land that has always been theirs, and which was taken from them after many broken promises." He gave a crooked smile. "My mother's Spanish ancestors fought the Indians for genera-tions. There was killing and abduction and slavery on both sides. Yet my mother's mother learned to love her man, and my mother bore the blood of both, as I do. Which do you find most alarming, Rowena: that I bear the blood of 'savages' or shapeshifters?"

For the first time in a long while she met his gaze. "Are they not the same?"

"Don't ordinary, civilized men commit atrocities in the name of progress?" he countered. "How can you find them so much better than those who merely defend their homes—or their right to live as they were born to live?"

"I was not born to live as a beast," she said hoarsely.

Instead of answering, he picked up the candle and stood, walking to the rear of the cave where the ancient figures marched across the blackened rock surface. "I discovered this canyon by accident, while I was . . . avoiding a pursuer."

"A man of the law, no doubt."

He saluted her. "Once this must have been part of a Spanish land grant, but the owners had long since abandoned it. It is not easily approached except by a winding path down from the cliff, so I knew it would be an ideal sanctuary." He brushed the surface of the rock with his fingertips. "Once it was a home for a native people who have disappeared—the people who made these paintings. In the time I've lived in this canyon, I have found artifacts they left long before the coming of the Spanish. They built houses from these caves formed naturally in the cliffs, and grew crops beside the little river and on the mesas. I think they were a people who loved life. They knew every day that they might die, like any other animal who shared the canyon with them."

Rowena's face showed real interest. "And what happened to these people?"

"No one knows, though the other Indians of this region have legends and stories. But they still speak to us over the ages." He pointed to a crude drawing of an arrow. "They drew what was important in life. They understood the heart of things." He pointed to another image. "The flute-player. They knew the joy of music. Here is an eagle, and a fish, and one of their gods. The moon and the sun."

Rowena rose and hesitantly came to join him. "And this?"

"The family. You see the man here, and the woman, and the child."

She didn't look away, though the pictures clearly distinguished male from female without benefit of covering. "I think family was important to them," he said. "Family and blood." He led her along the wall. "And the making of new life."

The joined figures he indicated were crude, but Rowena must have guessed what they portrayed. She froze, staring at them with unwilling fascination.

The male and female figures were drawn as one being, caught in the act of love. Beside them were other animals engaged in the same activity.

"Maybe it was their way of asking the gods for abundance and many children," he said. "Or perhaps they simply enjoyed this as much as they did their music."

Rowena breathed out harshly and moved on to the next grouping of figures. These were animals, safely detached from any others.

"And here are the wolves," Tomás said, following her. "There are many wolf symbols in these caves."

"Is that supposed to be significant?" she asked tartly.

He moved closer to her, holding the candle behind him so that her face was barely skimmed with light. "Isn't it, Rowena?" he whispered. "Don't you feel the magic of this place?"

She turned from the cave wall and retreated to safety beside the wall of adobe brick. "I do not believe in magic."

"But you do. You think you are cursed. Isn't that magic?" He knelt beside her, setting the candle down. "This is a place of ancient beginnings, Rowena. The earth's heartbeat is just beneath these rocks. That is what the native people of this land understand. You can hear it, if you wish. Sometimes I come here just to listen."

Her face grew still, and her eyes held a puzzlement that stripped her of arrogance. "I do not understand you, Tomás Alejandro Randall."

"Because even outlaws can hear the earth speak?"

"Because they should want to."

Impulsively he touched her face. Her skin was velvet under his calloused fingers. "Ah, *mi vida*. There is so much of me you could learn, if you desired to. I didn't bring you here to make you a prisoner. You call the Apache savages, but they do not imprison their enemies. And you are not my enemy." He stroked her cheek from temple to jawline, feeling her skin quiver in response. "I wanted to share this place with you, to let you feel it as I do. Here you don't need to be afraid of what you are. You can't fight it, for it is all around you."

"No," she said. "It's just a cave."

"But you are not just a woman." He lifted his other hand to cup her face. "Stop denying it, Rowena."

"Why—why are you doing this to me?"

Very gently he leaned toward her. "It is my nature," he said, "just as it is yours."

She didn't resist until his lips skimmed hers. Then her mouth tightened into a rigid line, forbidding him entrance.

"Release me," she said.

The command was oddly without conviction. He thrust his fingers into her hair. "You are afraid," he taunted. "You're afraid that if I kiss you, you will become what you most fear. You will have no control against a ruffian and scoundrel such as I. All your fine ways and discipline will vanish as if they'd never been." He wouldn't let her look away. "Are you so weak in your convictions, Rowena? Will you grant me such power?"

"I told you before. You . . . have *no* power over—"

He covered her mouth with his, and this time her lips softened in surrender.

She'd intended the kiss to be nothing but defiance.

He thought he had power over her, did he? He thought that with a few caresses he could undermine the habits and training of a lifetime, that he could unleash the beast with a single kiss, like a prince awakening a bewitched princess?

The Lady Rowena Forster was not so easily broken— neither with threats nor seduction. She would teach him that lesson once and for all.

His mouth fitted itself over hers as if it belonged there. She felt his firm masculinity, the heat of his body, his breath spilling into her mouth as she opened it to draw in a gasp. She didn't fight, for to struggle would prove he was right.

But as his arms came around her and his tongue teased the edges of her lips, she began to forget her purpose. With an effort she tried to focus on the memory of Cole's last kiss, when his usually restrained good-bye had become something much more passionate and possessive.

Cole's kiss. It was really no different from this. She could simply pretend it was Cole kissing her now. Accept it, just as she accepted Cole's liberties with her person as the privilege of a husband-to-be.

Yes. Remember what it was like when Cole kissed her. How he'd held her, how his lips had worked over hers and demanded entrance, but didn't push beyond when she resisted.

Before Cole, only one other man had kissed her, her first human beau in England. His kisses had been chaste. Tomás's kiss was anything but. And as he pulled her closer still, she became aware that she was not feeling what she'd always experienced in Cole's arms. There was none of the detachment and sense of obligation she'd believed was a woman's part in such exchanges.

Instead, she found her breath coming short, and waves of

heat coursing through her body. Tomás's hands spread across her back, kneading and rubbing until her spine felt soft as butter. Her breasts were remarkably sensitive where they pressed against his chest, as if her bodice and corset and chemise were no protection at all.

None of this had happened with Cole. It was as if a stranger had taken over her body—a stranger who willingly opened her mouth to accept Tomás's gentle invasion, who began to tremble with strange excitement when his tongue stroked hers. And this other Rowena did not wait passively for the kiss to end. She arched her back and responded, returning the pressure of his lips, her own hands stealing about his broad back.

The other Rowena had been waiting for this moment ever since she met Tomás Alejandro Randall. Ever since the train and the vivid, shameful, enticing images that invaded her thoughts. Ever since she had felt the ecstatic jolt of sensation when he'd touched her on the way to Rito Pequeño, and when he'd stood over her bed in the village and joked of sharing it with her.

It wasn't a joke. His kiss told her so. She had not the slightest urge to laugh.

She felt, absurdly, like crying.

Abruptly he let her go and rocked back onto his knees. The pupils of his eyes were dilated and his nostrils flared with every breath. She scrambled away, hands flying to her hair as if by putting it in proper order she could as easily tidy her emotions.

If he had not stopped it first . . .

"Well?" he said.

"Are you asking for my opinion?" she said, fighting to keep her voice level and dispassionate. She balanced on unsteady legs and found the wall's support. "It was an . . . interesting experience."

"Interesting?" He shook his head and laughed. "You are the first woman to use that word."

The nerve of the man. She glared down at him. "I have higher standards than your usual female companions."

"And Cole, I assume, met those 'standards'?"

Her immediate response was to snap out an agreement, but the words caught on her tongue. Until now, she wasn't sure she'd ever seen a truly smoldering gaze. His fit the description perfectly.

"Cole would never treat me as you have," she said.

"Like a clever, spirited, passionate woman?"

He countered her every statement with yet another question, each one meant to bait her. "I thought this was to be a test of my convictions. As you see, they have not wavered."

"I think you are not being honest, Rowena." He stood up to face her. "It was more than merely *interesting* to me."

A warm flush started from the base of her neck. She should be insulted, not pleased, that he found her kiss more than merely interesting. Kissing was nothing novel to a man such as he. She was an absolute amateur by comparison.

God help her if she accepted such a compliment. If she allowed herself to think that it might ever be repeated.

"I don't think it likely that I'll be able to give you a more accurate rating of your abilities," she said, straightening her skirts with a twitch.

"No?" He slipped up beside her and brushed her ear with his lips. "Here we have a saying: *'Con el tiempo se maduran las verdes.'* It means, 'In time green fruit ripens.' "

"I doubt," she said, refusing to retreat so much as an inch, "that this fruit will ever be to your taste."

"Only time will tell. And now I think it is time for you to rest." He started for the door.

"You do mean to leave me here."

"Just for one night, while your lodging is being prepared."

If she said anything more, he would guess the depth of her unease. She'd be a fool to give him ammunition. He might even offer to stay with her.

"The furs and blankets are soft," he said, "and the night is warm. Unless there is something else you require?"

"Nothing that you could provide."

"Then I wish you a good sleep." He opened the door and paused. "If you open your heart, Rowena, the earth and the ancients will speak to you. Listen, and you may learn how to live."

Tomás came for her the next morning when the canyon was still in shadow and the thickets of trees and shrubbery along the river rang sweet with birdsong. Rowena tidied herself with the water and her few personal belongings, determined not to let Tomás see how poorly she'd slept.

It hadn't been because of the primitive accommodations, or the temperature of the air, or even the confinement—for the door was latched, she'd found soon enough. She had lain awake all night, listening for the voices Tomás had promised, half afraid she could hear them calling. Telling her that she must let go. Give in to that other Rowena. Submit to the wolf.

Surrender to Tomás Alejandro Randall.

But when dawn broke, she was still herself. The figures on the wall had not spoken. She met Tomás's searching gaze with a raised brow and faint smile.

"Good morning," she said.

"Buenos días." He looked around the cave room, as if he expected to find some manifestation of his mysterious ancient voices. "Your casa is ready. If you please?"

She avoided his extended hand, went to the open door, and started down the ladder before Tomás could offer to precede her. A single horse was waiting at the bottom, side-saddled for her use; Tomás helped her mount, took the reins, and led the animal onto the path.

Nothing about the canyon would have been familiar to her a week ago—not the red-and-gold earth and rock, nor the stunted pines, nor the birds that called from the water's edge. She had little reason to appreciate its sere beauty. And yet she found herself drawn to it against her will and all recent experience. Spiny cacti unpredictably sprouted fruit and blossoms; wildflowers clung to the most unlikely crevices; the tall cottonwood trees with their bright, rustling leaves marched along the stream, towering above undergrowth as thick as any in an English wood. Birds kept up a ceaseless melody.

"So this is the place you call home," she said.

"It has its advantages," he said, glancing up at her. The sun, just clearing the top of the eastern mesa, gave his skin a rich, warm glow. "Do you like it?"

His eyes were so very striking in this particular light, she observed. Had she noticed the height of his cheekbones before, or the curling hair behind his ears, or the way his lips . . .

"You seem overly interested in the judgment of a prisoner," she said hastily.

"Not a prisoner, but an honored guest. As you will see."

And, indeed, as they approached the little village Rowena had her first glimpse of the welcome awaiting her. In the dusty square formed by the five or six adobe houses, a small crowd had gathered. At first glance it appeared to be made up largely of children, ranging in age from babes to gawky adolescents. They darted forward in a flock like eager birds, their arms filled with wildflowers.

Behind them came the adults. With a start, Rowena recognized the men of Tomás's outlaw gang: Mateo and Carlos, bereft of their guns and clothed in the simple garments of farmers, and three others similarly disarmed and dressed. They looked like ordinary villagers. With them was an older man with a sun-seamed face and hair white with age.

And there was Esperanza. She ran toward Rowena, stopped, and ducked her head shyly.

"I told you she'd be well cared for," Tomás said. He helped Rowena dismount and called out in Spanish to the crowd of children.

They formed a ragged row before Rowena and began to sing, voices earnest and slightly off-key.

"They are singing a song to welcome you," he said.

Rowena bit her lower lip, completely at a loss. Children were the last thing she'd expected to see in a den of thieves. They appeared healthy enough, and cheerful in their singing, but she was very much afraid this was all a plot to charm her. A plot that was succeeding.

"Did you arrange this?" she hissed to Tomás.

"I told them about you," he said. His mouth quirked in a wry smile. "We do not have many visitors here."

"Do they believe I am an honored guest?"

"Of course. Do you wish to tell them otherwise?"

Esperanza crept up beside Rowena and took her hand. Moved by the girl's trust, Rowena wondered that she felt so, so . . .

Needed. Wanted. Accepted, utterly without question. All because of a mute girl, a chorus of barefoot cherubs, and the winning words of a smooth-tongued scoundrel.

The children finished their song and two of them, a round-faced girl of ten and a sturdy boy some years older, came forward to present Rowena with a handful of yellow flowers.

"This is Enrique," Tomás said, "and his sister Pilar."

Rowena accepted the flowers gravely. "Thank you, Enrique. Pilar."

Pilar grinned, showing several crooked teeth, and spoke in a whisper.

"She says you're a very beautiful lady," Tomás translated.

"*Gracias,*" Rowena said to the child. "Do they not speak English?"

"They seldom leave the canyon." He beckoned the other children forward. One by one he named them for her:

Aquilino and Gita, the son and daughter of Mateo, and Miguel, Gertrudis, and Catalina, the children of Carlos. Gita was the smallest at two or three years, and Enrique the eldest, on the brink of young manhood. They were wide-eyed with curiosity and bubbling with questions Rowena couldn't understand or answer.

She had a number of questions herself. "Where are their mothers?" she asked.

"Mateo's wife was very ill and died a year ago. Carlos lost his woman before he joined us. Enrique and Pilar are *huérfanos*—orphans."

It explained much. She studied Pilar and noted the ragged hair, undoubtedly cut with the dull edge of a knife, and the too-large baggy trousers she wore under a boy's shirt. She was every bit as dusty and unkempt as the boys, whose clothing was streaked with dirt from rough-and-tumble play. The other girls were in much the same condition. How long had it been since they'd enjoyed a woman's personal care and instruction, or worn anything resembling a dress?

This was what came of children living among thieves. At Greyburn, Braden's estate in England, the children of tenants and laborers had been assured of regular medical care, good sturdy clothing, and a basic education. Rowena had helped distribute charity to needy families. Even at Rito Paqueño the children had complete families and a stable life. What could these children expect? The girls, especially, must suffer in such a place.

But Tomás did not seem in the least concerned. He knelt among them and shared a joke that sent them into gales of laughter. He was hardly more than a heedless boy himself. With a roar he made a frightening face and raised his arms as if to pounce on any child too slow to escape. They scattered with happy shrieks. Only Enrique hung back, gazing at Tomás with naked worship in his eyes.

Tomás ruffled the boy's hair, pushed him toward the others with a companionable slap, and turned to Rowena. "You must wish to see your house. Nestor will have the morning meal prepared."

She realized that she was very hungry, and the prospect of a real chair and a table set with breakfast was tantalizing. She gazed with troubled eyes after the children. *They are not your concern,* she told herself. *How can they be, when you're a prisoner yourself?*

Yet Esperanza had become her concern, unleashing within her instincts she'd scarcely known she possessed.

Instincts are dangerous. It is discipline and prudence that must guide you.

Resolutely she turned to follow Tomás across the square, Esperanza at her side. Tomás paused to confer with the older man she presumed to be Nestor. She was reflecting upon the disadvantages of not speaking Spanish when Esperanza pulled her to a stop, her fingers wrapped around Rowena's in a death grip.

Rowena felt the reason before she saw it. Sim Kavanagh stood in the shadow of one of the houses, simply staring at her. Or at Esperanza. At this distance it was difficult to tell. His gaze alone was enough to raise the small, loose hairs on the back of Rowena's neck. She dropped the flowers in her free hand.

Enemy, instinct cried. And for once it was in perfect agreement with common sense.

nine

Violence.

That was all Felícita could feel, trapped under the hot, fierce stare of the man called Sim.

She was intimate with the sensation of hatred not her own. It had surrounded her like foul air in Los Milagros after her uncle's death. She might almost have forgotten such torment, if not the confusing emotions constantly swirling between Tomás and Rowena.

But she hadn't been prepared for Sim Kavanagh. The hatred of the villagers came from fear, and fear she understood. Whenever Sim Kavanagh was near, something far more terrible invaded her awareness. He was not like Tomás, or any of the others who rode with him. Men of violence had sometimes come to Los Milagros, but her uncle had always kept them away from the casa. They were never real to her . . . until now.

Tío was not here to protect her from Sim. She hadn't even known his name until the journey to this place was nearly over, but she had learned very quickly to avoid him, just as she would stay away from a scorpion or deadly *serpiente*.

It did no good. For reasons she did not understand, he watched her. Again and again, she sensed his stare following her—when she rode, when she ate, when she slept. He wanted something from her, something she knew she could not give. His mind was a great darkness of rage and engulfing need. If not for Rowena, she would have been lost in the bottomless chasm of that darkness.

Once he had tried to touch her, and the lady had stopped him. That was the first time Felícita knew that his menacing emotions were not only for her. He hated Rowena.

Now, in a place that should have been a sanctuary, Sim Kavanagh's hatred struck like the blows of a hundred switches. He pulled and pulled at Felícita, but Rowena was the one he wished to hurt.

Unable to cry out a warning, Felícita whimpered and clutched Rowena's hand.

Rowena pressed her fingers. "Don't be afraid," she said. "I won't let him hurt you."

Felícita shook her head in despair. Rowena must know that Sim was not her friend, but she did not feel what Felícita felt.

The lady was in danger.

That certainty awakened in Felícita an unfamiliar impulse. She wished . . . she wished to *protect* her friend. She, who had lived her life in her uncle's shadow, hardly allowed to stir beyond her own doorstep, wished to protect a great lady who kept *el lobo* for a friend.

Loca. She was weak and ignorant, unable to take care of herself, let alone another. There were too many new voices in her head, too much hidden pain. If she could not stop them from filling her up, she would break like a clay pot used too many times.

Sim Kavanagh sauntered toward them, his black hat shading his eyes. "*Buenos días,* pretty señorita," he said, ignoring Rowena. Felícita shrank from the hunger in his gaze.

"I told you to stay away from this girl," Rowena said.

He drew the makings of a cigarette from his waistcoat and rolled the tobacco in its paper. He lit it with a *cerilla* and inhaled deeply. "Maybe I've taken a fancy to her."

The lady seemed to glow with tension and anger. "Not if you value your life."

"Is that a threat?" Sim blew a cloud of smoke into Rowena's face. "Maybe you forgot our conversation."

A bolt of sheer power shot through the lady and singed Felícita's hand like a lightning strike. Felícita had never felt such awesome energy before—except in the wolf who had rescued her. Rowena was more than angry. Her pale golden-brown eyes narrowed to slits, and her lips drew back from her teeth. Her face . . . her *face* . . .

She was on the verge of becoming something a hundred times more dangerous than Sim Kavanagh.

"I have not forgotten," she said, her voice low and hoarse. "Make your quarrel with me, but do not touch her."

He hurled the cigarette to the ground. "Funny how Tomás is never here when you need him."

"I do not need him to deal with *you*."

"That's good, because you'd better not go running to him for protection—not if you want this little girl safe and sound."

Rowena flung up her arm, fist clenched. She didn't even touch Sim, but he jerked back as if he'd been punched by a man twice his size.

Felícita swayed, battered by the weight of emotion: Rowena's rage at Sim and horror at that rage; his answering hatred and shock. His face had grown as white as the lady's.

"You're like Tomás," he said harshly. "You're what he is."

Rowena's silent denial washed over Felícita, *no, no, no,* like the tolling of a bell in her head. She opened her mouth to scream what Rowena would not: *No, no, no . . .*

"Rowena?"

Tomás. His voice was stronger than the unbearable denials. They died away, leaving an aching quiet. Felícita blinked up at his face.

"I thought you were coming with me," he said. "Sim?"

Kavanagh and Rowena stood almost side by side, pretending that nothing had happened. Sim looked straight into Tomás's eyes. "I was just welcoming the ladies."

The lie was a howling tempest at the center of his words. Rowena gathered Felícita into her arms, trembling so slightly that no one else could see. "Esperanza requires peace and quiet," she said.

"And you'll wish to rest and refresh yourself," Tomás said. "I'm sure that Sim can save his welcome for a better time."

Without another word Sim spun on his heel and strode toward the fields that stretched behind the *pueblacito.* Tomás watched him go, the hint of a frown tugging at his dark brows. "My lady, Nestor is here to show you to your casa."

The old man Felícita had met last night came forward to greet Rowena. She let Nestor lead them away, meek as a lamb, but underneath she seethed with anguish and shame.

Felícita did not know how to help her. All she could see, when she looked inside, was the tragic, beautiful face of a ghost-white wolf.

The wooden door to the adobe house closed with a rattling thump and Rowena leaned against it, concentrating on taking long, steady breaths. Esperanza sank into a huddle beside the wall, her arms wrapped around her knees. Rowena was inclined to join her.

She was grateful that Tomás had not insisted on remaining. She'd come far too close to disgracing herself in front of Kavanagh, Esperanza . . . and Tomás worst of all. There'd been a moment, confronting Kavanagh, when she'd faced the wild, appalling urge to strip off her clothes and Change.

It had never happened before. She had been compelled to Change, at Greyburn, but not since adolescence had she felt remotely tempted. Nor had she suffered such mindless anger.

Sim's threat to Esperanza, not herself, had triggered it. *"Tomás is never around when you need him,"* Kavanagh had said with belligerent mockery.

But he'd also threatened to hurt Esperanza if she told Tomás. That chance she wasn't willing to take . . . not yet.

She turned from the door and drew Esperanza to her feet. "Come. Shall we take a tour of our new—" Prison? It wouldn't help Esperanza to speak so bitterly. "—our new home?" she finished.

The house was very similar to the one in which she'd spent the night at Rito Pequeño, though it consisted of only two rooms. The main chamber was sparsely furnished with a crudely made table, four wooden chairs, shelves, and a cupboard. A hive-shaped fireplace was built into a far corner. The windows were small and deep and set with shutters instead of glass. A woven rug provided the single covering for the earthen floor.

An open doorway led to the other room, which was fitted with a narrow bed, a carved chest bearing a bowl and pitcher for washing, and a second cupboard that she guessed must serve as an armoire. A clay jug of flowers rested on the windowsill.

The place was clean enough, in spite of the primitive furnishings. But it lacked warmth or personality. Who had lived here? The house hadn't been built for Rowena's use alone.

She availed herself of the water to wash her face and hands. Esperanza copied her.

"Shall we see about breakfast?" she asked the girl. Esperanza nodded, the fear already fading from her eyes. As promised, a meal awaited them on the table in the main room. Rowena was long past balking at tortillas and frijoles; she'd even begun to enjoy the unique flavors and textures of the local cuisine. To her surprise, someone had provided more strawberries, fresh bread, butter, and real tea, served on chipped china.

Who else but Tomás?

Let him play the generous host. She wasn't fool enough to reject a good meal. In England, it was not the custom for ladies to do more than sample their food. The wilderness demanded quite a different attitude; one could not predict the regularity or size of the next meal. Rowena intended to keep herself strong and ready, and set a good example for Esperanza.

The girl, to her satisfaction, ate with real appetite, though she was obviously not familiar with butter or tea. She watched Rowena carefully for cues. Rowena showed her with gestures how to spread butter on neatly sliced bread, and pour out tea.

While they ate, Rowena directed her thoughts to the most pressing problem in her immediate future: Tomás Alejandro Randall.

Last night already seemed like a dream. The cave, and Tomás's kiss, had temporarily stolen her discernment as well as her self-control. Now that she was safely within man-made walls, however crude, she could think properly again. As she sipped her tea, the pattern became clear.

Until last night, she'd managed to treat his sensual badinage and too-intimate behavior as attempts to demoralize and intimidate her, establish his dominance as any beast might do. Even the erotic mental images had seemed like some sort of disagreeable game, just another part of his revenge on Cole that extended to her.

The kiss had forced her to reconsider that theory. It hadn't been given in jest, nor used as yet another weapon to confuse and subdue her. Tomás had meant it quite sincerely—as sincerely as a man like him ever could.

All in all he'd behaved much better than she could have anticipated. He'd never truly hurt her, and had gone out of his way, on occasion, to make her comfortable. There was no earthly reason that he should spend so much effort to beguile a mere hostage . . . unless he meant not only to hold her for ransom, but to seduce her as well.

Had he planned seduction from the beginning, when he'd first stolen her from Weylin in Colorado? His conduct had been overly familiar from the start. The more she resisted his provoking insinuations, the more determined he became to—how had he said it? To treat her "like a clever, spirited, passionate woman."

He believed she was passionate. He believed she could be won.

And she *had* been won, in the cave, for a few stunning moments. How hard had she fought him? The memory filled her less with mortification than with wonder. She touched her parted lips. They throbbed with a phantom ache, as if they yearned for something lost.

Admit it, she told herself. *Until you admit it, you cannot fight. You're defeated before you begin.*

She closed her eyes. Very well. She did find Tomás attractive. She had felt so within the first hour after she'd met him. She could find no good reason, for she ought to be above being impressed by handsome looks and blatant enticement.

Was it his soulful eyes, or the musical voice capable of both strength and gentleness? His easy laugh? His complete disregard of consequences, so utterly unlike her own view of the world? Or the way he commanded such loyalty, and rescued damsels in distress? How could these qualities outweigh his crimes?

Or was that the very attraction—that he could do all the things she denied herself?

It was madness. But his voice responded in her mind: *"There is a certain satisfaction in madness. But you've never allowed yourself to discover that, have you?"*

She'd most certainly discovered it. And she knew she was in very grave danger.

Her hand shook so much when she set down the cup that cooling tea splashed onto the table. There, the admission was made. She recognized her danger; she felt both liberated and ashamed at the acknowledgment of her weakness. Her determination and self-control could no longer be relied upon. Tomás was a thief out to steal what she valued most, and what he would steal couldn't be recovered.

Every day she remained here, the danger would grow. Now that she had reached the place where Tomás meant to keep her, she had two clear choices: remain his prisoner and risk the consequences, or find a way to escape. The encounters with Sim Kavanagh convinced her that Esperanza could not stay here without her. The escape must be planned for two.

She didn't deceive herself that it would be easy. The canyon had no convenient exits, and she'd arrived blindfolded. She'd have to test the limits of her freedom here, and carefully study the canyon from one end to the other without seeming to do so.

It would be far more plausible with allies. But Tomás's men were loyal to him, Kavanagh most of all. She couldn't expect the children to help a stranger.

The children. She frowned over her last strawberry. It was a pity that they were deprived of the possibility of a normal life and education, among law-abiding people of decent morals.

Tomás was, in a sense, the master of these people. There must be a way to make him aware of what he owed the children. But she would have to be very careful not to place herself in his debt.

She dared not forget that he was Cole's enemy. And hers.

The door creaked open behind her. The old man, Nestor, poked in his head.

"I have come to clean the table," he said, his mild brown eyes both curious and guarded. "If you are finished?"

Rowena rose and nodded to Esperanza. "We are, thank you. Señor—"

"I am only Nestor," he said. He shuffled into the room and picked up the plates carefully. "Was the meal to your liking?"

His English was accented but clear, the gentleness of his voice soothing. Rowena smiled. "Very much so, Nestor." She'd been looking for allies, and while there was no reason to suspect Nestor would be any less loyal to Tomás than the others, he might be more communicative. It wouldn't hurt to try. "Did you prepare it?"

"My wife taught me to bake the bread, but it was Don Tomás who brought the fruit and butter."

"The bread was delicious."

He ducked his head. "I will take these things away now."

"But you will return? I know we have just met, but I have so many questions about this place. Perhaps you might help me." She folded her hands in entreaty. "Please."

He hesitated by the door, balancing cutlery and china, and then his eyes lit up with pleasure that outweighed caution. "*Sí,* Doña Rowena. Don Tomás has spoken much of you. I will come back."

She hurried to hold the door open for him. Unless she was very much mistaken, Nestor could prove a most valuable source of information.

With a little effort, she convinced Esperanza to lie down on the bed. The girl soon fell into exhausted sleep. Rowena composed herself to wait for Nestor's return.

He knocked a half hour later. Rowena knew that the door had been locked, but she greeted him like a proper hostess, showing him to one of the chairs.

She made a few polite comments about the weather and the beauty of the canyon, and then began her interrogation.

"I wish to thank you again for breakfast," she said.

"It is nothing, Doña Rowena."

"Fine hospitality is never to be taken for granted, señor," she said. "This is a lovely house. I hope that I did not turn anyone out of his home."

Nestor smiled. "It is Don Tomás's casa."

"I . . . I see." Why should she be surprised? The bed in which Esperanza slept must be his, as well.

"Don Tomás had it prepared for you," Nestor said eagerly. "He wished you to be comfortable."

"How kind of him." She doubted that Nestor would grasp her irony. "Tell me, Nestor—how much has Don Tomás said of me? Has he told you why I am here?"

The guarded look came back into the old man's eyes. He shrugged uncomfortably. *"Suficiente."*

Best not to belabor her status as a prisoner, then. "You understand that there is so much I do not know about Tomás."

"Sí. Many do not know him, but I have been with him since his childhood."

Rowena's interest doubled. "You must have known his mother, then."

"Doña Adelina. She was a brave and handsome woman."

"Tomás's family did not always live in this canyon."

"Once he was heir to many *varas* of fine land in the east. But when his enemies came—" He broke off, rubbing his cracked lips. "Perhaps he has told you this."

"A little." *You are not here to learn about his past,* she chided herself, *unless it helps you escape.*

Nestor studied her face for a long moment. "You do not think well of him, Doña Rowena."

Does he believe that I should, under the circumstances? Her thoughts strayed back to the kiss and tripped over themselves in confusion and chagrin. "You must know that I did not . . . expect to come here."

"He thinks very well of you."

Suddenly she was aware of her heartbeat as she hadn't been an instant before. She bit down on her lip to keep from asking how he knew.

Nestor rose and paced several uneven steps away from the table. "You judge him on only a part of what he is. Not all is as it seems." He faced her with an earnest frown. "Many who have come to El Cañon del Rito de las Lágrimas were saved by Don Tomás."

"Saved?"

"You were with him when he rescued the girl. It was not the first time, nor will it be the last." He sat down again, working his thick brown fingers. "Ramón was accused of a murder he did not commit. Tomás learned of this, and risked his life to save him from hanging. Ramón is safe here."

Ramón, she remembered, was the man without children. "What of the others who follow him?"

"All owe Don Tomás their loyalty. They are good men."

Is that why they are so willing to join him in thievery and lawbreaking, not to mention threatening murder to Weylin MacLean?

Such blunt speech wouldn't be wise. "Did he rescue Sim Kavanagh as well?"

He must have recognized her sarcasm. "They have helped each other many times," he said. "Señor Kavanagh . . . is a hard man."

"Indeed."

"Don Tomás brought the *huérfanos,* Enrique and Pilar, to live here when their parents died," he said quickly. "There have been others like them, who have stayed and gone again when the time is right."

Nestor spoke as if the canyon were a sanctuary rather than a den of wanted criminals. He was anxious to convince her that Tomás was as much heroic benefactor as outlaw. She'd seen him play that role at Rito Pequeño, and again with

Esperanza. She was remarkably unsurprised that he'd done it before.

Did he do good out of a need to atone for what he knew to be evil? There was a great deal of difference between aiding a man like Kavanagh and providing a home, however, imperfect, to young orphans. Nothing Nestor had told her made Tomás more comprehensible.

It only made her doubt herself.

If she continued to question Nestor, she'd surely hear as much as she wanted to know about Tomás's past and motives. The story would be one-sided, however, skewed in the outlaw's favor, and thus worthless. She had no choice but to continue to trust her own judgment.

Did she dare to do so?

"You spoke of the orphans," she said at last. "Who cares for them?"

"All of us. They lack for nothing."

Except parents, education, and a decent upbringing, she thought. But she didn't wish to antagonize Nestor with more criticisms of his master. Best to turn the conversation in a more fruitful direction.

"Do you know," she asked cautiously, "if I am to be permitted to walk outside this house?"

"Don Tomás said that you could go where you will in the canyon," he said. "But it would not be best for you to stray too far alone."

So. Tomás must believe that there was little chance of her finding a way to escape—or that she lacked the courage to try.

"I shall certainly be careful," she said, "but the desert is less strange to me now than it was a week ago."

Nestor brightened. "Do you like our land, Doña Rowena?"

"I have . . . come to recognize its finer qualities."

"Excelente." He brought his tanned and wrinkled hands together. "You will soon see the beauty of our canyon."

Nestor, it seemed, was eager for her to explore. What were his motives? Did he have some notion that she would remain here of her own free will?

Or was he hoping that by growing to love this land, she must also grow to love . . .

"I was blindfolded when I came to the canyon," she said hastily. "Is that the way all people enter?"

"Those who are new, *sí.*"

Then there must be some risk that one could find the exit, by accident or careful investigation. The prospect gave her hope. "I suppose there are few towns of any size in the area."

He cocked one shaggy white brow. "The nearest villagers are all friends of Don Tomás."

A warning that she could not, even if she escaped, rely upon help from the locals. So be it. She would find a way.

"Well, Señor Nestor, your conversation has been most enlightening," she said. "And your cooking most delicious. I look forward to the next opportunity to sample it."

"Ah, yes, Doña Rowena. I almost forgot. Don Tomás asks if he may have the honor of attending you at dinner this evening."

The request was a mere formality, since she could hardly bar him from his own house. "Of course," she said. "Esperanza will be welcome, I trust?"

Nestor nodded and rose to go. "I will leave the door open, Doña Rowena."

"Gracias." He smiled with pleasure at her attempt at Spanish and bowed slightly by the door as he took his leave. She tested the door latch behind him; it was indeed unlocked.

Esperanza was still sleeping when she went to check on her. Neither of them had any demands on their time. There was no reason to put off the first informal survey of her larger prison.

The square just outside the door was, at the moment,

deserted. She looked curiously at the handful of houses, wondering where Tomás spent his nights.

No concern of yours, she told herself. *He may sleep on a cactus if he chooses.* The image cheered her. She wandered out of the square and caught sight of men working in the fields. Farmers now, not outlaws, doing what farmers did the world over. The children must be out playing, or helping the adults.

She was debating a walk to the fields for a closer look when the boy Enrique came running from behind the nearest house. He stopped short when he saw her.

"*Buenos días, señorita,*" he said. His face was smudged with dirt, but his eyes were shining and happy.

"*Buenos días,*" she pronounced carefully. "It's nice to see you again, Enrique."

"And you, señorita." He squared his thin shoulders. "I speak *inglés,* better than anyone but Nestor and Don Tomás."

"So I see. Where did you learn?"

"Nestor taught me. I was his *aprendiz.*"

Apprentice, she translated. "Does Nestor take care of you and Pilar?" she asked.

He shrugged. "I don't need anyone to take care of me. I take care of Pilar."

All at once he reminded her of Quentin at that age, scorning any limits on his boyish freedoms. Believing that he had no more need of adult supervision. At that time, their parents had been dead for years, and Grandfather was a tyrant to be feared, not loved. Orphans in virtually every sense.

"Where is Pilar?" she asked.

"Trying to make a doll." He made a face. "I am going to go help Isaaque with the sheep, up there." He gestured at the mesa topping the western cliff. "I know all about sheep."

So the boy had a trade of sorts, and had learned to speak English. Perhaps the children were not so badly off. . . .

"I will not always be *un pastor.* Some day, I will be like Don Tomás."

Rowena frowned. "What do you mean, Enrique?"

"I will be *un caballero,* a man of importance whom others respect," he said, lifting his chin.

Was that what he believed Tomás to be? "What does Tomás do that you admire so much?"

"He punishes the wicked, who steal from the poor," he said proudly. "They are all afraid of him. I was at Los Valerosos when the Tejanos came. I want to fight them with Don Tomás."

She didn't grasp the significance of the part about Los Valerosos and Tejanos, but the rest was clear enough. Tomás deceived the boy, or allowed others to deceive him. Enrique actually admired his outlaw patron.

"Do you know why I am here, Enrique?" she asked, hiding her consternation.

"Oh, yes. You are like Don Tomás—*un hombre-lobo.* I mean, *una mujer-loba.*" He thought for a moment, then grinned. "A . . . werewolf."

Good Lord. "How did you know?"

"Nestor told me. Don Tomás told him. I wish I could be like you and Don Tomás." He smiled wistfully. "Then I could run as silent and swift as moonlight. You are *muy afortunada.*"

Fortunate? How could she begin to make this boy understand? "It is not what you—"

"There are not many like Don Tomás in our country," he interrupted. "Now that you are here, he will no longer be lonely."

Rowena closed her eyes. Nestor knew the truth about her presence here, but even he seemed ready to play matchmaker. Enrique assumed a relationship that did not, could not, exist. Good-hearted the boy might be, but he was badly misguided. He lacked both manners and a suitable mentor.

"You are pretty enough for Don Tomás," he said, as if to encourage her. "You will make him *una buena esposa.*"

She'd begun to learn how to pick out the roots of Spanish words, and she was appalled to realize what he implied. *Esposa.* Spouse. Wife.

It was absolutely essential to set him straight—and anyone else who labored under this gross misapprehension. "Enrique . . . there is something you must know—"

"I am sorry, señorita. I have to go to Isaaque now. I will talk to you later!" He bounded away like a young deer, without a backward glance.

Rowena wrapped her arms about herself and shivered. This was not going well at all. She was in no state to meet one of Tomás's men now.

She walked back to her house, eyes fixed on the ground. She pushed the door open without really noticing that it was already ajar.

A little girl, hands full of white fabric, started up with a guilty expression as Rowena crossed the threshold. Pilar. The garment in her hands was Rowena's nightgown.

Pilar pushed it onto the table and backed away. "I am sorry, señorita," she whispered.

Closing the door behind her, Rowena smiled reassurance. "It's all right, Pilar. I was just speaking with your brother."

The girl's face remained wary. She was, Rowena observed, barefoot and still clothed in worn and patched trousers and shirt. She must have rifled Rowena's saddlebags to find the garment.

But Rowena felt no indignation, only pity. Far from a surprise that the child was drawn to a woman's garments. She was just at that age.

"Won't you sit down?" Rowena asked. She moved casually to the table and retrieved the nightgown, draping it over the back of a chair. "I'm glad to have visitors."

Pilar edged into a seat. "You are not angry that I looked at your dress?"

"Not at all." She sat across from the girl. "I see that you speak English as well as your brother."

Pilar's face relaxed. *"Sí."* She squirmed. "You are such a pretty lady. You have such pretty clothes. I have never seen such things before."

"Thank you." She touched the nightgown. "This is a . . . dress to sleep in."

The girl's eyes widened. "Oh. It is so soft." Her gaze ran hungrily over Rowena's much-stained and battered traveling suit. "Do all the ladies wear dresses like yours?"

How was she to answer that? "Some do." She cleared her throat. "Do you have a dress, Pilar?"

"I did once." She sighed. "When *mi madre* . . . before we came here."

Rowena felt a renewed indignation. It was not right that a girl her age should be forced to wear a boy's attire, driven to creep about a stranger's dwelling just to see what she might wear under normal conditions.

"Enrique said that you were making a doll," she said.

The girl dropped her gaze. "I am not good." With a shame-faced glance, she withdrew something from her trouser pocket. The misshapen form was made out of scraps or rags, with wide uneven stitching, one leg longer than the other, and no clothes.

"How did you learn to make it?" Rowena asked gently. "Did someone teach you?"

"No. I know it is ugly." She tossed the awkward doll onto the floor, scooted off the seat, and fled for the door.

Rowena caught her there. "Pilar . . . it isn't ugly. It's just that you haven't the right materials to work with."

Pilar turned a tear-streaked face to her. "I could learn, señorita. I could."

"Of course you can."

"Will you show me?" A hopeful smile quivered about her mouth. "I will not touch your things again, I promise."

Rowena swallowed hard. She'd meant to comfort the girl, and somehow had presented herself as a teacher. Goodness knew the child had no skill in stitching, and probably had never so much as embroidered a handkerchief in her short life. Those were the least of her disadvantages.

She needed a woman to guide her. Rowena made an impetuous and dangerous decision. "You would like a dress, wouldn't you?"

"Oh, yes!"

"Let me see what I can do. I cannot promise, but I'll do my best. And perhaps, then, you will have what you require to make a dress for your doll as well."

Pilar was speechless. She rushed back to her doll and scooped it up, cuddling it possessively. *"Gracias, señorita. Gracias!"*

"You are quite welcome."

Once Pilar was gone, she collected her scattered wits. How had it come to this? Now she must move heaven and earth to see that the girl got her dress . . . and there were the other children to consider. Yes. The girls, especially, must have at least some of the benefits of womanhood.

She would have to ask Tomás. Even beg, if necessary. But first she intended to make him face his responsibilities. Humiliating herself, and putting herself in Tomás's debt, was a measure of last resort.

After a moment of painful self-reflection, she looked up to see Esperanza by the bedchamber doorway. The young woman was sleepy-eyed, but Rowena sensed she'd witnessed some part of her conversation with Pilar.

"Well," Rowena said. "What do you know of needlework, Esperanza? Do you think you could help me teach a few children how to stitch and embroider?"

Esperanza smiled and nodded, more animation in her eyes than Rowena had seen in days. It occurred to Rowena that purpose was the very thing the girl needed, distraction from her own sorrows through helping others.

Purpose. Tonight's dinner with Tomás would certainly have a purpose, and that would make her stronger in facing him again. She would maintain the upper hand.

Tonight Tomás Alejandro Randall would learn just how determined she could be.

ten

Tomás found Sim tossing stones from the mouth of a natural cave halfway up the eastern canyon wall, where there were enough footholds for an ordinary man to climb. Considering the reek of smoke from Sim's favorite cigarettes, even an ordinary human could have located him by scent alone.

He pulled himself up over the ledge of the shallow cave and crouched beside his friend. Sim continued to blow smoke and toss pebbles in meditative silence, but his acknowledgement of Tomás's presence needed no words.

"A fine morning," Tomás said.

"You've come about the woman."

All the contempt in Sim's voice was for Rowena, not for him. He bristled nonetheless. The reaction was alien and unpleasant, as if he'd looked in a mirror and seen, not himself, but the twisted features of Cole MacLean.

God save him from such a fate.

"Her name," he said mildly, "is Lady Rowena. I would ask you to remember that."

Sim ground the cigarette butt under his palm. "Lady. She must have been mighty fine in bed."

Tomás bit back his anger. "What's wrong, Sim? Too long since you had a woman?"

"That's your problem, not mine. You always had too many scruples."

"They can be inconvenient at times."

"Scruples, or women?"

Tomás forced a laugh. He studied Sim's ragged profile under the black slouch hat, the scars and creases of many years. And the bitterness. "You have little enough use for either," he said.

Sim rolled another cigarette. "Females are good for one thing. The ones like your bi-" He broke off and spat into the canyon. "Your *lady*, ain't good even for that."

Tomás stood up, half bent to keep from hitting his head on the cave ceiling, and circled behind Sim. Only the slight stiffening of Sim's shoulders revealed his wariness.

Not fear. Simeon Kavanagh wasn't afraid of anything, or anyone. He didn't care enough. That was one thing he and Tomás had in common. As he'd told Rowena, it was simply their methods that differed.

"I saw what passed between you and Lady Rowena this morning," Tomás said softly.

"Did she go running to you after all?"

"What did you say to her?"

"I was trying to strike up a conversation with the little señorita. The lady took exception."

Tomás had seen the way Sim's gaze followed the girl Esperanza, and how Rowena had kept the child securely under her wing like a quail hen with one chick. He'd never thought Sim's interest in Esperanza was genuine. In the years they'd ridden together, Sim kept his dealings with women to himself. The last woman Tomás had seen him visit was a cheap whore in Santa Fe. A mute child like Esperanza wouldn't interest him.

Except as a way to provoke Rowena. Since the minute

they'd met in Colorado, he hadn't bothered to hide his hostility. He scorned the fairer sex, but this blunt hatred was something new.

Tomás circled around to Sim's other side and stood braced against the wall of the cave, staring across the canyon. "Don't lie to me, amigo. It was Rowena you wished to offend."

Sim took a long drag on his cigarette. "Offense isn't what I had in mind."

Tomás dug his fingers into the pitted stone of the cliff. He wanted to laugh and shake off this tension that filled his body. He had no use for such seriousness. Since his mother's death, he'd resolved never to mourn again; laughter served him far better. Only the MacLeans could rouse his darker passions, and those did not last beyond the moments of triumph when he took one more small part of his revenge.

Revenge was his life, and all life was a grand joke. A challenge to defeat death as long as possible, and take the MacLeans down with him when he went to hell.

This did not feel like a joke.

"There is one thing you must understand," he said. "The lady is under my protection—"

"Your protection?" Sim snorted. "You kidnapped her. Done a helluva lot more than that, I reckon. MacLean'll piss himself when he finds out you already picked her cherry."

The vulgarity left a foul taste in Tomás's mouth. It had never bothered him before. "I asked you not to speak of her in that way," he said.

Sim twisted his head to regard Tomás. "Don't tell me you kept your hands off her?"

"I don't take unwilling women."

"Good for you." Sim narrowed his eyes. "Maybe you're smarter than I thought."

Tomás knelt level with Sim. "Speak your mind, amigo, or I may become angry."

They stared at each other. "All right," Sim said. "You're

too damned blind to see the danger. You kidnap this female because she's Cole MacLean's woman, and bring her here—"

"You know the reason."

"I know what you started out to do. I warned you at the beginning—"

"That it was a bad idea." Tomás hung his legs over the ledge and kicked the rock with his boot heels. "I don't understand this caution. It isn't like you."

Sim cast him a stony look. "Someone has to keep you from getting yourself killed."

"You?" Tomás laughed in astonishment. "How many times have we risked our lives together, my friend?"

"How many times have I kept you from dying when you were bent on it?" He looked away. "How many times have you saved my life?"

Tomás fell silent. It seemed a century ago since he'd found Sim staked out in the desert, half-naked and badly injured, left for dead and to the tender mercies of vultures and coyotes. His tongue had been too swollen for speech at the time, but afterward, in his feverish babblings, he'd said more in a day than he would for the next several years.

Wild talk. Promises of bloody retribution. Tomás had pieced together his brutal life from those curses. Curses for the enemies who'd left him to die—and most of all for the woman who had betrayed him. A woman he'd loved.

Later, when he knew Sim's name, he heard other bits and pieces, enough to know that Sim had been a killer, a *pistolero* who hired out his gun with no questions asked. Tomás never inquired about his past. Whatever sins the man had committed, he had no further interest in them. Once recovered, the sinister Sim Kavanagh began to shadow his rescuer with the grim persistence of a dangerously loyal dog.

In time, that obsession had grown into something else. The change came when Sim saved him from a hunter's trap, and saw for the first time what he was. Tomás had nearly torn off his own hind foot in an effort to escape—and then Sim was there.

And Sim understood, without words. He stopped shadowing Tomás's every move, but he was always ready to fight at his side. Only he had the influence to restrain Sim from the violence that came as easily to him as the Change came to Tomás.

The bond that had grown up between then was never spoken. It ran far too deep to dismiss, even for the sake of Rowena's pride. Or his own.

"You shouldn't worry about me, amigo," he said. "I take life as it comes. To worry is to die a little at a time. Better the swift death met boldly, *no es verdad?*"

Once, Sim would have agreed without hesitation. He took a long drag on his cigarette and didn't answer.

Tomás began to lose his patience. "What is it about Lady Rowena that you hate so much? Because one woman betrayed you—"

"Because a MacLean hurt you, you steal from any *rico* who has dealings with them."

"They killed my parents, stole our ranch—"

"Hell, I don't care how much you steal from snakes like MacLean. But when you take a hostage and then get so hot for her that you start thinking with your *cojones,* you're setting yourself up for the noose. If she drags you down, she's my enemy."

Tomás jumped up again. "Damn you, Sim. What I do is my business. Don't make me choose. If you ever harm a hair on her head—"

"You'll kill me?" He drew a burning trail of ashes across the back of his hand, oblivious to the pain. "You play at being a killer, Tomás, but you don't have it in you."

Tomás snatched the cigarette from his hand, and Sim spun

into a crouch facing him. The urge to Change was suddenly very strong, responding to threat, needing to prove dominance. Few men had ever triggered such a formidable compulsion.

"Maybe you forget what I am," he said, breathing fast.

"I don't forget."

"I could force you to leave this canyon. You'd never find your way back."

"Or I could kill you first." Sim's ivory-handled Peace-maker was pointed straight at Tomás's chest. He grunted a laugh and pushed the gun back in its holster. "Why bother? MacLean'll get you anyway."

The blood-song of danger was loud in Tomás's ears. "It will take more than a bullet to kill me."

"Shit." Sim shook his head. "You've lost your head, hom-bre. You want the . . . lady. That I can almost understand. But you're after more than her body, or revenge."

"Estás loco."

"Am I? I've seen how you look at her. The way you treat her. And she's your breed." He cocked his head. "Maybe you can't help it."

Tomás wasn't shocked that Sim knew of Rowena's were-wolf nature. He would have learned sooner or later. But the rest was sheer insanity.

"I didn't know you had such a fine imagination," he said. "No one controls me, Sim, not even the wolf. And as for the lady—she's only a challenge. It amuses me to lay my trap with kindness. She'll come to my bed of her own choice. Be-fore I'm done, she'll spit on the name MacLean."

Sim met his stare. "Believe that, if you have to," he said. His expression altered; it softened, like jagged rock miracu-lously worn to smoothness in an instant. "Give her up, Tomás. Let her go. She'll be your death."

For a moment Tomás believed him. More than believed; he sensed what Sim feared so greatly that he'd challenge his friend and stretch his loyalty to the breaking point.

Tomás laughed, unable to bear the alternative. "A pleasant enough way to die. But I don't intend to let Ma--ean win." He grew serious and caught Sim's gaze. "Ther -s but one thing I demand of you. Swear, Sim—swear that you will never hurt Rowena."

"You could try to force me, like you said."

"I want your word. Your free word."

Sim was quiet for a long time. "I won't hurt her," he said in a gruff whisper. "I swear."

"And you must leave the girl Esperanza alone."

"All right."

A great weight lifted from Tomás's body. *"Muy bien."* He relaxed the muscles of his neck and shoulders with a roll of his head. "Now I have other business to attend to."

Sim stared eastward, jaw set. "When do we ride out again?"

"Patience, my friend. Soon."

He left the *pistolero* to smoke his last cigarette and toss pebbles into the canyon. Whatever else Sim might be, he'd never broken his word to Tomás. Rowena was safe. He had simply to keep the two apart, until . . . until . . .

There is no future. Only now.

But he found himself looking forward to tonight like the besotted fool Sim so mistakenly thought him to be.

Weylin rode far out onto the plain before he Changed.

How long had it been? He tried to remember as he dismounted and left his horse to graze on the rich grass. Eight years? Ten?

He knew all the reasons why he'd stayed human so long. Father hadn't liked Changing; he'd disliked it so much that he pretty much ordered his sons not to do it themselves. In those days, you didn't defy Father easily, and Weylin had never been particularly rebellious.

Cole was. There'd been a time, years ago in Texas, when he'd Changed out of sheer cussedness and hunted other men's sheep and cattle. Weylin had been a boy then, but the senseless slaughter and wickedness of it had sickened him.

After Cole lost his arm in the battle with Fergus MacLean, he'd refused to Change again. A wolf running on three legs was a pathetic creature; Cole would not tolerate any hint of vulnerability. When Father died, Cole made it clear to the family that he expected them to follow his example. And because in their kind the wolf was never entirely absent from the man, no matter what the shape, instinct had demanded obedience . . . or challenge.

Weylin wasn't interested in challenge. He'd come to see Changing as undesirable, but not for the reasons Cole and Father had.

The fact was that being a werewolf meant you had the advantage over every other man. It meant you could smell a thousand times more keenly, move faster than human eyes could follow, hear a needle hit the floor from five rooms away. It meant you could always win, just by using powers you'd been born with but hadn't earned.

It was too easy. It proved nothing of a man's worth. And Weylin had realized that he didn't want what he hadn't come by through his own honest efforts.

So he'd walked and ridden, fought and worked as human. He could still smell and hear better than most men, and he was damned hard to hurt. That he couldn't alter. But he prided himself on meeting other men on equal terms. No unfair advantages, no trickery, no deceit.

He'd held to that code until now. Today. Because the man he hunted was *un hombre-lobo,* and he'd run out of human ways to catch him.

Slowly he began to shed his clothes and weapons. When he was done, he packed them neatly in his saddlebags. His horse was well trained to stay ground-tied, but the mare hadn't been tested in the proximity of a wolf.

There was no reason to be self-conscious here. No observers.

He took in a long breath and set off at a jog. When he'd run just short of half a mile, he stopped. And concentrated.

And Changed.

Liquid lightning ran through his veins as if he were the center of a desert storm. He flung back his head, transfixed. He felt his edges soften and blur, turn into mist, begin to solidify again in a new shape. There was no pain. No awkwardness. Only a deep sense of rightness . . . and joy. His coat was thick and fair. On four strong legs he bestrode the plain, his senses bombarding him with a thousand temptations. He knew that he could run for hours, days, almost invincible. Why had Father been so reluctant, Cole so afraid?

This was what they were meant to be.

Drunk with jubilation, he gave way to impulse and tested the power of his body. He ran, and leaped, and slid to absolute stillness. He stalked a butterfly. He caught an unwary rabbit and let it go. And the human part of him realized as never before what he'd given up in pursuit of duty and justice.

Duty and justice. The words were of man, not wolf, but they broke through his trance like a bullet through paper. He wasn't led by the wolf, living wild with no regard for human law, like Tomás Alejandro Randall.

Randall was his reason for becoming the wolf once more. He shook himself and concentrated on his human form. The mist closed about him, and he stood on two feet, bereft of the magic but not of purpose.

His horse was grazing where he'd left it. He shook out his clothes and dressed again, buckling his gun in place.

Soon he'd return to Rito Pequeño, where the villagers had been so reluctant to help him. But he'd go as a wolf, and as a wolf he had hope of finding what he'd missed: the elusive scent, the one faint track that hadn't been erased by man or weather.

Timing was everything now. Weylin had a good idea what would happen if Cole found Randall first. Word had already gone out that Cole was hiring up every loose *pistolero* and drifter in the Territory. They'd have no qualms about using harsh methods to get people talking—people like those villagers in Rito Pequeño. The longer it took to find the outlaw, the greater chance that innocents would suffer.

And the greater chance that Weylin would be obliged to brand his own brother an outlaw.

Weylin mounted and turned toward home, considering last-minute preparations. From now on he'd be traveling light on his own four feet. He'd have to rig up some kind of pack to carry his clothing and perhaps a knife; clearly a rifle was out of the question.

He wouldn't need a man's weapons. No more hesitation; no more failure. When he defeated Randall, it would be with tooth and claw and his own werewolf strength.

Nestor lit the last candle and stepped away from the table. From her seat in the corner of the room, Rowena had watched him transform the plain little casa into a romantic bower, complete with wine, fresh wildflowers, crystal wine glasses, and the good china. Even the sun was cooperating, spilling velvet shafts of golden-red evening light through the square windows.

All this was, of course, for her benefit. In a matter of minutes Tomás would appear at the door, undoubtedly prepared to charm her to the utmost of his considerable ability. Perhaps he thought this a more appropriate setting for seduction than a cave of ancient primitives.

Ironic; should she consider herself his hostess, or his guest? The one role she refused to play was that of helpless victim. Nevertheless, she was grateful that Esperanza would dine with them. Her presence, like that of a trained chaperon, must surely put a damper on Tomás's amorous intentions.

Above all, it would be vital for her to control the conversation. She'd already settled on a pertinent topic that would serve more than one goal.

She pulled two chairs away from the table, set Esperanza in one of them, and waited with clasped hands. When the knock came, Nestor, who stood in the shadows like a well-trained waiter, moved to answer it.

Tomás was attired in what must be his best finery: a black jacket of cloth embroidered with braid and silver buttons, black close-fitting trousers with the same buttons running the outer length, a wide red sash, polished boots, and a broad-brimmed black hat rimmed with silver cord. He bowed deeply as he entered, his hat nearly touching the floor.

"Señoritas," he said. "I see that we have no need of candle-light. Your beauty is as the sun in brilliance."

Esperanza dipped her head and glanced from Tomás to Rowena. Rowena rose slowly. "Don Tomás."

He set his hat on a wooden hook on the wall by the door and swept his hand through his hair. Rowena found herself staring at its curling disarray. The way it tumbled over his forehead, refusing to be tamed . . .

"Should I find a barber?" he asked. "A pity you gave away your brush."

She stood straighter. "I doubt very much that a barber can improve you in any way, Tomás," she said.

He grinned. "I can see that we'll have a very interesting evening."

Rowena took Esperanza's hand. "Indeed."

Like any gentleman, Tomás carried the chairs back to the table and seated first Rowena and then Esperanza. "I apologize for the lack of elegance in our dinner appointments," he said, "but some luxuries are not easy to come by in our little canyon."

"No?" Rowena arched a brow. "I'd have thought you could contrive to steal almost anything."

"The finer the object, the more easily broken."

"Not always, I assure you," Rowena said sweetly.

Tomás gave her a long look and gestured to Nestor. The old man brought forth a bottle wrapped in white cloth.

"Would you care for wine, Lady Rowena?"

"No, thank you."

He didn't seem surprised. He also didn't, Rowena noted with approval, offer any to Esperanza. Nestor poured him half a glassful and retreated.

"It's excellent," he said after his first sip. "Do you abstain?"

"Only in certain circumstances."

He finished the wine and saluted her with the empty glass. "It's true that preliminaries can be tiresome." His eyes glinted with amusement. "You may serve dinner, Nestor."

The food the old man brought was much the same as they'd had in Rito Pequeño—strongly spiced mutton stew, tortillas, and beans. But there was also more freshly baked bread, butter, and fruit. Even after the small luncheon offered hours ago, Rowena found her mouth watering.

Esperanza ate as daintily as Rowena, every so often glancing up from her plate to study her companions with anxious eyes. Tomás smiled at her and spoke in quiet Spanish. She nodded and ducked her head.

At Rowena's questioning look, he translated. "I asked her if she is comfortable here," he said. "I trust you find these poor accommodations tolerable?"

"I regret that my presence has displaced you from your own home," she said coolly.

"That could be rectified, *dulzura*."

"Yes. All you need do is let me go."

"That wasn't the solution I had in mind." He nodded to Nestor, who gathered up the china and all remaining food but the fruit and bore it away.

"I hardly think there's room in this house for three people," she said, refusing to blush.

"True." Idly he sipped his second glass of wine. "But a few things—a very few—are worth waiting for. Dessert, perhaps?"

Nestor brought out fresh dishes bearing squares of puffy fried bread. Esperanza's solemn face lit up as one was set before her. Rowena tasted hers; the hollow inside was smothered with honey that melted on her tongue with sinful abandon.

"The young know how to live," Tomás said softly, watching Esperanza savor each bite. "They enjoy everything life has to offer, and don't waste time worrying about the future or the past."

It was exactly the opening Rowena had waited for. "Speaking of children," she said, mustering her determination, "I have a number of questions about yours."

"Mine?"

"Enrique, Pilar, and all the rest. You've taken responsibility for them, have you not?"

She was gratified at his expression of surprise. It was obviously not a subject he'd intended to cover. She continued her sally. "Yes, *your* children. What becomes of them when you ride out to kidnap and rob?"

"Becomes of—" His expression cleared. "Who cares for them? Nestor and Isaaque, our shepherd, are always here. You've met Nestor—"

"One aged man can look after so many? Surely a shepherd spends most of his time with his flock."

Tomás stood up and walked across the room, coming to a stop at the door. "Your concern is touching, but you have no need to fear for them. They are perfectly safe here."

"Safe, perhaps. What of the other essentials of a reasonable life?"

He turned to face her. "They have what they require— food, shelter, amusement—"

"Naturally you would list amusement as one of life's essentials. What of suitable clothing, especially for the girls? What of education? Can any of them read or write? And what sort of example do you set them—you and your band of cutthroats?" She rose, bracing her hands on the table. "These poor children must think that thievery and kidnapping are seemly occupations. Have you done anything to counter such a depraved and immoral view of life?"

This time he had the grace to look abashed. "I do not encourage—"

"But you do not discourage, either. You must see how the boy Enrique looks up to you, and wishes to be exactly like you."

Tomás stared down at the tips of his boots. "He . . . is a good boy."

"For how long, before he follows in your footsteps? You must realize that you've failed in your responsibility toward those who have no choice in how they live."

"I am relieved to hear that you think me capable of such sentiments."

"I am appealing to whatever decency you still possess," she said. "And I believe you do care for them, in your own way. That is why—"

She broke off as he strode toward her. "I see that you know far more about such matters than I do. What do you suggest?" He stood toe to toe with her, his face inches from hers. "Shall I separate them from their fathers and send them to some cold and proper school where they'll learn to be good, conventional citizens like your Cole MacLean?"

Rowena took a step back. "You could do much worse—"

"I doubt it." He sighed. "You do not understand. Family is important to us. These children have lost one or both parents, and I will not send them away."

"Nor will you give up your occupation," she said. "Nothing will change. You have not a single woman in this place to care for these children. No nurse, no teacher—not even a kindly housekeeper."

He laughed, though the sound was strained. "What would

I do with a housekeeper? Enrique is too old for a nurse. But—" His eyes clouded in thought, and then focused on Rowena with the half-lidded gaze of a self-satisfied cat.

"I suppose that I could find myself a mistress and bring her back. I would not lack for volunteers."

Rowena set her jaw. Trust him to turn the conversation in that direction! Boasting yet again about his conquests . . .

"You cannot imagine that such a woman would be a fit caretaker for children," she snapped.

"I see your point." He grabbed the nearest chair, turned it about, and sat with his legs straddling the seat and his arms folded across the back. Rowena was momentarily distracted by the flex of his muscles under the snug trousers.

"Who would be appropriate, eh?" Tomás said. "A chilly Eastern schoolmarm? But how could I get such a one to stay here? I have so little to offer. Unless—" His eyes narrowed. "I could kidnap her, of course."

Rowena pushed her fingers through her hair, disarranging the pins. "Is criminal behavior your only solution to every problem?"

"I can think of one other." He rested his chin on his folded arms and gazed up at her without so much as a smile. "I could find myself a wife."

eleven

The idea was so preposterous that Rowena burst into a laugh. The look in his eyes choked her mirth into silence. No. It wasn't possible. He couldn't mean—

Of course not. How completely absurd to even consider it. Marry? El Lobo?

"Marry?" she repeated aloud. "You would never go so far. You've made clear how much you relish your freedom." She clenched her fists on the table. "You have so many female admirers who do not demand the sanctity of marriage. And any woman willing to marry you must be tainted by your crimes and your bestial nature."

He blinked, as if he hadn't expected her reply, and his unaccustomed gravity hardened into a glower. "As any man would be tainted by yours," he said. "Except another of our kind. Like Cole MacLean." He sat straighter and held her trapped with his werewolf's gaze. "Is that why you wish to marry him? Because he knows what you are and cannot be disgusted?"

Rowena backed up another few steps. "Cole has renounced his animal blood," she said, "as I have."

"Ah. And that makes up for his many other defects."

"We are not speaking of Cole."

"But we are speaking of mating. However you may choose to live, your children will be *hombres-lobo*."

Rowena tried to block out his words. "It is the children here I am concerned about," she said, too loudly. "Will you help them?"

He released her gaze, and she felt that she'd held him off, even obtained a small victory.

"How?" he asked.

Her courage returned. "I scarcely know where to begin. The children can't possibly be getting any sort of education in this place; they need books, several primers at least. They also require new clothing—especially the girls, like Pilar. She hardly knows what a dress is. A good length of calico, a bit of plain lace, ribbon . . ."

"A dress?" His brows arched. "And who will sew it? Nestor? Myself?" He spread his hands. "These weren't made for such work."

She well knew the work they most enjoyed. She swallowed. "If you can supply the materials, I might cut a simple pattern and show Pilar how to sew it. She can teach the younger girls, when they are ready."

Tomás cast her a look of amazement, only half feigned. "You astonish me, Rowena. I didn't think fine ladies knew dressmaking."

"We've discussed how little you know about fine ladies."

"I also promised to be a most willing student." He swung one leg back over the chair and stood. His expression softened into something like tenderness. Rowena was very much afraid that he was going to touch her. "You are generous to help the children of the cañon."

"It is common decency to do so," she said, glancing away.

"Then I must warn you that to obtain the materials you

need, I will have to steal them—or use my ill-gotten gains to pay for them." His look was a challenge, balanced between mockery and intense watchfulness.

Rowena bit her lip. "I have money," she said, "in New York. If you let me go, I can send for it."

"Another generous notion, but impractical. If I let you go, who will teach Pilar? And if we wait for your . . . release"—he gave the word an odd emphasis—"you'll certainly lose interest in the children."

"I certainly shall not!"

He folded his arms across his chest. "I leave it up to you, *mi alma*. Shall I ride forth to find what you want, or leave the children as they are?"

She closed her eyes and weighed necessity against immorality. These children were innocent and didn't deserve to suffer for Tomás's wrongs. If he could be made to see the difference small changes made in their lives, he might be persuaded to make bigger ones.

"I ask," she said stiffly, "that you try to purchase what you can before you try . . . anything more drastic."

His mouth twitched into a wide grin and he caught her hands before she could escape. He kissed them, one by one.

"*Rubia mia,*" he said with a catch in his voice, "you are a queen among women."

She blushed and despised herself for basking in the compliment. Naturally he was pleased that she'd lent her sanction, however constrained, to his illegal profession.

But that rational thought didn't prevent her from trembling at the strong, possessive warmth of his hands. For once, he and she were in accord, bound by one goal. It felt remarkably wonderful.

"I only regret," he said, "that I cannot dress you as a queen. But you, too, must have something else to wear." He pulled back, looking her up and down. "That gown will not last much longer."

Indeed. She was reminded of how she'd come to be in such a state, and her gratification vanished. "Thank you for the observation," she said tartly. "I had noticed, but you didn't allow me to bring my wardrobe."

"Is that a joke, my lady? *Excelente.*" He tugged on her hand. "Come with me."

"What about Esperanza?" She realized with a start that the girl was gone. She must have slipped out during the heated discussion, embarrassed or frightened by it.

"She can come to no harm in the cañon," he said.

"Not even from Sim Kavanagh?"

"I've spoken with him. He'll not bother her again."

Rowena felt a rush of gratitude. Tomás's loyalty to his violent friend apparently had its limits. "Thank you."

"De nada." He led her into the bedchamber and knelt beside the carved wooden trunk set against the wall. He lifted the lid with a flourish.

Within was an array of colorful clothing—women's skirts, blouses, and petticoats. He drew out a skirt of bright green cloth and shook his head. "Too big." He rifled through the garments until he found another skirt, in brilliant red, and a white, short-sleeved blouse embroidered along the low neckline. "Ah. *Perfecta.*"

He held the skirt and blouse against his body for Rowena to inspect. "What do you think?"

"Are you asking whether or not I think it would flatter you?"

"Very funny." With a sly smile he held out his arms and laid the garments along the front of her dress. "Only you could do them justice, *dulzura.*"

Rowena's mind went blank, and the empty space filled with the memory of those fierce, erotic visions of the other Rowena, wanton and hungry. *She* dressed like this. No stays, no bustle, not even proper underthings—only the loose, flowing, sensual brush of cloth on bare skin.

And he wanted her to wear these clothes. He knew exactly

what they represented. Who but he had put the visions in her mind?

"Your fine gown will become rags soon enough," he said. "You can barely move in it. With these, you'll be comfortable. Free."

Free. She shuddered and pushed the skirt and blouse back at him. "I . . . cannot. It is out of the question—"

"Why?"

She could not possibly answer honestly. "You must have stolen these from some poor woman."

"Not at all. They were gifts to me from women in a village very much like Rito Pequeño."

Gifts in exchange for his stolen largesse, or for other "favors"?

"Women in my country," she said, "don't wear such garments."

"I see." He nodded solemnly. "You are too fine for the simple attire of my countrywomen. You would be ashamed to dress as they do and be thought one of them."

"No! I mean . . ." She floundered. "It would not look at all . . ." She flushed. "I should look ridiculous."

"You? Never." He smiled wickedly. "You would look *magnífica* beyond all words."

That was what she was afraid of. "I shall . . . give it some thought."

He laid the skirt and blouse across the top of the chest. "Take all the time you need. I wouldn't have thought you'd be content, like cattlemen or miners, to wear the same clothes for a month."

She turned away. "I said I would consider it. I assume that Esperanza may find something to wear in that trunk?"

"She may take her pick."

"Thank you for the dinner. Please thank Nestor again for me. And if you see Esperanza, I would appreciate it if you would send her back."

He gave her an ironic bow. "I shall give some thought to your request for children's dresses. I hope we reach similar conclusions."

Before she could ask him if he intended blackmail, he was gone. The front door clicked shut.

She forced herself to look again at the skirt and blouse. Wearing a corset underneath would be highly impractical. And as for the skirt . . .

With a sharp sigh she fell back on the bed and rested her arm across her forehead. This felt altogether too much like the first step down a very long and slippery slope to dishonor.

She laughed. No; she'd taken that step when she met Tomás Alejandro Randall. Her only choice was to climb back up or let herself fall.

Tomás watched the casa from his vantage behind a screen of trees by El Rito de las Lágrimas. He'd found Esperanza beside the stream, kicking her bare feet in the cool water. She'd looked up at him with a slight frown and nodded at his request that she return to Rowena, but he could see that something was troubling her. He simply didn't know what it was.

Rowena might have better luck. And he hoped for luck of his own.

Though it was dark in the cañon, he could see the door of the casa clearly. He knew his waiting might be in vain, and yet something told him that he'd be rewarded for his patience.

His notion proved correct. The door opened, and Rowena emerged. She paused and turned her face up to the night sky.

Victory.

The red skirt and white blouse caught the moonlight, caressing the curves she'd hidden so carefully under layers of tight English clothing. He couldn't tell if she'd kept her stays, but her breasts seemed fuller, plumping above the scooped neckline of the blouse. The skirt revealed a small waist that required no cinching. Even her hair flowed loose about her shoulders.

She was glorious, and the single false note was her insistence on wearing her walking boots.

He'd teach her the pleasure of going without shoes. And without any clothing at all. One day she'd run at his side as a silver-gold wolf, abandoning herself to the moment.

He winced at the tightening in his groin. When he rode out to retrieve the goods for the children, he should seek out one of the many women who'd be more than happy to lie with El Lobo.

It wouldn't work. He—of all men—had been chaste since he'd stolen Rowena away from Cole MacLean. And he couldn't imagine any other woman in his bed.

Of course his mention of marriage had been a jest. He'd known she'd see it as an insult. Once he bedded her, he'd leave this yearning behind, and send her on her way a very different woman. One who'd never marry Cole MacLean. And MacLean would know who had changed her.

He adjusted his snug *calzoneras*. Some diversion was what he needed now. Tonight he would run as a wolf, and in the morning . . .

In the morning he would get a much closer look at his newborn Lady of Fire.

Rowena woke to the sound of singing.

She lay still, half asleep and unwilling to stir, as the song washed over her. Though nine in ten of the words and the melody itself were unfamiliar, the voice that sang them was unmistakable.

As were its sentiments. Rowena stared up at the adobe ceiling of the bedchamber and tried not to listen. Esperanza sat up beside her. She cocked her head toward the small window and glanced at Rowena.

She knew, as must everyone in the village, for whom

Tomás Alejandro Randall sang in that golden voice. As the deceptively homely tune coiled like a lazy breeze about Rowena's body, raising gooseflesh on her arms and forbidden longings in her heart, she vowed that she would not go to the window and look for the singer.

The song began its third verse. The thin sheets on the bed seemed far too warm even for a cool dawn. Esperanza pushed them away and slipped from the bed. She was dressed in skirt and blouse and out the door before Rowena found the wit to stop her.

Esperanza's presence offered no safety, after all. Not even the most rigid *dueña* could protest a subtle incursion such as this.

What was he declaring with his music, to her and all the residents of this hidden valley? His intentions for romantic conquest? Never had a man done so more sweetly. Rowena found herself humming the refrain and unsuccessfully tried to quell the impulse by covering her head with a pillow.

"Señorita?"

She came up for air to find Nestor's brown eyes regarding her from the doorway. He looked away politely while she straightened her nightgown and pulled the sheets to her shoulders.

"I hope I did not disturb you," he said. "Your breakfast is prepared."

Evidently he expected her to be an early riser . . . or he'd known perfectly well when and how Tomás planned to wake her. She abandoned any idea of feigning sleep until he gave up and went away.

Somehow she wasn't surprised to find her soiled traveling suit absent from the place she'd left it last night. That was the risk she took when she'd decided to try the garments Tomás had provided for her. The skirt and blouse were still neatly folded on top of the trunk.

If Tomás had his way, she'd wear those and nothing else.

Fortunately, she'd had the foresight to hide her corset and petticoat under the bed. She fitted the corset over her chemise as best she could, well aware that the lacings were too loose to provide anything other than a degree of modesty under the thin peasant blouse. She fastened the bustleless skirt with a sigh of resignation.

Yet, just as last night when she'd first put them on, she was unavoidably aware of the movement in the garments, their lightness and lack of binding over her body. They had the additional advantage of being far less hot than her suit—and they were clean.

She was struck by an immodest desire to dance about the room to Tomás's sultry tune, swirling the skirt from side to side in a solitary waltz.

Instead, she sat down to don stockings and her once-elegant half-boots, aware of how incongruous they looked with the rest of the ensemble.

Esperanza was already at the breakfast table. The food was, as usual, simple but delicious, and Rowena should have had ample distraction from the noise outside the casa. She gave up eating after the third bite.

"Do you hear that singing, Nestor?" she said.

"*Sí, señorita.*"

"Could you tell me . . . what it's about?"

"The song?" Nestor pulled up a third chair and sat down, setting aside his usual formality. "It is a love song."

No more or less than she'd feared. She'd be a fool to ask for details.

"What does it say?"

He smiled and began to recite:

> " *'En una mesa te puse,*
> *Un ramillete de flores.*
> *Rowena, no seas ingrata,*
> *Regaláme tus amores.*

I placed for you on a table
A bouquet of flowers.
Rowena, don't be ungrateful,
Give me your love.' "

Rowena held her breath, waiting for another verse. It didn't come. The song was finished.

Nestor sighed and gathered up the plates. Only when he left the room did she jump up from the table and run to the window.

It was not Tomás who stood there, eyes snapping with mischief and seduction, but the dark brown wolf she'd seen once before. He opened his mouth wide and waved his tail from side to side. Gracefully he stretched out his front legs, performing a bow for her benefit.

"Am I supposed to applaud?" she said.

His wolf's jaws opened as if in a laugh. With an agile twist he leaped sideways, dashed toward the wood along the stream, spun about and regarded her with unconstrained invitation. Her arms tensed on the windowsill, as if she braced herself against the urge to follow him.

She *wanted* to follow him, run with him, explore the world at his side. As a wolf.

As his mate.

Stifling a cry, she stumbled away from the window and fled into the bedchamber. She flung herself full-length upon the bed and beat her fists into the mattress until her arms were too numb to lift.

Esperanza's inquiring touch was gentle, but it nearly made Rowena jump out of her skin. The girl looked genuinely frightened; did Rowena appear as much the lunatic as she felt? She was afraid she knew the answer to that question.

"I'm sorry," she said, making a halfhearted attempt to tidy her hair. "I didn't mean to disturb you."

Esperanza shook her head. Rowena climbed from the bed

and went to the window. It faced a different direction than the one in the main room, but she knew Tomás was gone.

"What am I to do, Esperanza?" she whispered. "I find myself in an untenable situation." She leaned her forehead against the cool adobe wall. "I'm a fool. Why is it that knowing one is a fool doesn't provide a cure?"

Esperanza joined her by the window, a warm and comforting presence. Rowena faced her with grim resolution.

"It seems I am as susceptible as any woman to a certain combination of good looks and charm," she said. "But it is all on the surface. Meaningless." She touched her mouth. "I know he doesn't care for me. Not . . . personally. Any woman would do as well, if she were promised to Cole MacLean."

Esperanza's lips parted on a sigh that might have been denial.

"It's all right," Rowena said. "One cannot hope to fight one's weaknesses without recognizing them for what they are. I would not accept that the beast in myself was still capable of influencing me. Now that it is out of the shadows, it can have no power."

And the best way to make sure it remained powerless was to take immediate action. The day was young, Tomás was gone, and she'd been given the freedom to explore this mysterious canyon.

"Come, Esperanza" she said. "I believe we both could benefit by a breath of fresh air."

And, indeed, she felt that benefit as soon as she stepped out into the sunny plaza. Like so many others she'd experienced in the West, this morning was drenched with sunlight, the colors crisp and radiant, promised warmth tempered by a light breeze that carried the scent of water from the stream.

The stream ran the length of the canyon and provided an easy landmark to guide her. If she turned north, deeper into the canyon, she'd find the steep and winding path by which she and Esperanza had been brought here—too close to the houses and undoubtedly watched. But southward the canyon was uninhabited. Her best chance for finding an exit lay in that direction.

She quickly discovered the faint streamside trail worn among the green spring growth that thrived along the watercourse. Here the thirsty trees known as cottonwoods arched high overhead, shading smaller shrubs that competed for moisture and light. Tall pines and slender birches made homes for countless birds, and where the dryer wall of the canyon sloped up to the mesa, wildflowers found purchase between the rocks. It was a miniature Eden surrounded by wasteland, and she could begin to understand why ancient peoples had chosen this place for their home.

Taking Esperanza by the hand, she started along the trail. At first it paralleled the steam, winding in and out of the cool wood. Then it began to climb along the hillside, becoming little more than an animal track. Esperanza, agile as a mountain goat on her bare feet, forgot caution and bounded ahead.

There was still no sign of a path directly up to the top of the mesa. Though not as steep as the opposite cliff, this side of the canyon was treacherous with loose rock.

Any werewolf could have managed it.

Rowena clenched her jaw and forged on. The canyon walls gradually came closer and closer together, rising high and steep to either side in narrows that forced the stream into a tight, sunken channel.

The delicate melody of flowing water changed to a more urgent drumming. Esperanza was out of sight beyond the next bend of the trail. Rowena hurried to catch up and slid to a stop at the sight of what the girl had found.

Glittering threads of water spilled over a sudden drop in the stream's course, forming a small but glorious waterfall. At its base twenty feet below, the fall had worn out a shallow pool that held the stream for a instant's stillness before releasing it again on its eastward course.

Esperanza smiled with real excitement and pointed at the fall.

"I see it," Rowena said. "It is lovely." But reaching the fall would require a bit of a scramble, even for a barefoot girl.

Esperanza didn't seem to mind. Before Rowena could recommend caution, she was halfway down the slope, sending a hail of pebbles into the water below. She slipped out of sight, and then reappeared at the edge of the pool.

Rowena watched with a stab of envy as the girl perched on a flat stone and plunged her feet into the water. She kicked up a froth of wavelets, smiling and waving to Rowena high above.

The place could not have been more perfectly designed for a restful, private bath. No hasty washing with a basin and old cloth, or worrying over privacy. An intruder would be seen before he got too close, even if one had the inclination to wander so far from the village.

It was sorely tempting. Esperanza slipped out of her skirt and jumped into the water clad solely in her *camisa,* ducking under and popping up again. All the scene lacked was the sound of joyful laughter.

Esperanza's unselfconscious happiness brought a tightness to Rowena's throat. Surely, by standing aloof, she would put a pall on this brief moment of pleasure. Esperanza deserved better.

Hitching up her skirt and petticoat, Rowena slipped and slid her way down to the water's edge. Only when she reached the pool did she realize that she'd lost the heel of one of her boots among the rocks above. With a hiss of disgust she unbuttoned the boots and tossed them aside. She wriggled her stockinged toes experimentally.

There was certainly no harm in wetting her feet. She

folded Esperanza's abandoned skirt and sat on the flat rock beside it. Esperanza came up for air again, sleek as an otter. The youthful curves of her body were clearly visible through the wet cotton of her blouse.

Rowena averted her eyes. *She* had a corset; even if she took off her blouse, she'd be at least partially covered. If she dared go so far.

She removed her stockings and eased her feet into the pool—ankle-deep, then to mid-calf. The water was cold, but not icy. She closed her eyes to savor the delightful sensation.

Something snatched at her toes. She yelped, only to see Esperanza darting away like a mischievous water sprite. There must have been magic in the air, for Rowena found herself responding in kind. She cupped her hands and sent a cascade of water pelting down on Esperanza's head.

That was the beginning of the game. It proceeded rapidly from light splashing to thorough soaking, and between one moment and the next Rowena found herself to her hips in the pool, laughing helplessly. The corset was already as good as ruined; she saw little reason for further restraint and bobbed down until she was completely submerged. Esperanza blinked owlishly under the surface, releasing a stream of bubbles from puffed cheeks.

They took turns standing under the soft shower of the fall. Rowena tilted up her face to drink the pure water. It ran in rivulets over her arched neck, between her breasts, along her hips like caressing fingers. The weight of it tugged at her petticoats until she had no choice but to wriggle free and toss the garment up on the rocks. Even the thin skirt felt heavy. The corset was quite unbearable.

Turning her back, she removed the blouse and then the corset, tugging at waterlogged laces. Esperanza came to her rescue. With a sigh of relief, Rowena laid it on the rock and put the wet blouse back on over the chemise. Two thin layers were as revealing as one, but she couldn't bring herself to care. The water, the sunshine, the setting were too enchanting for such mundane concerns.

The water had another unexpected effect. As she half floated on her back, her skirt billowing about her, she was intensely reminded of the parts of her body she'd tried to ignore since Tomás had made her all too aware of them. She felt the way her nipples tightened like bold sun-worshipers yearning for the warmth high above. She shivered as hidden currents slipped under her skirt, between her thighs, seeking and stroking until she ached.

Drowsing, she imagined that the water took form. Human form, potently male. The currents and ripples became questing fingers bent on taking unheard-of liberties with her person.

And she didn't resist. She let those hands have their way. Tomás's hands. The erotic waking dreams returned with redoubled vividness, but this time she forgot to be outraged or afraid.

There was a rightness to it in this enchanting place, this oasis in the desert. Only Esperanza witnessed her languid sensuality, and the girl couldn't guess what went on in her imagination.

Imagination had the power to transform her into the wanton of her visions. But she maintained control. She allowed the slow wave of excitement to build from the tips of her bare toes to the crown of her head, breathing more quickly as the new and rousing awareness centered at the apex of her thighs.

Yes. This had happened with the real Tomás, when she'd had no warning. It was quite incredible, but there was no reason that she could not master it like any other impulse. With a little concentration she could pull herself away from the brink and make her body bow to her will. All she had to do was open her eyes. . . .

She opened them. The dark brown wolf stood on the

flat rock, watching her. Esperanza was submerged to her neck in the water under the fall, transfixed by some overwhelming emotion.

The wolf crouched as if he would leap into the pool. His form blurred and melted into mist, pulsing with its own internal light.

When the mist dispelled it was Tomás who stood on the rock. Tomás, sleek and naked, smooth muscles sliding under tanned skin.

He'd Changed once before in her presence. Then, she'd looked away. But the tantalizing spell of warmth and water refused to disperse. She stared at him, half dazed. How handsome he was. How elegant in his lines, like a fine classical statue.

Statues were not quite so . . . anatomically detailed. She hunted vaguely for a better word. Not detailed—defined. Not like this. Not so pointedly.

She giggled. The pulling, tickling sensation between her legs grew stronger. How odd. A part of her wondered how she'd come to feel as if she'd consumed several large glasses of Quentin's favorite brandy.

The other part didn't care.

Tomás slid one leg into the water. She observed the progress of his descent with fascination. The water lapped caressingly about the athletic line of his calf. His other leg joined the first, until he stood thigh-deep in the pool.

The interesting point where the water ended made the rest of his body all the more noticeable. Especially the undeniably male portion of him. She looked up at his face.

Hunger. It was naked in his eyes. It matched the quivering, expectant, on-the-brink feeling that claimed her body. Brazen images crystalized in her mind. Two bodies, made to fit together like interlocking pieces of a puzzle. Wet skin upon wet skin. Water above and beneath and all around, like the most luxurious bed.

Fingers caressing. Lips parting. Soft cries. Pleasure.

Pleasure. The muscles in her stomach contracted. He would give her pleasure such as she'd never known, unimaginable sweetness and ecstasy.

All she had to do was give in, and he would do the rest. She smiled and opened her arms.

twelve

Tomás had never been one to question his good fortune.

The invitation was plain in Rowena's eyes. How this miraculous moment had come about he couldn't begin to guess and didn't intend to try.

He'd followed her and Esperanza to the falls without any expectation that she would succumb so swiftly to the lure of this hidden sanctuary. The tiny pool was one of his favorite places in the cañon; if she'd used her werewolf senses, she would have known that at once and been on her guard.

But she had not. Indeed, she'd behaved with gratifying impetuosity from the second she'd set foot in the water. Esperanza was partially responsible: She, too, had lost her fear and became the playful child she must once have been. She had led the way.

And Rowena followed willingly. From his vantage point high above, Tomás watched her splash about and laugh as if she hadn't a care in the world. Corset and petticoat had come off in a matter of minutes, leaving her in light cotton that clung like a second skin and left little to the imagination.

He stayed out of sight, savoring the shape of her full, unbound breasts, the proud thrust of her nipples, the outlines of her thighs, with a frustration balanced between pain and delight. The musky perfume of her body, enhanced by the water, made him reel like a drunkard. In his imagination she was readying herself for him. In his thoughts, like so many times in the past, she was giving up the fight.

Several delicious moments passed before he realized that not everything was in his imagination. The games were over, Esperanza had retreated to one end of the pool, and Rowena was floating on her back, legs parted, like a lascivious river goddess invoking the sun's caresses.

Tomás was no stranger to lust. Rowena roused it in him every time she came near. But what he'd felt the other times was a mere shadow of what possessed him then.

She didn't touch herself. He was quite sure she didn't know how. But he could picture the water seeking out the warm, pulsing core of her womanhood as he longed to do, invading her defenses with a cunning even he could not match.

The water became her lover. She sighed and yielded, eyes closed in voluptuous carnality.

Tomás was down the slope and beside the pool in an instant. He Changed and stood before her, naked and aroused and reckless with desire.

She opened her eyes, and then her arms.

In a final moment of sanity, Tomás looked for Esperanza. She had fled. He and Rowena were alone.

Her slender body was warm and weightless when he took her in his arms. He captured her mouth with a throaty laugh of triumph and a sense of complete unreality.

Surely this was a dream. Surely his Lady of Fire would vanish in a puff of smoke if he dared to blink.

Inexperienced as she was, she answered his kiss in such a way that he couldn't mistake it for anything resembling a dream. She had learned very quickly from that one encounter in the Indian cave. She curled about him, her water-logged skirt like a mermaid's tail meant to entangle him and drag him into her watery bower.

After the first kiss he held her away to gaze on what he had won with such unforeseen ease. Her face, beaded with tiny droplets, was unearthly in its beauty. Unbound hair drifted on the surface of the water like a flaxen halo. The white column of her neck arched smoothly from the scooped neck of the blouse that slid from her shoulders and revealed her breasts more enticingly than any nakedness. Darker nipples puckered under wet cotton, inviting his closer inspection.

He bent to touch the tip of her right nipple, molding the fabric with his tongue. She gave an almost soundless gasp. It was the sweetest encouragement he knew. Her breasts seemed made for his mouth, like the tenderest of oranges. He cradled her in the water and suckled gently.

Her eyes were wide, but she didn't seem to see him. Her hands reached blindly and caught in his hair. He tasted water flavored by her desire, moved his hands lower to find the fastening of her skirt. His fingers were unusually clumsy. Impatiently he pushed the billowing cloth away from her legs and above her waist.

Softly, softly, he warned himself. This was not something to be rushed. If she thought the water a satisfying lover, he had much to teach her.

Smooth as water itself, his fingers slid along the insides of her thighs. It was like stroking wet velvet. Even when he reached his goal, she did not flinch. Nor did she speak. Only her breath sighed out as he touched her tender petals. They, too, were wet, but not only with the moisture of the stream.

She was ready for him as she had never been before. He should have known that words were not the way to win her. Not for her the romantic songs, teasing innuendo, and practiced seduction that sufficed for other women. She tried to shield herself with words, true enough, but that was because she knew where she was most vulnerable.

She wanted to be taken. She wanted to be forced to admit the wildness within herself, to be shown by one who understood and accepted and embraced that very wildness. Fear and misplaced propriety would always hold her back . . . until the right man set her free with decisive action.

He was that man. She, too, must have always known. Some wondrous conjunction of time and place and fortune had finally allowed her to admit it. He did not dare delay longer, neither for her pleasure or his.

Quickly he set her upright, positioning her thighs to either side of his hips and supporting her bottom with a steadying hand. He reminded himself that she was a virgin. She must be. No other could touch her, possess her like this.

He pulled her head down to his shoulder and smoothed back her hair. "Don't be afraid, *mi flama*. You won't regret this. When I am done, you'll never go back to what you were. You'll be free. . . ."

He readied himself for the thrust. Her hand wedged between them and felt for him as if she were eager to guide his entry.

"Yes," he murmured, closing his eyes.

"No!"

Her choked voice gave him scant warning before she pushed him away. Sensitive flesh protested the rejection most emphatically. He flailed backward and lost his balance. Water closed over his head. A froth of bubbles marked Rowena's swift retreat across the pool. He broke the surface, whipping sodden hair from his eyes.

Rowena was scrambling up on a rock, dragging the hem of the skirt from the water in a vain effort to cover herself. She no longer bore any resemblance whatsoever to a nubile and uninhibited river goddess. Her teeth chattered and her face was tight with distress.

"What did you do?" she demanded in a harsh whisper.

He ducked under again and shook himself vigorously before he trusted himself to answer. "What did I do?" *Nothing,* his body shouted. He crouched waist-deep in the water. "I was doing exactly what you invited me to do."

"What? How dare you! I—" She sat down in a puddle of bunched skirts. "I came here . . . with Esperanza. We were only—" Her hand brushed her cheek, her throat, her breast. "Where is she?"

Oh, no. He wouldn't let her dodge the subject so easily. "She left us alone. Don't you remember what happened, or is it too inconvenient?"

"We were bathing. You interrupted—"

"I don't think so, *dulzura*. You were enjoying yourself, but you were happy enough to see me."

She stared at him as if she'd just noticed his nakedness. Hot color rose in a tide that stained her skin from breast to hairline. "Are you implying that I—asked you to come into the pool . . . like that?"

"Not in words. No words were needed." He cast her a mocking smile. "Is that your excuse for offering yourself to a man and then refusing him so rudely? Because you did not say, 'Come, Tomás, and take me?' "

In the usual course of events, she would have angrily refuted anything he claimed, gathered up her dignity, and marched off to lick her wounds. This time she surprised him. "Is that . . . what you think I intended?"

"Didn't you?"

She bit down hard on her lower lip. "It wasn't me." She looked at him with pleading in her eyes, more humble than he'd ever seen her. "You must believe that it wasn't me. I am not the kind of woman who would . . ." She stammered and swallowed. "I am truly sorry if I misled you."

His anger melted. She blamed herself, not him—and yet she remained safely locked within her own comfortable deception. To remain there she'd sacrifice everything, even her own pride.

He could be merciless, if he chose. He could push and push at her until she broke down. He hadn't been wrong; she wanted to be taken. She begged to be convinced, seized, mastered, so she could be absolved of guilt for the hungers she found so disgraceful.

"When I found you here," he said, "you were already dreaming of my touch."

"That is . . . not true."

"You're a poor liar, Rowena. You dreamed of my touch, as you've dreamed of it since the day I took you from Cole."

"Please." She averted her face. "Don't."

"You're no more a coward than a liar." He waded closer, rising from the water. "Look at me. Look at me, and tell me that you took no enjoyment in my caresses. Tell me that you were possessed by some spirit that robbed you of will and forced you to endure so great an affront. Tell me, and I'll never touch you again."

The world itself seem to hang breathless upon her answer. The canyon wren ceased its song, and even the sound of rushing water fell to a murmur.

She looked at him as he demanded. Her brown eyes swirled with tiny golden sparks, set alight by her inner battle.

"Very well," she said. "I will tell you the truth, Tomás Alejandro Randall. You are very good at what you do. You could charm a snake from its nest, and I have no doubt that you could seduce any woman you choose." Her hands twisted into a knot in her lap. "I am no exception. You have . . . affected me. You have caused me to forget myself and lose sight of my strongest beliefs. You have made me ashamed."

He felt as though she'd calmly reached out and struck him across the face. "That is not what I—"

"The flaw is in me. It is the part that wants to become a beast and run at your side."

The dull resignation of her tone robbed his victory of any

satisfaction. He reached out to her, and she made no move to pull away.

"Yes, Tomás, you could have me," she said. "You could make me betray Cole and myself. I might even enjoy it." She looked down at his hand on her arm. "But it's only the beast you will win. There is a part of me you can't touch—the part that is human."

He curled his fingers around her wrist. "Rowena," he said thickly.

"You needn't worry," she said. "You don't care about anything but this." She grasped his hand and placed it on her breast. "Once you have this, the rest scarcely matters, does it? You'll have no reason to make me stay."

He felt her nipple harden under his palm. "Ah. You'll sacrifice your virginity in exchange for release?"

"Why not? Will you agree to such a bargain?"

She wasn't serious. Her words came of anger and bitterness, and a desire to hurt. Surely she didn't think she could wound him merely by suggesting she would give herself for freedom from captivity, but not for pleasure—that she'd give him the shell of her beauty and not what lay beneath.

"That is not the sole reason I brought you here," he said, snatching his hand away. "MacLean must pay far more than the loss of your maidenhood. I'm afraid I can't accept your bargain."

"Then I am at your mercy." She lifted her chin and held his gaze with brittle dignity. "Do what you will."

Even if he'd gone womanless for five years he wouldn't have been tempted now. He made for the opposite side of the pool and pulled himself up on the rocks. He shook himself again, from head to toe.

"Your mistake," he said, "is to believe that you know my will—or your own. You separate the human from the wolf as if they are two different things. I look forward to the time when you realize they are not." He smiled, showing all his teeth. "I'll come to you again, Rowena, sooner than you think. But it will only be because you beg me to take you."

"We have a saying in England: 'Not for all the tea in China.' "

His heart lifted at the return of her stubborn spirit. "And we have one here: '*De lo contado come el lobo*—The wolf eats from what is told.' You would say, 'Don't count your chickens before they are hatched.' "

"Are you reduced to eating chickens, Don Tomás?"

"I prefer a spicier dish." He licked his lips. "One more piece of advice, *dulzura*. You'd be wise to stay in the water. *'Donde lumbre ha habido, rescoldo queda.'* Where there's been fire, embers remain."

It was over at last.

Felícita knelt behind a rock at the top of the rocky slope, pressing her hands to her chest. The brown wolf scrambled up from the stream and ran past her without stopping, but she made herself as small as she could until he was long gone from sight.

Even after Rowena gathered up her things and left, it was many minutes before Felícita found the energy to walk again. Her head still hummed like a hive full of bees. Not only her head, but her heart and every part of her body. She'd been caught at the leading edge of a storm, helpless amid the seething emotions of the two who had come together at the pool.

She still did not understand everything that had happened. One moment she had been happier than she could remember, playing in the water with her friend at her side, and the next she was watching the great brown wolf become the man who'd saved her life.

It was not that which shocked her. If Tomás was a *brujo*, he was not bad. She had already guessed that he was no ordinary man, as the lady was no ordinary woman. And they had saved her life.

But when he came to the pool, he chased away the fragile contentment she and Rowena had found. Felícita no longer existed, for all the world converged on the two who looked at each other across the water.

All the world became what they felt for each other.

Felícita picked her way down to the poolside to retrieve the skirt Rowena had folded and left on the rock. The place was safe now; raw emotion no longer vibrated in the stones at her feet or filled the water with heat that did not burn. She could almost put from her mind the sight of Rowena's face when Tomás began to touch her.

The sight, but not the passion. Felícita could run away from what she did not wish to see, when the feelings of others became too strong and confusing in her head. But she was not safe. Not even here.

Now she knew why the people who paid Tío to speak with her were so eager to believe the good things she told them, even when she could only guess what they wished to hear. *She* had wished to believe that running away from the village would be enough.

She had chosen to come to this cañon with Rowena and Tomás. They were strong; they would rescue her from the dangers of a world she did not understand.

But the lady could not protect her completely. If her strength was great, her feelings were just as irresistible. Felícita heard them, no matter how hard she tried not to. When the lady thought of Tomás, they became almost frightening—as frightening as those of Sim Kavanagh.

Yet there had been times, like this morning in the casa, when she wished so very much to help the lady in her distress. She had . . . *needed* to help, but she didn't know how.

If only she were not so stupid. If only she were not so very much afraid—afraid that if she reached too deeply into another's soul, she would lose the little bit she had of herself, however worthless it seemed.

Shivering, she put on her wet skirt and started up the trail toward the village. She was torn as the lady was torn. She wanted to leave the valley, but she wanted to stay; she was desperate to escape the tumultuous feelings shouting in her mind, and yet she could not bear to be alone.

If she could find a way out of the cañon, she could take the lady with her. Wouldn't that solve both their problems? Rowena would be free of Don Tomás and all the unbearable things he made her feel. And Felícita would have peace.

Peace, and quiet in her mind at last—

"Why in such a hurry, pretty señorita?"

She froze. Sim Kavanagh blocked the path like a great black raven. All at once the vast heavy cloud of his violent need rolled out to swallow her, and she reached for something, anything, to hold onto.

He grabbed her wrist. "What's wrong with you?"

Wrong, wrong, wrong. She opened her mouth to gasp for air. Moments ago she'd nearly been lost in the yearnings of Tomás and Rowena, but at least they had thought only of each other. The danger came from being too near the scalding white heat of their passion, like a moth drawn to its death in a candle flame.

With Sim Kavanagh she stood on the crumbling edge of the very pit of hell. He hated Rowena, but his need was all for *her.* His furious wanting battered at her like a fist on a wall, as if she could give him what he must have to live. But she had nothing to give.

Let me go, she screamed. The cry stopped in her throat.

"I'm not going to hurt you," he said, his voice laced with disgust. "Sit." He pulled her off the path and forced her down on the trunk of a fallen pine. She shrank in on herself, arms wrapped tight about her chest, while he plucked a rolled cigarette from his *chaleco* and lit it.

"Now we can have our talk," he said. He flicked ashes onto the end of the tree trunk inches from her hand. "I wouldn't go running to the English bitch, if I were you. Not if you want her safe."

She closed her eyes. No, Rowena couldn't help her now.

"They say you're a witch," he said leaning close. "Witch. *Bruja, comprende?*"

His feelings made his meaning clear. *Bruja* was what the villagers had called her after Tío died. They would have laughed to know how little power she had.

"I hear those villagers were mighty scared of you," he said. "Can you cast spells? Make someone go away? Scare them off?" He knelt so that his hard, bitter face was level with hers. "Don't lie to me, *paloma.*"

Make someone go away. Felícita knew who he meant. He wanted Rowena to go away. He wanted her to help.

It was so close to what she'd been thinking, that she and Rowena could both leave the cañon and find another place to be safe. But Sim Kavanagh didn't want the lady to be safe.

She shook her head emphatically. He stared at her with narrowed eyes, and she was afraid he didn't believe her.

"No witch," he muttered. "But there's something about you . . ." His heavy brows wrinkled in something like bewilderment. "What is it? What are you?"

Compelled to meet his gaze, Felícita had no way to answer. Again his wanting overwhelmed her thoughts. Wanting . . . and fear. Fear just like hers or Rowena's or anyone else's. Fear of losing what he had.

Out of the void of her own terror, a tiny seed of understanding struggled toward the distant light.

He turned his head and spat, crushing the seed before it could begin to grow. "To hell with that," he said. "You'll be of use to me one way or another." He paused to listen to the silence of the wood, as if he thought someone might be eavesdropping. "You do want to save your lady friend, don't you?"

She tried to croak out a sound, any sound. He laughed. "Of course you do. Because if you don't do what I tell you, I'll hurt her. Either she leaves this canyon the way I plan, or she's dead."

Nauseated by his hatred, Felícita pressed her palm to her forehead where all the sickness gathered. He meant what he said. He was not afraid of killing.

"You won't have to do much," he said. "You may think you're betraying her, but you'll be saving her life." He seized her wrist again. "It's a good thing you can't speak. I wouldn't want you to tell anyone about our conversation."

This time she found the courage to resist his hold, but he wasn't ready to let her go. He drew her so close that his lips were almost upon hers.

"I'll be gone for a few days, *paloma*. When I come back, I'll be looking for you." And then he kissed her—not the way Tomás kissed Rowena, but hard and angry, as if he hated both her and himself.

And he did. He did.

She hardly noticed the tears that filled her eyes and ran down her cheeks. Her hands moved of their own accord to touch his back. To hold him, as he wanted so much to be held.

He pushed her away roughly. "You're just like the rest of them," he said, scrubbing at his mouth. "But you won't betray me. *Adiós, señorita.*"

He strode away. Felícita's legs began to shake. She sat down on the log before she could fall. The tears dried on her cheeks and swollen lips.

Hope was a new thing to Felícita. She'd had no need for it when her whole life was bounded by the walls of her uncle's casa, touched but briefly by the strangers who came to consult the *adevinadora* of Los Milagros. She didn't care about those strangers. She didn't even care about herself. Future and past were the same, unchanging.

Until Tío died, and then there was no time to discover

hope before the village men came to beat her from the village. Only when the wolf and the lady saved her had she understood what it was to hope for something better.

Sim Kavanagh had stolen that dream. He would carry her away into his darkness, and there was nothing she could do to stop him.

There was no one to rescue her now.

Cole had never met Sim Kavanagh, but he knew everything he needed to know. Kavanagh was a rustler and a train robber, with a reputation as a ruthless killer of few loyalties and no scruples.

He was the kind of man Cole understood and wasn't fool enough to trust. He was also Tomás Randall's *compañero.* Under any other circumstances, Cole would have killed him at first sight.

These were not ordinary circumstances.

He paused in the doorway of the Las Vegas Exchange Hotel's saloon, scanning the faces above the gaming tables and along the bar. Being a wanted man, Kavanagh wasn't likely to sit in plain view of the law—or of the San Miguel, Colfax, and Mora County ranchers who'd suffered his plundering.

I can get your woman, the crudely scrawled note read. *I know where she is. Meet me at the Exchange tomorrow at noon.* The note had come to him yesterday, at the hands of a grubby child, while he was pursuing family business in Las Vegas; the messenger had disappeared before he could question him. One glance at the signature made Cole forget his business.

He hadn't been able to trace the note to its origin, nor learn how Sim Kavanagh knew he was in town. It was only another in a string of infuriating failures. Today marked the seventeenth day since Randall had kidnapped Rowena, and no further progress had been made in recovering her or locating Randall's lair. Weylin, defying Cole's authority, had set off to track Randall on his own and hadn't returned. The supposedly relentless men Cole hired wandered in circles like stupid sheep without a shepherd. He hadn't even considered bringing in the law.

The note was the first sign that something was about to break. If it was a trick, Kavanagh would die one way or another. If it wasn't, it was worth the small risk to himself.

Especially if Kavanagh betrayed El Lobo.

"Mr. MacLean?" A skinny bartender sidled up to him nervously, bobbing his head. "I was told to take you to the back room. Please come with me?"

Cole nodded. If Kavanagh thought he was safe in the back room, he was a fool. He'd have to know that Cole's men were watching every exit, and that he'd damned well better have something good if he wanted to get out of the Exchange alive.

He must want something from Cole very, very badly.

The back room, usually reserved for business or private meetings, was empty save for the man sitting alone at the large table. Clouds of smoke obscured his face and his scent, but Cole knew immediately that he wasn't afraid.

"Kavanagh," he said.

"MacLean." The smoke cleared. Kavanagh looked every inch the outlaw he was, the way tenderfoot easterners liked to portray men of his kind: dressed all in black, even to his hat; steel-eyed and of dangerous mien; scarred and seamed in a thousand battles with sun, wind, and a host of enemies.

In another man it would have been affectation or bluff. Not in this one. Most of Kavanagh's enemies were undoubtedly dead.

Cole smiled. "I hope you aren't going to waste my time," he said.

Kavanagh deliberately leaned back in his chair, balancing it on two legs. "Not unless you want Randall to keep the woman."

"Is she well?"

The outlaw's narrow lips curled in contempt. "Now that's heartwarming, seeing how you're so worried about her."

Cole brushed back his coat and hooked his thumb into the waistband of his trousers. Kavanagh's chair crashed to the floor. His revolver was pointed at Cole's chest.

"I'm unarmed," Cole said, leaving his hand where it was.

"Like hell. I know what you are."

"Then you know if you shoot you may wound me, but I'll kill you. If my men don't get to you first."

They stared at each other. Moving slowly, Kavanagh laid his gun on the table. For a man like the outlaw, letting go of his weapon would be like losing an arm.

"I'm glad we understand each other." Cole pulled up a chair and sat at the table. "Though I wonder what could possibly be worth the risk you're taking to come here, or why you think I should deal with you at all before I see you hanged." He gestured to the bartender. "Bring glasses and a bottle of whiskey, then leave us alone." The bartender scurried out the door.

"I wonder," Kavanagh said, "why you need men to back you up, being what you are. Or is it because you're a cripple?"

Cole reacted instinctively, focusing his rage on the outlaw in the same way he used his will on sharp eastern businessmen to bilk them of their money. Kavanagh didn't so much as flinch when he should have been gibbering on his knees for mercy.

"Tomás told me that your kind could do things to men's minds," he said casually. "He doesn't go in for that much, himself. Doesn't seem to be working on me."

It was true. The man's mind was opaque and completely resistant to any influence. Cole felt a moment of panic. Men always did what he said. Always. He reached for the gun on the table.

"You kill me, and you never get your bitch back," Kavanagh said. "I'm the only one who can deliver her to you."

"My men—"

"Your men are useless. None of 'em saw me when I rode into town. How're they going to find Randall?" He scratched the underside of his arm. "You won't find him, and he don't plan on letting her go, no matter what ransom you pay. And you won't pay a plugged nickel."

His words drove the rage from Cole's mind and left it cold and clear. Randall, too, must know he wouldn't pay so much as a fraction of the demanded ransom. The desperado's purpose had always been revenge: to take what was Cole's and laugh while he tried to get it back.

"Is her life in danger?"

"You said not to waste your time, MacLean. Now you're wasting mine. I don't like this town." He spat with perfect aim into the nearest cuspidor. "You want her back, or don't you?"

Cole reminded himself again that this man might be of use before he died. "You're ready enough to double-cross your friend."

Kavanagh leaned over the table, eyes narrowed. "I don't have any friends, MacLean. Tomás betrayed all his *compañeros* when he decided to take your woman. He did it for himself. I won't go down with him when she gets him killed."

"You just said I'd never find Randall."

"Not where he is now, and not soon. But you won't give up, will you, MacLean? Tomás think he's tough, but he's not like you. You'd do anything to get him, kill anyone who stands in your way. Like I would in your place."

"Don't compare yourself to me, you son of a bitch."

Kavanagh shrugged. "Like you said, we understand each other. You're powerful because nothing stops you. I know you'll get Tomás eventually. I don't plan to be on the losing side of the final war."

"You should have thought of that before you rustled MacLean cattle."

"Maybe I've seen the evil of my ways. Maybe I've gotten used to living."

"Is that what you want for bringing back my fiancée? Your life?"

"I don't expect gratitude, MacLean. Just a pardon from the governor, and your word to let me leave the Territory alive."

Cole laughed sarcastically. "That's all?"

"You have the influence. The governor will do it if you ask him."

Scum or not, Kavanagh knew the way of politics in New Mexico. He didn't underestimate the MacLeans' clout in the Ring that made the Territory's unofficial law.

"Yes," Cole said. "I have the influence. Why should I believe you can get Lady Rowena way from Randall?"

"Because Tomás trusts me."

And that was Randall's fatal flaw, that he could trust a man such as this. It was an error Cole would never have made. Nor would Kavanagh. Self-interest, not trust, would bind any agreement between them.

Until Cole had what he wanted. Then all bets were off.

Cole ran his finger up and down the ivory grip of Kavanagh's Peacemaker. "I'll guarantee your life if you bring me the lady—and Randall."

"No."

The answer was too swift. "I thought you didn't owe him any loyalty."

"Stealing the woman is one thing. Going up against Tomás—that's suicide."

"Do you think it's safer going against me, Kavanagh?"

The outlaw pushed his chair back from the table. "That's why I'm here. Have we got a deal?"

As far as Cole could see, the advantages were all on his

side. If Kavanagh succeeded, it would save him the time, trouble, and expense of finding Randall's weakness. And Kavanagh wouldn't survive to use his governor's pardon.

"All right," he said. "I'll let you leave Las Vegas alive, this time. I'll give you two weeks to return with the Lady Rowena, unharmed. And untouched."

The question was evident in the outlaw's eyes: *What if she has been touched?* Cole didn't bother to answer. Rowena's virtue was unassailable; she'd die before submitting to any would-be rapist.

"Bring her back," he said, "and you'll have your pardon and a week to get out of the Territory." The door creaked open behind them; Kavanagh's gun fairly leaped from the table and into his hand. The bartender stood knock-kneed in the doorway with a pair of smudged glasses and a bottle balanced precariously on a tray.

"Your drinks?" he said in a high voice.

Kavanagh holstered his revolver and snatched the bottle from the tray before the bartender could set it down. He took a long pull and wiped his mouth with his sleeve.

"You got a deal," he said, thrusting the bottle at Cole.

With open scorn Cole took the bottle, set it on the table, deliberately cleaned the mouth with his handkerchief, chose a glass and poured himself a measure. "Deal."

He accompanied Kavanagh to the rear door of the saloon and signaled his men to let the outlaw go. Kavanagh's sharp eyes picked out the hidden observers one by one.

"Tell them not to follow me," he said.

Cole had already considered and discarded that plan. Kavanagh was too smart to let them trail him far. Only a werewolf could succeed in pursuing such a man without being detected and stopped.

Damn Weylin for being gone when he might finally prove useful.

As Kavanagh mounted and rode west out of town, Cole

was almost tempted to follow himself. To see Randall dead, once and for all . . .

Phantom pain thrust into the stump of his arm like a white-hot branding iron. No. Randall wasn't worth his personal effort. Not until every other possibility was exhausted. And he had a very strong premonition that trusting Sim Kavanagh was the first of Tomás Randall's final, most deadly mistakes.

Weylin picked up the horseman's track at midmorning, just beyond the village of Tecolote, roughly ten miles southwest of Las Vegas at the edge of the Santa Fe Trail.

He recognized the scent immediately and felt the grim pleasure of long-awaited victory. After only four days of running as a wolf, out of contact with his brother or any human being, he'd found what he'd sought for so many years.

He followed the spoor with an ease impossible in his human form, running silent and unseen at a steady, ground-eating lope. The rider pushed his mount hard, keeping away from the main trail where settlers and merchants drove their carts and wagons. It was well past sunset when he stopped to rest at the place called Glorieta Pass.

Weylin lay among the trees downwind from his prey and watched Sim Kavanagh make camp for the night. In all those years of tracking Randall's band, he'd never come so close to the outlaw said to be even more ruthless than Randall himself. Sim Kavanagh was wanted in several states and by the federal government for crimes too innumerable to count; the man who brought him in would be acclaimed a hero.

It took great discipline for Weylin to remain quiet and still. So long, so long he had waited for a moment like this. His wolf's blood cried out for action; the hair remained stiff and erect along his spine, and he hardly cared about the emptiness of his belly or the ache in his paws. Kavanagh might run with a werewolf, but he was no match for one.

Weylin growled deep in his throat. Power flowed through

him, muscle and sinew and bone, begging to be used. All this he'd given up in refusing to Change, just for some antiquated notion of fairness and honor.

Men like Sim Kavanagh didn't hesitate to use their advantages to get what they wanted. Skill with a gun, cleverness, or a convenient lack of scruples—those were human talents to be wielded in the service of greed and cruelty. There was no reason in the world that one born more than human shouldn't embrace his birthright in the service of something far greater.

Weylin stretched, feeling the strength in a body made to run and leap and hunt with perfect efficiency. If he'd ignored Cole's disapproval and done this from the beginning, Randall's career of harassment, theft, and murder might have ended before it began.

As Kavanagh's might be ended here and now. But he was Weylin's best chance of finding Randall's hidden lair.

Kavanagh finished his scanty meal of jerky and lay down on a thin blanket with his saddle for a pillow. His horse stood hip-shot beside him, dozing. Weylin laid his head on his paws and waited. He fell into a light sleep and jerked awake, only to find Kavanagh turning onto his side with a restless motion.

The next time he woke, Kavanagh was standing over him, his gun fixed on Weylin at point-blank range.

He leaped up. The gun fired, and searing agony sliced into his side. He fell, all four legs splayed as if in the throes of death. Then he lay still.

Kavanagh nudged him with his boot. Weylin knew he could kill with a well-aimed shot to the heart or the head; his only hope lay in pretending that the first shot had hit its mark.

Perhaps it had. Weylin felt blood mat his fur as his limbs lost all sensation. Was this death? Was this what Kenneth and Father had felt in their final moments?

His breaths came too shallow for Kavanagh to detect. After a little while the outlaw walked away and left him to finish dying alone.

thirteen

Four days. Four days Tomás had been gone, and instead of the relief and sense of freedom his absence should have brought her, Rowena felt only restless worry and a strange sort of loneliness.

She felt it now as she stood by the window and gazed out at the pale salmon cliffs, watching for his return. He, Kavanagh, and another of his men had left the canyon the very same evening of her devastating encounter with him by the waterfall. She remembered, quite painfully, the hours following that meeting, when she'd tried to prepare herself for their next inevitable confrontation. Planning what she'd say to him. How she'd act. What she would do to make sure such a thing never happened again.

But her thoughts had been all confusion and her emotions in turmoil long after she returned to the village. She'd allowed herself to breathe a bit easier when he didn't show up for dinner that night. And then Nestor had told her he'd ridden out.

Just like that, without a word to her. Leaving her to imagine what reckless and dangerous acts he might commit to defy and impress the world. Consigning her to relive the dreamlike moments in the pool beneath the waterfall and suffer the aches and fears and ecstacies those forbidden memories evoked.

Compelling her to find some purpose and occupation here in this robber's nest—or go quite mad.

"Señorita?"

Pilar tugged on her sleeve. She glanced down with a smile, making a serious effort to cast off her distraction.

"Look, señorita!" The girl held up the small, chipped slate proudly. "I can write 'cow' in English and Spanish!"

"So I see. Excellent work, Pilar."

And, indeed, it was—better than Rowena could have hoped after a mere three days' instruction. Pilar was her most advanced student, eager to learn. Rowena had little enough to work with in this makeshift schoolroom, and her pupils were not always attentive during the handful of hours they spent with her.

But it was a start. The day following Tomás's disappearance, when she'd first conceived the idea to begin teaching the children of the canyon, it had seemed an unlikely scheme. She couldn't abide spending all her time searching for a way to escape, especially not when she saw that she might do some good for the children even before he returned.

She'd gone to Nestor for help; much to her satisfaction, he had agreed. He'd accompanied her that very morning to see the children's fathers as they went to work in the fields along the stream. The men had reacted to her proposal with reserved surprise at first, and then with growing interest. In the end, they'd agreed to let the children come to her for basic schooling in English for a few hours a day.

Pilar and Enrique, the orphans, were another matter. They had no family demands on their time and few chores to perform. Pilar was enthusiastic at the prospect of learning, Enrique less so; the boy had thus far come to school but once in three days.

The others made up for his lapses. Rowena glanced around the main room of the casa. Gita, too young yet to begin any formal instruction, sat in the corner and played with a carved wooden dog. Pilar, Gertrudis, and Aquilino sat at the table, sharing the slate to practice their letters, while Miguel and Catalina sang the English nursery song she'd taught them, carefully sounding out the new words.

Considering that only Enrique and Pilar spoke much English, they'd made remarkable progress. Nestor had been invaluable as translator and familiar figure of authority. Moreover, he'd miraculously conjured up several schoolroom supplies she hadn't dared to hope for: the slate for writing, a box of broken chalk and stubby pencils, a pair of books in English. Nestor couldn't tell where they'd come from or who had last used them.

They would certainly be put to excellent use from now on. Not only was she able to begin teaching the children basic English, but she was learning Spanish as well. The boys and girls found it most entertaining that she was so ignorant. The first day had been spent trading common words back and forth in both languages—including *"vaca"* and "cow," accompanied by much posturing and appropriate animal cries.

It was nothing like what she'd done in England. She had taught tenants' children on her brother's estate, as many young English gentlewomen did. It was a part of the duty those of her rank owed the less fortunate.

Duty, order, normality. Those had always been her watchwords. In England her place among the tenants and their children was firmly established. She was accustomed to the respect and awe with which they regarded her, their unquestioning obedience.

Here, she had no place but what Tomás had made for her or what she made for herself. She was neither fine lady nor wealthy aristocrat. The children were not dependent upon her, nor did they hold her in any particular awe.

So she found herself gradually forgetting all the careful formalities she had planned to establish. She laughed helplessly when Miguel imitated a bleating sheep, or when Gertrudis showed remarkable flair for imitating Tomás's swagger. She beamed with pride when Pilar gravely congratulated her for correctly pronouncing a new Spanish word. And she reflected, again and again, how much these untutored children already knew of life and happiness in spite of their disadvantages.

Did Tomás have any idea who they truly were, or what they were capable of?

Tomás. She glanced toward the window. He'd better return soon with the fabric and patterns she'd requested, if he didn't wish to hear her very pointed thoughts on his delinquency.

She touched her hot cheeks. No. She and Tomás could never return to that peculiar raillery that had made up so much of their conversation since her kidnapping. She had come to realize, during his absence, how used to it she'd grown. She had even begun to enjoy it.

But the time at the waterfall had changed everything. An important barrier had been breached; *she* had breached it with her carelessness and unconsciously wanton behavior. She had encouraged him to take liberties. The only way she could mend the chasm between them was to begin with words: cool formality and absolute courtesy. She must at all times keep her distance and reserve with Tomás, regardless of how much he provoked her. The children gave her a perfect reason to discuss things with him in a reasonable manner.

To wish for his swift return was sheer foolishness. And she'd made little headway in finding a reasonable exit from the canyon. Esperanza no longer accompanied her on the morning and evening excursions up and down the canyon floor; the girl had grown almost reclusive since the waterfall incident. Rowena felt somehow to blame. For the child to witness such a shocking lapse on the part of her mentor . . . no wonder she avoided Rowena's company.

At least Sim Kavanagh had left the same day as his master, and could not trouble Esperanza in her solitude.

Turning away from the window, Rowena clapped her hands. "*Atención, niños!* It is time for Nestor and me to read to you from *Little Women.*"

The children stopped their work and play with varying degrees of alacrity and settled cross-legged on the packed earth floor. Pilar sat at the foot of Rowena's chair, her round face turned up like a flower toward the sun.

Rowena began to read. At the end of each sentence, she paused for Nestor to translate the words into Spanish and watched as magic worked in the minds of the children. Somehow she must find more books for them, in their own language as well as English. There was so much of the world to show them.

Her gaze drifted from the page. She wouldn't be here long enough to make a real difference in their lives—just as Tomás, in spite of his efforts, could make no difference in hers.

"Señorita?"

She started at the sound of Nestor's voice and found her place again. " 'Call yourself any names you like, but *I* am neither a rascal nor a wretch and I don't choose to be called—' "

The front door burst open before she could finish the sentence. Enrique ran in, out of breath and flush-faced.

"Está de vuelta! Don Tomás ha regresado!

Any hope of order in the classroom was lost as the children bounced up from their places. Rowena remained frozen in her chair.

Tomás. Tomás has returned.

She tried to prepare herself. She thought she had reasonable control of her face and manner when Tomás walked in the door a minute later.

He looked just as she remembered. Why should he be any different? He was still handsome, dashing, lithe as the predator he was. And just as shameless.

In his arms he carried a large canvas bag, which he set down in the middle of the floor with an air of drama.

"I've been to town, *muchachos*," he said, ignoring Rowena.

A series of happy shrieks greeted his words. Like a little flock of mudlarks, the children pounced on the sack. Tomás scattered them with a gentle sweep of his hands.

"*Con cuidado, muchachos.* I have a present for each of you." From the depths of the sack he produced what he'd promised: toys for each of the children, including a pair of plain but well-made dolls, a top, a rubber ball, and a handful of wooden soldiers. Each one found its way into the eager grasp of a child. Even Pilar, who hung back, received one of the dolls. She gazed at it as if it were an undreamed-of luxury from some exotic land. Chattering and laughing, the children tumbled out into the plaza.

Rowena had sworn to herself that she wouldn't be the first to speak, that she would greet Tomás's return with complete disinterest. Let him accuse her of deception if he wished. Let him try to impress her with his generosity to the children, belated as it was. She would not be moved.

Quickly she got up and went to the window. Two people were talking several yards away, just out of her hearing. She recognized Esperanza—and Sim Kavanagh.

He'd wasted no time in bedeviling her again. Clenching her jaw, Rowena turned and strode for the door.

"Don't you want to know what I have for you in my magic bag, *mi alma*?"

She stopped. Tomás stood right behind her. If she turned too swiftly, she'd all but fall into his arms.

She pressed her back to the open door and faced him warily. "Unless you've brought the fabric I asked for the children—"

"But I have." He reached into the sack again and withdrew a paper-wrapped bundle, and then another, and a third. He cut the strings with his knife and tore open the paper. Fabric tumbled free—strong, practical broadcloth and calico, one bolt printed with tiny flowers, perfectly suited for a little girl's frock. He draped the lengths of fabric over the table and piled the rest of his bounty on top: patterns, thread, needles, all she could possibly require to provide the children with sturdy, simple clothing.

She swallowed the sudden thickness in her throat. "I suppose you stole all of this."

Tomás touched his chest above his heart. "How good it is to come back to your gracious words of welcome, señorita," he said. "But I'm afraid I must disappoint you. I used no theft or trickery in obtaining what you see. All this I was given, or purchased in the usual way."

With stolen money, Rowena thought. She bit her lip until she lost the urge to speak. *Courtesy. Formality. Give neither him nor yourself a single excuse . . .*

"Then both I and the children owe you thanks," she said, inclining her head.

"The children are too busy for gratitude," Tomás said, pointing his chin toward the open door with a wry smile. "But I'll accept yours willingly."

She stepped over the threshold. "If you'll excuse me, there is something I must see to."

By the time she reached the place where she'd observed Esperanza and Kavanagh, both were gone. She shaded her eyes and looked up and down the canyon.

"Who are you looking for?"

The increasingly familiar tingling in her body had already warned her of Tomás's approach, but worry lowered her defenses. "Esperanza has been behaving oddly for the past several days."

"And you are concerned about her."

"Shouldn't I be—especially when Kavanagh continues to annoy her?"

Tomás frowned. "I've spoken with him about this. Perhaps I must do so again. More firmly."

She relaxed a little. "I'm glad you see the necessity of keeping such a man under control."

He kicked at the dirt with the toe of his boot. "Nestor tells me that you've been busy while I was away."

"Since you left without any indication of when you might return, I felt it best to find myself some useful occupation."

"Teaching the children." His gaze slid up to hers, warm with approval. "Nestor says they are learning very quickly because of your patience. Now it is I who must be grateful to you, for taking such good care of my people."

It was difficult not to let herself be affected by the honest admiration in his words. "Any decent person would wish to help."

"Why, *dulzura,* is it so hard for you to accept thanks?" The back of his hand brushed hers, as if by accident. "Just as you won't accept the pleasures your body knows are its due." His breath teased her ear. "I thought of you every night while I was gone, *mi cielo.* I couldn't forget a single moment in the pool, when you almost gave yourself to me."

His suggestive words no longer had the power to shock her, but his touch was more than she could bear. She had learned what it felt like to be aroused. Erotic images filled her mind again, made inescapable by their reality. She *had* been in that pool. She *had* nearly given herself to him. . . .

"You have not said you missed me, but your body cannot lie," he said. His hand came to rest on her hip, curving about it possessively. "I can feel what you feel. I smell it in your scent. If I were to invite you to my bed, your mouth would say no, but your body would say yes."

Yes. The wolf within her howled in unholy joy.

She took it firmly by the scruff of its imaginary neck and bid it be silent.

"I thought you said you'd make me beg for it, Señor Tomás," she said.

His hand jerked from her hip. She caught the dazed surprise on his face before he smoothed his expression into one of indolent amusement.

"So I did," he said. "Thank you for reminding me."

"You're welcome. And since you are a man of your word, I think perhaps you ought to find your friend Kavanagh and remind him to leave Esperanza alone."

There was a peculiar light in his eye that belied his easy posture. She could have sworn it was anger—genuine anger that came from being thwarted—and . . . hurt. Could El Lobo be hurt?

"Don't you want to know if I saw your precious Cole MacLean while I was away shopping?" he asked.

With a jolt of guilt she realized she hadn't thought of Cole once in the past several days. Of escape, yes, but not of returning to her fiancé. His face was already becoming frighteningly dim in her memory.

"Did you?" she said, covering her confusion.

"No, but I saw the men he hired to find you." He laughed. "Fools, every one of them."

"If you had come face to face with Mr. MacLean himself, I doubt that you would be standing here now."

He grew very still. "Are you so anxious to see me dead?"

The question hung in silence, as terrible as a blow. It was not what she had meant . . . not that Cole would kill him, only that he would be facing retribution for his crimes, as all lawbreakers must.

Now all Rowena could see was Tomás's body, sprawled dead upon the ground at Cole's feet, his joy in living ended, his laughter forever silenced.

"No," she whispered.

In the space of a heartbeat she felt a stunning transformation in the emotional current flowing between them. Desire, lust, anger, suspicion—all were swept away by something far more intense. It was as if they had both forgotten every feeble defense they used against each other . . . against the fearsome prospect of an intimacy, not of the body, but of the soul.

Rowena was too transfixed to remember why she should be afraid. She couldn't look away from Tomás's eyes and what she saw within them. Slowly she lifted her hand.

Tomás drew in a breath and let it out again. He raised his hand to take hers. His skin was hot as with fever.

"Thank you." His voice was hardly more than a croak. It startled them both; the bizarre spell was shattered. Tomás flashed his teeth and pumped her hand up and down with hearty goodwill.

"Thank you," he repeated mockingly. "I'm grateful to know that you find me more interesting alive than dead." He let go of her hand and backed away. "I fear I won't be able to attend you at dinner this evening, but I wish you good sleep. *Hasta mañana,* my lady."

Esperanza appeared for dinner at the usual time. She might as well not have been there at all; Rowena's cheerful comments and careful questions were met with averted eyes and a bowed head. Something was most definitely disturbing the girl—some*one* by the name of Kavanagh—but she also seemed to have lost her trust in Rowena.

The explanation was simple. Rowena had failed to protect her. Why should she be surprised that Esperanza, who had suffered such abuse from her own people, should draw away from a near-stranger who'd broken her most solemn promise?

It was not Rowena's only failure. What, after all, had she accomplished? Since coming here she'd broken nearly every resolve she'd made: to escape, to protect Esperanza, to remain indifferent to Tomás's blandishments. The single one that remained intact was her determination never again to become a beast. How did she dare think she could help anyone else when she could scarcely help herself?

Deeply ashamed, she took her own refuge in the painful silence. Esperanza remained at the table just long enough to swallow a few mouthfuls of food, and then slipped from the house as quickly as she'd come. Rowena felt for the glass of wine beside her plate.

She was not like Quentin to lose herself in drink, but she had taken a glass or two every night during Tomás's absence. She finished the first glass, allowed Nestor to refill it, pulled a chair to the window, and watched as the sunset stained the cliffs with red and gold and the canyon filled with shadow. A pleasant lassitude settled over her.

"I think this wine is past its prime, Nestor," she said, frowning vaguely at the dregs in the bottom of her glass.

He emerged from his corner and took the glass from her hand. His nose twitched. "I did not realize. I'm sorry, señorita."

"Please do not be. It was . . . adequate." She leaned her head against the hard, carved back of the chair. "Thank you, Nestor. You've been a good friend."

He bowed. "Sleep well, Lady Rowena."

Sleep well. She'd be lucky to sleep at all, but if she did . . . If she did, she was going to dream of Cole instead of Tomás. Yes. She'd had quite enough of Tomás Alejandro Randall, waking or sleeping. She would banish him from her dreams entirely.

"Cole," she murmured. She fixed her mind on his image and worked her way unsteadily into the bedchamber. Was she so dizzy because of a scant two glasses of wine? The prospect of removing her blouse and skirt was daunting. After a moment of indecision, she toppled facedown onto the bed fully clothed.

"Cole," she said. How odd the named sounded. How alien. *I am going to think only of . . .*

Her thoughts unraveled. She let herself float away on a gray cloud of indifference.

Sometime later, faint noises stirred her awake. A figure moved beside her bed. "Esper . . . anza?" she mumbled.

No. The figure too large. Male. *Tomás.* Tomás was coming into her room. He wanted to seduce her. He wanted to make her beg him to . . . to . . .

A hand closed over her mouth. Not Tomás. Kavanagh. Sim Kavanagh.

The cloud of indifference remained wrapped about her like a muffling shroud. Someone far away was urging her to fight; her arms and legs made halfhearted attempts to resist as he dragged her from the bed and tied her hands together. Then she was out of the room, moving in fitful jerks through the night. Concentration was impossible. She forgot who it was that half carried, half shoved her across the open space beyond the door and pushed her face-first against the warm body of some smelly animal. The man, or the animal, grunted as she was thrown over a broad, hairy back. Her head dangled just above the ground. More grunts, and then her nose was in the stiff mane of the animal while her legs straddled its barrel.

That was the last she remembered of how she came to be outside the canyon. She regained her senses in darkness, lit by flickering light that pierced her eyes like a knife. Her mouth tasted foul, and her head ached; there was no soothing haze to shield her from the reality of her situation.

She was lying on the bare earth, bound hand and foot, at the base of a low pine. From this ignominious position she could see that the light came from a small fire a few feet away. Around the fire sat five or six men, strangers, whose faces held the remorseless brutality of hardened desperados.

One of the men was Sim Kavanagh.

She struggled into a half-sitting position, wincing at the discomfort in her arms and legs. Several pairs of eyes fixed on her with hungry interest. Kavanagh got to his feet.

"So you're awake," he said. He crouched beside her, a cigarette dangling between his fingers. He examined it as if it were of far greater importance than she was. "I thought maybe she gave you too much."

Her mind was finally working well enough to grasp his meaning. "I was drugged," she said thickly. "The wine—"

"Yes, the wine." She heard the expected contempt in his voice. "A local concoction I picked up from an old *curandero*. He said it would kill with a strong enough dose, but I wasn't taking any risks with a werewolf."

Werewolf. He meant *her*. He'd drugged her to make her compliant when he snatched her from the bed and took her . . . to this place. She made a swift appraisal of their surroundings, glad for once of her ability to see in the dark. The camp was in a clearing, surrounded by a low forest of piñon pines and junipers. They could be anywhere in this harsh country; she knew she wasn't in the canyon.

"How long have I been asleep?" she demanded.

"A night and a day."

So the situation was as bad as she feared; it must be well past sunset.

"What have you done with Esperanza?"

"Nothing. She served her purpose, like a good little girl. Who do you think put the drug in your wine?"

"Esperanza would never—"

"She did."

"Not willingly. Now I understand what has been bothering her these past few days." She clenched her fists, all too aware of her helplessness. "You *are* a monster."

His eyes reflected the firelight, glinting with infernal amusement. "If you want me to untie your hands, you'll keep your mouth shut."

She considered a retort and bit it back. He finished his cigarette, ignoring her completely, and tossed the butt to the ground. After another long and deliberate delay, he twisted her about and worked the ropes free from her wrists.

The bindings had numbed her wrists and chafed them raw, but she wasn't about to complain. She levered herself upright and rested against the trunk of the pine. Kavanagh got up and went around the fire. There was a murmur of voices; he returned with a dented tin cup of water and a plate of beans.

"Drink," he said.

She gave him her iciest glare. "I don't suppose it will do any good to ask you where I am."

"Not much."

"Who are these people?"

"Don't recognize them? You met them before. Some of the men from Rialto's gang." He snickered. "Lucky for you Bill Hager ain't here. He took quite a fancy to you."

Bill Hager she remembered—the man Tomás had negotiated with when he'd sold the stolen MacLean horses. The other men were only so many unfamiliar faces, Anglo and Hispano both.

"Do I take your presence here to mean that you've changed your allegiance from Tomás to this . . . Rialto?" she said.

"You don't know a damned thing about it."

"Then just what am I doing here?"

His eyes narrowed to slits, giving his face a fiendish cast. "I warned you," he said. "I told you to stay away from Tomás. Now I'm making sure he's rid of you for good." His smile chilled her. "You're poison, and I'm the antidote."

She kept her voice admirably level. "You once implied that you would kill me. Is that your intention?"

"Not as long as you're worth something to MacLean. We have a deal." He spat into the fire. "You should be grateful, Lady Rowena. I'm taking you back to your fiancé."

His statement was so unexpected that she laughed before she could stop herself. "Taking me back . . . to Cole?"

"You heard me."

"He would never bargain with a man like you."

"Sooner me than Tomás."

This was all happening too quickly. "Is Cole paying you to do this?"

His voice took on a strained, almost defensive tone. "I'm getting rid of you and giving Tomás back his freedom."

He spoke as if she were a weighted chain that would drag Tomás inevitably into some unspeakable captivity, or worse—as if he were the helpless victim of her wiles and not the reverse. It was ludicrous, but Kavanagh believed it. He truly believed she was dangerous to his friend.

His friend. For all his evil, Kavanagh was capable of a twisted loyalty. But it was a mad sort of loyalty that betrayed the friend in an effort to save him.

"And you think," she said, "that Tomás will thank you for what you're doing, after all the trouble he took to kidnap me?"

He turned his face away.

"He will come hunt you down when he discovers I'm gone," she said.

"I arranged a little distraction for him," Kavanagh said. "If that doesn't work, Rialto's men owe me a favor. They'll make false trails and slow him down. He won't catch up."

Obviously he had the whole thing well planned. She was the one at a crippling disadvantage. Her mind was still muddled, her once-solid principles turned upside-down. Instead of feeling satisfaction at being on the verge of escape, however unlikely the means, she was angry on Tomás's behalf and outraged that his supposed friend had betrayed him. Her irrational instinct was to fight Kavanagh tooth and nail and ride straight back to the canyon.

Back to Tomás.

She swallowed hard. Hadn't she proven her mastery over mere instinct, time and again? She could turn this entire situation to her advantage. All she need do was let Kavanagh take her to Cole. Tomás would come to no harm, and she'd be safe from him at last.

And safe from herself.

"Very well," she said. "You have what you want, Kavanagh. You're giving me what I've sought since the day I was kidnapped." The words caught in her throat. "There's no reason to keep me tied."

One of the men behind him said something in Spanish; he laughed. "You'll stay tied up until we reach Las Vegas and Cole pays me for delivering you."

"Then you are doing this for profit—"

"Just like MacLean." He leaned closer, resting his hand on her bent knee. "You shouldn't hate me, Lady Rowena Forster. MacLean and I are the same. We both take what we want, and we don't give a damn about anyone else."

"Mr. MacLean has nothing in common with you."

"Wrong." His hand slid higher, pushing up her skirt. "There's just one difference between us. I use a gun. He uses the power he was born with. He makes people like you believe he's a fine, upstanding gentleman while he steals everything they have."

She'd heard and dismissed slurs like this before—in New York, from envious rumormongers who implied that Cole's wealth and influence came from questionable business practices, and again from Tomás himself. His words remained etched in her memory: *Didn't you know that your fine Cole MacLean has many enemies? Of course he would not tell you. The stories would hardly be to his credit.*

He had never elaborated on his accusation, nor explained his reasons for preying on the MacLeans. He'd let her believe the worst of him, even as he tried to seduce her. And yet . . . it had become more and more difficult to think of him as a villain.

But if *he* were not . . .

"I wonder what MacLean sees in you," Kavanagh said. He stroked her leg from thigh to knee. "He uses women like everyone else. You must have more than a little money, or he wouldn't want you back." He shrugged. "If he knew the way you acted with Tomás, he'd leave you to rot. Unless he found a way to use you as bait. I'm making sure that never happens."

"I believe you've been out in the sun too long."

His fingers dug into her skin through the cloth of her skirt. "Tomás is too proud to tell you what MacLean did to him. He pretends he doesn't care what you think. But you're going to know what you're going back to. Cole MacLean killed Tomás's father."

fourteen

Rowena tried to push herself to her feet, remembering too late that they remained tied at the ankles. Kavanagh let her go. She lost her balance, caught at the branches of the pine, and fell onto her rump. The shock was far less than that of Kavanagh's words.

"I will not listen to your lies," she whispered.

"You don't have any choice." He turned and spoke to Rialto's men in rapid Spanish. One of them rose and vanished into the darkness. The others drew closer to the fire.

Kavanagh smiled with grim satisfaction. "The *trovadores*," he said, "still sing *corridos*—ballads—about Tomás's mother, who tried to take revenge on her husband's killer when he came to destroy everything she had. They sing about Tomás and how he won't stop fighting MacLean until one of them is dead." He nodded toward the man returning to the fire with a guitar in his hands. "Américo is Rialto's finest *cantante*. He's going to sing you a song of El Lobo and Cole MacLean."

"I do not speak Spanish."

"I'll translate," he said. "And you will listen."

The man with the guitar, Américo, spoke a soft introduction. The men around him murmured and nodded. He strummed the guitar and began to sing.

The Spanish words and melody seemed simple, just as such songs did when Tomás sang them. But there was something different about this ballad, a sense of reality within the entertainment.

"In the land of Scotland," Kavanagh said, "one hundred years ago, they say, a great fight began between the men of two families."

Kavanagh's voice changed, losing its harsh and brittle edge to become something almost spellbinding, as if he were possessed by the soul of some ancient bard—or by Tomás himself. It rang with truth. It compelled her to hear him as no use of force could have done.

And she wanted to know. She had to.

She listened.

"Don Fergus Randall came to New Mexico,
here to find peace for himself and his kinfolk.

"He took as a bride the daughter of good family,
and made his fortune on the land of Don Arturo.

"It was named Los Valerosos for the courage of its
      people,
a grant on the long Canadian River.

"Don Fergus found no peace on the rancho,
for his old enemies had followed him from Texas.

"The MacLeans were proud and had many cattle,
and most of all hatred for the Don and the Randalls."

As Rowena followed the cadences of the song, Kavanagh continued to translate, telling how the War came to New

Mexico, pitting north against south; how the southern soldiers came to Glorieta pass, where Don Fergus met his enemies and warned them away; how the MacLeans refused to leave, and Fergus was forced to kill one MacLean in battle; and how the MacLeans swore vengeance.

"When the war was ended, Don Fergus went to
        Mexico;
There he was killed, they said by the Apaches.

"But Cole and Frank MacLean had ambushed and
        killed him;
in cowardice they killed him, to leave his wife a
        widow.

"Many years passed, and she sent her son away,
Young Don Tomás, to learn American ways in the
        East.

"Then she found how her husband had died, and
        cried in great anger,
'I will take revenge on the killers of Don Fergus.' "

So the feud continued. Doña Adelina, Tomás's mother, vowed revenge on her enemies, stealing the MacLeans' cattle and horses. For many years the MacLeans couldn't catch her, until one day they brought powerful allies to destroy all of Los Valerosos and drive off the people.

"But Doña Adelina found the trail to follow them;
they say she took the shape of a wolf to follow their
        tracks.

"When she found the MacLeans, they had no pity on
        a woman;

it is said that they killed her as they killed her
            husband.

"Then Don Tomás returned, singing songs of his
            country;
he knew nothing of all that had happened.

"He was a man of joy and laughter, much loved,
a gentle *caballero* who bore no man ill-will.

"All the women sighed for him, and he sang like
            an angel;
But he came home, and everything he left was
            changed."

Tomás had found his ranch destroyed, the people scattered. He learned of his mother's death, and in grief and rage
vowed vengance.

"After many months, he found Frank MacLean alone;
they fought with great fury, each as strong as the
            other.

"But El Lobo fought for justice, and so he was the
            stronger;
he took his vengeance, in the name of his mother and
            father."

Cole MacLean learned of his father's death and made
Tomás an outlaw, ever hunting and hunted, a hero of the
people and scourge of the MacLeans.

"He knows he will die one day, but he is not afraid;
let all who hear this ballad remember the tale of
            El Lobo."

The guitar fell silent. The men were quiet for a few moments, and then they called out in raucous appreciation. Rowena sat very still, eyes closed. Odd, how a few stanzas that didn't even rhyme could be so moving. Perhaps it was the music that made it so.

She remembered what Tomás had said of his father, and how he'd met and married Adelina. He'd even mentioned a feud—and she had changed the subject.

But this was a song, a fairy tale, a legend.

"The *corrido* leaves a few details out," Kavanagh said, the music gone from his voice. "Like how the MacLeans came to Las Vegas nine years after Fergus's murder with a bunch of other big Texas ranchers, to round up beeves rustled by the Comancheros and Indians and sold to the poor farmers in the Territory."

"The . . . Comancheros?"

"Indian traders. Some of them started buying cattle stolen by the Indians or rustling beeves themselves. Didn't figure they owed loyalty to the big cattlemen who were taking over. Adelina made them her allies when she went up against the MacLeans." He stared into the fire. "The Texans said they just wanted their property back. But that was only an excuse for the MacLeans. They wanted a legal way to wipe out Los Valerosos and everything Fergus Randall left behind, including his wife and son and all the people who lived on their land and worked for them.

"They got Adelina, but Tomás didn't return from the East until after they destroyed Los Valerosos. He followed their trail, and found one of Frank MacLean's men with a wolf pelt on his saddle. His mother's."

Rowena shook her head in disbelief.

"That was when Tomás went after Frank MacLean. Cole and his men found Tomás badly wounded from the fight. They tortured him and left him for dead."

The horrible events played out in Rowena's imagination. She'd seen, in England, what such hostilities could do. Two families on opposite sides of a divisive, brutal war. One grudge building upon another, each new death demanding recompense. A father and brother, half-mad with grief, pursuing Fergus Randall. Tomás seeking his revenge in turn . . .

And Cole, respected and eminently civilized, hunting Tomás down and torturing him to the very edge of death.

She rejected the vision. Cole was not perfect, but he could not have committed such atrocities. He was no Stefan Boroskov, depraved and perverted by his tainted werewolf power.

And if the song were true, Tomás, too, had killed.

You knew he was a killer. Weylin said so. Tomás did not deny it . . .

But the song gave him a reason for his terrible act, some purpose other than mere bloodlust and greed. "He was a man of joy and laughter, much loved, a gentle caballero who bore no man ill-will." She had seen that man in Tomás.

When was vengeance justified? If Tomás's father had killed Cole's brother in the War, could there be any right in murdering a soldier after the war had ended? Was Tomás evil in seeking revenge on his father's killers? Must the pattern continue until every last Randall and MacLean was gone?

No. She turned her back on the fire and bent her head to her knees. The song took Tomás's side without apology, and cast the MacLeans as the villains. She would *not* make a similar judgment. Some great misunderstanding lay at the heart of this feud, twisted and romanticized by the overactive imaginations of the local balladeers.

Why don't you take the part of your own fiancé? an inner voice chided. *Shouldn't it be obvious where the truth lies?*

I will make no judgments! she answered. With a twinge of startlement she realized that she'd spent nearly all her life making such judgments, never questioning her right to do so. She found herself, at last, in a situation where any choice she made must lead to pain.

Yes, pain . . . even at the likely prospect that Cole was innocent and Tomás the villain. Wasn't that the assumption she'd made at the beginning and carried with her ever since?

When had she begun to change her mind?

It didn't matter. In a few days she'd be with Cole again. She would simply ask him for the truth. He might wish to shield her from the unpleasant aspects of his family's past, but he would not lie. Then she would know both sides of the story. Then she could decide. . . .

"You still don't believe, do you?" Kavanagh said close to her ear.

She didn't give him the satisfaction of drawing away. "I believe there has been a great tragedy," she said, "and much suffering—"

"Caused by your high-and-mighty MacLeans," he said. "It wasn't only Tomás's family they destroyed. From the time they came to New Mexico, they used their power to trample anyone weaker than they were. Frank MacLean was a big man in Texas since the Mexican War, but that wasn't enough. He wanted an empire. He started by driving his cattle north through New Mexico on the Goodnight-Loving trail when almost no one else had the sand. The Indians left him alone. Even men like Hittson and Chisum backed down when he came around.

"He wasn't human, and he didn't see humans as threats. He could make them do whatever he wanted—just like Cole does now. He used people and threw them away when he was finished. If someone had land he wanted, he got rid of them one way or another—poor squatters, small farmers, people just trying to survive. Wasn't just land, but anything he could take. He was a thief who got the law and the politicians on his side. Pretty soon he had one of the biggest spreads in the Territory, not counting his land in Texas." Kavanagh's face was rigid as a skull. "Only the Randalls had the power to stand up to him, because they were *hombres-lobo*. He had to get rid of them. The feud and the War gave him a reason."

Never had she heard Sim Kavanagh speak with such passion. This had gone beyond loyalty to a friend. It was as if . . . yes, as if he himself had suffered some personal injury at the hands of the MacLeans.

"I never met Cole's father," she said. "Cole respected him greatly, and so did many men of influence and integrity—"

"Because they were scared of him. The same way they're scared of Cole." He smiled. "You're afraid of him yourself."

"I most certainly am not." She shivered. "Even if Frank MacLean did some of the things you claim, Cole . . . Cole was not the head of the family. He has been in New York since 'sixty-six."

"He helped kill Fergus before then. He came back to try to kill Tomás. He took over all the family's business when Frank MacLean died. You think because he lives in the East he doesn't control everything that happens here? He's carried on his daddy's fine tradition of stealing and killing."

"All you've given me is hearsay and the opinion of a wanted criminal."

He rocked back on his heels. "I reckoned you'd approve of the way the MacLeans do business. Must be the same with your kind in England."

She bit back a swift denial. It was because of their innate abilities that werewolves naturally rose to positions of wealth and authority wherever they lived. Kavanagh implied that the MacLeans practiced *loup-garou* influence on humans; hadn't Braden done the same thing in England, to safeguard the Forster secrets? But her brother had never manipulated humans for his own profit, nor employed them to steal and kill.

How she hated owing anything to her savage heritage.

"At the moment I see little to choose between you, Tomás, and Cole," she said.

Kavanagh laughed. He kept laughing even as he tossed a dirty blanket over her shoulders and lay down a few feet away, watching, always watching with those merciless eyes.

Rowena spent the next sleepless hours trying to chase the Ballad of El Lobo from her mind.

Weylin woke from a profound sleep, his first memory that of pain.

He still wore his wolf's body. As he lay under the low boughs of a sheltering piñon, he struggled to remember how he had come to be there, and why. His senses told him it was not long after sunset—of which day, he did not know—and that his fur bore the scent of dried blood.

Blood from the nearly mortal wound he'd received at Sim Kavanagh's hands. A wound that would have killed an ordinary wolf. Or man.

Only his inhuman werewolf nature had saved him. Somehow he'd dragged himself into deeper shelter where no passerby could chance upon his apparently lifeless body. There, his driving instinct for survival had taken command, drawing him into a deep, healing torpor.

He might have died. He was still extremely weak, and desperately thirsty. He wasn't sure he had the strength to Change, even if he wished. But he lived.

He *lived*. Not since childhood, when the whole family was together and life seemed full of wonder, had he felt such unexpected, spontaneous happiness. "Right" and "justice" and "revenge" were meaningless human words that he cast aside with a snap of his jaws. He wanted to point his muzzle to the stars and howl for joy, to leap and dance like a foolish colt.

Dancing was beyond his ability. He banked his jubilation and concentrated on the simple act of standing. After two tries, he managed to do so without losing his balance. His muscles groaned and protested; the shoulder where he'd taken the bullet worked like an old dog's. Taking small and uneven steps, he followed his nose to the trickle of a stream-let winding down from the mountains.

He drank for several long minutes, glorying in the pure taste of clear water. Slowly the dreamlike rapture faded. As he lay beside the brook, purpose returned to his thoughts. Almost, almost he ignored it. There was a part of him that wanted to remain a wolf and never return to the world of duty and discipline that he'd made for himself.

Wasn't this world just as real? He could live, not for some abstract notion of justice, but for moments like these. For the freedom to run at will and think no further than tomorrow, with nothing to prove and beholden to none—not Cole, not his father's memory, not the rule of man's law. Not even to himself.

But the habit of years was too strong.

He was Weylin Arthur MacLean. That meant something, more now than ever. A MacLean didn't give up just be-cause it was easier or more pleasurable. He didn't run away from responsibility.

He had work to do.

He pulled himself to his feet and concentrated on his goal until the last, tattered remnants of temptation slipped away and his mind was clear again. His first task was to find his modified saddlebags. They were where he'd left them before Kavanagh's attack, undisturbed even by animals.

It might have been wiser to wait and heal another day or two before Changing. But many days might have passed, each one robbed from his pursuit of Tomás; he must return to the haunts of men to regain his bearings and hear the latest news.

If he'd lost the chance to follow Kavanagh to Randall, he had gained one advantage he hadn't possessed in the past. He had faced death and survived. Father, Kenneth, Cole—all of them had stood face to face with their own mor-tality, fighting for what they believed. He'd never been part of that brotherhood. Deep in his heart he'd been ashamed of that lack, of not knowing how he would face the moment when it came. If he'd prove a true MacLean in the end.

That doubt was gone. He was worthy. He could stand in Cole's presence without wondering if his choice, his way, was right.

In the pack was plain clothing to cover his human body, and money enough for a fully equipped mount. The nearest village of any size was less than ten miles distant. There he'd find what he needed to resume his hunt, this time as a man. But he knew he could take either form as it suited his purpose, without hesitation or apology or forgetting who and what he was.

Gathering all his strength, he stood alone beneath the light of a thousand stars and willed himself to Change.

Night was well advanced by the time Tomás rode Delfín into the plaza at El Cañon del Rito de las Lágrimas. He hadn't slept since the previous night; Sim had sent him to a village many hours' ride from the cañon, but when he'd arrived in the late afternoon, the man he was to meet was nowhere to be found. He'd lingered a full night and half the day before turning for home.

Sim was not one to make such mistakes. If he said there was a man seeking El Lobo's aid against cruelty and injustice, that man must exist. But no one in Cañada del Rocoso had known anything of him.

Tomás consoled himself during the wasted journey by flirting with the señoritas and enjoying the obliging hospitality of people who claimed El Lobo as their hero. *They* did not constantly waver between welcome and rejection, nor question his methods and motives. *They* did not leave him torn between laughter and insanity. Among them, he never doubted what he felt and what he wanted.

Not like that last encounter with Rowena, when he was damned by the certainty that he had gone beyond the borders of mere wanting and entered a deadly, alien territory he'd avoided all his life. A country fraught with perils and traps and bottomless pits into which he would fall and continue falling for all eternity.

He was expert at roaming no-man's-lands where others dared not stray. He'd walked many perilous borderlines before meeting Lady Rowena Forster, and had always chosen to stay free of allegiance to any but himself. No one, not even Sim, had traveled the whole journey at his side.

Then the lady held out her hand and beckoned him across that final line. He had very nearly taken the irrevocable step from Wanting to Caring.

He dismounted in front of his casa—Rowena's, now—and leaned against his horse's warm barrel. "There are times, my friend," he said, "when I'd rather be a horse than a wolf. The stallion has many mares, and each one knows she'll never be his only *amor*. Nor has he any wish to confine himself." He sighed and slapped the gelding's neck. "Not that you'd know of such things. I'm beginning to think you and I have a little too much in common." He led Delfín toward the stable, noting that no lights shown from any of the houses. Why should there be?

"Do you suppose she has found life unbearably dull in my absence?" he asked. Delfín nickered, doubtless longing for his grain and a good rubdown. Tomás was thinking less of food and a bath than what he was going to do about Rowena.

He could let her go. The thought had come to him more than once, never so strongly as during that last conversation. His intent to use her to humiliate and injure Cole MacLean had lost its savor somewhere along the way. He didn't believe that MacLean would give him what he demanded in exchange for her release.

So Rowena would remain. And though he would find satisfaction in her realization that Cole was a faithless rogue, who then would be responsible for her? Though she would eventually give herself to him, what would come after?

No future. Rowena believed in such laudable ambitions as marriage, children, law and order, proper etiquette, and a settled life. Such things were real to her. His reality lay in the moment, and in knowing there was no certainty, no permanence in the world.

He should take her back—back to the world she knew. If he did not, she would suffer. Her suffering might be more than he could bear.

He paused at the stable door and pressed his face to Delfín's soft muzzle. "Am I not noble, to think of her welfare at this late hour?" he said. "Or is it myself alone I think of?" He laughed. "You see what's become of me. She's like a poison in my blood. *Sí, mi amigo*—the sooner I get rid of her, the better I—"

"Huuuuh!"

Delfín tossed his head. A small shadow slipped around the corner of the stable and stopped before him. It reached out to catch his sleeve with unmistakable urgency.

Esperanza.

She opened her mouth, and the same hoarse sound emerged. Not a word, not yet, but more noise than she had made since they'd found her at Los Milagros. "Sssuuuh—"

He dropped Delfín's reins and grasped the girl's shoulders. "Esperanza! Can you speak?"

Her hand flew to her throat. Her face was smeared with dirt, her clothes torn as if in some recent struggle. His stomach tightened with the foreknowledge of disaster.

"What is it?"

"Rrruuu—eee—nahh," she gasped.

Rowena.

He let her go and ran across the plaza. Rowena's door swung open at his first touch. He plunged into the bedchamber, only to find the sheets rumpled and cold. Her scent was the barest trace in the stale air.

Esperanza waited for him just outside, her eyes shining

with anxiety. He touched her shoulder in passing and strode to the door of Nestor's casa. His knock went unanswered. Nestor was not within.

One by one he visited the other houses, Esperanza at his heels. His people welcomed him and sleepily answered his questions with puzzlement and concern.

No, none of them had seen the lady Rowena since the evening before last. Why? He himself had left a letter saying that she was sick and must not be disturbed while he was gone. Enrique had found the letter on the door to her house this past morning. No, Nestor was not here; they had heard he was called away the night before to see a dying relative in a village some miles distant.

Something was very much the matter. Tomás cursed too softly for the curious children to hear and reassured his men with a few casual words. False words; Nestor was gone without a clear explanation; Rowena hadn't been seen in a full day; and Esperanza—

"Ssseee-" The girl tugged on his sleeve, forcing him to look at her again. "Sseeemm."

Sim. His blood became ice. "Sim Kavanagh?" he said, grabbing her hand. "Speak to me, Esperanza. Where is Rowena? Did Sim—"

She nodded. "Sseeem. Took—" She pointed toward the trail that led up the cliffs to the mesa above. "A . . . way."

Sim had taken Rowena out of the cañon.

Only a few times in his life had he known the fell emotions that claimed him in that moment. Rage was uppermost among them—rage and despair and overwhelming fear. The roots of his hair stiffened, and his lips curled in a snarl.

Sim had betrayed him. Sim had taken Rowena. Sim had stolen his mate . . .

And he would kill to reclaim her.

He flung back his head, ready to howl out his challenge. Esperanza snatched her hand from his.

"Nooo," she moaned. She slapped her hands over her ears as if to block out some unbearable noise. "Nooooh!"

The sheer terror in her voice stopped him. His vision cleared to find her crouched on the ground at his feet. Several of the older children watched the drama from the sidelines, half in fascination and half in fear. Their fathers and guardians had far more sense.

"You, *niños*!" he said sharply. "Go back to your houses. Enrique, see to Delfín. *Vamos!*"

If ever they thought to disobey, it was not now. They ran inside, and the casa doors remained firmly closed behind them. Tomás caught his breath and knelt beside Esperanza.

"Come," he said. "I will not hurt you."

She looked up, hands still pressed to her head. "Help—"

He lifted her easily and supported her slight weight. "*Sí.* Rest easy, *muchacha.*" Though she was dirty and afraid, her face bore no bruises or the marks of blows. Yet he was sure that she had personal knowledge of what had become of Rowena, and how. Sim had done far worse than ignore his commands about bothering the girl.

He had warned Sim about it again, yesterday afternoon—at the same time Sim told him of the man in Cañada del Rocoso who required his help. That man hadn't been waiting for him because Sim had invented him. He'd doubtless found a way to lure Nestor from the village at an appropriate time, and written the letter that supposedly came from Tomás. Only a few in the village could read, and none could distinguish his handwriting from any other's. No one would be looking for Rowena.

Had Sim underestimated Esperanza?

Tomás cupped the girl's chin. "I am sorry I did not protect you and Rowena from Sim," he said. "Can you forgive me?"

She nodded, a heartbreaking gravity replacing fear and panic.

"This time I will make certain he does no further harm. Do you know where he was taking the lady?"

Her lips moved but formed no coherent word. He didn't require her answer. "Cole," he whispered. "Why, Sim? Why?"

Esperanza touched his chin with her fingertips. Her eyes spoke eloquently—of sorrow, sympathy, and an understanding that humbled him. He, like Sim, had overlooked Esperanza.

"Don't worry," he said. "I will find them. It was last night that he took her?"

She nodded. So, Sim had a day's head start. He'd planned well; he knew what a werewolf could do. But even he couldn't guess the limits of a werewolf's strength and stamina, when that werewolf had cause to test those limits. Tomás had used the Change for convenience and pleasure and to aid in harassing the MacLeans, but seldom had he faced such a pressing need as now.

He was sure as hell that Sim hadn't planned nearly well enough.

"*De acuerdo,*" he said. "Go into the house and rest, Esperanza. I will bring her back."

"No!"

Something in her vehement protest made him think of the one possibility he hadn't considered. Rowena had wanted to escape him from the very first. Wouldn't she grasp at any opportunity to return to Cole, no matter how offensive the method?

His tongue felt thick and heavy in his mouth. "Esperanza— she did not go with him willingly?"

A faint smile touched the girl's mouth. "No," she said softly. "No."

He closed his eyes. Just because Rowena had not encouraged Sim did not mean she wouldn't recognize the benefit of cooperation once the deed was done.

You could still let her go. It was what you considered—

The thought smashed headlong into a wall of unreasonable rage. Let her go, with Sim? Let her return to Cole, when the decision had not been his to make?

Nothing so easy.

He turned from Esperanza's too-knowing eyes and went to rouse Mateo, Carlos, and the others from their beds. They had no reason to fear he would blame them for Rowena's abduction—he had been the one to trust Sim—but they were quick to follow his instructions. While they prepared fresh horses and supplies, Tomás took Esperanza aside.

"You know that I can become a wolf," he said. "I must do it now, to catch up with Sim and Rowena. My men will follow with the horses. You will stay here and wait for our return."

She shook her head fiercely. "I . . . go," she said. "I must go."

"You can't."

"I must."

"There is nothing you can do for Rowena."

"I . . . can help."

She'd found not only her voice, but a strange and stubborn courage to defy him. He had no choice but to take drastic action. With no concession to her modesty, he stripped out of his clothes and Changed.

His wolf's eyes found her standing where he'd left her, shaken but every bit as determined. There was no more time for arguing. Courage she might have, but she wouldn't be able to follow him or his men once they left the cañon.

He nudged her curled fingers in farewell and ran for the eastern cliffs.

Sim's trail was easy enough to follow: two horses and a mule, moving at a steady pace, one horse and the mule bearing riders. He'd taken the quickest route down from the plateau to the Rio Grande, making no effort to conceal himself.

But after hours of tireless running into the rising sun, across mesas and valleys and the Rio Grande, faster than a true wolf or even the strongest horse, Tomás encountered the obstacles Sim had left for him. The camp had been abandoned before dawn; he smelled Sim and Rowena and five or six others, desperados of Rialto's band. They had been clever. Horses and clothing had been exchanged, scents intermingled. Tomás followed several false trails before he recognized his error. Once he caught up to the maker of one such trail; the man panicked and tried to shoot him. Tomás had him off his horse and whimpering in the dirt before he had time for a second shot.

He released the bandit with a healthy fear of repeating such tricks and doubled back to leave marks for his own men to follow. Sim's other companions were easy enough to dodge until he found the correct path. By mid-morning he reached the outskirts of a little town called San José del Vado, on the Pecos River, and knew Sim and Rowena were very near.

It wasn't merely his senses that told him so. Rowena's spirit hovered about the place, as if she reached back with her will to summon him. He shook off his weariness, circled the village and forded the Pecos at a run. A mile beyond he found two riders, one leading the other. Their figures were unmistakable.

Rowena must have sensed him first. Her back stiffened, but she didn't turn. Tomás skimmed over the ground, belly to the earth. Sim heard him when he was but twenty feet distant.

Tomás gathered his haunches to leap. Sim's horse wheeled and reared as the outlaw snatched his gun from its holster. He steadied his mount and aimed the pistol with lethal confidence—at Rowena.

Whirling in midair, Tomás fell back. Sim yanked on the second horse's lead rope until the animal was barrel to barrel with his and the muzzle of the Peacemaker was pressed to Rowena's temple.

"Stay where you are, Tomás," he said.

Betrayal. Tomás snarled and looked up at Rowena. She

appeared disheveled but unhurt; her face was pale and calm and unafraid. But her eyes . . . her eyes blazed, their brown depths glinting with golden sparks.

That alone gave him warning. Sim never saw it coming. With the speed of a striking rattlesnake, she flung up her arm and knocked the gun from his hand. In almost the same breath she twisted in the saddle and hurled her weight against him. His horse shied at the unexpected movement. The two of them balanced precariously on the sidling animal's back, and then Sim tumbled from the saddle. Rowena fell on top of him.

By the time Tomás reached them, Rowena was straddling Sim, her hair flying about her face like a harpy's. She struck at his face. Shaking off his amazement, Sim struck back.

His blow never connected. Tomás caught his wrist in his jaws and clamped down hard. Sim gave an explosive breath of shock. Rowena jumped off and crouched beside Tomás, leaving a row of four scratches on Sim's cheek where her nails had scored him.

But the battle wasn't over. Ignoring the pain of Tomás's grinding fangs, Sim curled his body and reached for his boot. A tiny Deringer came up in his hand. He buried it in the fur of Tomás's mane.

"Stalemate," he said, gritting his teeth. "I don't want to shoot you, Tomás. Let me go."

The taste of blood was both bitter and sweet on Tomás's tongue. With just a little pressure, he could sever Sim's hand from his wrist. And Sim would shoot him, perhaps fatally.

Rowena gazed at him with feral eyes. *Kill*, they seemed to say. The very insanity of such a notion cleared Tomás's mind.

He released Sim's wrist and jumped over him to shield Rowena. Sim pulled his wounded arm against his chest. He rolled sideways to work his legs beneath him, the Deringer loose in his grip. Tomás let him get to his feet.

There were three choices now: remain a wolf and punish

Sim for his treachery, Change and confront him as a man, or let him go. All at once Tomás felt unutterably weary. He kept himself between Sim and Rowena as the outlaw stumbled to his horse and mounted awkwardly, dripping blood with every motion.

"Curse you, Tomás," Sim said hoarsely. "Take her, and be damned."

He kicked his horse savagely and turned it north toward the mountains. Tomás let his legs buckle and collapsed where he was.

"Tomás?" Rowena's fingers slipped into his fur. "Are you hurt?"

Laughter was beyond his wolf's abilities, nor could he mimic a human smile with bloodstained teeth. He simply wagged his tail and leaned into her steadying hand.

She stiffened. He waited for her to draw away from his beast's form, but she sat beside him and stared blankly the way Sim had gone. He waited for her to speak, but she remained silent. They rested quietly for several more minutes, and then he rose and gestured with his head and body until she understood that she was to collect her horse and follow him.

They sought more private shelter in a cluster of junipers well clear of the trail, and there Tomás prepared to remain until his men found him. Rowena moved as if in a dream. She could have made an attempt to ride off, but she showed little interest in anything, not even taking advantage of the small stream Tomás found for her. She rested a short distance from him, knees drawn up and arms wrapped about them.

The last thing he wished now was to Change. Rowena was like an exhausted creature hunted to its limit. He might push her past that limit if he stood before her in all his naked humanity—and *he* would be vulnerable.

Because he wanted to do more than touch her, lie with her. He wished to comfort her, hold her in his arms, speak softly of unimportant things until she slept peacefully against his chest. He wished to tell her that all would be well, forever. He wished to promise her a thousand things he knew he could not give.

He growled to himself and licked a scratch on his paw. El Lobo was not vulnerable. Such a word was for women and children and those who needed too desperately.

Rowena needed *him*. She needed to talk, and as a wolf he was mute. It was not such a big thing to grant. There were questions only she could answer.

Surprised at his own reticence, he retired behind a convenient bush to Change. She hardly glanced at him when he emerged again.

He took up a relatively modest position with his body turned away from her and picked up a twig to draw in the dirt.

"Well?" he said.

Her eyes were almost dull, the golden sparks snuffed out. "Why didn't you kill him?" she asked.

He thrust the stick into the earth so hard that it snapped. "Did you hope I would? You behaved as if you'd kill him yourself."

"I . . . don't wish to speak of it."

"Did he hurt you?"

"No."

Tomás closed his eyes. "He was my friend. My good friend."

"He was taking me back to Cole."

It was what Tomás expected, but still the knowledge cut deep. "Did he tell you why?"

"To protect you from me."

This time nothing stopped him from laughing, but the sound held a bitter edge. "Of course. How often he warned me that you would be my downfall. But I never—" His throat closed on the laughter. "He swore he wouldn't hurt you. He kept that promise, at least."

She didn't reply. Her gaze remained downcast, closed, distant, not with pride but with despair. Something had driven her within, where he couldn't reach her. He hadn't thought it possible.

"Esperanza said he kidnapped you, that you did not go with him willingly," he said.

"Esperanza *told* you?"

He heard the edge of hope in her voice. "She did. More than that, Rowena—she spoke. She wanted very much to rescue you."

"I knew," she whispered. "I knew she would not—" She shook her head. "I'm glad."

He leaned toward her, forgetting modesty. "You were not tied when I found you with Sim."

"I was until we reached Santa Fe. Then I . . . convinced him that it might look peculiar if I were bound. He agreed."

"Then you had one civil conversation."

"Yes." That single word hid a wealth of meaning, but it was clear she would not elaborate. "He had a deal with Cole. I don't know what he was to receive in return for bringing me back."

Not money. Not Sim. That was too easy. "Why didn't you cooperate, Rowena? Wasn't he giving you exactly what you wanted?"

"I am not a pawn, to be handed back and forth between a pair of ruffians like—" She seemed suddenly to realize that her voice had risen in anger. She crumpled in on herself again. "It doesn't matter now."

But it did. Tomás's heart pounded with the compulsion to make her tell him exactly why she hadn't gone along with Sim Kavanagh. Why she hadn't taken his side when Tomás caught up with them. Why she'd attacked Sim, even after he was down, like a wolf fighting for its mate.

And if she told him? If she surrendered, and admitted at last that she . . .

He closed his mouth. She hugged herself more tightly.

The day passed with aching slowness. Only at sunset did he scent the approach of his men, and go to meet them.

"Don Tomás," Mateo said, sliding from the saddle of his sweating mount. "*Gracias a Dios.* Is the señorita well?"

"She is." He looked behind him. Rowena had risen and was looking out from among the junipers. "Sim is gone."

Mateo shook his head as the other men gathered about them. "*Ay!* I have bad news." His expression was very grave. "We met Kavanagh on the way here."

"What?"

"It is true, Don Tomás. And worse. He had the girl Esperanza with him."

Someone gasped. Tomás clenched his hands. "That is not possible."

"The girl had more courage than we knew. She followed on Delfín, after we left the cañon. I do not know how she did it, nor how Kavanagh passed us on the way here, but he found Esperanza somewhere on our back trail. He holds her now." He cast a glance at his fellows. "Forgive us, Don Tomás. He gave us a message to take to you. He says that you may have Esperanza back—but you must go to Las Vegas to get her. And you must bring the Lady Rowena."

fifteen

Matco's words penetrated Rowena's numbness, dissolving it in a wash of pain like sensation returning to a paralyzed limb.

Sim Kavanagh. The very name revived the vicious impulses that had brought her so close to violence hours before. She hated it almost as much as she loathed herself.

Sim Kavanagh had not been defeated. Tomás had let him go, and now he had Esperanza.

She grasped at that fact with desperate tenacity; it was something straightforward to focus on when the rest of her world had lost its moorings. There was salvation, however temporary, in knowing what she must do.

Pushing aside the screen of juniper branches, she picked up her skirt and ran to join the others. Tomás was pulling on the clothing his men had brought him. He looked at Rowena searchingly.

"You heard?"

"Yes." Belatedly she noticed the stares of the men and gathered her tangled hair behind her head. She lacked even a single pin to hold it in place.

What did they see when they looked at her now?

Esperanza. Think only of Esperanza. "We must go to Las Vegas at once," she said.

Tomás tilted his head, wolflike. She could recall with vivid clarity the way his fur had felt under her hand—and how close he'd come to severing Sim Kavanagh's. He was beauty and ferocity inextricably commingled.

As she was.

"You seem to be feeling better," he said. His voice offered concern and discomfiting warmth, as if they were still alone. "I have been worried."

Well he might be, wondering if he'd lost his hostage. But since coming for her, he hadn't threatened her with captivity, nor made any move to hold her. He might not have stopped her if she tried to run.

"I am perfectly well," she said. "It is Esperanza who concerns me now."

He finished buttoning his shirt and shrugged into a worn woollen waistcoat and patched coat. "Now you undoubtedly wish I'd killed him. I've only traded one hostage for another."

She heard self-condemnation in his words. Was he as torn as she was, by opposing compulsions to protect both himself and those he . . . cared for? Did El Lobo, who willfully and recklessly lived life for the moment, finally face the consequences of his actions—and his own impossible choices?

She felt a surge of closeness to him, and a deep desire to comfort. "He was your friend," she said. "You could not have known that Esperanza would do what she did."

His half smile lacked even a hint of its usual cockiness. "You are generous."

No, she thought. *Only weary of this endless battle.* "Do you think he will . . . hurt her?"

"He has no reason to." He took a canteen passed down by one of the man and offered it to her. "It is not Esperanza he wants."

Rowena drank the water, scarcely noticing its warmth and the taste of metal. "He wants me," she said. "He simply used Esperanza."

He drank as well and tossed the canteen to Mateo. "So it appears. This is a trap, because he knows I—we—will come after him."

She'd expected him to exclude her, to demand that she return to the canyon. She'd been ready for an argument, to offer solemn promises that she would not try to escape as long as they had a hope of rescuing Esperanza.

How ironic. If Kavanagh had succeeded in taking her back to Cole, Esperanza would be safe. If Rowena hadn't fought him . . .

She forced herself to think back to the moment when the beast had taken control of her will. Tomás had shown up as she'd known he would—she'd heard him approach well before Kavanagh did—but that in itself was not enough to make her take action. The turning point came when Kavanagh set the gun to her temple. It was meant as a threat to Tomás, and she'd known, in that final flash of sanity, that he'd never risk her life. So had Kavanagh.

The decision to attack had been instantaneous and lacking all reason. She'd told Tomás that she wouldn't be any man's pawn, but nothing so sane had entered her mind. She had done what her werewolf blood demanded. Knocking the gun from Kavanagh's hand wasn't enough. She'd knocked him from his horse as well, and then leaped upon him as if she would tear out his throat. Inhuman. Hating. Utterly savage.

If she had remained herself, Tomás would have backed off. Kavanagh was clever enough to keep him away until they reached Las Vegas. She was every bit as much to blame for Esperanza's predicament as Tomás was.

At least she hadn't Changed. The beast was still at bay. It was the only solace she had left.

"Sim must have worked out a very good deal with MacLean to go so far," Tomás said. "He wouldn't do this just to save me. He knows what he's up against." He bowed to Rowena. "My lady, you'll get what you desire. I am sending my men back to the cañon. We will ride to Las Vegas, and you will have your chance to return to MacLean—one way or another."

How baldly he put it, as if he didn't care. After everything that had happened, he'd let her go so easily?

"How very inefficient of you," she said coldly, "to have gone to all this trouble to kidnap me only to give up. What of your revenge, El Lobo? And the ransom? What of your reputation? You should have saved all of us the inconvenience and left me alone that day in Colorado."

"You're probably right, señorita. I apologize for the annoyance I've caused you."

"Apologize to Esperanza," she said. "I suppose it's natural for a man like you to change his mind at whim, regardless of who else it may hurt." She turned away from him, hugging herself. "In any case, I will not simply give myself up to Kavanagh like a sack of trade goods, even if he does intend to turn me over to Cole immediately. I've had quite enough, and no reason in the world to trust him. There must be a way to outmaneuver him."

His posture relaxed into the familiar, lazily mocking stance, but his eyes glinted with challenge. "You can always run to MacLean for help. He has business offices and many employees in Las Vegas, and the men and influence to outnumber Sim a hundred to one."

"An excellent notion."

"Of course, your Cole will have no reason to save Esperanza once he has you again. Why should he care about a poor peasant girl? Unless, of course, he considers it worth his while to kill Sim, in which case Esperanza may get caught in the crossfire."

"He would not—" She faltered, remembering the *corrido* and the festering doubts it had planted in her mind. She drove them out again. "He will not pursue Kavanagh if I ask him not to."

"Then you have a decision to make, *dulzura*." The casual endearment caught at her heart. "Go to MacLean—" Mockery vanished, leaving him solemn and earnest as a boy requesting his first dance. He all but whispered the next words. "Or stay with me, and we'll outsmart Sim Kavanagh together."

"You will let me go?"

"I will find Sim myself, and . . . convince him to surrender the girl." He gave "convince" an ominous edge, exposing the anger he concealed so well. It was not aimed solely at Kavanagh. Rowena recognized the signs of self-contempt. Tomás was the last man in the world to judge himself, and yet somewhere, sometime, in the few short weeks she'd known him, he had learned to do it. She did not know what flaw or mistake or weakness he condemned the most.

But he would punish himself. He gave her the choice to decide, and thought he knew what that decision would be. He would not only give her up, but put himself at risk, against both Kavanagh and the MacLeans. Even if—though— she never told Cole of his presence in Las Vegas, he'd be walking into a potential trap.

And he wouldn't even care.

She'd told Tomás she could persuade Cole not to go after Kavanagh. She couldn't possibly claim the same influence on Weylin or Cole where Tomás was concerned—not after hearing the *corrido*.

Whatever Tomás had done, she didn't want . . . couldn't bear . . . the thought of him dangling at the end of a rope. That was the way they dealt with horse and cattle thieves here, even the common variety. And Tomás was anything but common, not with the MacLeans his deadly enemies.

Once, the decision would have been easy. Lawbreakers

deserved punishment. They earned their fates, however severe. But just as Tomás had begun to judge himself, she had begun to cease judging. When no man was without sin, how could she choose among them? How could she hope to weigh one wrong against another, or even know which was true and which false?

She could no longer rely even upon the moral scales within her own heart.

If the only way to make sure of his safety was to accompany him until Esperanza was free, so be it. She could return to Cole when he was gone. Gone and out of her life for all time.

Her eyes and nose prickled with incipient tears. She didn't know which was worse: such misplaced sentimentality or the brutish viciousness of the beast.

"Esperanza is as much my responsibility as yours," she said at last. "I will not run away while she is in danger. I will come with you."

Tomás grinned his old heedless grin. "*Muy valiente.* That's my brave Rowena." He trapped her hand in a tight grip, and she didn't even think to pull away. His elation pulsed through her like some foreign drug. "You and I, *querida*—you and I together can do anything."

Oddly enough, she believed him.

The *jacal* to which Sim brought Felícita was run-down and long abandoned, with one small window and a roof near to collapse. The door was half off its hinges. A crude bed stood in one corner; Sim pushed her down on the dirty mattress and closed the door, plunging them into gloom broken by stripes of dust-filtered light.

Felícita was afraid. For a while, in the cañon, she had been brave enough to think she could catch up to Tomás and help him rescue the lady. Rowena, whom she had betrayed.

But Sim had stopped her, and her courage dissolved like

rainwater into parched earth. While the bravery had lasted, it had made her more than a little crazy. She had hardly been aware of place or time, riding all night and into the day until her thighs were raw and her legs felt heavy as adobe bricks. She vaguely remembered hanging on the back of the borrowed horse as he walked without her guidance and she dreamed of water and sleep and an end to pain.

Then Sim had come out of nowhere, riding up in a fury of dust and rage, radiating hatred and hopelessness and grief. She was shocked awake by the sheer power of his feelings. He bled heavily from the right wrist, which he had clumsily bound up in rags. Scratches marked his face. She knew that Tomás had found him, and that Rowena was free.

And she knew Sim Kavanagh was not done with any of them.

In the close mustiness of the *jacal*, he drank from his metal bottle and tossed it to her. She wet her cracked lips. The ride had been long. They had rested through part of the night before, but by dawn they had set out again. The torment of her raw skin grew blessedly numb along with all the muscles in her legs. For many hours they rode east through the pass, turning north at last into the hills west of Las Vegas. Now it was late afternoon, and she thought she might lie down and sleep forever. If she were not so terribly afraid.

Sim snatched a three-legged stool from the wall and drew it up beside the bed. "What did you think you were doing?" he demanded harshly. "Going to rescue your precious lady?"

They were the first words he'd spoken to her, beyond brusque commands she didn't dare disobey. Without thinking she touched her throat, and then her lips; she could speak, now—when she thought of words, they came to her mouth, instead of remaining locked in her heart—but she did not wish to. He still thought she was mute.

"Tomás got her back," he said, kicking the dirt floor with his boot heel, "but that don't mean he wins a damned thing.

He'll come—and she'll come with him." He felt in his vest pocket with his uninjured hand and found a half-smoked cigarette. He threw it to the ground in disgust. "Don't think he'll let her? You don't know Tomás. She's got him in her spell. If she was going to run to MacLean, she would have let me take her. She's playing some game, and I'm going to stop her."

Felícita closed her eyes. He caught her by the chin and forced her to look at him.

"Oh, she'll come. She has a real fondness for you, *chiquita*. Maybe the only real thing about her. She'll come, and when she does—maybe I'll sell her to MacLean, or maybe—" He smiled. Felícita had no trouble understanding what he meant.

He hated so much. So much that her head rang constantly, making it impossible to think, let alone resist. His body's hurt was more direct, more understandable, maybe even something she could control a little, and so ease the chaos in her mind.

She reached for his wounded hand. He flinched. In spite of her terror, she kept hold. The rags he'd used to bind the wounds were almost soaked through.

With small, cautious gestures she pretended to unwind his bandage. A strange look came into his eyes. He got up and went to the saddlebags he had dropped on the ground. From them he drew a shirt, ragged but clean. He sat back down on the stool and held out his arm.

Carefully she began to unroll the bandage. The wound was ugly, but she did not look away. Fresh blood washed over her fingers. She picked up the shirt and tried to tear it, but the cloth was too heavy. There was nothing with which to cut.

"Here." Suddenly Sim was holding a knife, offering it to her with a twisted smile. "Take it."

The knife, like Sim, was full of violence. Now it could be used to heal. A little of her fear went away. She cut the shirt into strips and gently laid them over the wound. Some inner knowledge told her what she must do, though she'd never helped anyone who was hurt in this way. The feeling it gave her was so sweet and wonderful that she almost didn't hear Sim's hatred.

Sim's breathing went from heavy and swift to low and steady. She finished up the last of the shirt strips to tie off the bandage. Maybe it wouldn't last very long, but it was better than before.

He raised his arm to examine her handiwork. She knew he still hurt, but that, too, was better than before.

"Damn," he said softly. For a moment he seemed at a loss; confusion replaced his anger. She felt dizzy with the changes in him. He snatched up the knife, overturning the stool as he rose, and strode across the room. Only the wall stopped him.

"You think I'm an evil man," he said abruptly.

She shook her head instinctively, and then realized she meant the denial. Sim was full of hate and anger and dreadful feelings, and yet . . . Maybe she was too ignorant to know what evil really was. Nearly all she understood of the world came to her filtered through the minds and emotions of others, and only a handful of those others had been more than strangers. She could barely remember her mother and father. Tío seldom spoke of the world outside their village, though he had once traveled far and wide. There were the villagers, including the men who'd driven her out, but until the end they'd usually avoided her uncle's house.

And then Rowena and Tomás, with their great, unspoken passion for one another . . . and Sim Kavanagh. If he was evil, there were too many things she could never hope to understand.

"I've done . . . evil things," Sim said. His voice dropped

low. "I know what I am. But there're worse men than me."
He swung around and knelt beside the bed, gripping its rickety frame. "Cole MacLean. Tomás's enemy. My enemy." He
laughed. "There's a lot Tomás doesn't know about me. He
thinks he does. I know what he's thinking now."

She held her breath. He was talking in a way he hadn't
done before, and his heart was opening to her. To *her*.

"He was the only man I ever trusted," he said. "Until *she*
came to the cañon. I knew what she'd do to him from the beginning, but he wouldn't listen." His eyes no longer saw
Felícita. "Women are good for one thing. I know better than
anyone. My mother was a whore. A stinking whore who
hated me from the day I was born."

There was no bandage in the world that could bind this
wound. Felícita touched his uninjured hand. He didn't seem
to notice.

"They said she was beautiful once, high-class—like Lady
Rowena. By the time I was born she was working in a whorehouse in Hat Rock, Texas. That's where I grew up. The
madam was my first lay. I knew everything there was to know
about females by the time I was thirteen. Ma never told me
who my father was. Not until she was ugly with sickness and
dying. Then she told me to run to him and make him pay for
what he did to her."

Felícita curled her fingers around his as if she might fall if
she let go. She could see only vague images of the things he
spoke of, could hardly begin to imagine them, but his self-hatred and sorrow were clear as a mountain sky. They shook
her to the core.

"I found him, all right," he said. "I found my daddy. Only
he didn't want no whore's son to be part of his nice, respectable, powerful family. He made sure no one else ever
found out about me or my loving mother. By then she was
dead. If she'd found out what he did to me, she wouldn't
have given a damn. She'd have cursed me from the grave."

What did he do to you? Felícita asked inside her mind. She wanted to speak it out loud, but the fear was still too great. Sim was too close, in every way. He had let down his walls, and it was just a single step from feeling what he felt to knowing what he knew. One step, and she would *become* Sim Kavanagh.

She snatched back her hands and folded them under her arms. Sim blinked, and the distant, lost look in his gave way to derision and scorn.

"Well, *chiquita*," he said, "maybe you wish you hadn't doctored me up. I'm still able to use this." He touched the butt of his gun. "When I go down, I'm taking someone with me."

"No," she whispered.

"What?"

"Please—no. No killing—"

"You can talk?" He grabbed her by the arms and shook her. "How long? Damn you, if you've been deceiving me—"

"No." She closed her eyes again, as if she could block his anger. "Only . . . a night ago. Before that, I . . ." She had given up trying to figure out what had happened when she lost her voice. It was after the village men came for her that she found herself unable to speak.

Until she had to save Rowena.

Sim let her go with a little push that sent her rolling back on the cot. "So you're not a mute at all. That's how Tomás got after me so fast, isn't it? I should have—" He clenched and unclenched his fists. "It doesn't matter. You can't stop whatever I decide to do." As if to prove it to both of them, he lunged at her and pinned her to the bed. He kissed her as he'd done in the cañon, but this time his mouth softened after a few moments. Felícita felt the difference, in his heart as well as his body.

The need was still there, just as it had been the first time, demanding and grasping. Before, she'd been afraid that the sheer force of it would swallow her up. She'd only begun to understand what it meant when he'd pushed her away. And then he'd made her betray Rowena.

Now the truth came to her like the singing of angels. He needed her, but he couldn't see it. He made himself blind with his hatred for the world.

Yet he came to her like an injured animal hiding in a safe place where he could heal. She was that place. Something in her was like . . . like the bandages she'd used on his arm, only the healing he sought was for his soul. The idea filled her with awe even as she trembled with the terrible weight of it.

She, of all people, had the means to speak to this man as no one else could. In Los Milagros, she had told people what she sensed they wanted to hear. It would not so easy with Sim.

What would she give to save Rowena and Tomás? Could she take such a fearful risk? Could she make him believe a truth not in her own heart?

When he loosened his hold enough for her to breathe, she spoke.

"I will not stop you," she said. "I cannot. But I will stay with you, Sim Kavanagh."

He held her away to stare at her face. "You're damned right you will."

"You can force me," she said. "But I will go with you willingly." She touched his lips. He flinched. "I will follow you to the ends of the earth and never leave you—if we go now. Far away from this place."

"Still trying to save your friends." He laughed unpleasantly. "Ready to trade your body for their lives. You think you're worth anything to me except as bait?"

"Yes."

Her simple answer left him without a retort. He wiped his mouth with a dirty sleeve and left her lying on the bed.

"Everything is for sale," he said. "Life is like a whorehouse—

any virgin'll sell herself for the right price. I'm buying my life from Cole MacLean. Tomás thinks he can buy revenge. You think you can buy mercy. Only you can't buy what ain't there."

"You are right," she said, wondering who spoke with her dry lips. "You cannot buy a life you do not have, Sim Kavanagh. But I know there is mercy in you."

His eyes were cold. "You're so sure. Is it because you are a witch, like they said? Maybe you can tell what people are thinking?" He smiled. "What am I thinking now, *chiquita*?"

"I can feel . . . what you feel."

He slammed his fist into the wall of the *jacal*, making the whole hut shudder. "And it doesn't scare you?"

"Yes." She made herself breathe in and out and in again. "You have suffered much. But you want to make other people suffer, too. You want to keep Tomás and Rowena apart. But you can't." She stood up. "They love each other." She was amazed once again at her own certainty, the ease with which the words came to her. How was she to know of such love, any more than evil? And yet it was so. She knew.

"And you love Tomás," she said. "You don't want to hurt him. Please—" She held out her hand. "Let us go away from here. I . . . can make you happy."

For a long time he didn't speak. His heart leaped from one emotion to another, unable to decide what to feel: anger, envy, sadness, loss, jealousy, hope, despair. When he looked at her again, his face showed nothing, not even indifference.

"Happy?" he said. "There's only one thing that'll make me happy." He spun on his heel and strode for the door.

This was not how it was to be. For once she had been so confident of herself. He was to understand, to listen, to let go . . .

She ran after him. "Where are you going?"

"To find Cole MacLean." The door swung shut in her face. She laid her cheek against the rough wood and wept.

After a while she went outside and saw that the sky was growing light in the east, the pale false light that comes an hour before true dawn.

Sim had left her horse wandering loose outside the hut. It hadn't gone far; she coaxed softly until it came to her. She patted its shoulder.

"Will you bear me a little farther, amigo?" she whispered.

She knew how to find Sim. She was no wolf to follow a trail by smell, but she had learned that men carried with them markers far stronger than any scent.

Sim Kavanagh most of all.

Rowena sighed and adjusted the kerchief over her head once more. With a sideways glance at Tomás, she scratched beneath the waistband of the ill-fitting garment that passed as a dress. He smothered a grin behind his hand and tried to look appropriately sympathetic to her plight.

He had "borrowed" the dress from a small farm, where it had been hanging on a line outside the run-down building. He'd left enough money to more than pay for five such dresses, but the lady had made clear that she wished the original owner had kept this one.

Indeed, it didn't do much for her beauty. But that was the point. There was no question of entering Las Vegas as Lady Rowena Forster and the wanted outlaw El Lobo. "You must look like an ordinary settler's wife," he'd told her. He had to admit she looked much more fetching in the skirt and blouse of the past few days, but he'd thought the faded calico, with its patches at the elbows and general shapelessness, would disguise her unique attractions beyond any recognition.

Little hope of that. Even the kerchief barely covered the bleached gold of her hair. He himself had donned his own set of worn farmer's clothing quite unlike his usual more flamboyant garb, but there were those who would know him on sight.

He considered the prospect and dismissed it. He had not been himself for weeks; his emotions had tossed and bucked him about like an unbroken stallion. At last he understood the reason why.

Rowena. Rowena was the reason, and it was her despair after the fight with Sim that had opened his eyes.

Rowena had worked a change in him greater than any he might have suspected. She'd not only awakened a deeper wanting than any he'd ever felt, an attraction beyond lust that he'd failed to resist, but she had made him do what he knew to be impossible. She made him try to control destiny. His, hers . . . it didn't matter. She had made him begin to believe in the future.

Once upon a time he'd accepted what life offered from day to day, thinking no farther than the next opportunity to harass the MacLeans and their allies. That was the one purpose to his existence. He knew an end must come eventually, but he didn't dread it. He had given himself into the hands of fate on the day he woke from death to become El Lobo. It was the pact he made: Let him have his revenge, and he would never attempt to alter what would be.

Luck and chance defined his actions and the revenge he took upon his enemies. Yes, others had entered his life and become part of it. He had encountered those who needed help and helped them as he could; he had shared his bounty with those who suffered. All of that was easy. Men and women crossed his path and went on their way . . . even Sim, who became his friend. But in the end there were only two people in his world: himself and Cole MacLean.

He had defied his master Fate when he kidnapped Rowena. She had not merely fallen into his path, a convenient tool to use against Cole. No; he had planned and schemed from the time he learned of MacLean's would-be werewolf bride and gone to England to see her for himself. He might have been saved had he left her alone after that. But he'd dared to make her the centerpiece of a grand design to steal her from his enemy, in disregard of all he had learned.

Worse still, he'd set out to woo her for himself, even in the face of her protests. Instead of walking away from her resistance, he'd set himself to altering the very qualities that made her what she was. At first it had been in the name of vengeance, but that had quickly changed. He usurped the powers Fate alone could hold, while letting another person shape his actions. That was the great sin of which he was guilty.

Fate had taken its own revenge. It had made him care too much for the object of his design. It had given him words such as "duty" and "responsibility." It had brought him guilt for the first time since the death of Frank MacLean; it had caused his friend to betray him.

He knew, had known for a day now, what he must sacrifice to win free of the curse he'd brought upon himself. But fate must decide the method of that sacrifice. He would no longer interfere.

"What are we waiting for?"

Rowena came up beside him, leading her horse by the reins. She'd dirtied her face as he'd recommended, but her natural elegance couldn't be sullied by something so mundane as earth. Her eyes swam with the gold sparks that revealed her excitement.

Let this be their last grand adventure, then. No fear, no expectations. Only now.

"Remember," he said lightly. "We are new settlers to the Territory, in Las Vegas to buy a few necessities, and you can't speak much English. You are very shy and retiring."

She looked down her nose at him. "You, of course, will do all the talking."

He gave his voice the guttural accent he'd heard used at Greyburn in England during the Convocation. *"Ja, mein liebchen."*

"And our purpose is to find Esperanza," she said.

"Sim will find us."

"Unless Cole does so first."

"Only if you give yourself away."

She tossed her head, sending the kerchief askew. "You said Las Vegas is several hours' ride from here. It's mid-morning, and Esperanza was taken last night. We've wasted enough time."

So they had. He checked her saddle and gear with a practiced eye, helped her mount, and signaled to his men. They wouldn't interfere with whatever was to come. If he left Las Vegas alive, they'd be waiting—safely, in the cañon.

Tomás well knew that Sim would be watching for his and Rowena's arrival. He had only two goals; to get Esperanza free, and to make sure that Sim didn't take Rowena again. Whatever else might happen was in *fortuna's* hands.

Las Vegas was a growing town, one of the largest in the Territory, pushing outward from the old Spanish settlement by the Gallinas River. Within a year, so the newspapers said, the railroad would lay tracks over the Raton Pass, and life in northern New Mexico would change forever. Already the speculators, gamblers, thieves, and those others who could most benefit by the wild growth of a new railroad town were making a place for themselves here.

That made it easy to pass into town virtually unnoticed. No one gave the dusty farmer and his wife a second glance, though they might have had they seen Rowena's face more clearly.

He took Rowena to a hotel on the plaza and paid for a private room where she could wait. She objected at first, but when he pointed out that the disreputable saloon across the street was his first stop in looking for news of Esperanza and Sim, she subsided. A decent woman attracted far too much attention in such a place.

He breathed easier when he was alone again. Yes . . . clear Rowena from his thoughts. Pretend he had never met her, and this was simply another feint against the MacLeans on their own ground. Return to the man he used to be.

The man known only as El Lobo.

The saloon was filled with thirsty men of every profession and description from shopkeeper to cattleman, lined up at the bar and seated at tables scattered over the earthen floor. Tomás recognized several faces, including men who were wanted for some minor crime or other. The lawmen in Las Vegas—police, town marshal, and the county sheriff himself—were not consistently effective and were often corruptible. That was why the subtler criminals like Cole MacLean preferred to take the law into their own hands.

Tomás took an empty stool at the bar and ordered a whiskey. The bartender responded with indifferent efficiency.

"Pardon me," he said to the man beside him, who was nursing a drink of his own. "I am looking for a girl. A Mexican girl of about seventeen years."

The man laughed coarsely and winked. "The willing kind, you mean?"

"A girl who works for us at our farm." He adjusted his German accent as he spoke, thickening it for effect. "She has run off, and my wife is much concerned for her."

The man squinted at him. "That's too bad. Can't help you. No lack of girls like that around here. You'll find another one easily enough."

"Then perhaps you have seen a man—a gunman by the name of Sim Kavanagh."

"What? What d'you want with him?"

"He is the one our girl ran off with."

The man pushed away from the bar. "Good luck." He swept Tomás with his gaze. "I haven't seen him and don't want to. I'd get myself a gun if I were you, and say my prayers." He slapped a coin down on the bar and hurried away.

So Sim hadn't openly shown himself here. The saloon would be buzzing with it if he'd come into town. But Tomás had no intention of spending all day asking pointless questions. If Sim didn't contact him by evening, he'd leave Rowena in the hotel and go in search of the outlaw—alone.

"Tomás? Tomás Randall?"

He went still and turned his head slowly. Another stranger had taken the stool beside him.

"Are you speaking to me, sir?" he said carefully.

"God damn, it *is* you," the fellow said. He was dressed like a cowhand who'd seen better days, with a ragged mustache and a pair of missing teeth in his grin. "You don't remember me." He lowered his voice to a hoarse whisper. "No reason you should. Two years ago you did me a favor when you broke your friend out of the Santa Fe hoosegow—I got free at the same time. Not before your friend told me all about El Lobo. I been hearin' about you ever since." He whistled through the gap in his teeth. "What the hell are you doing here? Good God, hombre. Don't you know MacLean's in town, and all his men with him?" He leaned forward eagerly. "Story's all over the Territory. MacLean tried to keep it quiet, but not in this town. How you rode off with his lady right under his brother's nose. Hell, that's a good one. Heard the female was some high-class English filly. You still have her?"

Tomás glanced about the saloon. No one else showed interest in the garrulous cowhand and his talk. "Would I be such a fool as to bring her here?" he said.

"The Wolf'd do anything, just to spit in MacLean's eye." His rather foolish face sobered. "Had my own little spread once, until MacLean cheated me out of it. Lots of folks want to see you win."

Fate was still on Tomás's side. "In that case, perhaps you'd better keep my presence here a secret."

"You bet." He grabbed Tomás's hand and shook it vigorously. "If I can do anything—"

"Have you seen a man called Sim Kavanagh?"

"Ain't he a friend o' yours, too?"

Tomás slipped the man a coin. "Get yourself another drink, amigo." He started for the door.

The cowhand grabbed his arm. "Better go the back way," he said. "Saw one of the sheriff's deputies out there when I came in. The one MacLean has in his pocket."

"Thanks for the warning." Tomás straightened his patched woollen waistcoat and headed straight for the main entrance.

sixteen

Rowena's heartbeat slowed by the merest fraction when Tomás came out of the saloon.

Obviously he hadn't been recognized. She leaned against the window frame and let herself draw a normal breath. Of course there was no way of knowing if his inquiries about Esperanza had borne any fruit, but she hadn't seen anything promising from the hotel room window.

She ought to be down there, with him. What was the point of this masquerade, otherwise? She watched Tomás intently as he left the saloon doorway to speak to a man standing in the dusty street.

"He must think his disguise is pretty damned good if he's talking to Vasquez."

Rowena spun around. "Kavanagh!"

He touched the brim of his hat. "Ma'am."

The greeting was mocking at best, but it was ironically the most civil she'd ever received from him. The right sleeve of his shirt was pulled down over a bandage tied about his injured wrist; the parallel scratches she'd left on his face were bright red. But his face was devoid of hatred and his gun remained holstered.

That couldn't last. She briefly wondered how he'd managed to enter the room without her knowing it, and how long she had before he made his move. Yet, of all the concerns and questions that flooded her mind, only one formed on her lips.

"Who is Vasquez?"

"MacLean's bought-and-paid-for deputy. Sheriff Jaramillo's out of town."

She forced Kavanagh from her mind and turned back to the window. From this vantage, the deputy might have been any other armed man, but Tomás must know who he was. He was deliberately risking exposure.

As if he'd sensed her thoughts, he looked directly up at the window. She could have sworn he smiled.

Damn you, Tomás . . .

"MacLean's men are all over town, waiting for me," Kavanagh said. "And you."

"How surprising," she said, her gaze still fixed on the men in the street. "I see you managed to elude them. Or did you?"

He moved to look out the window over her shoulder. "They haven't seen me yet."

Given their last encounter, the fact that she and Kavanagh were holding any sort of conversation was nothing short of amazing. "You left us a message telling us to come to Las Vegas to find Esperanza," she said. "Where is she?"

"I let her go."

She closed her eyes in relief. "Is she here?"

"Aren't you more concerned about yourself?"

"I don't think you'd hurt me, Kavanagh, when you can still sell me to Cole."

"Why aren't you with him now?" Sim pulled her about to face him. "If Tomás brought you here, he knew you could run back to Cole any time."

Rowena felt the hairs on the nape of her neck rise with instinctive hostility. In an instant she could once again become the fury who'd attacked the outlaw and come so close to wanting him dead. She grabbed a handful of curtain in her fist to keep from striking out.

"Why are you up here instead of telling MacLean about Tomás?" Kavanagh hissed. "Is it because you love him?"

Her body heard him before her mind did. The curtain tore in her hand. "What?"

"Do you love him?"

The question, from Kavanagh, was ludicrous. But he wasn't mocking her now. The perpetual sneer was gone from his face. And as she realized his perfect seriousness, she felt his words strike her heart as surely as any bullet.

"Answer me," he said. "I'll know if you're lying."

He couldn't. Not unless he were a werewolf, and perhaps not even then. And why should she lie? She had nothing to hide. The very idea of her being in love with Tomás was simply—

She covered her mouth with her hand. After a moment she remembered that it was necessary to breathe upon occasion, and that the world had not stopped to wait for her recovery. Tomás was still talking to a possible enemy, and Esperanza was in Kavanagh's hands, and . . . and . . .

"Yes," she whispered.

She didn't move when Kavanagh withdrew. He looked out the window again and sat on the edge of the bed.

"Do you know how to use a gun?"

The second question was so startlingly different from the first that it brought her back to sanity. "Yes," she said. Should she curse Quentin for having shown her the workings of a pistol when they were hardly more than children, or thank him?

"Take this." Kavanagh thrust a length of cool metal and polished wood into her hand. Instead of dropping it, her fingers closed over the grip. He pressed his hand on hers until she held it correctly, and stepped back. "It's loaded."

Had she wished, she could have shot him then. She pointed the weapon toward the floor. "Why are you doing this?"

"Get Tomás out of here." She couldn't think of a single response while he went to the door, looked up and down the hall, and walked away.

The revolver hung like a dead weight from her hand. She looked out at the street. Tomás and the deputy were no longer in sight. With a feeling of mingled dread and unreality, she stuffed the gun in the canvas sack that served as her farmwife's reticule and ran into the hall.

She saw Tomás as soon as she reached the street. He was walking briskly toward her; the deputy was talking to someone else at the door of the saloon. She paused to look up and down the length of the street.

Perhaps her senses, so much on edge, were keener than usual, or it might have been sheer luck that she saw the one recognizable face among a group of men clustered in front of a row of low buildings two blocks away.

Cole. He stood at the center of the group, tall and commanding even from this distance. The others were dressed as Westerners, every one armed; he wore the same type of expensive, neatly pressed suit he adopted in New York, incongruous among the rough gunmen to whom he spoke.

Cole. She'd expected to feel strong emotions when she saw him again, but not this . . . this dread in the pit of her stomach. As if she believed the tales Kavanagh told of him. As if he might shoot Tomás down right here in the streets of Las Vegas.

Tomás stopped in mid-stride and followed her gaze. His muscles tensed into complete stillness. She knew that within a few moments Cole would turn his head and see him—if Tomás did not act first.

"Get Tomás out of here," Kavanagh had said. Clutching the canvas bag in a stranglehold, she rushed to Tomás and grabbed his arm.

"Come on," she said. "It's time to leave."

"Cole," he said softly.

"Tomás, don't be a fool. We must go."

He turned his head to meet her gaze. "Still worried about me, *dulzura*?"

She hissed under her breath and walked quickly to the horses Tomás had left tied in front of the saloon. Tomás remained where he was. The group with Cole was breaking up, the men going their separate ways. Cole was still occupied. But one of the gunmen looked directly toward Tomás, and something in his posture set an alarm ringing in Rowena's head.

She put down her sack and worked at the slipknot in the first horse's reins, fingers clumsy with agitation. Tomás's gelding swung his head sideways and bumped her temple. Her kerchief fell over her eyes. She yanked it off and dropped it on the ground at her feet. The reins slid from the hitching post, and she wrapped them around her arm while she untied the other horse.

Only then, as she led the horses into the street, did she dare to look toward Cole again. He was not in view, but his gunman had begun to walk toward her. She could have sworn that his gaze focused directly upon her face. And upon her uncovered hair.

He stopped. His right hand shifted to his gun, his gaze to Tomás. He stared.

"Mr. MacLean!" he shouted.

Rowena didn't wait to witness the results of his warning. "Tomás! Hurry!"

Tomás might as well have been a statue for all his response. Cursing him with words that would have astonished anyone who had known her in England or New York, Rowena freed one hand to tug open the mouth of the sack. She grabbed the gun and let the sack fall. Shoving the revolver into the waistband of her skirt, she summoned her werewolf strength, released one of the horses, and leaped into the saddle of the other.

The gunman was in the midst of drawing his weapon when Rowena cocked and aimed hers at his chest.

"Don't move," she said. "Drop the gun."

He blinked. "Lady—"

"Put it down!"

He moved, but not to obey. His gun pointed straight at Tomás. "Randall! Mr. MacLean, it's Randall!"

Rowena felt the change come over her then, the first waves of ferocious, protective anger swamping all reason and civilized restraint. Her senses grew preternaturally keen, and the blood pounded in her ears: *Enemy, enemy, enemy.*

She adjusted the aim of her revolver and fired it. Dirt exploded a few inches from the gunman's feet. He yelped and danced aside. She prepared to shoot again. He dropped his weapon. Behind him, men were responding to his shout and the commotion, preparing to intervene. If Cole was there, she couldn't see him. She couldn't think of anything but Tomás and the need to fight.

She felt more than saw or heard Tomás break free of his paralysis and chase down his skittish horse. Then he was beside her.

A bullet whistled close to Rowena's ear. Startled, she looked for the new enemy. There, and there—men half hidden at the corners of buildings, armed with rifles. Cole's men, like the first.

She bared her teeth and kicked her horse into motion. It burst forward with a jump. A rifleman stepped out from cover and sighted down the barrel, at her or at Tomás. It made no difference. She drove her horse directly at him.

An obstacle appeared as if by magic in her path: a mounted man, swinging his horse sideways to hers. Her horse half reared and skidded to a stop. Another bullet passed, very near; the man on the horse twisted in his saddle and shot back. "Get the hell out of here!" he snarled.

"Rowena!" Tomás rode up beside her and snatched her horse's reins from her hands. "Ride! Now!"

They rode. Rowena caught glimpses of gaping mouths and heard shouts and the boom of gunfire behind them. Tomás led the way, dashing full out down the street and careening around a corner toward the edge of town. Her mount followed almost without her guidance.

Elation beat in her heart to the rhythm of drumming hoofbeats. Not fear, not shame, but a turbulent, fiery joy. They had won. They had beat the ones who'd catch them and cage them up like hopeless creatures in a zoo. Tomás was at her side, crouched low over the back of his horse, graceful and beautiful. She felt the strength in her own body, free of all constraint.

Nothing could stop them now.

The hired gun staggered back from Cole's blow, colliding with the man behind him. He regained his feet, and the hate in his eyes suggested that he might actually try to fight back. Cole braced himself, hoping the man would give him the excuse he needed.

At the moment he very much wanted something to kill. Slowly.

The human wiped his bloody mouth instead. "I'm sorry, Mr. MacLean—"

"Sorry." He smiled and flexed his fist. "You're lucky you didn't hit the Lady Rowena. If you had, you'd be dead."

"But we didn't know it was her—she was with Randall, not—"

Cole simply looked at him. The gunman's mouth worked, blood running in a dark trickle from his cut lips. The other men melted from his path as he backed away, turned, and began to run.

Cole let him go. The rest never turned their attention away from the man who'd hired them, not even to watch their colleague's flight. Not one dared to move his hand anywhere near a gun.

Cole fought down the urge to reduce them all to whimpering, cowering, mindless slaves. They'd be of no use to him in that state. It was almost enough to look at them one by one and watch them cringe.

"You've failed in everything I hired you to do," he said, "all of you. You couldn't find Randall, let alone his hideout. Now he walks right into town, and only Beck had the brains to see it."

Beck also had the brains not to look smug. He'd failed as much as the rest—because Rowena had pulled a gun on him.

Rowena. It was the first time he'd seen her in three weeks, but it was nothing like the reunion he'd anticipated. She might not have been in the best of circumstances when she returned with Sim Kavanagh, but he had envisioned her sinking gratefully into his arms and then retiring to be cosseted by his servants while he dealt with the outlaw. He'd see to it that her admiration for him didn't suffer—that, in fact, it increased when she heard the story of his tireless quest to recover her from Randall.

Not in his wildest dreams had he imagined she would return with Randall himself.

He had only observed the farce from a distance, after the gunfire began. It had taken him a full minute to realize that the woman on horseback was Rowena. By then Kavanagh had appeared . . . but not to steal Rowena from Randall and deliver her to Cole. He'd actually given them the chance to get away.

He, too, was gone now, in the opposite direction. But he was the last thing on Cole's mind.

Cole clenched his fist so hard that his knuckles threatened to split the fine kid of his glove. Randall hadn't merely kidnapped Rowena and eluded all pursuit, but he had somehow corrupted her. How else to explain her bizarre and treacherous behavior? How else could she be seen to dress in a poor settler's rags, hold a gun on one of his men, and help Randall escape instead of attempting to escape herself?

It was possible. More than possible. Randall was a werewolf, with the potential power to make others do as he wished. Some of the *loups-garous,* like himself, could even influence the minds of others of their kind, and Rowena's rejection of her werewolf heritage made her doubly vulnerable. If Randall had that power . . .

He bared his teeth. "Listen to me," he said. "This time there will be no excuses. You will follow Randall and bring him back—with the lady. You will not allow anyone or anything to get in your way. If you haven't returned in twenty-four hours, I will get Deputy Vasquez to gather a posse and ride after you. And if I am obliged to go myself—" He swept the men with his gaze, letting them complete the statement in their own weak minds. He was a far more merciless enemy than Randall could ever be: Most of these men were wanted on some charge or other. He could see each of them hanged. Or worse.

"We'll get him, Mr. MacLean," Beck said. "If we ride now—"

"Go." As Beck and others turned to leave, he caught the gunman by his sleeve.

"Remember, the lady isn't to be harmed, whatever she does." It wasn't necessary for him to restate the penalty should any of the men fail in that provision.

Beck nodded and Cole let him go. The men mounted and rode off in uncharacteristic silence. A handful of the less cautious townsfolk stood and gawked at him until he turned his stare on them, one by one. They retreated quickly back to their respective occupations. Deputy Vasquez, he noted, no longer lingered by the saloon. Beck said he'd been seen talking to the man who turned out to be Randall himself. How Randall must have laughed.

They were half-wits and oafs, these humans. He knew how far he could trust them. Vasquez would gather a posse in record time, or know the reason why. Rowena would be in his hands again, soon.

The sound of tearing pulled his attention to his left fist. The glove had split over the knuckles. He yanked it off with his teeth and tossed it to the ground.

He would have sworn he could trust Rowena to remain pure and utterly loyal to him, no matter what trials she suffered. He'd never felt the need to use his will on her, so well had he trained her to obey.

That Randall had touched her mind and turned her against him . . . the idea filled him with revulsion. That he might have touched her body as well . . .

He would know when he recovered her. The truth would be easy enough to ascertain. Then he'd have no more doubts about her reasons for helping Randall. No nagging question of her going with the outlaw because she chose it freely.

Should such a thing be possible, it could not be forgiven. But it was impossible. Rowena had everything she'd ever wanted in him, and loathed what was bestial, coarse, and uncivilized. Like Randall.

To become like Randall was a worse punishment for her than anything Cole could devise.

When this was over, Rowena's shame and horror would make her more humble and cooperative than ever before, eager to make up to him for her faithlessness. He would enjoy seeing her humiliation as he pointed out her disgraceful weakness. And reminding her who was master.

Placing his heel precisely over the discarded glove, he ground it into the dirt.

.   .   .

Unnoticed and all but invisible, Felícita watched the deadly scene play out in the streets of Las Vegas.

She had come upon a strange silence when she rode into town. The reason had not been far to seek. Every face was turned toward the golden-haired woman with the gun and the men she confronted.

Lady Rowena. Felícita would have recognized her anywhere, even in the plain dress she now wore. And Tomás was with her, oddly disguised but unmistakable. The men ranged against him and Rowena were many and filled with violence, but Felícita did not know them. They were afraid.

They had reason to fear. Once Felícita had compared Rowena to a cactus that stood alone, prickly with self-protection. Now she glowed as brightly as Tomás himself—more so, for Tomás was shrouded in a pall that dimmed the brilliance of his mind like a cloud over the sun.

Felícita clutched her horse's reins and whispered a prayer. Tomás and Rowena had come to help her, as Sim predicted—but she could not help them. There were too many people here, too many voices, too much anger. She was but one girl, and a coward.

She drew her breath to shout out a warning just as she saw the man with the rifle aim toward the lady from behind the corner of the building.

No warning was required. The man missed, and then Sim Kavanagh appeared out of nowhere to place himself in the lady's path. His intervention allowed them to escape before he, too, rode away.

Felícita did not go after him, though her heart was warm with thanks. She could have followed Tomás and the lady by the beacon of their souls, but a sharp premonition stopped her just as she prepared to mount.

Sim had said that he was going to find Cole MacLean. He had called MacLean his enemy. Tomás's enemy. She had heard Tomás and Rowena speak of him in the same breath as marriage—Cole MacLean's marriage to Rowena. The *pistolero* facing Rowena had shouted that same name.

He was here, the man Sim had called worse than himself. In a moment she would see him. She waited while the *pistoleros* roiled about in confusion at the flight of their quarry, waited until another man strode out among them and claimed their attention without a single word or gesture.

He was their master. They bent to him like corn tassels before the wind. His very essence pulsed with a hideous cruelty and power that devoured the empty spirits of the others with ease.

Cole MacLean.

She had been afraid more times than she could count since the day her uncle died and left her to face the world alone. She had been afraid of Sim. She was far more desperately afraid of Cole MacLean. But she led her horse as close as she dared, listening to his voice as he scolded and threatened his followers for their failure. She heard him speak of the lady with possession in his voice, and knew he would not harm her with anything so obvious as a gun.

But he had claimed her. He would kill Tomás to get her. And when he had killed Tomás, he would destroy her as well.

This, then, was evil. And she knew, with a certainty she had felt but once before, that this man was at the very heart of the sorrow and hatred and pain that hung above Tomás and Rowena, that stood in the way of their true destinies.

She leaned her forehead against her horse's warm neck and shuddered. She could not know the future. But as she'd once felt that her own fate was tied to that of the lady and the wolf, so she now understood that Sim and Cole MacLean were a part of the same tangled web. And she was the only one who could observe MacLean without being noticed.

No. She was not strong like Lady Rowena. She was nobody, nothing. She could ride away, find the others and warn them, be safe from the horror of twisted souls like Cole MacLean's.

But she would still be haunted by the memory of how she had betrayed Rowena at Sim's command. He and Cole MacLean were almost like brothers. If there was a way to stop MacLean, she might be the one to find it.

Swallowing the thickness in her throat, she tried not to feel what came from MacLean's mind until he was finished speaking and the men had scattered. She watched him drop his glove and crush it into the dirt as if it were his enemy. His victim.

And then she followed him.

Tomás didn't let the horses stop completely until the hour before sunset. By then they had covered many miles, and Las Vegas lay far behind them to the west. There was no visible pursuit, but Tomás did not expect it; the place to which they'd fled was the last hideout MacLean would ever suspect.

How could El Lobo dare to take refuge on the MacLean's own land?

He dared because this land had once been his. It was home, the home he had lost so long ago. The home he would not have again.

He dismounted and lifted his arms to Rowena. She sat her horse without any sign of weariness, but her gaze rested on the country around them as if she didn't really see it. She let him ease her out of the saddle without once looking at his face.

She didn't see *him*, just as she hadn't listened to him in Las Vegas. His doing, all of it: the risks she'd taken, the danger she'd faced so recklessly, the fact that all the town had seen her wielding a gun in open defiance of Cole's men. A gun he had not given her.

If not for Sim, she might be dead, hit by a stray bullet meant for him while he stood waiting for his Fate to be decided. His doing, his error, his responsibility.

And after the great daring she had shown, she was sinking

back into the despair he had seen in her when she'd attacked Sim. He could not bear that as well, knowing he had brought it upon her. Forced her to become what she was not, for his sake.

He alone was to blame.

He caught her arms and shook her until her eyes lost their blankness, the golden flecks sparking to life like embers in a banked fire. Her hair, blown loose from its bindings, was a lustrous flame. Her body tensed to resist him. When he saw the anger wake in her face, he let her go and waited for the conflagration.

"You addle-brained, rattle-headed buffoon," she snapped. "What ever possessed you to stand in the middle of the street waiting to be killed?"

Two weeks ago Tomás would have laughed with relief. But he had gone well beyond laughter. It was anger he felt, a fury so deep that it took him back to the day he'd returned from the East to find Los Valerosos burning, its great herds of sheep and cattle driven off and its people scattered.

The day his mother had died.

"You should not have interfered," he said between his teeth.

She put her hands on her hips. "Oh, no. I should simply have watched while you showed off in your typical reckless manner, speaking to sheriff's deputies and generally behaving as if you wished to be captured."

Her words cut too close to the truth, and he could think of no retort. "I told you to stay in the hotel, where you would be safe."

"And I had no intention of passively obeying your commands like—like—"

"Like a proper, docile English lady?"

"If you were in any respect a proper gentleman, none of this would be happening!"

He looked away, across the plain. "Once I was a gentleman," he said, "the son of an old and respected family. Once all this land would have been mine, along with ten thousand cattle and sheep and horses."

She fell silent and followed his gaze. He knew what she saw: yet more desert grassland cut by arroyos and rocky mesas, carpeted with shrubs, cholla, yucca, scrubby junipers, and understated patches of yellow, white, and purple wildflowers. He knew it would mean little to her, a creature from a land of lush greenery and constant rain. She wouldn't understand the pride and happiness he'd once known at Los Valerosos: herding sheep, swimming in the river when the water was still cold from winter, riding with the *vaqueros* to round up the cattle, sharing jokes with the people of Los Valerosos.

That had all been before he went east for his "formal" education. Before the old feud had become personal. The traditions of fifty years had been wiped out in a day, traditions and a way of life that his mother's father's ancestors had made for themselves in New Mexico two centuries ago.

"It's MacLean land now," he said. "One more part of his vast holdings in northern New Mexico."

"I . . . don't understand."

"He stole it from my family, after he and his kin killed my father and mother and left me for dead."

Rowena caught her breath. Of course; he'd never told her so much of his past, merely hinted of wrongs done and an ancient feud. Why should she believe anything he said if it meant accepting that her fiancé was a black-hearted villain and murderer?

And yet, in Las Vegas she had turned against MacLean's men and fought for his life. She knew Cole would kill him without hesitation. If she believed that—if she risked her very future to save him in spite of his reputation—she'd guessed something very close to the truth. Or someone else had shared the details.

Only two men might have done so: old Nestor, or Sim.

"The MacLeans burned the old hacienda and drove off

the families who worked for my mother," he said. "Some had been with us for generations. The livestock they claimed for their own. The law looked the other way." He showed the edges of his teeth. "It took longer for them to claim the land. Cole had to find the surviving heirs and intimidate them into signing it away for pennies."

He saw Rowena absorb what he'd said, her face expressionless. "But you're alive."

"*Sí,* I survived. As a desperado. The MacLeans have the law in their pockets, and I am a wanted man. Of course it will be far more convenient when I'm truly dead. Which, thanks to you, must wait for another day."

She ignored his sarcasm. "When Kavanagh captured me," she said, "he translated a song about you. It told of the feud and what happened between your family and Cole's. It made you into a hero. But it also said that you killed Cole's father."

"Did you believe it?"

The fierceness returned to her eyes. "The song was written by those who admire you for your deeds and hate the MacLeans. It was sung in an outlaw camp."

"Then of course the things it said of my enemies must be lies."

"I have not seen Cole since you took me from his brother," she said. "I've heard only your side of this terrible history, but I have seen you break the law out of revenge." She clenched her fists. "I've . . . become no better than an outlaw myself. I will make no judgments until I speak to Cole again."

"Yes. As I said before, doubtless he'll tell you the truth."

"I don't know what he'll tell me."

"If you wanted his opinion, why didn't you run to him when you had the chance? After all, he is exactly what you want."

She stared at him, her face taking on an arrested look as if he'd said something astonishing. And then she changed again, as surely as if she'd shifted her shape into the wolf she rejected.

A she-wolf, stalking her prey. She took a step toward him.

"Do you think you know what I want, Tomás Alejandro Randall?" she asked, her voice a husky, dangerous purr. "Why don't you show me?"

Challenge and desire hung in the space between them like the musky scent of lovemaking. It caught Tomás like a bullet in the gut. The madness of it worked through his body and filled his mind with the alluring image of the Lady of Fire.

But it was no image. His Lady of Fire was here—awake and alive and real.

And she wanted him. At last, consciously and deliberately, she wanted *him*.

He trapped her face between his hands and kissed her.

She did not draw back, or quiver in outrage and denial. For an instant she was still, and then her arms locked about his neck and her lips opened beneath his. He felt the reckless strength of her fingers working in his hair, the drumming of her heartbeat under the full firmness of her breasts. And above all, he felt the ardent burning of her need.

Her need. His. There was no difference. The virginal Lady Rowena was swallowed up by it, leaving the hungry, feral creature who kissed him like a wanton. *His* wanton, his woman, his mate. He'd waited all his life for this surrender.

But she was far from submissive. Her fingertips trailed from his hair to his neck, touched the hollow of his throat where the pulse beat so fast, and began to push the coat from his shoulders. His amazement was lost in triumphant exultation. He shrugged from the coat and let it fall to the ground. He felt the trembling in her hands as she worked at the buttons of his waistcoat.

Trembling, but not from fear or modesty. She was beyond those barriers now, as he was beyond the questions and doubts of mere moments ago. He finished unfastening the waistcoat, and then it joined the coat at his feet.

He kissed Rowena again, more deeply. Her mouth welcomed the thrust of his tongue. His practiced fingers made short work of the buttons of her simple bodice, revealing the thin fabric of her chemise. No corset lay beneath. The blush of her nipples made small, bold peaks against the pale cloth.

He'd caressed her breasts before, at the pool. Then she had been in a waking dream, only half aware of what he did. Her desire for him now was a thousand times more arousing. This time he'd be neither subtle nor gentle. She didn't want him to be. He pulled the chemise over her head, bent her back in his arms, and took her nipple into his mouth.

The sounds she made were not gasps or cries but something in between. She arched up eagerly, offering still more of herself to his lips and tongue. The unique scent of her skin mingled with a richer perfume. He licked every curve of one breast and then the other, suckled until her nipples were the lush pink of roses and as hard and aching as his manhood.

Driven as much by her desire as his own, he removed her chemise and kissed her slender throat and her ears and her shoulders. He eased her down to the earth, spreading his coat to shield the tenderness of her body. The grass was their only bed, the desert plain their vast bedchamber, the emerging stars their candlelight.

She lay gazing up at him, fire dancing in her eyes and spread about her face in an aura of pale golden hair. Through his hunger he was vaguely aware that she was no longer fierce or seductive but fully awake to everything he did, watching with an odd inner stillness. She called him to account with that look, and he felt the weight of obligation settle about his neck like a yoke.

He broke it with a thought and claimed her lips in a rough kiss, seizing the hem of her skirt. She moved to let him pull it up above her hips. To feel her naked beneath him was what he'd wanted from the beginning, but there was a still greater urgency. He parted her thighs and unfastened his trousers as if life itself depended upon their joining.

And it did. This *was* life, holding Rowena in his arms. Today he had stood in the middle of the street and openly courted death rather than face a future he'd never believed could exist.

What had Sim told him that day in the cañon? "How many times have I kept you from dying when you were bent on it?" Kate had said something similar in New York, about his wanting to die.

He hadn't believed it then. He loved life too much, life and adventure and the satisfaction of thwarting the MacLeans. But Sim had been right. Just as he'd been right about the danger of Lady Rowena Forster.

Rowena, who'd made him see himself clearly for the first time: not a charming rogue who so easily captured the loyalty of the common people, the fear of his enemies, and the hearts of adoring women, but a man who neglected the welfare of those he pretended to help, who sought oblivion and his own destruction behind a mask of cheerful indifference.

She had stolen his self-deception like a skilled thief, but she could give it back for a few precious hours. This *was* the moment, the only one that mattered. When he buried himself in her hot, yielding flesh, Cole MacLean, Sim Kavanagh, memory, hatred, duty, revenge—all would cease to have meaning.

He did not need to touch her to know she was ready for him. The scent of her arousal worked like a drug on his senses. He slid his hands along the insides of her thighs, urging them apart. She made no resistance. He positioned himself above her, resting his weight on his arms. Her body's heat and wetness summoned him to enter with a siren's silent call. He hesitated, and she reached up to him with strong, slender hands that demanded the ultimate worship of his body.

He covered her mouth with his as they celebrated the most ancient rite of all.

seventeen

The world exploded in a shower of pleasure and pain, awe and terror.

Rowena could make no sound as Tomás plunged deep inside her, his manhood pushing into the very core of her body. The brief pain vanished, replaced by something she could not have imagined possible within the strictures of her carefully planned life.

Ecstasy. A word she hadn't known the meaning of until now. A word far too tame and insipid for the miracle of the gift Tomás gave her with his body, the gift she at last dared to receive with all the desire of her heart. She arched her back to take him deeper still, claiming him even as he marked her as his.

This is what it is like, the lost part of her mind observed. *This is what you feared.* Then all such thought was drowned by the waves of still greater pleasure that swept through her as Tomás began to move.

She could not have described the myriad sensations he created within her. Explanation was impossible. Her body quivered and pulsed with every rhythmic thrust. She clutched at Tomás's shirt and gripped his hips with her legs, exulting in his potent masculinity, reveling in her own female power.

If there was an inner voice that reviled her for what she'd become, she could no longer hear it. Tomás's hungry possession inflamed her. His mouth was on her neck, her shoulder, her breasts, driving her to higher and higher peaks of delight. The sensuous smell of their joined bodies made her dizzy. She wanted to return pleasure for pleasure, but she could feel herself beginning to slide toward some inevitable ending. Excitement peaked at the place where their bodies joined—cast her up like fire from a surging volcano—sent her spinning in space where the colors had intoxicating scents and celestial music flowed over her body.

It all came crashing together in a rapturous burst of sheer joy. She cried out. Through a haze of stunned amazement, she saw Tomás fling back his head and answer with a cry of his own. He moved within her again—once, twice, three times—and then his body stiffened. She felt the rush of his seed. And then she lay still beneath him, dazed by the wonder of it, as he kissed her forehead and cheek and hair.

"Rowena," he said. "Rowena, *mi amor*."

My love.

Her flesh still throbbed where he rested within her, but her mind would not listen to the flawed and deceptive communication of mere speech. More than her body had been aroused.

The wolf was here. She had been released, wild and hungry, and she was not ready to be put back in her cage. Lady Rowena Forster had nothing to say about it.

Nor did Tomás. Tomás Alejandro Randall, El Lobo, had dominated her with his body and taken her to a place of miracles where the outside world ceased to exist. Now it was her turn.

Rowena-the-wolf laughed. She pushed herself up on her

arms and kissed Tomás on the mouth, using her tongue as he'd used his.

He reared back, separating from her. "Rowena—"

She followed him, laying her hands flat on his chest. His shirt was in the way, so she removed it, tearing at his collar. At the last minute he preserved the shirt by undoing the final few buttons.

Then his bare chest was under her palms, lightly dusted with dark hair, beautifully muscled and sleek. She'd seen him thus before, but only through the eyes of fear. Now she was touching him because she wanted to touch, wanted to feel, wanted to know.

His body was alien to her still. Alien and fascinating. She traced the line of his collarbone and then down the center of his chest. He shuddered, but his face was rapt.

She brushed her lips against the firm skin of his chest. His hair, rich with masculine scent, tickled her nose. She found his nipple and touched it with the tip of her tongue.

His hands shot out to grip her arms. "Rowena!" He sounded almost shocked. She wanted to shock him still more. She pushed his arms away and teased his nipples as he'd done with hers. Then she carried him to the ground with her weight, stretched out upon his body. His manhood stirred against her stomach.

She kissed him, lacing her fingers in the curls of his hair. The angry jubilation that had filled her on their escape from Las Vegas returned in all its force. He was *hers*. He thought he could command her, humiliate her, tease her again and again? He was wrong. She was his equal in every way. His superior. She could make him feel what she felt.

She pinned him to the ground and kissed the strong planes of his face, brow and cheekbone and jaw. When he tried to raise his hands to embrace her, she trapped them with hers. Copying what he had done, she licked the vulnerable pulse point of his throat and the hard curve of his shoulder. He breathed in and out roughly, fingers working in the grass beneath him.

"Rowena—"

Rowena was not there. She silenced him with another kiss and moved her legs to straddle him. She explored his body with hungry wonder, chest and ribs and flat belly. How perfect he was. Nearly flawless. The ideal mate. Hers.

But she had not seen all of him. She must; the wolf demanded it. She reached for his trousers and struggled to remove them. Tomás's hands covered hers and finished the job with practiced ease.

How many women had he lain with? How many? She growled in her throat and pushed him down again. There would be no other females from this moment on. He must *know* it.

She slid back to study the part of him that had given her so much gratification. It was strangely fascinating, so alien from what she knew. Brief glances on previous occasions didn't do it justice.

Without hesitation she reached for him. Her fingers touched the firm length and closed about it. Tomás jerked under her and gave a soft oath. Carefully she ran her fingertips up and down, watching his face.

Wanton, Lady Rowena cried. *Shame, oh shame!*

The wolf felt no shame, did not understand its meaning. She knew mingled triumph and joy at her mate's astonished pleasure. He wasn't laughing now, and his eyes were dark with passion.

Passion. At last she knew what it was. It was more than lust or physical hunger. The act that joined their bodies wasn't a thing to be endured for the sake of children, or performed with remorse and dread out of a sense of duty. It was a precious gift, a binding, a sealing of unspoken vows. Rowena-the-wolf had made that vow when she lay in the grass with El Lobo, and she did not regret it.

Once more she straddled his hips, fitting herself to him. He circled her waist with his hands as she claimed him with her body. She led the way, moving slowly at first, steadied by Tomás's hold, guided by his touch on her buttocks.

At this moment she was master, but the triumph of conquest gave way to the pure exaltation of complete wholeness. She saw Tomás's pleasure and knew it for her own. The barriers made by nature, of form and shape and gender, melted away. Tomás-wolf and Rowena-wolf became one as their joined bodies carried them over the crest of completion and into a world of jubilant union.

It took nearly an hour for the happiness to fade. The wolf remained strong in Rowena's mind and heart as she lay in Tomás's arms. Thoughts were irrelevant; feeling was everything, and sensation—the scents of earth and man and woman, the sounds of insects in the grass and brush, the rustle of a cool evening breeze, the sight of stars emerging through the wash of fading color that was the sky above them.

But the bodies they wore were human. Human reason worked its way into Rowena's mind, insidious at first, then shouting at her to listen.

What have you done? it demanded. *What have you become?*

She tried to ignore it, burrowing deeper into the crook of Tomás's arm. He shifted to accommodate her, his eyes closed as if he, too, were fighting some inner command.

They are after you, Lady Rowena whispered in the she-wolf's ear. *Do you think you can lie there like a whore and escape the consequences of your actions?*

The wolf bristled and growled in defiance. Beast and lady confronted each other on the battlefield of her soul, neither willing to retreat. In the end, the wolf was the first to look aside. But she did not slink away to hide in some hidden corner. She watched and waited with animal patience for another chance to emerge.

And Rowena, too, waited—for humiliation and self-contempt to send her spinning into despair once again. It had come after her attack on Sim Kavanagh, paralyzing her with horror at what she'd done. And it had gradually consumed her heady sense of victory when she and Tomás fled Las Vegas, feeding on the memory of the frenzy that had driven her to raise a weapon and attack Cole's men in violent defense of El Lobo.

It might hold her even now, if not for Tomás's challenge. *". . . why didn't you run to Cole when you had the chance?"* he'd said. *"He is exactly what you want."*

She still wasn't sure what had happened, or how the wanton she-wolf was set free by his words. She'd desired only one thing then: to prove Tomás wrong, whatever it took. To show him exactly what she *did* want.

She had succeeded. Her virginity was lost, her self-control abandoned, her devotion to propriety turned into a farce.

But the shame didn't come. That was the frightening part, that she looked at Tomás lying beside her, his face relaxed with sleep, and felt not humiliation and anguish but a bittersweet happiness. Happiness she did not deserve.

She disentangled herself from his arms, careful not to disturb him, and gathered her clothing. She shook grass and dirt from the dress and put it on. It should have made her feel more human, but it only reminded her of what she'd chosen to throw away.

Yes, chosen. However much she might wish to blame the wolf in her soul, she wouldn't be such a coward as to hide from the truth.

The truth was that her body ached and her heart turned over in her chest as she watched Tomás sprawled naked on his back, oblivious to his danger. She wanted to lie down beside him, wake him, begin the caresses and loving all over again. In this instant of crystal-clear understanding, she understood herself.

For so many years she'd fought her werewolf blood, standing

rigid against all threats to her resolve. Instead of bending, even a little, when flexibility might have eased her way, she held firm against every challenge to face her bestial nature. And just like the proverbial tree in a storm, she snapped when the stress became too great.

Tomás was her storm. He'd blown so gently that she hadn't realized how close she was to breaking. Once shattered, a brittle tree could never be restored to its former strength. At best it might be mended.

But only if she fully accepted her failure, and that the wolf was part of her. She could not cage it without facing the same risk of losing control. If she acknowledged her dual essence at last, kept the wolf tied within view rather than behind hidden bars, she could learn to tame it. She need never be taken by surprise again. There was still hope of saving her humanity if she refused the final degeneration into wolf's shape as well as wolf's nature. And, in time, the wolf's nature would be mastered.

All she needed was time.

Slowly she walked back to Tomás and knelt beside him. Her fingers trembled as she touched his brow. How quiet he was, still without a care in the world. How far she'd come, from regarding this man as a contemptible enemy to lying in his arms. From despising all he stood for to all but embracing it. From hating him to . . .

Loving him.

She didn't flinch from the word. Kavanagh had forced her to speak the truth when he'd asked her if she loved Tomás. She'd told herself then that she'd lied to satisfy the outlaw, but the joke was on her.

Somewhere along this rash and fateful journey, she'd fallen in love. When had it begun—that first night in the adobe ruins, or when he'd rescued Esperanza, or those heart-stopping moments by the waterfall? What about him had captured her in spite of all her resistance? His irreverent disdain for propriety, his laughter, his unexpected kindnesses and generosity, his roguish gallantry, the wild spirit that no danger could break or tame—the very fact that he was the opposite of everything she'd ever believed herself to be?

It made no difference. The deed was done, irrevocable, signed and sealed by their loving under the wide desert sky. This love was not the idealized emotion she'd once felt for an upright young man in England, or her respectful admiration for Cole. It extracted a much greater price. It stripped her of her complacent ignorance, and made each decision a test she might fail at terrible cost.

But love had also given her a new kind of courage—not the arrogant bluster she'd used to shield herself from Tomás's threat to her heart, but the fortitude to accept what had been and what must be.

She brushed the thick hair away from Tomás's forehead. Even if she had the choice to undo what had happened in Las Vegas and afterward, she wouldn't. And if she could go even farther back in time, and never meet El Lobo at all . . .

She might have been content. Content, married to Cole, ignorant of passion, unsuspecting that her husband wore a mask of refinement and gentility over a criminal's soul.

But of that she still had no proof. If he'd had a role in the death of Tomás's parents, she would find out. And if Tomás had murdered Cole's father . . .

God help her. Once she'd asked him how many men he'd killed, and he hadn't answered. She could no more believe he was a killer by nature than she was. The black-and-white certainties that ruled her life had faded to shades of gray, distressingly ambiguous. Could she love a murderer?

She was sure of but one thing: She couldn't bear the thought of a world without Tomás Alejandro Randall.

She stretched out beside him and closed her eyes. She

would make peace with herself one day, even with her wolf and its savagery. But there would be no such reconciliation with this love, for she knew that Tomás did not share it.

He'd set out to seduce her from the moment they met—as a challenge, revenge, amusement. He'd found her beautiful and desirable. He had protected her as he did any of his dependents. She thought he'd come to feel genuine affection for her, in spite of their constant sparring.

But the emotions she had discovered weren't for the likes of El Lobo. Anything else he might give with his whole heart, but not this.

Love, they said, made everything possible. Without it, the vast gulf between them was insurmountable.

She could swallow her pride and ask Tomás to abandon his quest for revenge and . . . what? Run away with her to a place where they were both unknown? Ask him to give up his freedom and settle down to the life she had always wanted—raise their children as human and grow old in a stable home with four real walls and civilization on every side?

Or she could go with him and become an outlaw's woman, forever hunted, watching the wolf engulf the woman until Lady Rowena Forster ceased to exist. . . .

Love had made her surrender her convictions and principles. Love had urged her into Tomás's arms, in spite of her vows to another man. But not even love dared demand the sacrifice of all she had ever been or could be. Nor could she demand that of Tomás.

There could be no shared future for Lady Rowena Forster and Tomás Alejandro Randall.

But, for a few more stolen moments, there was now. She drew closer to Tomás and rested her cheek on his shoulder. He sighed into her hair without waking, and his arm curled around her in unconscious possessiveness.

I cannot be yours, she thought. *Not because I love another, but because it is the only way to give my love for you some meaning.*

Cole filled her mind's eye, as she'd last seen him—sophisticated, elegant, exuding the supreme confidence and self-assurance that drew everyone to him. Everything had changed since that day in New York. She'd heard tales that made her doubt she'd ever known Cole at all. Tales she still couldn't bring herself to believe. For, if they were true, her fragile plan would collapse.

She had no doubt that Cole and his brother hated Tomás, and would kill him on sight. Her abduction would only have hardened their resolve. But, no matter how dangerous the chance she took, she knew what she had to do.

"Tomás," she said. "Wake up."

He murmured sleepily and tried to pull her atop him. She braced herself. "Wake up, Tomás. I must talk to you."

His eyes opened to slits and his lips curled into a seductive smile. "Talk?" he said. "Why talk, when there are so many more interesting things we could be—"

"Not any more." She looked away. "Tomás, I must go back to Cole."

Tomás came fully awake in an instant, as if a gunshot had gone off beside his ear. He was on the verge of laughter when he saw the look on Rowena's face. She backed away and sat with her arms wrapped around her knees, avoiding his touch.

"This has been a mistake," she said, "and there is but one way to correct it."

He sat up and pulled himself into a half-curled posture that mirrored hers. "A mistake?"

"Yes. You know that as well as I do. But there is still a chance that it can be made right—if I return to Cole immediately."

He heard her words clearly enough. They acted like whips on his bare flesh: He wanted to howl and dance like a true lunatic, to Change and run for miles and miles to the very ends of the earth, to caress Rowena again and again until she gasped his name and begged him to take her flying over the moon.

He did none of those things. He merely stared at her until she met his eyes.

"You wish to return to Cole," he said.

"I must." She held out her hand and let it fall. "What has happened between us was an error in judgment that can lead nowhere except to more suffering. If I go back, there is a chance to end it—the feud, the hunt for your life, the threat to those around us. Can't you see that it has to end?"

Tomás closed his eyes. *It has to end.* He'd known that, hadn't he? He'd known it all along.

The curse of understanding had come to him when the loving was over, when they'd lain side by side, avoiding the words that might shatter the miracle. Understanding fully what he'd done to her—and to himself.

He'd never felt before what he'd experienced in Rowena's arms, in her body. She'd given herself fully, with no thought to the consequences, just as he had done. And though he had lain with many women, not one had ever given him reason to walk away with regret.

Rowena did.

He had wanted her. Perhaps if he'd won her that day at the pool in the cañon, it would have been easy to regard it simply as a most pleasurable revenge against Cole MacLean. Today, so close to death, he'd thought that losing himself in her body would give him the release he sought, release from the unwanted burden of guilt and anger and too-powerful emotions.

There was no release. Not when he knew what must happen when she woke and realized what she'd sacrificed.

What had he told her that day by the pool when he'd nearly taken her? *"When I am done, you'll never go back to what you were. You'll be free. . . ."*

Free. Free to risk her life in defense of his . . . free to lose all she'd ever known.

Or free to return to Cole MacLean.

Oh, her pleasure had been real enough. She had touched him and accepted his caresses with true passion, even abandon. She was everything he'd wanted in his Lady of Fire.

But the Lady of Fire was not Rowena. She was a figment of his fantasies; *she* would never force him to see what he did not wish to see.

Rowena did. She was his mirror, mercilessly reflecting back upon him the emptiness of what he thought of as freedom.

"How," he asked, "how will returning to MacLean end the feud?"

She lifted her chin. "I will tell him that you are dead."

Dead. With that one word she told him what greater eloquence could not. She wished to put him from her life completely. And he couldn't blame her.

What had he given her but pain? When had he ever thought of her welfare and happiness?

"You don't care about anything but this," she'd said by the pool, putting his hand on her breast. *"Once you have this, the rest scarcely matters, does it?"*

That was what she believed. He'd gotten what he wanted. But she didn't know how much more he'd received than he reckoned on.

There was a binding that could occur between two werewolves who were perfectly matched. It went far beyond what humans knew in marriage. It was said to be unbreakable when sealed by the act of love. His own mother and father had shared that bond; Adelina was never the same after Fergus died.

Rowena was the first *mujer-loba* to share Tomás's bed. He hadn't thought for a moment that such a link might occur between them.

If he allowed his imagination free rein, he could almost picture a future no more substantial than a dream: Rowena at his side, riding across the plain and back to their secret cañon; living with him, lying with him every night, keeping him humble with the occasional stringent observation about his reckless behavior and irreverence.

Rowena as his companion. His mate. His wife. A woman to whom he must be faithful, forsaking all others, forsaking the feud and the life that had been his since his mother's death.

He imagined himself on bended knee, begging Rowena for her hand. By the rules of her station, she'd been ruined and could only be saved by honorable marriage. But he remembered one more thing she'd told him: *". . . it's only the beast you will win. There is a part of me you can't touch—the part that is human."*

She didn't feel the binding. She couldn't accept the passion of the wolf—not as an abiding part of her life, to be enjoyed and cherished. And she wouldn't accept the wolf within him. She needed the kind of mate he could never be: upright, law-abiding, human. A man who'd offer her the future she craved. The future she thought she would have had with Cole MacLean.

Tomás had planted doubts in her mind about the man she'd planned to marry. Obviously those doubts weren't enough. Did she still think that MacLean would take her back without question, after what had happened in Las Vegas? And here, tonight . . .

"So you would tell him I'm dead," he said at last. "And of course he will believe you."

"He will if you don't ruin it by contradicting me with your presence. You can have your freedom and your life, if you leave this country and don't return—"

He stood up. "You'd have me run away to save my own skin. And you—you will walk back into Cole's life, and he'll accept you with open arms because he loves you so deeply."

She rose to face him. "That is my concern. He will forgive me. I will tell him that I finally escaped. I'll tell him—"

"That I used my will to make you attack his men, and then give yourself to me?"

She paled. "If necessary. There are surely ways to . . . conceal the physical alterations. I'll convince him to take me back to New York immediately. He'll have no reason to suspect that I ever . . . cooperated willingly with you."

Because you'll play the remorseful, chastened and deferential female? Because he wants your influence and connections and money too much to reject you? Do you think your life will be anything but misery with a man who considers you damaged goods?

He will find out, Rowena. He'll never look at you without being reminded of his deadly enemy.

And when you learn that I was right about him, will you sit quietly by and let his wrongdoing go unopposed? No. You will smash yourself on the rocks of his evil. . . .

Tomás turned his back on her and bowed his head. This was guilt, guilt such as he'd known only once before, on the day of his mother's death. He knew why he'd spent his life avoiding all such emotions. Guilt, shame, sorrow, rage, worry, jealousy, devotion . . . love.

She was his responsibility. He had made it so. She told herself lies to secure her safety from the wolf within and without. He must be the rational one now.

"I am sorry, *dulzura*," he said. "I cannot allow you to return to him. He is mine to deal with. I think it would be best for both of us if I see you to a safe place from which you can make your journey east."

"Is that your command?" she said, her voice shaking. "Will you use force to make me go away as you once did to capture me, simply so that you can continue seeking your revenge? Isn't what you've done enough?"

No. It was not enough. He saw his path as clearly as if a shaft of sunlight had broken through a mantle of clouds to point his way.

The wolf in him understood the needs of survival.

Rowena's survival. Useless to even try to explain what he knew: that Cole would have control over her as long as he lived—over her mind and spirit and heart—that a MacLean did not forgive. Her single hope of happiness lay in her return to New York, where the Lady of Fire and the wolf had no place.

And she must go alone.

Rowena had asked if he'd murdered Cole's father. He hadn't answered. For years he'd pushed the image of Frank MacLean's body from his mind: an old man lying still in the brush because the son of his enemy had killed him.

An eye for an eye, a tooth for a tooth. But when he remembered, the sickness came all over again. He could not kill like Sim, coldly and without remorse. And yet he'd let the MacLeans build his reputation as a ruthless outlaw who would strike down anyone who stood in his way.

At last he'd earn that reputation.

It's all I can give you, mi rubia. To make certain that you truly are free to create your own destiny. I know what mine must be.

"You are stronger than you know," he said. "But I am strong enough to make you obey. We will ride to Trujillo, where I have friends who can see you back to Colorado." He looked toward Las Vegas, where his enemy waited. "Come."

He expected her to argue, but she was more distant now than ever. They rode the miles to Trujillo as if they'd returned to that very first day when he had taken her from Weylin MacLean. It was easier so.

Trujillo was dark and silent as they approached the village. Tomás brought them to a stop a quarter mile away. "We will wait here until just before dawn," he said. "In the meantime, I suggest that you try to sleep. I'll make sure all is safe."

She dismounted without his help and saw to her horse. He did the same, and then walked a short distance away to Change. Rowena didn't so much as glance in his direction.

He ran from her, driven by all the helpless anger his human body could not express. He ceased to think, even in the way of a wolf in a territory not his own. Only after he'd run several miles did he remember that he must not leave Rowena alone.

By then it was too late.

eighteen

If it weren't for Weylin's perfect night-vision, he would never have seen the wolf as it ran across the desert plain below. From his viewpoint at the top of the low mesa where he rested his mount, the animal was little more than a blur to the southeast.

It might have been an ordinary wolf. A few canny beasts still avoided the hunter's traps and bullets, but most of the survivors lived in the mountains, where they were harder to catch.

This wolf made no attempt at concealment. It glided over the ground at a pace too swift for any normal animal, headed north toward the town of Trujillo.

Weylin knew who it must be.

His newly bought horse shied at his sharp movement in the saddle. He quieted the mare as best he could, but his heart raced with the knowledge that the long hunt was at an end.

El Lobo had finally miscalculated. This was close to the old Randall land, now the MacLeans', and Randall had made the mistake of returning at the worst possible time. For him.

Weylin calculated Randall's speed and the best way of intercepting him. The chance would come but once. There was a deep arroyo in Randall's path he'd have to cross if he held to his course, and Weylin was slightly north of him. If he descended from the mesa at an angle heading east, he should reach a certain sheltered place of brush and rock where he'd be able to intercept Randall with little risk of being seen or scented.

He set the horse at a good speed down the slope, grateful that he'd bought a sturdy mount with strong wind and firm muscle. While the mare ran, he uncoiled the rawhide rope hung from his saddle.

Luck was with him. The moon gave just enough light to ease the mare's way, and she put her heart into the run. He came to his destination ahead of Randall and brought her to a stop.

This was it. He checked the lariat once more. The rope wouldn't be strong enough to hold Randall for long, but he didn't need much time. Just a few moments to get El Lobo at a disadvantage, and then . . .

He all but pricked his ears as he heard the faint scrabbling of paws on stone and earth. His mare raised her head and quivered.

The wolf burst from the arroyo. Weylin swung the rope with a precision born of years of practice. The loop came down over Randall's head just as he whirled to face the unexpected threat. His lunge nearly ripped the rope from Weylin's hand.

Instead of fighting the pull, he snatched his rifle and leaped from the mare's back. Randall snapped at the rope, twisting this way and that, muscles straining and hair on end. Weylin dropped the rope and took aim.

Randall froze. The noose was about his neck, but he could have severed it with another bite. He might even have risked attack, since there was a good chance he could survive a bullet anywhere but in the heart or brain.

He did not attack. He simply stood, watching Weylin, ears cocked sideways and tail low in a stance that wasn't quite submission. It was as if he'd made a conscious decision not to fight.

Or it was a trick.

Weylin held the rifle steady. "I will shoot you if you resist," he said. "I'd rather bring you in alive."

Randall opened his mouth in a silent laugh and performed a bow over lowered forelegs.

"Don't waste your shenanigans on me," Weylin said. "I'm taking you back to Las Vegas, but I'm not bringing in a wolf. I don't think you want me to, either."

Dropping onto his haunches, Randall used teeth and paws to dislodge the rope from around his neck. Under Weylin's pointed gaze, he Changed. He shook himself, dark hair falling into his eyes. Weylin could have sworn he was smiling.

"Do you plan on bringing a naked man into Las Vegas?" Randall asked.

Weylin was sorely provoked to wipe that smile from the outlaw's face, preferably with his rifle butt. The thought of facing Randall down, wolf to wolf, was even more tempting. But he knew how to control his anger—and he had come too far in the name of law to abuse it now.

"It'd be what you deserve," he said.

Randall's eyes glinted in the moonlight. "You don't happen to have an extra pair of trousers?"

Weylin reached behind his saddle and unrolled the spare clothes he'd bought at the same time as the mare. He threw them within Randall's reach. "You can wear these."

Randall shook out the shirt and trousers, tugged them on, and gave Weylin an elegant half-bow.

"*Gracias,*" he said.

"Don't thank me," Weylin said. He kept the rifle trained on Randall and drew a pair of handcuffs from his saddlebags.

"Put these on," he said, tossing them to the outlaw.

Randall hesitated, then slowly fastened them over his wrists.

"I know damned well that you can break those," Weylin said. "But by the time you do, you'll be dead. Understand?"

"Perfectly."

"What have you done with Lady Rowena?"

"Ah, yes. That *was* the last time we met." He held his bound hands up in front of him. "I believe your final words were of tracking me down, come hell or high water. How does it feel to know you've won?"

Weylin stared at him. This was all too easy. Why had Randall made such a token resistance when so much was at stake?

It didn't matter. He *had* won. After all this time—after the humiliation of Rowena's capture, Cole's incessant contempt, and near-death at Sim Kavanagh's hands, he'd succeeded in his quest. And he'd done it his way.

Victory should be sweet. This was more than a personal triumph; it was for Kenneth and Father. It'd make Cole eat his words about Weylin's shortcomings; one man had succeeded where all Cole's hired *pistoleros* failed.

But Weylin felt little satisfaction at seeing Randall prisoner. He'd relearned what it was to run as a wolf; he could guess what it would be like to die in chains and captivity. For a man like Randall, death would be preferable. All El Lobo had to do was make a rush at him, and he'd have his quick death.

He hardened his heart. "I asked you about my brother's fiancée."

Randall's shoulders dropped. "She is well," he said, without a trace of mockery.

"Where is she?"

"Free to seek her own destiny."

"Give me a straight answer, you bastard."

"Or you'll shoot me?"

"No. That's just what you want me to do, so you won't have to choke your life out at the end of a rope."

"A pleasant thought," Randall said. "If it will set your

mind at ease, the lady is very near a town where she will find any assistance she requires. I have let her go."

He wasn't lying. Weylin felt truth as if it were something solid in the air between them. "Maybe that's the one decent thing you've done in your life."

"It may be. I assume you are delivering me to your brother?"

"It's the law you have to face, Randall. That'll be enough."

In the dim moonlight Randall's face betrayed the first hint of consternation. "Surely you wish to share your conquest with your kin, to personally complete your family's revenge."

It was as if Randall wanted to face Cole again, though he knew he'd get less mercy from him than from a judge and jury. There was only one reason he'd want to be taken to his worst enemy.

He thought he'd get a chance to bring Cole down before he died.

"We'll get our vengeance," Weylin said. "The law will see to that." He gestured with the rifle. "It's thirty miles to town, and you're going to be walking all the way."

"Naturally." Randall gazed across the plain. "We wouldn't want to keep the hangman waiting."

It was by far the grandest casa Felícita had ever seen, finer than any other in Las Vegas. It was also one of the few houses made of wood rather than adobe, two stories high and neatly painted white and blue.

The house belonged to Cole MacLean. It stood alone on its own square of land, just on the edge of town. No one, least of all Cole MacLean, had noticed her following him to the house and watching from a safe distance. She'd seen him go inside and had waited for many hours, trying to decide what to do. At last night had come, and she'd spent it in the shelter of a cluster of bushes, her horse tied up beside her.

Darkness was fading with the first light of dawn. She

brushed the dirt from her skirt, ignoring the rumble in her stomach, and fed the horse a bit of the grain she had in her saddlebags.

"I am sorry, my friend, that I couldn't remove your saddle," she told it softly. "I know nothing of horses. It would be better to let you go, so that you can find someone to properly care for you." *And I have delayed too long in what I must do.*

There was a big stable right here at the house. If a strange horse were to wander in among the others, the people here would take it in.

Cautiously she led the horse as close to the stable as she dared. She gave it a push on its broad rump; maybe it smelled other horses, for it pricked up its ears and started for the stable at a fast walk. Felícita waited until she saw the horse disappear into a stall. Then she looked for a way to get closer to the house.

As the sun rose, people arrived to begin various tasks. A boy groomed the horses, an old man weeded the garden of flowers by the door, and a girl—about her own age, Felícita guessed—was hanging clothes out to dry on a line in the back of the house. She was not much better dressed than Felícita, and might have come from the same village.

If such a girl worked for Cole MacLean, maybe she could pretend to be a servant as well. She brushed off her clothing once more and moved quietly to the back of the house, trying to pass the girl hanging clothes.

"*Eh, tu!*" the girl said in Spanish. "Who are you?"

Felícita bowed her head and tried to think. "I have come . . . I am here because—"

"Oh, you must be the new girl to work in the kitchen." The girl rubbed her nose with the back of her arm. "Sebastiana will be very glad to see you. She's in a temper."

Felícita smiled timidly. "I am not too late?"

"You will be if you don't hurry up!" She flapped her

skirt toward Felícita. "It's not so bad working here. Señor MacLean is only at the house a few times a year. He is now, so keep out of his way."

Felícita nodded and hurried to the *terraza* at the back of the house. At once she could smell cooking, and heard a querulous voice arguing with someone. She opened the door into a short hallway and followed her nose to the kitchen.

It matched the house in every way, with a huge iron stove, a great table and every sort of pot and pan imaginable. A stout woman, her arms coated with flour, turned from her work to stare at Felícita.

"Are you the new girl?" she said. "It's about time." She wiped her hands on her apron. "Don't just stand there. Come in, come in! I hope you are better than the last one, who ran off with a man just before dinner!" She looked Felícita up and down. "Is that all you have to wear? *No importa.* I will do the serving myself. *Rápido, rápido!* Señor MacLean has important guests for the noon meal. Cut up that chicken, and then . . ."

Felícita listened to the cook's instructions and did her best to follow them. She'd cooked enough for her uncle to understand what was required of her. She also knew how lucky she was, to find a place so quickly in MacLean's household. But that was only the beginning of her task.

She had to get closer to MacLean. If she remained in the kitchen, not even allowed to serve, she'd be just as far away from him as she'd been on the street.

"Ay, Dios!" the cook cried, throwing up her hands. "That fool María never even bought the eggs!" Her gaze flashed to Felícita, who was cutting up an onion. "You, girl—" She went to a shelf on the wall and brought down a basket, and a handful of coins from a jar. "Go at once to the store and buy a dozen eggs. And don't think you can run off with the money! Señor MacLean knows everything, and he'll find you and beat you." She pressed the coins and basket into Felícita's hands. "Well, what are you waiting for? Go!"

Felícita hurried out of the house and across the yard. She paused to glance in at the stable, where her horse was being brushed by the stableboy. He grinned at her and waved. Ducking her head, she set off for the general store she'd seen yesterday on the main street of Las Vegas.

She had to wait for a man buying a sack of flour to be finished before the storekeeper sold her the eggs. She cradled the basket carefully and was turning from the counter when she heard the first customer exclaim as he stood by the window.

"Will you look at that," he said. "Ain't that the woman who pulled a gun on Beck yesterday?"

Felícita nearly dropped the basket. She took a firmer grip on it and went to the door.

Lady Rowena, looking just as she had yesterday, rode down the center of the street. She glanced neither right nor left at the gawking spectators; her chin was high, and in spite of her ragged dress and her horse's heavy Spanish saddle she managed to ride like an elegant gentlewoman.

Tomás was not with her.

Felícita became aware of the emotions among the watching people: curiosity, excitement, anticipation. Everyone was expecting something to happen. Rowena's feelings were impossible to sense apart from all the rest. But if she had come back to town, alone . . .

A man stepped out into the street, and Felícita recognized him as the one called Deputy Vasquez. He blocked Rowena's way and spoke to her, shifting nervously from foot to foot. She answered in a soft, flat voice. After a moment the deputy took her horse's reins and began to lead her away.

Felícita knew where Vasquez was taking the lady. She ran back to MacLean's house as fast as she could without dropping the basket of eggs.

The kitchen was deserted when she reached it. She left the eggs on the counter and peeked through the door leading into another hall. No one was there. She slipped into the hall, followed it deeper into the house and around several corners, and found the room where Cole MacLean was talking with another man.

All she needed now was a place to hide.

Rowena had told herself she was prepared to face Cole again.

She'd reached the outskirts of Las Vegas by late morning, having covered the roughly thirty miles from Trujillo during the dark of night, alternately leading one horse and riding the other. She could not have said how she knew the way without benefit of maps or directions; she didn't bother to question. She found it best if she didn't think at all.

Her half-formed plan could not have proceeded more smoothly. Tomás had never returned when he'd left her just outside the village of Trujillo; he'd Changed and run away, and for all she knew he was still running. After his blustering talk about keeping her from Cole, he'd obviously changed his mind as well as his shape.

No . . . he'd come to his senses, and realized she was right. He conceded the logic in her argument by leaving her to make her own choice. In so doing, he gave up his precious revenge, all the complications she'd added to his heedless life . . .

And *her*.

She should be relieved. This was the way it had to be. She told herself that every mile of the ride: *How it has to be, how it has to be, how it has to be*, each word falling with the rhythm of the horses' hooves.

Too much to expect Tomás to bid her a decent farewell, or admit that he felt any personal regret in granting her the victory. Too much to expect anything, except that he honor her decision. He'd made the greatest sacrifice he was capable of, simply by relinquishing his vengeance.

That much she had done to change him, and it was remarkable enough. He was safe, now. And so was she. Tomás knew what she intended to tell Cole; he'd be worse than a fool to contradict her by failing to leave the area.

It only remained to find Cole, throw herself on his mercy, and convince him that the story she told was true.

"You are stronger than you know," Tomás had said. Now she'd prove him right.

She ignored the constant ache in her heart as she rode into Las Vegas. She heard the whispered exclamations and felt the stares as people recognized her from yesterday's violent scene. Instinctively she drew herself up, as if she were attired in a fashionable habit and riding sidesaddle like the lady she'd once been.

Her first test was when the deputy sheriff came out to meet her. She half expected him to arrest her. Instead, he answered her request by offering to take her to Cole.

She'd never been to the MacLean house in Las Vegas; had her life continued along its anticipated course, she likely never would have. It was modest by her previously high standards, though the locals doubtless thought it imposing.

But she found that her hands were shaking as a stableboy helped her dismount in the yard and the deputy took her arm with a murmur of apology. She wasn't fooled by his nervous solicitude. The poor man probably didn't know whether to treat her like a criminal, or as a stolen valuable being returned to its owner.

No matter what she felt from now on, she must remember to behave exactly like the latter.

The deputy took her through a side door into the house. Rowena caught glimpses of people who might have been servants, but none of them lingered to watch her humiliation.

Cole was standing by the window in a parlor decorated to a man's taste, filled with furnishings that must have been expensive to bring so far west. Rowena tore her thoughts away from such trivialities and forced herself to look at her fiancé.

There was no change in him. He was still impeccably dressed, dignified, charismatic. He was everything she'd so come to admire and respect in New York, the opposite of Tomás Alejandro Randall. Her heart felt encased in a layer of ice.

He turned to look at her, and she knew he had been warned that she was coming. His face had lost any sign of shock or gratitude or relief, and he merely stared at her as if he felt nothing.

As if he were testing her.

She closed her eyes and drew a shuddering breath. "Cole," she said. And then she let her legs buckle and sank to the carpet.

He was at her side even before the deputy. With casual strength he lifted her into his arms.

"Go for the doctor," he told Vasquez. "See to it that we're not disturbed until he comes. And send a servant with water and brandy."

The man left with alacrity. Rowena kept her eyes closed and leaned against Cole heavily. He took her to the settee near the window and eased her down, arranging the cushions to support her.

"Are you all right?" he asked. "Is there anything you require until the servant comes?"

"No. I am sorry. I'm . . . quite all right. Just a little tired." She didn't let go of his hand, though she felt a profound desire to push him away.

"My poor Rowena," he said, sitting beside her. "It's no wonder you feel ill after all you've been through. You have nothing to be frightened of now. You are safe."

She let out the breath she didn't know she'd been holding. "Yes. It was . . . quite terrible." She opened her eyes. His expression was still composed, neither anxious nor angry, only marked with the polite concern he might show any woman in her circumstances. Of course he'd never been maudlin;

that was one of the things she'd appreciated about him. Had she hoped he would throw open his arms and weep in joyous relief at her safe return? "I hardly know where to begin—how to explain—"

"Weylin told me everything," he said. "Randall fooled you into believing your brother needed your help, and you came west with him."

The words sounded like a condemnation. "He tricked me," she whispered. "I didn't know who he really was. I didn't realize he was your enemy—"

"Of course you didn't." He pulled his hand free of hers with utmost gentleness. "But I am surprised at your impulsive actions. You should have consulted me before even considering leaving New York."

"Yes. I know." She dropped her gaze. "It was entirely my fault—"

"It was also Weylin's fault. He let the outlaw take you."

"The outlaw held a gun on him. There was nothing he could do." She shivered. "Oh, Cole. It was dreadful, and all I could think of was how worried you must be, and the trouble I should cause you—"

"Yes." He rose and went to stand beside the window. "You must forgive me for failing to rescue you."

His voice was so remote. "I know you did all you could—" she began.

"Paying the ransom was out of the question." He glanced back at her. "He did not hurt you."

This was the difficult part. "Not . . . physically," she said. "But something else happened—it is painful to speak of it. . . ."

He looked at her. "You are perhaps referring to what occurred yesterday."

Her flush was not contrived. "Yes. You are aware . . . that those of animal nature can sometimes control others with their wills—"

"And that is what Randall did to you. You would have no defenses against such an attack."

"Yes." He was making it easy. "I attempted to escape at first, but he had his men watching me. And then—he began to control me." She clutched her temples. "He made me come into town yesterday. He wanted to taunt you with my presence, while all the while he . . . forced me to behave like a criminal. I tried to fight it, but . . . oh, Cole. What you must think of me."

It would have been the perfect time for him to come to her and embrace her in understanding and forgiveness. But he kept his distance. "Was there anything else he forced you to do?"

She started at his bluntness. Her flush deepened. If he could imagine what went through her mind at this moment . . .

"No," she said. "He did not. He . . . looked at me. That is all."

"I see. Then we have cause to be grateful."

Grateful—because her value had not been damaged in his eyes? She pushed the thought aside. First she must convince him to take her back to New York, and then—then she could deal with the things Tomás had told her.

"I am simply glad to be back," she said. "To be free of him and his band of cutthroats." She swallowed. "He did not succeed in his plans. You must wish to know all that happened—"

"There will be time for details later," he said. "You have not told me how you managed to escape his control."

His coolness went beyond emotional restraint and well-bred formality. Could he care so little if he thought, as he should, that she'd suffered? At the very least, he'd know she had experienced humiliation, discomfort, physical hardship, and loss of the dignity that was essential to her being.

"I escaped," she said carefully, "because he is dead."

His head jerked, and he lost his aloof demeanor. "Dead? Randall is dead?"

"Yes. The one who rode with him—Kavanagh—they quarreled. Kavanagh shot him. It released his control over me."

He continued to stare at her. "Kavanagh. Where is he?"

"I don't know. He rode off . . . I think he was wounded in the fight."

"Did he try to get you away from Randall?"

Best to stick close to the truth. "Yes. Two days ago, he got me out of the—the place where Randall hides." She gave Cole her most humble look of gratitude. "He told me you had hired him to save me. But Randall hunted him down and took me back. That was why he decided to come into Las Vegas, because we were so close."

Cole's jaw flexed. "Then Kavanagh did betray El Lobo," he said. "But why did he help Randall escape yesterday? Did he also fall under Randall's control?"

"I don't know. I was . . . not in my right mind. I only know that they fought last night, and Randall was killed." She had to fight to clear her mind of the image of Tomás lying dead. She covered her face with her hands. "So much violence—"

"Do you pity him?"

"Pity him? The man who kidnapped me?" She reminded herself not to show too much outrage. *Humility, Rowena.* "All I could think of was returning to you, and to New York. To leave this horrible place behind forever."

He smiled faintly. "I do so admire you, Rowena. Any other woman would be reduced to a puddle of jelly by now."

Was that it? She hadn't been fragile enough to suit him? "I did not think . . . that you would wish me to behave so," she said. She let hurt creep into her voice. "I thought you would be glad to see me safe."

"But I am, my dear. More than you can imagine." He knelt beside the couch and took her hand. "I'm sorry if I've seemed cold. I've been quite preoccupied by this trying situation. Now that I know he is dead, we can put this unfortunate incident behind us."

"Oh, yes. That is all I wish, Cole. Only that."

He squeezed her fingers. "Where is that servant? You must have the best of care from now on."

"Thank you. I shan't disappoint you again."

"No." His gaze held hers. "What did you think of Randall?"

"Think of him? He was a barbarian, a savage." Once she would have spoken with complete conviction. "He was merely a beast in human shape."

"You knew he was a werewolf."

"He . . . flaunted it. Cole, must we talk about—"

"He took you to his lair."

"Yes. It was some sort of canyon in the desert far from here, but I was blindfolded."

"You weren't when Kavanagh took you out."

"No . . . but I recognized nothing."

"A pity. If you had, we could wipe out the nest of his followers once and for all."

Wipe out. He meant Nestor, and Enrique, and Pilar, and Mateo. As if they were insects to be crushed underfoot. Her fingers stiffened in his hold.

"They have lost their leader," she said. "How much harm can they do now? All I wish to do is forget about them." She let her eyes become moist. "Take me home, Cole. Back to New York."

"Of course," he said, but his gaze remained intent. "What did he tell you about me?"

"Randall? I don't—"

"Surely he spoke of me in most unflattering terms. He had no reason to be discreet. He must have told you why he hated me, and why I hated him."

She hesitated. This was a way to hear his side of it, but there could be just as much risk in revelation.

"He boasted," she said. "I didn't listen. Why should I? He was a thief and a liar."

He cupped her cheek in his palm. "Did he tell you that I killed his father?"

She allowed her shock to show. "I presumed it was only another lie—"

"It's no lie." His expression hardened. "Fergus Randall, his father, shot my brother Kenneth in the back during the battle of Glorieta Pass. We are MacLeans; we couldn't allow my brother's life to go unavenged."

He admitted it freely, as if he were proud of such a barbarous philosophy. This was not the Cole she'd known. How much else of Tomás's story was true? "Randall . . . mentioned a feud—"

"It was over years before the War. Fergus Randall started it again when he killed my brother."

"Kenneth? You've never spoken of him—"

"Kenneth was my father's eldest son. He was nothing like my father—he didn't have the ambition or the strength. But he knew how to do just what Frank wanted." Bitterness edged Cole's voice. "He was the favorite, the perfect one, the brave hero. Father chose him to inherit everything he'd built in Texas." He looked away. "All my father's dreams lay with him. When he was murdered, my father went crazy with grief. He swore vengeance even before the War was over. I went with him to find Randall. But he underestimated Randall's cunning. Instead of accepting a fair fight, Randall tricked us into an ambush. He was the one who did this." He touched the empty sleeve of his right shoulder. "I saved my father."

Rowena stared at his old injury. She'd believed—he'd led everyone in New York to believe—that he'd lost it in the War, fighting honorably. She thought back to the words of the *corrido*. It had said that Fergus killed Kenneth MacLean in battle, after asking the MacLeans to leave the Territory. It said that the MacLeans had ambushed and killed Fergus in Mexico.

"Did Randall tell you that we killed his mother as well, and stole his land?" Cole asked. "The weak will always twist the facts to justify their cowardice and treachery. The Randalls were all thieves and killers. We recovered the cattle they had stolen from us. Fergus's wife abandoned the land and disappeared. She probably returned to her own savage kind."

He must mean the Apache. Was it possible that Tomás and the *corrido* were wrong about his mother's death? Perhaps, in his grief, he'd mistaken the wolf pelt he'd seen for his mother's.

Tomás might be a thief, but he was far from stupid. He believed in the reasons for what he did.

Someone was lying.

"After that," Cole said, "Randall hunted down my father—an old, sick man by then—and murdered him. It was butchery. He got away and declared war on my family. His whole ambition has been to destroy everything we have done for this Territory." He turned Rowena's face toward his. "But if he's dead—" His fingers tightened just enough to pinch her skin. "He is dead, isn't he, my dear? You're quite sure of that?"

She held very still. "Yes, Cole."

He dropped his hand. "Of course. How absurd to think that you might lie to me."

"No more," she said softly, "than you would ever lie to me."

"Do I hear doubt in your voice?" Cole asked. He gathered up a lock of her hair. "Have I ever misled you, Rowena?"

"No."

"But I sense that you are somehow dissatisfied with what I've told you." He fanned her hair between his fingers. "We are to be married, my dear. It's time to do away with any final secrets between us, don't you agree?"

"Then . . . the wedding will go on as planned?"

"Is there some reason it shouldn't?"

"Not at all. But a slight delay, a few months perhaps . . . I shall be able to think so much better in New York—"

"You puzzle me. I'd think you'd be more eager than ever for our union. Has my past distressed you, that fact that I killed a man?"

"I . . . understand your reasons."

"Now you *are* lying," he said. "You think that a truly civilized man could not do such a thing and remain unsullied. Yet humans behave so all the time. Why should we be different?"

"We?"

He sighed. "I've coddled you too long, Rowena. You can't be a fit mate unless you understand my purpose." He coiled her hair around and around his fingers. "I have always told you that I reject the animal nature in myself, just as you do. I quite agree that to become a filthy beast and run on all fours is a grotesque debasement of what we are. What we are is so much greater."

Sickness rose in her throat. "I don't understand."

"I think you do." His gaze grew distant. "When I was young, my father showed us that our kind has certain powers—the very powers Randall used on you, my dear. He believed that it was foolish to deny them. He believed in the fundamental right of the strong to rule the weak." He laughed softly. "Ah, yes, he taught us well. And I learned. Even the most powerful humans proved to be weak compared to him. He made his empire by controlling or removing anyone who stood in his way." Cole kissed the tips of her hair. "My father was a great man, but even he made mistakes. His ambitions were too limited and his methods crude, at best. When I went east to be educated, I saw how much more of the world there was than Texas and New Mexico Territory. I knew that New York was the true center of influence, a fitting seat for our kind. And so it has proved to be."

Sim Kavanagh's warnings, dismissed as falsehoods, filled

Rowena's mind: *"From the time the MacLeans came to New Mexico, they used their power to trample anyone weaker and less ruthless than they were. Frank MacLean wasn't human, and he didn't see humans as threats."*

Cole was saying that he agreed with his father, that he followed Frank MacLean's ways—and deliberately employed his werewolf abilities to rise to wealth and preeminence by any means. *Loup-garou* senses alone provided a huge advantage over ordinary men. When you added the deliberate misuse of a werewolf's mental influence . . .

"You seem shocked, my dear," he said. "I did not wish to deceive you, but it did seem a sensitive topic at the time. You were too adamant about forgetting one entire half of your nature."

"Then—you never did intend to live as fully human," she whispered. "Even if you didn't Change—"

"I've done only what it is my right to do. My duty, as one who is of a superior breed. It is the very nature of evolution that the weak perish while the strong survive. Your brother understood that, did he not? He would tell you that it is really quite simple for those like us to make even the most eminent and influential men and women believe that we are whatever they wish to see. Simple to gain their confidence and learn secrets they'd never share with one another. Manipulate, intimidate—separate lies from truth, sweep aside the obstacles and take all we have coming."

Rowena listened with numb understanding. She'd always assumed that Cole's great successes had come from his natural wit, intelligence and commanding personality. He had been utterly convincing in his desire to live, like her, as human: honest, upright, charitable toward the weak and destitute. She had seen what she wanted to see, believed in an ideal because it seemed to offer her a way to have the life she wanted without fearing exposure of her werewolf heritage.

It was not merely the rich and powerful old families

whom Cole had deceived into supporting his rise to the top of New York society. Rowena herself had broken down the last barriers to final acceptance of the charming *arriviste* by allowing him to escort her, by accepting his proposal of marriage. He'd gained the perfect platform from which to play puppet-master to unsuspecting humans.

In a single conversation he had removed the blinders from her eyes and revealed himself to be exactly what Tomás and Kavanagh had warned her he was. Ethics would not trouble this Cole MacLean. He could ruin his rivals and steal whatever he chose. It would even amuse him to topple those who aspired to the greatness he thought only he deserved.

There was no limit to what he might achieve—in business, politics, the highest echelons of power in the United States. And beyond . . .

"We both take what we want, and we don't give a damn about anyone else," Kavanagh had told her. *"He makes people like you believe he's a fine, upstanding gentleman while he steals everything they have."*

And he'd said something else, of Frank MacLean: *"Only the Randalls had the power to stand up to him, because they were* hombres-lobo. *He had to get rid of them. The feud and the War gave him a reason."*

That was just as true of Frank MacLean's son. But she didn't dare reveal the depths of her horror and disgust.

"You knew how I felt about the werewolf blood from the beginning," she said, striving to speak calmly. "You knew why I left England. Was it all deception from the moment we met?"

"It breaks my heart that you should ask such a question," he said. "Haven't I told you that I love you?"

She looked into his eyes, searching for even a sliver of truth. "Do you, Cole?"

"I've wanted you since the moment I saw you. You were meant to be mine. I knew you would be the perfect ornament to my career." He laid his hand on top of her head. "Your family has great influence, my dear, in your own country. And wealth—your own and your brother's. You have beauty, grace, natural presence, and rank to add luster to my reputation. All this is why I will still take you, though you have been lying to me since the minute you entered this room."

nineteen

Cole took great pleasure in watching Rowena try to cover her dismay. He focused on that dark satisfaction rather than the rage that tore at his body—and the stink of Tomás Randall on her clothing and in her hair.

Anger could be controlled. The real punishment could also wait. For now it was enough to let Rowena begin to understand what her fate would be.

"Oh, yes," he said. "I know. I know that you betrayed me of your own free will, not by Randall's. And I know you lay with him like a bitch in heat." He tilted her head back, baring her throat. "You're a hopeless liar, my dear. No talent for it at all. I wanted to see how far you'd go to deceive me—and protect him."

He waited for her to refute his accusation, the feigned outrage that surely must come. He was surprised when she simply gazed at him, her skin very white, especially along the exposed curve of her throat. Rapid breaths flared her delicate nostrils.

"I confess I am more than a trifle shocked that you, of all women, should discard your honor and succumb to your most primitive instincts," he said. "It's fortunate that I discovered what you are now, instead of later. There will be no more pretenses between us. I will call you what you truly are, and you'll answer to me as your master." He bent to kiss the pulse in her neck. "You will do so because you wish to save your lover, who is very much alive."

She swallowed. It was all the confirmation he needed. He was briefly tempted to bite into that white flesh, but he'd spoken the truth when he said he'd discarded the outward bestiality of the werewolf blood. He'd not give way to it now.

"I see you do understand," he said.

"Understand what?" she whispered. "That you'll let Tomás go if I obey you?"

"How sweetly you speak his name. I wonder how long it took you to forget your vow to me." He ran his finger along her jaw. "No matter. I'm curious to know what he taught you of bed-sports, my little whore. I'll certainly test your knowledge as often as possible. It will be a pleasure to drive the memory of him out of your body."

It was a measure of her corruption that she didn't even shudder. "You can have everything," she said. "My body, my wealth, my position, everything. Only let us return to New York, and forget about Tomás—"

"Forget?" He released her hair with a jerk. "I don't forget. But I may bargain."

She remained very still, as if she feared any movement might cause him to attack. "What do you want?"

"All I can take. And you'll help me." He looked out the window and noted that Vasquez was keeping the curious townsfolk at bay. "Where is Randall?"

"I don't know. He left me before dawn—"

"Don't lie to me. He let you go. He was after revenge when he took you. Does he think he has it because he marked you with his seed?"

His crude words brought a hectic flush to her cheeks. So it

was still possible to shame her. He'd counted on that. Shame could be an exquisite form of torture.

"He wanted revenge," she said, her voice shaking. "He thought he had ruined me, and so he let me go."

Randall was capable of that, but Cole sensed the lie. Lies upon lies. "So he does not love you," he said, going along. "But you love him. You will always love him."

She turned her head as if to shake it and stopped. No sound emerged from her lips.

"Very well," he said. He poured himself a whiskey from the sideboard. "We will return to New York. I won't hunt Randall down and kill him. But there will be rules, Lady Slut. And the moment you break a single one, I'll have Tomás hanged."

She closed her eyes and opened them again. "Yes."

"When we are married, you will not speak his name. You will not think of him. It will be as if he never existed."

"Yes."

"You will make all your assets and inheritance available to me and never question my use of them. You'll be my perfect hostess and do everything within your power to smooth my investments and contacts here and abroad, even among your own family. You will not reveal anything of my life to anyone."

"Yes."

"You will strive to please me and obey my slightest wish. You will come to my bed when I ask, and do whatever I ask. 'No' will be a word forbidden to you. If it pleases me to have you serve me at table naked, you'll do it. If I choose to put a collar around that lovely throat—" He smiled at the image the thought presented. "A collar for my little bitch, gold, studded with diamonds. What do you think of that?"

She made a faint choking sound. "I will . . . obey you."

"So you say now. But when you're far from this place . . ." He left the window and stood behind her. "If you hadn't betrayed me, you would have done what I wanted in any case. But it would have been much more pleasant for you. I'd have treated you as a lady, Rowena. I thought you were worth preserving, like an expensive and fragile piece of art." He smiled. "I'm grateful now that you've shown me more interesting possibilities." He touched the fly of his trousers and stroked the growing hardness there. "I'd like to see what experience I'm buying in exchange for my mercy."

Still she did not break, though she was close. Power was his greatest aphrodisiac, and he couldn't remember the last time he'd been so aroused. He worked loose the buttons of his trousers. "You've had a taste of the outlaw life, Rowena. I'll give you a taste of your future. Get down on your knees."

She hesitated only an instant. There were no corsets to creak or heavy skirts to rustle as she slid from the settee to the floor. Her loose hair fell forward like a screen behind which she could hide. She did not look up as he moved to stand before her.

"I've always wondered if a lady could do this as well as a whore," he said. "I don't even have to choose between them. Look up, sweet harlot. Look up and open your mouth."

The door to the parlor banged as it rebounded against the wall. Cole jumped back, his hands splayed over his erection. Rowena scooted around on her knees.

A girl, not a gunman, stood in the doorway, a silver tray balanced on her hands. Her eyes were wide and stupid.

If Cole had been within reach of her, his blow would have sent her flying across the room. He buttoned his trousers and pulled Rowena to her feet as if she'd merely stumbled.

"I see the water and wine have finally arrived," he said. He glanced at the girl and realized she must be a new servant to replace one of the recent deserters. One looked exactly like the next. "You took your time. Put it down over there," he ordered.

She bobbed a very clumsy curtsey and mumbled something in Spanish. By the time she reached the sideboard she'd managed to spill water from the crystal pitcher and nearly toppled the wine bottle. Then she stood waiting, gaping at Rowena as if she'd never seen a woman not of her own kind.

"Get out," Cole snapped.

She fled. Cole strode after her to see that the door was shut and locked. But the moment was ruined. Rowena had had just enough time to recover herself, and she sat on the couch with her dignity restored, calm and indifferent.

But not for long. He took a handful of her hair, drew it out to its full length, and wound it around her throat like a noose.

"I'm sorry we were interrupted," he said, "but tonight we'll continue. If you please me, we'll leave for New York tomorrow. In the meantime, I suggest you think about the consequences of your lover's touch." He tugged on her hair. "You'd better pray that Randall didn't start a brat in your belly."

Tomás whistled. He did it not because it annoyed Weylin MacLean, but because music had always kept him from thinking too deeply. Now was not the time to think, when he could so easily spend every moment worrying about Rowena.

She was all right. She must be. It would have been simple for her to ride into Trujillo when he didn't return, and get help there. But if she'd held to her foolish notion to go to Cole . . .

It was doubly urgent that he get to MacLean as quickly as possible, by any means necessary.

Thinking about it wouldn't help until the right opportunity arose. So he whistled. He kept the beat to the rhythm of his footfalls across the plain to Las Vegas, wandering from one old folk song to another, while Weylin rode stolidly behind him.

"Did you whistle when you murdered my father?"

Tomás stopped. He turned to face his captor, meeting Weylin's expressionless gaze. Strange, how one brother could be so different from the other. Try as he might, he could not hate Weylin MacLean as he did Cole. There was a certain honesty in Weylin, a fundamental decency, that Cole had no part of. And Weylin hadn't been involved in his mother's and father's deaths.

Yet this was the man who had hunted him for years, while Cole remained in New York. He was a MacLean, loyal to his family, and thus an enemy. But Tomás had never considered killing him. Not even now.

He crouched on the dry earth in the manner of his Apache forefathers and dangled his manacled hands over his knees. "I did not rejoice in his death," he said softly.

Weylin dismounted and stood beside his horse's head, stroking its muzzle as if to steady himself as much as the animal. He didn't like to show his feelings, this one, but they betrayed him nonetheless.

"Like hell," Weylin said. "You enjoyed it, all right. You beat him to death."

Tomás bent his head as the sickness of memory returned. "All I knew was that he had killed my mother—"

"That's a lie."

"No lie." He looked up, letting Weylin see his open face. "I saw my mother's pelt on the saddle of one of your father's men, the very day after I returned to Los Valerosos to find the hacienda burning and went to find her. Did your brother never tell you how Frank MacLean came to destroy my family's holdings?"

"I know how your mother's people raided our property and stole our cattle, with the help of Comancheros and Indians. Her ranch was a den for outlaws and rustlers."

"My mother took that path in revenge for my father's death. Cole must have told you that story as well."

"I know you'd pervert the truth like any criminal, to make

it sound like Cole killed an innocent man when he fought your father."

"Because it is said that my father shot your eldest brother in the War without provocation or a soldier's honor? Because your father and Cole offered my father a fair fight when they came for revenge, and he used treachery instead, tearing off Cole's arm before he was killed? Yes, I have heard that story. Your brother made everyone in the Territory hear it." He closed his eyes, and the morning sun danced behind his lids. "You were not there—not in the War, not when they came for my father, not during the destruction of Los Valerosos. All you know is what Cole has told you—"

"My *father* told me about the battle at Glorieta."

"Did your father witness Kenneth's death, or was it Cole?" He sighed. "Of course it is not possible that Cole tells anything but the truth. He has always been the fine gentleman of your family, most respectable and worthy of admiration. The MacLeans are beyond reproach. All that has happened to you is the doing of my evil clan, acting without provocation. *No es así?*"

He thought he might at last have planted a doubt in Weylin's mind. The stern face relaxed into uncertainty, reflecting the thoughts behind it. Weylin might be the one MacLean capable of seeing beyond his own name.

Not that it made any difference. There was still only one way to keep Rowena safe from Cole MacLean.

He laughed, though his heart was clenched in a heavy fist. "We have a saying: *"El lobo pierde los dientes pero no las mientes.* A wolf loses his teeth but not his ways."

"You're right," Weylin said, mounting again.

Tomás got to his feet. "Still, you are an honorable man, Weylin MacLean. Honorable enough to promise protection to one who will need it when I'm gone."

"Who? One of your band of cutthroats?"

"The Lady Rowena."

Weylin sat very tall in the saddle. "She'll be safe enough when you're dead."

"Not from your brother." He held up his hands. "It is said that even those sentenced to die are allowed a final request. I ask but one thing: that no matter what happens, you will guard the lady from all harm. Do everything you can to see that she's free to decide her own fate, even if your brother tries to interfere."

"Why should you care what happens to her?"

"I came to . . . respect the lady. And to believe she deserves better than marriage to Cole. Not because of my own vendetta, but because of what she is and what he will do to her if he has the chance."

The expected angry reaction didn't come. Weylin's face had gone blank once more. "He has no reason to hurt her."

"I ask that you judge for yourself. Observe your brother and how he treats her. If what I believe is true, she will not wish to stay with him, and he will not let her go without making her suffer." He gazed up at Weylin, narrowing his eyes. "Or is it that you fear your brother too much? *Ay*, it's loco of me to think you could stand against him—"

"Cole doesn't control me," Weylin said. He tugged at the brim of his hat as if the sun had grown too bright. "I don't need an outlaw to tell me my duty. She'll have my protection as long as she needs it."

"Even from your brother?"

"If just one thing you say is true, damned if I won't see her back to New York myself."

Tomás let his hands fall and bowed his head. *"Muchas gracias."*

The horse snorted and pawed the ground. "Get moving," Weylin said. "I want to be in Las Vegas by—" His sudden silence caught Tomás's attention. A moment later the scent came to him as it had to Weylin—the smell of many men and horses. Cole's men, whom he'd confronted in town.

It took Cole's band a few minutes longer to spot Weylin and Tomás. Weylin pulled his rifle from its scabbard and held it loosely in his arms. Whatever he thought of his brother, he didn't trust Cole's hirelings with his prisoner. He watched intently as they approached in a ragged line, their overworked horses slick with sweat and flecked with foam. Cole was not among them.

"Well I'll be damned," Beck said, yanking his horse to a stop. "Here we been ridin' to hell and back lookin' for this son of a bitch, and who's got him but Cole's little brother." His tone was that of a man whose long-sought prize had been snatched right out of his fingers. He spat, a missile which Tomás dodged easily enough, and mopped at his face with his filthy bandana. "Won't the boss be surprised."

Weylin stared at Beck, his hand resting lightly on the rifle. "I'm taking the prisoner back to Las Vegas. To the sheriff."

"Well, well. That's mighty nice of you, to catch him for us 'n' all. Someday you'll have to tell me how you did it. But you don't have to worry about Randall no longer, Mr. MacLean. Me 'n' the boys'll just take care of your 'prisoner' from now on."

Weylin raised the rifle and held it ready. "You're not touching him, Beck."

Beck clucked his tongue. "That's a problem, Mr. MacLean. Cole told us to bring him back and not let anyone get in our way. I'd sure hate to get in a quarrel over this."

"Make one move, and I'll shoot you," Weylin said calmly.

He was so obviously in earnest that Beck hesitated, calculation moving behind his slitted eyes. Saddle leather creaked as his men shifted uneasily. *Pistoleros* and ruffians they might be, but they'd think twice before attacking Cole's brother. There was a good chance they'd back off.

That Tomás couldn't allow. He had to get to Cole. While the standoff continued, he feinted as if to attempt escape and affected a stumble that brought him almost under the hooves of Beck's horse. Beck wasn't stupid enough to let the opportunity pass. He kicked his mount in between Weylin and Tomás and signaled to his men, who enclosed Tomás in a cage of milling horseflesh. Someone put a gun to Tomás's temple.

Beck and the rest of them had every other weapon trained on Weylin. "Never heard El Lobo was loco," Beck said, grinning at his own rhyme, "but I guess he took himself right out of your hands, Mr. MacLean. I think you'd better just throw your rifle down."

Weylin lowered his rifle, uncocked it, and bent over the saddle to let it fall. Under Beck's prodding he unbuckled his gun belt and dropped it as well. He looked grimly at Tomás through the screen of horses and riders.

"I'm sorry," he said, so low that only Tomás's werewolf hearing might make out his words. "You made too many mistakes, Randall. Maybe you could have proved some of the things you told me. The law would have given you that chance—"

Tomás shook his head. "No, caballero. But thank you for your honor. In a place better than this one, we might have been friends. Remember your promise." He saluted. *"Adiós."* He glanced up at Beck. "Shall we proceed, gentlemen?"

The gunman lost his grin. "Hatch, your horse is freshest. Ride ahead to Vegas and tell the boss that we have Randall—" he produced a length of rope and tested its sturdiness between his hands"—and that we'll meet him at the old hangin' tree out by Sonrosado Creek."

Felícita remained in the hall to watch and wait long after Cole ordered her out of the room where he held the Lady Rowena. She returned briefly to the kitchen to make sure that the cook had not come back, and that the deputy, who had discovered her in the hallway and sent her to fetch the water and wine, was still safely outside the house. He and

Cole had both taken her for a servant, faceless and unimportant. They had made it possible for her to interrupt what Cole was doing. What he was *feeling* when he had Rowena in his hands.

She leaned against the door, as much for support as to listen through the heavy wood. For the last hour there had been a kind of aching stillness from the lady in the room, ever since Cole MacLean had locked her inside and gone up the stairs alone. Felícita felt her spirit, beaten down and despairing but not yet defeated.

It was a miracle that the lady could bear the things Cole had said and done. Felícita knew why she had let herself be treated so, and what had given her the strength.

Love. Her love for Tomás. Love stood like a shield between her and the vicious cruelty that hung about Cole MacLean like choking fog.

But the lady didn't understand that she could not bargain with the devil. Felícita did. She had looked straight into the heart of Cole MacLean.

She trembled in sheer amazement that she had gone into that room and come out still able to remember her own name. There had been times, even before her intrusion, when she'd been certain the roaring maelstrom of Cole MacLean's desires would plunge her into madness.

Like Sim, he sucked her into the dark chasm of his being. But with Sim she could stop herself from falling too deep. Cole MacLean was far beyond anything or anyone she'd ever known. He howled where the rest of the world whispered. If she had dared to touch him, she could have heard his thoughts as if they were shouts.

Hearing his words was bad enough. Feeling him take pleasure in causing pain and humiliation was at the limit of what she could endure.

And she must keep enduring it, for Rowena's sake. Cole was the key. He was the one who had to be . . . she hissed between her teeth, caught by a frightening image. *Sí.* He had to be exposed, like a poisonous scorpion scuttling under a rock by day and afraid of the sun. Cole appeared to the world as a bird of brilliant plumage, hiding the scorpion's sting beneath the beautiful feathers.

If he were stripped of those feathers, he would lose his power—over the lady, Tomás, everyone. Felícita felt now as she had the day Rowena and Tomás saved her, as she did with Sim Kavanagh: Her destiny was bound up together with Cole's as it was to the others'. She must stop him. But she did not know how.

Footsteps sounded on the staircase at the end of the hall. Felícita darted around the nearest corner just as Cole descended the last step. He drew Felícita after him with the force of his hungers, down the hall and to the large double doors that faced the street. She shrank behind them as he stepped outside.

A man was dismounting in front of the house—one of Cole's hombres, whom she had seen yesterday—surrounded by a flock of people that included the deputy. Vasquez listened to the man's rapid speech, pointed to Cole, and disappeared into the crowd. The man ran up the walkway.

"Mr. MacLean!" he said between heavy breaths. "We found Randall!"

Searing triumph flooded through Felícita's mind as if it were her own: hot, lustful, hating. She couldn't hear the words Cole spoke aloud; they were lost in the fractured images and emotions that replaced her own thoughts.

She *was* Cole. She breathed through his lungs and saw through his eyes; she was a giant looking down upon a whole world of scurrying ants. Enough of herself remained to feel the terror of thinking as he thought, seeing every other person as a means to an end or an annoyance to be discarded. And she saw farther . . . into a past not hers, a string of deceptions covering death and treachery. Now that past could never be discovered. The last dangerous link would be choked to death at the end of a rope.

She looked forward to seeing Randall die.

Felícita screamed without sound. Cole was tearing her apart, scattering the fragile pieces of self that she had hoarded since Tío's death. She beat her head against the wall, once, twice, three times, until the pain jarred loose Cole's grip on her mind.

She collapsed to the floor, listening to his footsteps going away from the house. He did not even know what she had done. He did not know she could get inside his thoughts. For him, she was less than the ants in his vision. She did not exist.

It is the things we do not see that can destroy us.

She crossed her arms over her stomach and heaved until nothing more would come out. After a while she heard the sounds of horses, and then quiet. Quiet in the house, in her mind. She wanted to live in that quiet forever.

There was only one way to do so. As long as she remained among people whose wills and spirits were so irresistible, what had happened with Cole could happen again. A doorway had opened within her—not the small window she could make into people's souls, but a portal that stood at the very center of her mind. Rowena and Tomás had begun shaping it, and Sim Kavanagh had built the framework that made it solid and real. Cole had burst through with his deadly power, and now she did not know how to bar it against further attack.

Until she learned, it wouldn't stop. Other, stronger minds could suck her in; one by one they would take little pieces of her with them when they departed, and leave the twisted fragments of themselves behind. Even now she could feel Cole's touch like something rotten crouched on the inside of her head. She would end a gibbering *loca*.

A rebounding crash shook the walls of the house. Felícita flinched and curled into a ball on the floor. She knew where the noise came from.

Rowena was trying to escape.

"I do not want this," Felícita whispered. "It is too much. I cannot bear it. Please, take it away."

The banging came again, less vigorously, and then silence returned. But Felícita knew what Rowena was feeling. She sensed that Tomás was in danger. There was a bond between her and El Lobo, a bridge between their hearts. Her fear of defying Cole and losing her last chance to save Tomás was driving her to her own kind of madness.

Felícita pushed herself to her feet. In one direction was the door that would lead to places far from here, and rest, and a chance to learn how to shut the world out. In the other . . .

In the other was the embracing of all she had become. Accepting this ability she had never wanted. Learning to control the portal, and to touch other spirits without fear.

Living without fear. Was such a thing possible? She had been forced unwilling into the world and found herself unprepared for the chaos of human minds. What Tío called a gift had become a curse.

It could be a gift again. All at once she saw how one with courage could turn it into a thing of wonder and hope. Such a one could feel the pain of others' souls and find a way to do more than merely endure. If she could learn to speak *to* their hearts, not only listen . . .

Was it possible not only to share pain, but heal it . . . even that of Sim Kavanagh, or Cole MacLean?

Slowly she turned back down the hall. Lady Rowena was no longer pounding on the doors of her prison. Felícita tried the doorknob, and then went up the stairs the way Cole had gone. She found a key lying on a big wooden chest in one of the rooms. She returned to the downstairs room and fit it in the lock.

The door opened. Rowena sat on the floor, her head between her knees. She looked up, hollow-eyed with desperation. Hope spilled into her soul like sweet water.

"Esperanza," she said hoarsely. "It *is* you. Thank God. When you come in with the tray, I thought I was dreaming." She struggled to her feet and touched Felícita's cheek with a shaking hand. "Kavanagh told me he'd let you go, but I never thought to see you here. You seem to be all right—"

"I am all right," Felícita said.

Rowena's eyes lit. "You *can* speak! Oh, my dear . . ." The brief joy left her, and she stared past Felícita's shoulder at the open door. "There is no time. Cole—the man who was with me—where is he?"

"He is gone."

"Gone?" She plunged toward the doorway. "Something has happened to Tomás. I can feel it—"

Felícita caught her arm. She closed her eyes, and imagined the portal in her mind opening wide—easily, freely, sending forth a part of herself to speak to Rowena's heart. *I am here, lady.*

Rowena flinched. "What?"

The test had worked. She *could* make herself be heard in feelings as well as words.

Now, if the lady could only understand.

Do not be afraid. Listen. . . . Felícita recalled what she'd learned from Cole's mind and offered it to the lady, images and thoughts riding on an illusory beam of light stretched between two minds. Rowena covered her mouth with her hand as if she were about to be ill. She half fell against the door and stared at Felícita with unseeing eyes.

"I . . . hear," she whispered. "I hear you. Cole's men have caught Tomás." Her hands fisted against the wood. "He swore to me—if I obeyed him—" She took a deliberate breath. "You know where they've taken him. Yes, I see it. A tree. A place outside of town."

Felícita slumped and let the portal close. The lady would take the lead now. All she need do was follow—until they found Cole MacLean.

"I know how to find them," Rowena said, and the pale golden wolf sprang to life in her eyes.

twenty

The hanging tree was blasted and bare, an enormous ghost of a cottonwood destroyed by drought and the changing path of the creek that had once fed its roots and broad trunk and many branches. Now a single heavy limb projected above a dry wash, creating a perfect beam for a rope.

Tomás admired the irony of it from his position a few feet away. He'd once rescued an innocent man from this very tree, but it seemed unlikely that anyone would do the same for him. The law could be bought in Las Vegas, especially since the sheriff was still doing business elsewhere in the county. Judge Lynch was most amenable to men like Cole MacLean. His jury was currently made up of hired guns who probably ought to be swinging themselves; Weylin wasn't likely to get a vote. No appeal was possible.

Tomás didn't expect one. He had only two concerns: that Cole should come within his reach before he died, and that Rowena did not suffer too much at Cole's hands before the deed was done.

Cole didn't make Tomás wait too long. He rode up with the messenger sent to find him, dressed as always in an eastern dandy's expensive suit but sitting his horse like the Texan he'd been raised.

He dismounted and swept the gathering with his gaze, pausing only an instant to note Tomás before moving on. "I see you finally did what I hired you to do, Beck," he said. "You and your men will be rewarded appropriately." Beck's smug smile thinned.

"Weylin," he said, acknowledging his brother at last. "I'm surprised to see you among us. I thought that perhaps you'd vanished from the face of the earth. Did you come to witness the carrying out of long-delayed justice?"

"This isn't justice, Cole," Weylin said. He stepped out from among the others, holding the pistol Cole's men had returned to him. "I was taking him to the jail, to stand trial—"

"*You* were taking him back?"

"It's true," Tomás said. The men around him drifted to the sides, leaving a clear path between him and Cole. "Your brother caught me, MacLean. Your men had nothing to do with it."

Cole's attention locked on Tomás, dismissing Weylin. "El Lobo. I've waited a many years to meet you again, face to face. When was the last time? Oh, yes—just after you murdered my father."

"*Sí.* You left me with a few mementos of that meeting. And you MacLeans took some from my family as well. Do you still have my mother's fur coat?"

"I never met your mother. I heard she was half savage. I know what your father was."

"You'd have good cause to remember him. Do any of your high-society friends in New York ask how you lost the arm?"

Cole's lips lifted away from his teeth. The expression was shocking in a face so sophisticated and carefully controlled. "It might be interesting to see how you would enjoy losing yours—before the hanging," he said.

Tomás laughed. "Would you take it yourself, MacLean? I'll be happy to give you the opportunity."

He thought he might have provoked Cole just enough to bring him within reach, but Cole was too practiced at subduing his impulses. His single hand twitched into a fist and opened slowly. "So you can die fighting? Oh, no, Randall. I know that's what you want. I'd planned something much more leisurely. And while my men are preparing your much-deserved trip to hell"—he signaled to Beck, who brandished the rope with its ready-made noose—"you might contemplate your final failure. The Lady Rowena has returned to me."

Tomás shrugged. "I knew she'd escaped."

"And you were no doubt pursuing her when Weylin caught you."

"Pursuing her? She wasn't worth the effort. Nothing but trouble, your fine lady. So bony and *vanidosa,* like ice; I don't know a man who'd touch her. Except you."

"So you didn't take advantage of her?"

"I, El Lobo? Women give themselves to me willingly." He cocked his head. "Tell me . . . does the loss of a man's arm weaken his other members as well? Perhaps that is why you chose such a cold one to share your bed—she'll not expect anything from you."

Cole took a step forward. So did Weylin. Tomás made himself ready. There would be but one chance, and he would die right after Cole, perhaps even by Weylin's hand.

Death would come as a friend. He'd prided himself on his love of life, but it was a false love. El Lobo was by his very nature unfaithful.

When he was dead, the feud would be over. He would leave no children to avenge him into another generation. Even the people of the cañon, the *niños* most of all, would be better off without him and the dangerous life he made for

them. The memory of his parents' deaths, of the murder he
had committed, the meaninglessness of his existence—all
would be so much ash carried on the wind.

And Rowena would be free to find a mate worthy of her.

He grinned and beckoned with his bound hands. "Come,
Cole MacLean. Where is the vengeance in watching from a
distance? Why not put the rope around my neck yourself?
But no—it was never you who chased me across the Territory when I stole your cattle and your woman. Perhaps you
were afraid. Perhaps you are still afraid."

Cole lunged at Tomás. His men grabbed Tomás by the
arms and shoulders and pushed him to the horse that waited
under the dangling noose.

"It's too bad you won't be able to give your farewells to
Lady Rowena personally," Cole said. "I'll pass them on for
you." He nodded to Beck, who shoved the muzzle of his gun
into Tomás's belly.

"Mount," he ordered.

Tomás glanced down at the gun in feigned bemusement,
rapidly calculating his next move. A belly shot wouldn't kill
him instantly. A few seconds was all he needed.

The gun jabbed harder into the muscles of his stomach.
His body tensed. At first he thought the fierce drumming in
the soles of his feet was his own heartbeat, but then he heard
the unmistakable sound that accompanied it: hoofbeats, drawing rapidly nearer. Cole turned his head sharply. The other
men noticed just as the two horses burst in among them.

Their riders might have been Amazons, or the Valkyrie of
old-world legends. Rowena sat astride, hair whipping loose
behind her, hand raised as if it held an invisible spear. Esperanza rode at her side.

"Stop!" Rowena cried. She all but leaped from her horse's
back. "Cole, what are you doing?"

Cole seemed transfixed, caught maskless by her sudden

appearance. She strode toward him, taking in the scene with one keen glance.

"So this is how you keep your bargains," she said furiously. "You promised to let him go, if I obeyed you. But you intended to kill him all along." Her gaze sought Tomás. "I thought you'd have the sense to go away," she said, her anger unabated. "You knew it was impossible. It was always impossible."

"Rowena," Tomás whispered.

"Is that the best you can do, my dear?" Cole said, regaining his composure. "Where are the ardent declarations of love and self-sacrifice?" He stepped away from Rowena and took the gun from Beck's hand. "Isn't it touching, Randall? She was so devoted to you that she would have been my willing slave simply to extend your paltry existence. I thought there was something of value in what you'd left of her, but I see that I was wrong. Look at her!" He flung out his arm in a gesture of disgust. "Behold the Lady Rowena Forster!"

It was clear what he saw in her: a sullied creature bereft of beauty or honor or dignity, a fallen woman, a virago, the object of any proper male's contempt . . . the very things she had most feared becoming. Yet she didn't shrink beneath his scorn. She raised her head higher, dirty and clothed in near-rags as she was, and held her ground. Tomás wanted to shout with pride. Or weep.

"You've ruined her for anything but life as a beast among beasts," Cole said. He smiled at Rowena with coaxing charm. "No words of courage for your lover? Perhaps you'll beg on your knees as you did before. I might agree to make his death quick and relatively painless."

Rowena stared at him. Something remarkable was happening, something beyond the comprehension of the humans who watched. Tomás understood. What passed between Cole and Rowena was the silent challenge of wolf to wolf, a struggle on levels of instinct that had remained unchanged for millennia.

Tomás's imagination tormented him with thoughts of what had happened in the hours since Rowena had gone back to Cole. She'd returned to MacLean to save *him,* but she'd made an error. She'd revealed too much of her relationship with Cole's enemy.

How Cole must have made her suffer. *"She would have been my willing slave,"* he'd said. Had he proposed the bargain, humiliation and perpetual servitude in exchange for her lover's life?

Rowena had accepted. It was an action Tomás had utterly failed to predict, and he hated himself for that failure and the irremediable flaws in his nature.

And now, after fighting so long to remain human, she loosed the wolf for his sake. She had finally accepted the source of limitless strength hidden beneath that veneer of aristocratic hauteur and disciplined propriety—and for what?

He had brought her to this moment, he alone. But there was one consolation: Cole wouldn't master her again. She'd thrown off the last of her shackles. Her courage and strength made Tomás burn with humility and gratitude and love.

Love.

This was love. He loved her. How strange: He'd thought to teach her the ways of passion and enjoy her body while seizing his revenge, or at least that was what he'd believed. Now he saw how much he'd deceived himself. Stealing Rowena from Cole was an open challenge to death itself, his last grand adventure. He'd meant to give nothing to Rowena but pleasure, take nothing from her but the same, until Cole and his minions brought about the inevitable end.

Rowena had turned the tables on him completely. He had nothing to teach her. All the lessons were his to learn. His control of her had always been illusion. His whole life was illusion except for this one thing.

This love.

It told him that what he did was right. As he watched Rowena stare Cole down like the magnificent lady she was, he knew that she would not simply survive but flourish when he and Cole were gone.

The time had come. He pulled his handcuffs apart and moved with uncanny speed, thrusting Cole's men aside like so many brittle cornstalks. Cole had no chance to turn. Tomás grabbed him around the neck in a grip that would snap his spine with only the slightest shift of his weight.

Cole froze. The gun fell from his hand. His men moved as if to intervene and stopped suddenly, falling silent. Seconds moved like hours. And in those seconds Tomás had a clear opportunity to act, to kill, to twist Cole's neck with a brutal sideways tug and break his spine beyond any hope of healing.

He did not. He could not. Death mocked him with his failure. He felt himself being torn in two by warring impulses: oblivion and life. Peace and suffering. Hate . . . and love.

As if in a dream, Esperanza appeared at Rowena's shoulder. Something passed between the two women, a sharing that excluded the men with their guns and violence. An expression of wonderment transfixed Rowena's face. Esperanza nodded gravely and looked into Tomás's eyes.

She was no longer the fearful, mute child he'd known, clinging tenaciously to Rowena's side. Her face was veiled in an aura of remote benevolence that made her seem as ancient as a crone. She gazed at Tomás with more than ordinary vision. He felt her spirit brush his own, warm and full of compassion and sorrow . . . and a profound surrender.

Hear me, Tomás Alejandro Randall, she said. No words were spoken, yet he heard them. *I know your pain and your guilt. I know how you seek death.*

He tried to hide his amazement and shock behind laughter, but his heart was too heavy to let him draw a deep enough breath. "You shouldn't be a part of this, señorita," he said hoarsely. "Rowena, take her away. I beg you. Go from this place—"

"No," Rowena said quietly. "I won't leave you."

"You think you are guilty of murder," Esperanza said aloud, "and now you would end your own life by taking another."

Abruptly Weylin pushed out from among Cole's men, his gun ready in his hand. "He is guilty," he said. "He killed my father." He took aim at Tomás's head. "Let my brother go."

Esperanza looked at Weylin. "You seek truth, Weylin MacLean. Was it not you who would bring him to justice, where all truth will be revealed? Or are you yourself afraid to face it?"

Weylin blinked. Esperanza did not know him. They had never met. And yet . . .

And yet she walked freely in Tomás's mind. Why not Weylin MacLean's?

He lowered his revolver. "Who are you?" he demanded.

"Nobody," she said. "Nothing." She turned back to Tomás. "It is time for truth, Tomás Alejandro Randall. You cannot run away any longer. You must choose. Life, or death."

Cole trembled with rage in Tomás's grip. "Kill him, Weylin!"

Weylin didn't move. No one so much as twitched. Tomás closed his eyes, and released the black knot of despair he had denied for so many years.

"Weylin brought me here to meet justice," he said. "There is no need for a trial." He gazed at Rowena, as if they were alone. "Once you asked me how many men I had killed. There was only one. I killed Frank MacLean, just as the *corridos* say. I saw my mother's pelt among his men after they raided our hacienda, and I gave way to my hatred. I was strong and young, and he was an old man. He could not match me." He swallowed. "Near the end, my hatred died, and I left him, believing he might live. But when I returned to find him, I saw what I had done."

"You beat him to death," Cole said. "There was nothing left—"

"And who killed your mother?" Weylin said, his voice without emotion. "Do you have proof that it was my father?"

Tomás turned his head to meet Weylin's gaze. "I know that your father led those who raided Los Valerosos, and my mother tried to defend her land and people. She died fighting them." He looked once again to Rowena. All this was for her, to make her understand. "I was in the East, at school, when my mother began raiding the MacLeans with her Comanchero allies. She had learned how my father was killed by the MacLeans, and swore vengeance by stealing all she could from their holdings in New Mexico. She never told me. But she didn't realize that I knew about the ancient feud, and that my father had admitted to killing Kenneth MacLean in the War. He said . . . he had no choice."

"He shot Kenneth in the back," Cole snarled.

"He told me that he had come west to leave the old feud behind, but when he and the MacLeans met on opposite sides of the War, he thought it would start all over again. My father took Kenneth and Cole MacLean prisoner. They attempted escape. My father found Cole gone and Kenneth standing over the bodies of their guards. He . . . shot Kenneth for the murder of the soldiers."

"*He* was the murderer—" Cole began.

"Was that how it happened, Cole?" Weylin asked. "Did you run away and leave our brother to face your enemies alone?"

Cole stared at Weylin. "He's lying. It didn't happen that way. Randall only wanted an excuse—"

"No," Esperanza said. "Your lies are strong, Cole MacLean. They are so strong that they feel like truth. The truth you fear."

"You," Cole said. "You're the servant girl. How dare you speak to me? I'll have you whipped—"

"You'll do nothing," Tomás said softly, tightening his

hold on Cole's neck. "The girl is right. It's time to throw away our masks."

"I'll see you in Hell."

Tomás pushed Cole down to his knees. Esperanza knelt before him and extended her hand to touch his wrist. She stiffened, convulsed, almost let him go. But then she straightened and gazed at him as she'd done to Tomás, and spoke in that same voice of ageless wisdom.

"Cole MacLean, you have caused much suffering."

He tried to snatch his hand away, but Esperanza laced her small fingers through his like a lover. "Can you feel me, Cole MacLean? We are together. I know all your fears and your hates and how they devour you. We . . . are one."

His eyes held the beginnings of panic. "Let me go. I'll kill you."

"No." She touched his face. "Would you kill yourself?"

"Get out," he said, panting. "Get out!"

Rowena cast Tomás an anguished look and fell to her knees beside Esperanza. "I don't understand what you're doing," she said, "but I know it can hurt you. Stop, Esperanza. Please."

"I cannot." She focused on Cole again. "I will not harm you, Cole MacLean. That is what you fear most, that others will have power over you. I have none. But I cannot leave you. I cannot let you kill again."

Cole knew what it was to be intoxicated, to feel the firm reality of the world slip away. As a boy he'd drunk himself into a stupor, until he realized that it made him vulnerable. As a man, he'd felt the inebriation that only victory could bring.

This was different. He felt reality and control slide away from him at the hands of this child, who spoke to him as if he were helpless to defend himself. As if she dared to think herself his master.

No man or woman, human or werewolf had ever mastered him—not Randall, not Kenneth, not his father, certainly not Weylin. His will was too strong. And yet this girl had breached all his defenses before he even recognized the threat.

But she was not a werewolf. She hadn't the ability to manipulate his thoughts, as he had done with so many humans in his climb to the top. Somehow, by some unknown path, she had come inside his mind. She insinuated herself into his emotions and laid them bare. She knew what he was feeling. And he felt *her* thoughts, her essence in a way he'd never managed with any other human; her consciousness was soft and sickeningly compassionate, stripped of anger or viciousness, like that of some angel sent to save him from damnation.

He wanted nothing more than to kill her. But he knew instinctively that what she'd said was true; if he killed her, he ran the risk of damaging himself.

He could feel them all watching—his men, Weylin, Randall who held him prisoner, even the bitch Rowena—watching and waiting for him to falter. They heard this girl call him afraid. Afraid of the truth.

What was the truth? That he'd bent fate as he wished, grasped opportunities that allowed him to take what he deserved? The girl called them lies, but they were the necessities of survival.

Survival built on absolute, ruthless conviction. Who were these creatures that surrounded him, with their petty concerns? Did they truly think they could defeat him? They had no conception of his power. He could destroy them, every one, with a gesture of his hand.

He laughed. "So you think you know what I am," he said to the girl. "You know all my thoughts. Very well. Why don't you tell everyone this great truth of yours? Come inside, little señorita. What do you see?"

She was silent for a long time, and all at once he felt memories surge up within him, memories he hadn't bothered with in years. His childhood, on a small ranch in Texas—a ranch that had grown into an empire.

"I see a boy," the girl said. "A boy with two brothers, one elder and one younger. A boy full of anger. He hates his elder brother because he is his father's favorite, his chosen heir. But the boy knows he is stronger and more worthy. His father . . . fears him, fears his strength even when the boy is very young. He tries to crush his son, but the boy only grows more determined."

Cole suppressed a shiver. "My dear father," he said scornfully. "Was he so afraid of me?"

She didn't answer. "The family grows rich and powerful in their country. The boy's father is glad to see him go to the East for schooling. The boy is very clever and comes home a man of great knowledge. But the War changes everything. The father and his two eldest sons join the side of the South. In Nuevo Méjico they meet an old enemy and the brothers are captured. They plan escape. But Cole kills his guards and leaves his brother behind to be blamed. He feels no sorrow, because now he is the heir. Now his father will know. . . ."

Weylin crouched at Cole's side. "You did run away. You left Kenneth to be killed—"

"Kenneth was weak," Cole said. He stared at Weylin, seeing the judgment in his brother's eyes. Weylin, as weak as Kenneth ever was, daring to judge *him*. "He brought it on himself with his puerile concepts of human honor, trying to make a truce with Randall. He forgot what we are. He didn't deserve to inherit what our father built."

"You wanted Kenneth to die."

"I wanted what was mine."

"You told Father that Randall shot Kenneth in the back, unprovoked—"

"*You* went with Father and me to find Randall after the

War. You said you wanted revenge as much as we did, but you lost your nerve. You ran away even before we had Randall in our hands. You couldn't do a man's work, a MacLean's duty." He sneered. "You're a coward. Father knew it, even though he tried to protect you and made you his heir. You weren't there when he died. You've been trying to make up for that ever since, haven't you, little brother?"

The corner of Weylin's mouth twitched. "Yes," he said. He looked at the girl. "What happened the day Cole killed Fergus Randall?"

She closed her eyes and tightened her grip on Cole's hand. "He and his father . . . track their enemy to Mexico. Frank MacLean wants to kill Fergus Randall himself, with his own hands. He sets an ambush, and sends Cole to draw Fergus in. But Cole warns Fergus and makes his own bargain. He—" She sucked in a sharp breath. "He says that if Fergus kills Frank, he will not take vengeance."

Cole struck out at the girl with such force that he sent her tumbling into a heap. Rowena gathered her up, a look of pure fury contorting her face. In an instant Cole was on his back, Tomás Randall crouched over him with bared teeth. He caught Cole's lapels between his fists and slammed his head against the ground.

"Tomás!" The girl sat up in Rowena's arms, her nose running with blood. "It is not finished." She tried to rise and fell back, boneless as a puppet. "You think you are powerful, Cole MacLean," she whispered, "but you are dead in your heart."

"When this is over, I'll be the only one left alive," he said.

She shook her head. Weylin stood over them all like a figure carved of stone, unmoved. "You wanted Father to die," he said.

"You believe them?" Cole said, struggling up. "Our enemies? You aren't even fit to lick MacLean boots."

"Can you make him tell the truth?" Weylin asked the girl.

"No. I cannot make him do anything. I can only see what

he remembers. What he feels." She wiped the blood from her nose and stared at her hand in a daze. "I will try—"

"She's had enough," Rowena said. She squeezed the girl's arm and laid her back on the ground. She advanced on Cole, head low, brown eyes limned by golden fire. "We are the same, you and I. I won't deny it any longer. You *will* speak—"

"Stay back, Rowena," Tomás said. He bent low over Cole, and for the first time Cole truly felt the threat of the outlaw's reckless despair. For the first time he felt the battering of Randall's will against his own, the most deadly and unpredictable of challenges.

"Weylin!" he cried.

"Stop, Randall," Weylin said. "I can't let you hurt him. He's my brother."

"Prove your loyalty," Cole said. "Kill Randall now. I'll deal with the girl and Rowena—"

"You wanted Fergus Randall to kill your father," Esperanza said, her soft voice effortlessly drowning out Cole's. She crawled to his side. "Fergus told you that he did not wish to kill Frank MacLean. He said that he came to believe that you killed the men who guarded you in the camp, and left your brother to take the blame. He said he would fight you, instead. If you did not, he would tell your father of your betrayals. You pretended to agree, but then you fell upon him when he was not prepared. He took your arm before he died." Tears ran down her cheeks. "When you recovered, you told your father that Fergus Randall planned to kill you both in your sleep, and you stopped him. It should have made you a hero in your father's eyes."

"A hero?" Cole said. "He always hated me because he was afraid, because he knew I was stronger than he was, and I'd take his power from him when he showed the slightest weakness. When I lost my arm, he thought I was safe. He told me how he was going to give everything to Weylin, and I could go back to New York and live like half a man, with all my luxuries and fancy friends. He thought he was rid of me."

"And that's why you hated him," Weylin said. The stern stoicism of his expression melted into grief. "I didn't want to see it. You and Father—you were family. MacLeans. We were supposed to stick together, but you only wanted him out of the way."

"And that is why," the girl whispered, "you killed your own father."

twenty-one

Racked by nausea and horror, Weylin nearly let the gun fall from his hand. He was vaguely aware of Rowena's shock, Randall's disbelief, the mutterings of Cole's men on the sidelines.

He knew in his soul that what the girl said was true.

He waited numbly for Cole to defend himself, to spin some new web of deceit with his smooth, educated tongue. But Cole, lying on his back with Randall crouched over him and the lady staring her contempt, began to laugh.

He laughed in the way Cole supposed an Eastern gentleman did, a measured chuckle that sounded crazier than the loudest guffaw or most hysterical bellow. He laughed and dabbed at his eyes and ended with a pleasant smile for all of them, as if they were guests at one of his fancy parties.

"The story has been left incomplete," he said. "Shall I finish it for you?" He gazed up at Weylin. "Father made you his heir, because he knew he could make you do exactly what he wanted. You were never a threat to him, any more than Kenneth. You stayed behind and looked after the ranches like any dutiful *peón*. But I was the one who made us what we are today. Father didn't bother to concede that the money I'd made in New York increased our holdings a thousandfold, that *my* influence, not his, got us more land and power in the Territory than anyone but the governor himself. He thought he was receiving his rightful tribute as the head of our clan.

"But Father was getting old and weak. He'd lost the ambition he once had, to conquer and hold. I came back to the Territory to make him remember. *I* was the one who convinced him to join with Hittson and the other big Texas cattlemen to replevin our stolen cattle from the New Mexicans and Comancheros, hitting Los Valerosos along the way to eliminate the Randall influence for all time.

"I was there when he and his men left Randall's place in ruins. I saw Randall's mother, the half-Apache bitch the *peónes* called Doña Adelina, tracking them as a wolf. I was the one who shot her and gave her pelt to one of my father's men."

Tomás made a low sound of mourning deep in his throat, and Weylin wondered if he would have to drag the gun up and keep the outlaw from killing Cole. But Tomás only closed his eyes and tucked his chin into his chest while Rowena rested her hand on his back in a gesture of helpless sympathy.

Cole continued in the same conversational tone, unmoved. "I knew when Randall followed his mother's scent, caught up to Father, and accused him of killing her. He was half crazy. Father didn't have a chance against him. But Randall didn't finish the job. He left Father still alive. I rectified his error."

"God," Weylin said.

"Sim Kavanagh told me that you hunted Tomás down," Rowena said, her face bleak and pale. "You tried to cover what you'd done by trying to kill him—"

"And Randall survived. But once he started attacking our property, no one questioned that El Lobo was the murderer of Frank MacLean. He built his reputation better than I could have done, robbing and stealing from us and our allies.

He made himself the hero of the small ranchers and peasants, but he had formidable enemies among the rich." He looked at Weylin. "You, with your obsession with 'justice'— it was easy to keep you busy hunting Randall. I assumed that Randall would kill you sooner or later, and all the property Father willed to you would come to me. And if you killed him—well, I knew you wouldn't stop me from running things the way I wanted. I'd shape the new MacLean dynasty, the way it was meant to be."

Weylin looked away quickly. Cole's men couldn't see the moisture in his eyes; they were too busy milling about, trying to decide what to do about Cole's revelations. They were all cutthroats themselves, but he had a feeling that they knew Cole was headed for a fall, and they didn't want to fall with him.

Was Cole too sick, too crazy to see what he'd done?

Justice. The only justice now was to take in the real criminal, the real murderer, the man directly responsible for three deaths and probably a dozen more. Weylin swallowed the bile in his throat and put his hand on Tomás's shoulder.

"Move aside," he said.

Tomás stared up at him, and their gazes locked. "You want me to let him go?" he said in a rasp.

"I can't let you kill him."

"Do you think *I* could?" He laughed brokenly. Rowena reached out to touch him. He glanced at her, and she dropped her hand.

"We are not so different, you and I," he said to Weylin. "Our family names left us a great burden we did not wish to bear. But you have borne yours with far greater honor and courage than I." He got to his feet and turned to Rowena, his mouth distorted in a smile of self-contempt. "And you, my Lady of Fire. You've been brave and true to one who does not deserve it, who used you only as an amusing diversion on the path to oblivion."

She said nothing. Weylin pitied her, little as he knew her, for he saw what lay in her eyes.

"When I was a boy," Tomás said, "my father told me about the great Randall-MacLean feud. It sounded so full of heroism and adventure to me then, coming from an ancient land in olden days of swords and shields and vows made in blood.

"My father was naive in believing he could escape the feud's curse by coming west. He knew it would not end with Kenneth MacLean's death. So he told me that if anything happened to him, it must be my charge to preserve the Randall honor, no matter what it took or what I must do. He made me swear never to rest until the feud was ended for all time.

"I was young, and very proud. But I did not believe it was real. I discovered that Cole MacLean had killed my father years before my mother learned of it, but I did not tell her. I failed in my vow. I did not seek vengeance. I went to the East to avoid the burden of retribution. Because of my cowardice, I returned to find that the MacLeans had destroyed my home, and that my mother had died in taking the role I was meant to play. At last I went after the man who had done it, intending to kill."

"But you didn't," Rowena said. "You couldn't. It wasn't in you, to kill like an animal—"

"You thought you'd killed, when you came back to find my father dead," Weylin said.

"Yes. And that was when I knew I was to be the last of the Randalls, that I did not have the strength of will and the blood to avenge my parents and my name. I could not kill again. I could only survive what Cole MacLean did to me, and find other ways to make him remember my father and mother. I became El Lobo for that purpose alone. With the money and horses and cattle I stole from him, I set others to watch him; I saw him grow in power, here and in New York.

I saw the weak and less ruthless fall before him, while I was but a straw in the wind. I harried and taunted him; whatever I did, it made no difference. And then I learned of his betrothal to you, Rowena. I went to England to observe for myself the woman he would marry. I saw you, and I—" He glanced at the sky. "*No importa.* I thought that at last I could steal something he valued more than his other possessions. I thought at last that he would acknowledge that one Randall remained in the world."

"And you wanted . . . to die," Esperanza said.

Rowena heard Tomás's and Esperanza's words with a sickness and fury that turned upon those, living and dead, who had set this tragic and senseless scene: Fergus Randall, Frank MacLean, all their ancestors who had begun and nurtured the feud; Cole, who'd used it and killed to further his own ambitions, and Weylin, who'd followed his brother's path so blindly . . . and Tomás. Tomás, who'd given up on life and existed only as a shadow, grasping at shallow pleasure and diversions when they fell in his chosen path of self destructive revenge.

Diversions like Lady Rowena Forster.

Tomás would not meet her gaze. Esperanza came to her swaying with exhaustion, and grasped her arm as if Rowena were the one in need of support. But it was to Tomás that the girl spoke.

"You tried to do as your father expected of you, because you loved him," she said. "And you did penance for the murder you thought you had committed, by helping those who suffered at the hands of men like Cole MacLean. You let the world believe you were the murderous outlaw MacLean called you. Still it was not punishment enough for your failures. There was only one way to end the feud and fulfill your vow: to kill the last of the Randalls. Yourself."

He stared at her, unprotesting, wordless.

Rowena turned her face away from him. "I never believed you a coward," she said. She found that her voice held a humiliating tremor, but her growing anger and sadness made such trivialities unimportant. "You deceived me. You deceived everyone. You pretended to love life, to help others, knowing all the while that you sought death with every reckless act. And called me afraid because I wouldn't face the beast within myself."

She felt profound pity for him, for the empty life he'd led, and ached with the pain he'd endured. At the same time, righteous anger simmered to a boil in her veins, her muscles, her nerves, rising and rising to crowd her head like fireworks ready to explode.

"You are a fraud, Tomás Alejandro Randall. But I owe you thanks for two things. You showed me what Cole was, and prevented me from making a dreadful mistake. You taught me not to fear my own life, my own heart, even if it was all just one more diversion before dying."

Tomás let out a shuddering sigh. "Then I have not totally failed," he said. "Thank you, my lady."

Rowena closed her eyes, fighting to hold back tears. Esperanza leaned her cheek against Rowena's shoulder. Weylin and Tomás were lost in their own thoughts. None of them were prepared when Cole made his move.

He lashed out with his legs in a violent thrust, kicking Weylin's feet out from under him. The gun went flying. Tomás whirled and crouched; Rowena turned in time to see Cole fling himself after the fallen pistol and clutch it in his single hand. He rolled at the same instant and swung the revolver up to fix on Tomás's chest.

"You want to die, Randall? I'll grant your wish."

Time could literally stand still. Rowena felt it happen as she made the crucial and agonizing decision, gathered her will and all the rage boiling in her body, and prepared to stop Cole MacLean.

She let the Change take her, painless and so simple that she wanted to laugh for the sheer relief of it. She kicked off her shoes; her ragged dress split along its much-mended seams as she tore it from her body. Naked and triumphant, she flung back her head in a cry that made Cole's men scatter in terror. Mist the color of gold-shot ice enveloped her like an ethereal cocoon.

She had made herself forget, but the knowledge of wolf-being was as natural to her as breathing. She tore through the mist like lightning on four legs. Her senses exploded in a thousand colors and scents and sounds unknown to man. She shook a lush coat thick enough to turn aside bullets and snapped keen jaws against the air; sleek muscles obeyed her every thought, and a powerful heart pumped blood through a body designed for adversity.

A body she'd hated all her life. The body of the beast that would save her mate.

Cole! she cried, and the word was a howl of promise and fury. She gathered her legs beneath her, preparing to spring. Cole's pistol swung toward her.

Tomás lunged, shouting Rowena's name. The sound of gunfire blasted Rowena's sensitive ears. Tomás fell, and Cole turned to her again. She roared, oblivious to the certainty of her own death.

Suddenly Esperanza threw herself between wolf and man, ready to take the bullet. Gunfire cracked from behind Rowena, and the revolver flew from Cole's bloodied hand. A mounted man at the edge of the crowd raised his own weapon in salute, wheeled his horse, and set off at a gallop.

Sim Kavanagh, gone as mysteriously as he'd arrived.

In that moment of confusion and dodging outlaws, Weylin retrieved his gun and aimed it at Cole's head.

Rowena ran to Tomás and Changed again, heedless of her nudity. She saw the blood soaking his sleeve and frantically tore at his clothing.

Cole's bullet had clipped his arm, producing an injury that must have hurt like the devil but was far from fatal. Rowena gasped out her relief and stretched herself over Tomás, avoiding his wounded arm.

"How . . . very pleasant," Tomás quipped raggedly. "What a pity that the moment is not more opportune for—"

His words were overwhelmed by an inhuman cry. Rowena crouched across Tomás to face the threat, and saw . . .

Cole. Cole stripping, *Changing*, wrapped in mist streaked with black and purple, emerging as a creature of hate incarnate. A three-legged wolf, awkward and stumbling, finding his balance, baring teeth in a rictus of insanity. Bending back on his haunches, tensing muscle, gleaming eyes fixed on Rowena with the unmistakable intent to kill.

He leaped. Weylin shot him as he stretched suspended in air. He fell, forepaws mere inches from Tomás and Rowena.

Weylin threw down his gun and ran to his brother's side.

The bullet had taken Cole through the center of his body. Rowena helped Tomás to his knees. Esperanza stood apart, tears falling unregarded from her cheeks.

"Cole," Weylin whispered. He lifted the great wolf's head in his arms. "Cole—"

Dark mist returned, and a naked man replaced the wolf. He gasped each laborious breath, and each came more slowly than the last.

"Cole," Weylin said. "You shouldn't have Changed. You could have healed—"

"No." Cole coughed so hard that his whole body convulsed. "I wouldn't die . . . as a beast." He smiled. "I was wrong about you, little brother. You weren't so weak after all." He strained to turn his head toward Rowena and Tomás. "The feud is over, Randall. And you, Rowena—you can live out your life as an animal in perfect freedom. I hope you are happy." He closed his eyes. "The MacLeans are dead." He let out a last, long breath, and his body went still.

Weylin knelt with Cole's head in his arms. Esperanza gazed back the way Sim Kavanagh had ridden off, and then walked to Weylin's side.

"*Lo siento,*" she said gently.

He looked at her blankly. "I killed my own brother." He bent his head to Cole's. Esperanza slipped her arms about his shoulders. Tomás took Rowena's hand in his and led her away from Weylin's silent grief. He eased out of his shirt, tore off the bloodied sleeve, and draped the rest of it over Rowena's bare shoulders.

Already the flow of blood was beginning to ease. Tomás was unaware of the pain when so much greater suffering was all around him. For the first time in many minutes he looked toward the hanging tree and the men who'd watched the drama unfold. Every last one of them had ridden off.

It would all pass into legend, of course—the legend of El Lobo, perhaps, or of the MacLeans. No one would believe any tales those men chose to tell. If they dared to speak at all.

Rowena was shivering. He drew her close, to share his warmth and what little comfort she might accept. She shook him off. In the fire of her gaze and the proud lift of her head he saw what she had become: the fierce she-wolf that had always lain dormant within her—the Lady of Fire he'd been so eager to liberate for his own pleasure.

She was sure of her own strength, now; she had seen her men betray her, and still she stood firm and unshaken. No one would ever dominate Lady Rowena Forster again.

He was proud of her, beyond any pride he'd known. And he mourned. *It is impossible; it was always impossible.* She was right. If there were degrees of impossibility, they had gone far beyond the last.

He looked at Weylin, grieving so stoically for a brother who'd despised him. El Lobo and Weylin had become brothers in all but blood. Both were the last of their family. Both faced the end of what had driven them for years, and a future stripped of purpose.

The future opened up before Tomás, a future he'd never imagined in his ardent courting of death. It terrified him. He must face the years stretching ahead, unknowable, demanding some ambition other than vengeance. He had chosen life. And he must live it without the woman he loved, for her sake.

"It's true, then," Rowena said.

He met her gaze. "What truth, my lady?"

"You captured me just so that you could force Cole to come after you and kill you. I was a tool, but not in the way I thought at first. It wasn't really even about revenge. It was about you, and your guilt. You turned my life upside down with no . . . no interest in what it might do to me, or to the others you pretended to care for."

He bowed his head. "I cannot dispute it. Or ask your forgiveness."

She caught her breath. "When we . . . when we lay together, that was your farewell to life, wasn't it? A last, desperate attempt to—to—" She broke off and turned away. "Are you still determined to die, Tomás Alejandro Randall? Will you go about your robbing ways and find some new enemy to hunt you down?"

He tried to laugh, and failed. "No," he said. "The strange thing is that you cured me of that desire, *dulzura*. I thought I was ready to die when I let Weylin capture me so he could bring me to Cole. I thought I'd save you by killing Cole, and end it all in one moment. You see, I had come to care for you. I did not wish to see you hurt any more, and I thought that if you were free of Cole, you could find your own life."

"While destroying your own," she said harshly.

"But then I saw you come to defend me. I saw you Change, when I knew it was the one thing you dreaded above all else, and it was as if you reached into my soul and burned out the thing that wanted me to die."

She turned back, her face as naked to him as her body. "Because I Changed?"

"You changed us both. I knew then that I wanted to live, to make something better of my life. But I do not know where or how. I have much to atone for."

"The people—the children in the canyon?"

"It is a place to start. I have enough money hidden away to give them a good life, in the cañon or wherever they choose to go."

"And you can begin to look after them properly—"

"No. That was El Lobo's lair. That life is over. We must all begin again."

"Yes," she whispered. "All over again."

He almost surrendered to the old recklessness, the careless disregard for consequences that had ruled his life so long. He almost asked her to help him find the purpose that would give his existence meaning again. He almost asked her to *become* that very purpose.

And do what? Take away the last of the life she'd known, a life she might still recover with time and forgetting? She deserved far better than he could ever give, were he the richest and wisest man in the world.

"Will you go back to New York, or to England?" he asked her, sealing his fate. "If I can help—"

"I do not need your help." She walked away, clutching his ragged shirt about her arms. He found that he had nothing to say that would not hurt them both in these final moments. Instead he went to stand at Weylin's side. Cole lay with his arm folded across his chest, covered by Weylin's coat.

Weylin looked up. His eyes were bleak, but Tomás saw no hatred in them.

"It's over," Weylin said. "The feud is over."

Tomás closed his eyes. "Thank you."

"No. You tried to ask forgiveness when you thought you'd killed my father. I pegged you wrong from the beginning. We were both deceived. I won't spend the rest of my life pursuing something as worthless as this."

"But I have stolen from you many times."

"My brother stole your land, your parents' lives, and my father's. You have the right to hate me. But I hope the time for hating is finished." He reached up to offer his hand.

Tomás took it in a firm grip and pulled Weylin to his feet. "The hating is finished," he said.

Weylin gazed toward the eastern horizon. "I reckon there's a lot to be done now. There's still the ranches to run, and the will, and I'll have to see to Cole's affairs in New York. I don't know a thing about that high-toned world. I'll have to hire a passel of lawyers, at least." He grimaced. "And you'll want your land back, the land taken from your family—"

"I thank you for that, but no. Not yet." He followed Weylin's gaze. "I think it's best if I leave the Territory for a time. El Lobo is no more; let it be said that he died fighting Cole MacLean. Let the legends take us both."

Weylin tipped his hat and sighed. "I'd almost like to ride with you, Randall. I don't want Cole's empire. Father's was enough, and he had his own men to run it the way he wanted. But maybe I can undo some of the wrongs they did over the years, make things a little fairer for folks in the Territory. It's time I grew up."

"It isn't an easy thing, to grow up," Tomás said. He smiled. "But perhaps there are some compensations."

"Like running as a wolf," Weylin said. "For a long time I thought it was just a kind of unfair advantage we had over ordinary folk, something to be resisted. But now I know it's natural—if it's not used for evil." He glanced at his brother. "Maybe I can find a way to use those powers for good."

"I am sure of it, amigo." Tomás offered his hand again. "I still ask that last favor of you. See that the Lady Rowena returns safely to whatever place she wishes to go. She was not at fault in any of this. She deserves only joy and peace."

"Yes," Weylin said. "I'll see to it." He smiled crookedly. "I never had a lot of use for petticoats, but she's gone a long way toward changing my mind. There may be a few other females like her."

"I doubt it," Tomás said softly. "But there is no harm in looking."

He nodded farewell and located one of the riderless horses, the one Cole had ridden from Las Vegas. He patted its neck and mounted, welcoming the pain in his arm. It reminded him that he was alive.

His last view of Rowena was the sight of her standing on a hillock, head flung back and hair tossing in the wind like a battle flag.

"Adiós, mi amor," he whispered. *"Vaya con Dios."*

Rowena didn't turn as she heard him ride away.

The shirt he'd left her smelled of his essence, his masculinity; she clutched it more tightly to her body, telling herself that she had to make some effort to hide her nudity, at least from Weylin. He and Esperanza were the only other living people here, now that the drama was over. Cole's men had fled, undoubtedly in horror at her transformation—and that of their master.

She wasn't afraid of their opinion or the rumors they might spread. She didn't care about the things that had once been so important.

She'd Changed. She'd abandoned her final and most crucial resolve, the one to which she'd clung for so many years: not to take the form and shape of a wolf. No matter what else happened, she had believed herself safe from that offense.

But she'd done it, for Tomás. And she knew she'd do it again under the same circumstances. The last certainty of her life was gone; she'd seen the others fall away one by one, stolen by the master thief El Lobo.

It had been too easy to become a wolf. She'd felt invulnerable, free, passionate, just as Tomás had promised. The Change was like an addiction, a weakness she ought to despise, and she didn't think she could ever give it up again.

Unless she went far from this place, returned to New York where she could ease back into Society as if she'd never left—except for the minor inconvenience of fabricating the explanations for her disappearance and her fiancé's death in the West. Once that awkwardness had passed, her money and rank would make it possible to resume the life she'd known and thought she wanted. And she could forget.

Surely that was the solution. Wasn't it what she'd been thinking when she walked away from Tomás? He'd said it himself, asking if she planned to return to New York or England. He hadn't even questioned that she might choose something else.

Why should he? He said he'd meant to protect her, *free* her by killing Cole, expecting to die himself. Even if he . . . even though he admitted that she had cured him of his desire for oblivion. Even though he said he'd come to care for her.

Care for her. How extremely generous of him. And after admitting so much, he'd ridden away without a good-bye, as if they were total strangers. Knowing that anything else was impossible, as she'd told him.

They were too different. Their worlds, their desires, the futures they envisioned. Tomás searched for his own future, now that he'd decided he had one. She still had the option of returning to hers—one of her own choosing, without the influence of either Cole MacLean or El Lobo.

"You taught me not to fear my own life, my own heart." Wasn't that what she'd told Tomás? Why, then, was she trembling?

Damn you, Tomás Alejandro Randall. You rode away from me. If you think for one minute that I'll go running after . . .

A hand touched her arm, warm and familiar. She waited for Esperanza to speak: Esperanza, who had proven to be so much greater than any of them could have guessed, whose eyes were filled with such boundless compassion and grief—not for herself, but for those whose lives she had so altered.

But the girl—no girl now, but woman—didn't speak in words. She communicated in the way she'd done before, with feelings and images that approached thought. And Rowena herself had no need to speak.

Love didn't require words. Love spilled from Esperanza and tapped the flow within Rowena, a love so profound that for a moment all the sorrow in the world was extinguished. And then the brilliant light of that love quieted, grew simpler and yet more focused. It was courage, and self-acceptance, and humility. It was the poignant understanding that some Changes could never be reversed.

Tomás Alejandro Randall had Changed her. There was no going back. Pride meant nothing. The future was whatever she wanted it to be. She . . . and Tomás.

She needed him. He needed her. He *needed* her.

And you love him. She couldn't tell if it was Esperanza or her own heart that exclaimed so passionately. *You love him. Don't let him go.*

With a cry of triumph, Rowena threw off Tomás's shirt. She cast a glance at Esperanza. The young woman smiled her blessing, and Rowena prepared to Change.

She didn't complete the act. The thunder of hoofbeats stopped her just as she gathered the mist about herself. Tomás came charging back across the plain, his horse at the gallop. He swept up upon her as he'd done not so long ago, eyes flashing in challenge. He bent low in the saddle and hooked Rowena around the waist with one arm, carrying her just above the ground until his mount came to a snorting halt. He pulled her up effortlessly to straddle his thighs, bare chest to breasts, lips inches apart.

"I couldn't let you go," he said, breathing hard. "Forgive me, *mi alma*. Forgive my selfishness."

She gazed down her nose at him, as regally as a naked lady could manage. "What do you think you're doing, you scoundrel?"

"Kidnapping you," he said. "Stealing you away to be my bride."

"You'll never get away with it. I've a mind to summon the law—"

He kissed her. The kiss was very long and very deep and very mutual.

He drew back enough to let her breathe, grinning with wicked pleasure at her disadvantage. Damn him, he enjoyed seeing her like this, nude and caught in a most compromising position. . . .

"Well?" he said.

"Well, what? I'm afraid I must insist that you put me down at once."

"But I do so appreciate the view."

"Is that why you continue to make war on women?"

"Only one very special woman. But—" He tapped his chin. "I might be persuaded to let you down, if you pay my ransom."

"Which is?"

"I know a certain old padre who could marry us quickly. He owes me a favor for services rendered."

"An illicit contribution to the church coffers, no doubt, made to benefit the less fortunate?"

"I trust that God will forgive me. If you will."

She kissed him. He held her very tight. "From now on," she said, "you will have to do without criminal activity. We shall find other ways to help those in need and satisfy your endless hunger for adventure."

"We?"

"*Sí.* If you promise to listen to reason, from time to time."

"Only if you promise to be reckless as often as possible."

"And if I don't?"

"Then I shall have to convince you." His hand crept up to touch her breast.

The sound of masculine throat-clearing interrupted them. Weylin was standing a little distance away, his face slightly averted and his tanned skin suspiciously pink.

"I don't reckon you're going to need me after all," he said. He glanced at Esperanza, who had gone to kneel beside Cole's body. "I'll see that the girl gets to wherever she needs to go."

Tomás leaned back in the saddle. "*Gracias.*" He looked at Rowena. "We have much to thank her for. We will see her again."

Rowena wondered how far down her blush extended. "Mr. MacLean, if you could escort Esperanza back to Las Vegas and to a comfortable lodging, we will fetch her as soon as may be. She will always have a home with us."

"Here in New Mexico?" Tomás asked softly. "When El Lobo is known to be gone forever—"

"The Territory will be safe for a proper home," she said. "I think I'll learn to love your desert, as I've learned to love its inhabitants."

They gazed at each other. Weylin coughed behind his hand. "Well, if you'll excuse me, I'll take my brother home." He turned away before Rowena could thank him again.

"He is not a man for *sentimentalismo,*" Tomás said. "But I think we can count him a friend."

"There is nothing more wonderful than when enemies become friends."

"*Sí, mi querida amiga.*" He cupped her face between his hands. "I have forgotten—have I told you that I love you?"

"Amidst all the confusion, it seems to have slipped your mind."

"Then you may give me as many tongue-lashings as you see fit, and I will endure without protest." He gave her a sly smile. "And then I will use my tongue just as freely."

She squirmed upon the hard seat of his thighs. "I think we had best find that padre of yours without delay."

"Agreed." He looked her up and down in open appreciation. "I was thinking . . . if you're willing, *mi amor* . . . we might leave this horse for Weylin. There is another way we can travel."

It was not a test. Rowena knew that he would love her whether or not she agreed. But she was no longer afraid.

She slipped from his embrace and jumped to the ground. Tomás murmured a word to the horse and followed her. He stripped out of his trousers and stood before her, naked as she, breathtakingly beautiful. Once more they kissed, and the vast blue sky wheeled over their heads in joy.

They Changed together. Side by side, they went to Esperanza and licked her hands in thanks. Shoulder to shoulder, pale fur mingling with brown, they set off across the desert.

twenty-two

Tomás and Rowena returned to the cañon unannounced, three days after their simple wedding.

For the two days following Cole's death, they had run as wolves—oblivious to the human world, traveling where they would, Changing to make love in sheltered places and under the sky. Rowena had overcome her shame and doubt, but enough modesty remained that she waited out of sight when, on the third day, Tomás ran to one of the villages where his true nature was known, and borrowed clothing and horses to suit their human shapes.

It was as humans that they rode back to the outskirts of Las Vegas and got a message to Weylin, who brought Esperanza to them. She was well, if very quiet, and ready to accompany them back to the cañon.

Of Sim there was no sign.

The three of them went in search of the old padre, who married the couple quickly and with little fanfare, Esperanza and a villager serving as the only witnesses. Rowena wore New Mexican clothing and a borrowed veil, but to Tomás she'd never been more radiant.

The tiny village of El Cañon del Rito de las Lágrimas

seemed deserted when they arrived. Esperanza, though she was merely human, was the first to spot the giggling child crouched behind a casa wall. After that there was no hiding, and the other children and Tomás's men spilled into the plaza with cheers and cries of welcome.

"Bienvenido!" old Nestor said, beaming through his wrinkles. *"Enhorabuena* to you both!"

Tomás helped Rowena and Esperanza to dismount, and the three of them ducked laughingly as the children, from youngest to oldest, pelted them with wildflower blossoms. Rowena knelt to accept the happy greetings of the children, while Esperanza watched with a quiet smile.

"How is it that you knew we were returning?" Tomás asked, drawing Nestor aside. "I sent the men back long before—"

"Before you were nearly killed in Las Vegas?" The old man said. "Before Weylin MacLean captured you and Cole MacLean died?"

Tomás shook his head in wonderment. "News travels fast, but so few know of this cañon . . ."

"One who knows it well brought us the tale," Nestor said. His smile faded. "Sim Kavanagh rode in four days ago, to tell us all that had happened since he left with the lady." The old man frowned. "I would have shot him myself if he had not convinced me that he spoke truth. But he said that you had rescued the lady, and he had taken Esperanza and then let her go. He told us, too, how you and the lady met MacLean's men in Las Vegas, and how she fought for you like *la fierecilla.*" He glanced at Rowena, who was bouncing little Gita on her knee. "I was much gladdened to hear that she had accepted you. She is one very much like your mother. At last you have a woman worthy of you."

Tomás flushed, an experience new to him and not without inconvenience. "No, my friend. She is by far my superior." He looked at Rowena with love and such happiness that he thought his heart must burst. "And it was Esperanza, too, who saved my life, and Rowena's. Cole MacLean brought his death upon himself, and set the lady free."

Nestor clasped his hands. "Then it is over, *gracias a Dios.*" His brow furrowed anxiously. "It *is* over? Señor Kavanagh was right when he said that you have made peace with Weylin MacLean?"

"It is true," Tomás said. He wondered how Sim could have learned so much, when he'd done no more than shoot the gun from Cole's hand and then vanish. "There will be peace—at least between me and Weylin MacLean. The wounds may take time to heal, but—" He looked again at Rowena. "Change is always possible, amigo. Change, and hope." He looked around the village, where nothing had altered. Only he saw it through new eyes. "Where is Sim now?"

"He rode on." Nestor drew a folded piece of paper from his sash. "He left this for you."

Tomás took the paper and tucked it into his own sash. There would be time for that later—time to consider what Sim had done, both betrayal and redemption.

Now there must be only celebration.

"Amigos!" he cried.

The noise died, and all eyes turned to him. He saw the faces of his loyal men—men who must, like him, now abandon the outlaw way and find another life. They trusted in him as they always had. And the children—Aquilino and Gita, Miguel, Gertrudis and Catalina, Pilar with her new doll, still waiting for a proper frock, and Enrique, his gaze full of worship. How much he owed them all.

He held out his hand to Rowena. She rose with all her natural grace and came to him. Her face was no longer pale, but shone with the warmth of the sun. Her eyes danced with golden sparks and sly mischief. Her fingers slid into his.

"My friends," he repeated. "I have the greatest honor and joy of introducing you to my wife, Doña Rowena Forster Randall."

One of his men hooted, and the others cried out their congratulations. Pilar beamed, old enough to understand and approve. Enrique nodded wisely.

"Did I not say it would be so?" he said.

Rowena beckoned to Esperanza. The girl came to stand beside them, her eyes downcast.

"I know that Tomás will translate what I cannot say in Spanish," Rowena said. "I wish to tell you how very happy I am to be back in the cañon, to be among you and have the chance to know you much better. I hope that I will be permitted to earn your friendship."

Tomás translated swiftly, and the men nodded approval.

"I would also like to introduce you once more to Esperanza, who has done so much for us and saved both our lives. I hope you will make her welcome here, so that she will know she has a home always where she is loved and needed." She hugged Esperanza tightly and kissed her cheeks. Tomás did the same. Esperanza seemed to glow from within, a fire that touched her skin and filled her eyes with soft warmth.

After that there was more general talking and laughter and many exchanges of goodwill. Tomás knew that a serious discussion must soon take place; the men had to decide upon their future, and that of the children.

So must he and Rowena.

He carried her off for a few moments to himself while Nestor set to preparing a small feast. The children went back to playing, and Esperanza wandered down to the wood by the stream. All at once the cañon was quiet with the profound stillness of peace.

They walked, hand in hand, to the waterfall where once Tomás had attempted to seduce Rowena. If she blushed when they sat beside the pool, he couldn't blame her. He had taken shameful liberties.

This time there was no hesitation or confusion when they kissed and caressed each other. Rowena sighed and leaned her head against his shoulder, trailing her bare feet in the water.

"I can't forget what happened to Cole," she said. "No matter how hard I try, I can't put it out of my mind, or stop wondering what I could have done differently. If I'd understood him—"

"Hush." He pulled her close to him and rested his cheek against her hair. "You were always blameless in this, *mi amor*. Cole MacLean was mad."

"Then you no longer hate him?"

"My hatred died with him. He punished himself, by casting aside all that made him human—in the finest sense of the word. His kind of sickness was not unique to our kind, but because of his power it was far more deadly. He believed that the whole world was his to use or cast aside as he willed. Including you." He kissed her temple. "You could have done nothing to mend his illness. Sooner or later, he must have destroyed himself. I thank heaven that I found you before he could destroy you as well." He smiled wryly. "Though at times I was little better than he—"

"Don't be ridiculous." Rowena sat upright and frowned at him. "You are a rogue and a rascal, granted, but you are not—quite—mad." Her frown resolved into a look of sadness. "Still, I will always wonder if someone might have reached him—"

"Esperanza reached him," Tomás reminded her. "If he could be healed, she would have done so. But she reflected back to him the cruelties of his soul, and he could not bear it. Just as she reflected to us our deepest desires, and made us see the truth in our own hearts."

"Yes." Rowena closed her eyes and laced her fingers through his. "She has a remarkable gift. And great courage. Perhaps it is something that we were able to save her. Perhaps she will go on to help others, as she helped us."

"*Que así sea.* May it be so."

"I didn't tell you what she said to me at our wedding. She told me that her real name is Felícita . . . 'happiness.' She could not speak it until after she escaped Sim—and then there was never time to explain. She lost her voice when she lost her old life, and I gave her a new name out of ignorance. But she said to me, 'You have given me Hope. I was named for happiness, but I was never happy. Now I have something more precious than happiness. I will keep the name that was your gift to me.' "

Tomás squeezed her hand. "A new name for a new life. It will be a new life for all of us, *mi rubia.*"

"And how far we have come."

They sat in silence for a while, hand in hand, listening to the water and the cry of canyon wrens high above.

"Did you know," Tomás said at last, "that Weylin asked Esperanza to stay with him in Las Vegas?"

Rowena stared at him. "She didn't tell me—"

"It is odd that Weylin confided in me. But he was much taken with her, more than he would admit. I don't know what passed between them, but she chose to return with us."

"Weylin and Esperanza," Rowena murmured. "How strange."

"No stranger than Sim and Esperanza," Tomás said. "I think he was in love with her."

"What?"

"You may well be shocked. Sim had contempt for women. He was obsessed with the girl in a way I've never seen. Perhaps the gentleness in her called out to his suffering. Perhaps he understood that she was the only one who could end it."

Rowena shuddered. "I wouldn't let him touch her. He's too much like Cole MacLean."

"Not so much. I think there is still hope for Sim Kavanagh."

He remembered the paper Nestor had given him and pulled it from his waistcoat. "Nestor said he left this for me."

He unfolded the paper and held it out so Rowena could see. The writing was painstaking, as if by the hand of someone who seldom had the need—or the desire—for correspondence.

" *'Amigo,'* "it began,

" *'By the time you see this, I'll be gone. I've had a mind for some time now to head out of the Territory and find new stomping grounds, and now that you're domesticated, there ain't much point in staying. Your lady and me don't see eye to eye. I grant she's better than I thought, but there never was a woman who didn't ruin a friendship sooner or later.'* "

Rowena snorted. "The nerve of the man, after all he did—"

"He saved our lives," Tomás said quietly. He continued to read aloud.

" *'I reckon you forgave me for taking the lady. I thought it was a good way to get close enough to Cole MacLean to kill him and get you out of trouble at the same time. Didn't work out as I planned. I wouldn't have turned you in. If you don't know that, you're a bigger fool than I thought.'* "

Tomás shook his head. "So I am."

" *'I never told you why I hated MacLean as much as you did. It didn't have anything to do with the time you found me in the desert. No reason you shouldn't know now.*

" *'Frank MacLean was my father—'* " Tomás nearly dropped the paper. "His father? *Maldición.* '—*and Cole was my brother.'* "

"How can that be?" Rowena said. "Surely that would make him—"

"*Hombre-lobo.* Like us." He snapped the paper flat, as if the words on it might alter. "It explains much. He says, *'My mother was a whore in Texas. Frank MacLean visited her when he got tired of his wife, which was often enough. She thought he'd set her up in a house and give her a fancy life. Then I was born, and he stopped coming. Ma blamed me for that. She started sickening a few years later. I didn't know who my pa was until Ma told me on her deathbed. I was sixteen. I went to find my daddy. MacLean didn't want anything to do with me. When I stood up to him, he sent Cole to get rid of me. I lived. And I meant so little to him that when we met in Las Vegas, he didn't even recognize me.'"*

"*Caramba*," Tomás murmured. "His own brother."

"How horrible," Rowena said.

"'Now, I reckon, you're thinking you should feel sorry for me. I chose my path, and I saw Cole MacLean die. I don't mourn my pa, either. Weylin MacLean is nobody to me. You were my brother, amigo, the only one I had. Maybe we'll meet again. Look after that pretty señorita, and if you hear I'm dead, shoot off a few rounds for me.

"'Adiós.'"

Tomás set down the paper and stared unseeing at the cliff above the pool. "I never guessed. In all this time—"

"How could you? If he had the *loup-garou* powers, he hid them completely. He got the revenge he wanted by using you—"

"No. I had few illusions about Sim. I wish him well." He sighed. "If only—"

"Yes. If only." She rubbed his arm. "Will you tell Weylin about this?"

"One day, perhaps. It may be that both he and Sim may find themselves in need of kin."

"I believe you are right. In time—" She sat up straight and met Tomás's gaze. "What of us? You said you wanted to leave the Territory, that the name of El Lobo must be forgotten. Is that still your wish?"

Tomás closed his eyes, breathing in the scents of the cañon and listening to its sounds as if for the last time. He took her hands in his and kissed her fingertips. "What is *your* wish, my lady?"

She tilted her head back to look at the sky. "When I first

came to this land, I hated it. It was the epitome of all I loathed in myself, and the beast I feared. It was a place I could never hope to limit or control. But now . . . now I cannot imagine living anywhere else."

"Not even New York, or England? El Lobo is unknown in those places. There would be no risk—"

"No risk. Safety. What I thought I always wanted. But you see, my dear husband, the Rowena who lived in those places no longer exists. She belongs here, in this land that Tomás Alejandro Randall loves."

Tomás swallowed his elation. "I am still a wanted man in the Territory. An outlaw cannot give you the life you deserve—"

"What I deserve is here beside me." She kissed him, delighting him with the agile motion of her tongue. "You remember what Weylin said when we retrieved Esperanza. If he has any of his brother's influence, he'll get the governor's pardon for you. If not . . . he'll make clear to everyone in the Territory that he doesn't want you hunted. I very much doubt that many men will defy the will of Weylin MacLean, however self-effacing he may be."

Tomás couldn't help but agree. Weylin MacLean was a man to be reckoned with. "And where," he said, "should we live if we stay in New Mexico?" He looked down at their interlocking fingers. "Now that I have foresworn thievery, the money I have saved will not last long. If I could build you a mansion—"

"I certainly do not want your money!" She withdrew her hand from his. "It so happens that I am a wealthy woman in my own right. It is my wish to see that the children here receive a proper education, so that they may become whatever they choose, be it farmer, shepherd, teacher, storekeeper, or officer of the law—"

"Anything but desperado?"

"Just so! Is there any reason why we may not remain here in the cañon for a while? I can purchase all the materials the children need for their initial schooling, and determine what will be best for them later. Your men must also learn new trades. They will need time to adjust. I doubt very much that they will insist upon remaining outlaws."

"You would be content to stay here?"

"You sound shocked. Have I not proven to you that I can live just as simply as anyone in this country?"

He pulled her close and gave her a resounding kiss. She didn't so much as feign resistance.

"There is one more thing," she said, growing serious. "I came west in search of Quentin. I still sense that all is not well with him. If he is anywhere in this part of the country, I must find him."

"Of course." He set her back and held her arms, as if she might struggle. "I have given it much thought. I was the one who brought you to the West; it is my charge to finish what I forced you to begin. Once you are well settled, I'll ride out and find him, and return him safely to you."

"Not without me. And we cannot abandon the children now. But there must be some capable tracker I can hire to locate him. I feel certain that Weylin would help."

He cocked his head and smiled wistfully. "Ah, if I were not now so responsible, I would insist that we go together. Days of great adventure, nights of love under the stars—"

"They are not lost forever, Tomás," she said. "We will have those days and nights." She glanced aside. "Or do you regret—"

"Never. Never." He drew her again into his arms. "You have given me a reason for living. You are my life."

An hour later Rowena adjusted her *camisa* and patted her hair into some semblance of order, and by unspoken agreement they rose and returned up the path to the village, where the men and children were hovering about the makeshift table Nestor had set up in the plaza. Mutton was roasting over an open fire, and the smell of frijoles and chile drifted out from Nestor's casa.

The people of the cañon had their own little *baile* that night, with Esperanza and Rowena partnering one man after another, and the children mimicking their elders with shrieks of laughter.

Tomás spent much of his time merely watching. These were his people; he was no longer afraid to admit how deep his affection for them ran. The future held room for such emotions. It embraced them joyfully.

There was a great quiet in Esperanza, a sense of waiting, though she danced and laughed willingly enough. Tomás saw Rowena draw the girl aside, and they spoke in low tones while the men paused to smoke and exchange boasts. Rowena returned to Tomás with a pensive air, but held private what she and Esperanza had discussed.

It was not until everyone was exhausted and wandering off to bed that Tomás took Rowena to the cave dwelling where once she'd been his prisoner.

She climbed the wooden ladder without hesitation and sat cross-legged upon the cool stone floor. Tomás lit a single candle, and the painted figures on the wall danced in celebration of their return.

"I think I can hear it," Rowena whispered.

"Hear what?" he said, laying out the furs for their bed.

"The ancient music in these rocks. You once told me to listen for it, that these were the bones of the earth. I think I finally understand."

She lay down on the furs, closing her eyes, and he lay beside her. He had never known such peace. But as the minutes passed he became aware of her scent, and the curves of her hip and breast, and the primal need for union that was never satisfied. As long as he lived, he would want her. Love her. He leaned on his elbow and drew his finger over her nipple until it puckered under her blouse.

She turned toward him, and they kissed.

"Do you think they'll mind?" she murmured breathlessly as he slipped his hand under her blouse.

"Who?"

"The people who once lived here."

He chuckled. "Did I not tell you that they loved life? They were like us; they lived, and ate, and slept, and made children. They understood the heart of things. They will not begrudge us."

And Rowena did not begrudge all the passion that was hers. This time their joining felt truly blessed, as if they had not been married until this moment.

They lay entangled until sunset, when Rowena rose to look out the windows at the cañon. She was unselfconscious in the beauty of her nakedness, but he put aside his selfish pleasure in watching her and got up to wrap a Navajo blanket about her shoulders. She sighed and settled back into his arms.

He saw then what she observed so intently: the lone figure walking the path along the cañon floor, a small female shape leading a saddled horse.

"Esperanza," he said in surprise. "What is she doing?"

"Leaving us," Rowena said.

She spoke without dismay and just a little sadness, and Tomás knew what she and the girl had discussed at the *baile*. "Why?" he asked, holding her close.

"She said she had much to learn, and if she remained here she would find it too easy to go back to the old life she knew," Rowena said. "She said . . . that you and I would protect her from pain and challenge, but she understands that what she must discover lies elsewhere. Out there."

Tomás rested his chin on her shoulder and rubbed her cheek with his. "She is wise."

"And very brave. I hope some day she comes back to us."

"She will." He turned her about and cradled her face in

his hands. "We have a saying: *'No se puede luchar contra el destino.'* One cannot fight destiny."

"Or one's true nature."

"My fighting days are over. I intend to devote the rest of my life to love." With a grin, he pulled her back down among the furs.

about the author

SUSAN KRINARD graduated from the California College of Arts and Crafts with a BFA, and worked as an artist and freelance illustrator before turning to writing. An admirer of both romance and fantasy, Susan enjoys combining these elements in her books. Her first novel, *Prince of Wolves*, garnered praise and broke new ground in the genre of paranormal romance. She has won the *Romantic Times* Award for Best Contemporary Fantasy, *Affaire de Coeur*'s award for Best Up-and-Coming Author of Futuristic, Fantasy and Paranormal Romance, and the PRISM award for Best Dark Paranormal in 1997.

Susan loves to get out into nature as frequently as possible, and enjoys old movies, wolves, dogs, books of every kind, classical and New Age music, history, mythology, the Southwest, fresh bread, and Mexican food. She bakes a killer chocolate cake.

A native Californian, Susan lives in the San Francisco Bay Area with her French-Canadian husband, Serge, a very spoiled dog, and two cats.

Susan loves to hear from readers. She can be reached by e-mail at: Skrinard@aol.com.

Her web page, with quarterly newsletter, links, and book information, can be found at: http://members.aol.com/skrinard/.

Or you can write to her at: P.O. Box 272545, Concord, CA 94527. Please include a self-addressed stamped envelope for a personal reply.